BLIND EYE

by
F. Lynn Godfriaux

WolfSinger Publications ~ Security Colorado

Acknowledgements

A first book requires a tremendous leap of faith on the part of the author, and an equally tremendous amount of support from friends and family. I apologize up front for being brainless and probably omitting someone important whose name I will remember as soon as this is published.

To Steve and Brenda, Sam, Elizabeth, Joe, Erin, Shelly, and Andrea: I would never have made it beyond the first few (okay, numerous) really bad drafts without your ability to recognize the potential in those early reads. Thank you for your time and patience, and for your ability to find a way to tell me what I needed to fix with minimal injury to a notoriously fragile author's ego.

To Lon and staff at the Fillmore Documart: Thank you for your patience and professionalism every time I walked in with a ream of paper and a thumb drive and a request for yet another copy of my manuscript. After all the revisions, I think I'm almost proficient now with uncoiling and re-coiling.

To Steve, Tim, Joe P., and the Colorado Springs ASIS Chapter: Thank you for your expertise and extensive knowledge, and for allowing me to pick your brains over and over. And over.

To Carol and Wolfsinger Publications: Thank you for taking on this project and for believing in me when no one in the publishing world would give me the time of day.

To Mom and Dad: Thank you for raising and loving all four of us kids. I would not be here if not for the two of you. I love you both.

To my husband and family: I saved you for last, just like one of my studio recitals. Your support and patience with my griping, my threats to rip everything up and never write again, and general manic disposition through this whole ordeal, got me through to the end. I truly would never have succeeded without you.

"There is no safety in denial."
LTC (RET) Dave Grossman, from "Sheep, Wolves, and Sheepdogs"

Prologue

George Digby Lamont blinked but his vision wouldn't clear. Butterflies filled his chest, fluttering around his heart with uncomfortable heaviness. He glanced at his wife, Ginnie, who seemed lost in thought as she gazed out the passenger window of their Land Rover.

Should he say anything? Pull over? Find an emergency facility?

He returned his attention to the two-lane highway and blinked several times in an effort to clear the blur in front of him. Flat, empty, brown Kansas prairie spread under an expansive Kansas blue sky. The January midday sun held no warmth. He rubbed the front of his thick plaid long-sleeved shirt as the discomfort in his chest increased. Sweat beaded his forehead and he fumbled with the collar buttons to ease the sudden constriction around his throat. He didn't understand what was wrong. He'd felt fine this morning when they started their trip to visit their daughter Mattie in Colorado. And though in his sixties, he'd never had heart-related problems.

He heard Ginnie moan and snapped his head in her direction. Her color looked awful. His eyes widened with alarm as she slumped over.

"Ginnie!" He tried to yell, but his voice barely made it beyond his lips. The sudden blast of a truck horn jerked his attention to the two-lane highway and he squinted, frantically trying to clear his worsening vision. Rubber bands wrapped tighter and tighter around his chest until he couldn't breathe. He caught a whiff of the sweet pickles he and his wife had been eating, felt his head begin to spin, heard again the thunderous, deafening blare of a truck horn.

Screeching tires, exploding glass, and impacting steel ripped the afternoon air as the oncoming eighteen-wheeler slammed head-on into the careening Land Rover.

Chapter One

I can't believe this.

The thought became a boulder that took up all the room in my head, then rolled slowly, painfully into my chest and stomach. I gazed through the tinted glass of the long, black limousine that belonged to the funeral company and wondered how everything outside could be light and normal when everything inside me was dark and strange.

The limousine crawled down Main Street in Shawnee, the small Oklahoma town where my sister Angela and I had spent our youth, where our parents had raised us with love, gentleness, and joy. It seemed as though every car in town joined the slow procession to the cemetery. Jeremiah, my husband of almost seven years, slipped an arm around my shoulders, pulling me close. His warm, solid body enveloped mine, and I leaned into his black leather jacket and wished he could lift the boulder away from my heart. Angela, motionless within the folds of her knee-length black wool coat, huddled against the opposite window. Long, thick, chocolate brown hair hid her pale face. A glance down at her nails, normally long and beautifully polished but now bitten to the quick, told me she felt the same boulder in the pit of her stomach.

My only recollection of our parents' graveside service was the January wind that lashed through my outer protection and froze my inner boulder into a massive chunk of ice. Even Preacher Pat's Irish lilt and consoling words could not penetrate the cold that engulfed me. Voices grated like nails on a chalkboard as friends filed by, hugging me close and patting my hands. The wind whipped my short black hair around my face, into my normally clear, ocean green eyes, pushed me with invisible power until I almost fell over. Jeremiah's gentle hands steadied me, then guided Angela and me back to the long, black car. Black, like the void sucking me into a pit never to let me out again. Black tires crunched along gravel until they reached thin black pavement, made the slow procession through town, the end of the awful trip no better than the beginning as we pulled up alongside the front staircase of our parents' estate.

As we drifted to a halt, a man wearing a charcoal gray wool overcoat appeared from the endless line of parked cars and strode to the left rear passenger door. He reached for the handle when the limo doors unlocked, opened Angela's door, and leaned down.

"My poor, dear Angela, come with me." Avoiding eye contact with both Jeremiah and myself, he helped my sister from the car. The collar of his heavy coat hid his face so I didn't get a clear look at him, but I felt Jeremiah tense. The stranger wrapped a protective arm around my sister then slammed the door shut. I watched through the tinted glass as he steered her away and wondered how he had known which side Angela would be on.

"Who was that?" I asked as we rose from the car, feeling Jeremiah's strong hands steady me when the wind threatened to blow me over again.

"I think it prudent we find out." The curtness in his voice startled me, his black eyes narrowing on the two figures ascending the broad steps that led to the front entrance.

My husband, Jeremiah Black Bear Tyler, a full-blood Southern Ute, stood slightly over six feet and had the build of a distance runner. He rarely answered questions, listened more than he talked. He did not use contractions, a characteristic which made his personality seem formal.

Jeremiah slipped his arm around my shoulders and pulled me close, protecting me as we climbed the stairs to the house I had called home for most of my twenty-eight years.

William, the family butler since Angela and I were old enough to walk, met us just inside the front entrance. The aged, bent little man hugged me with surprising strength. Flowers and potted plants crowded the large entryway, leaving only a narrow path along the broad hardwood floor. An undulating body of friends, colleagues, and strangers crowded the large room to our left. I didn't want to talk to any of them, so I stood there and stared at the plants.

William's shiny pink bald head nodded towards the sea of colors. "Anna and I will see to these, Miss Mattie. Don't you worry." He ducked his head from my stare, but not before I saw the wetness on his face. He took our coats, and Jeremiah coaxed me into the throng. Muted sounds of familiar music whisked me away from the present torment, and the boulder lifted just a little from my heart as I slid into a fog of memories.

My father, George Digby Lamont, born into immense southern wealth, left the Lamont Alabama plantation to pursue degrees in piano at the University of Oklahoma. He met my mother, Virginia Marigold Tessence Campbell, on the Norman university campus as she was working on her last doctoral piano recital. Together they devoted their lives to university and private teaching, local and regional performing, and raising and loving Angela and me. Music echoed through this house throughout my youth, continued after I married Jeremiah and we moved to Colorado. It had been a wonderful, warm, welcoming, way of sharing their love of life and music.

Gut-ripping truth forced itself back into my thoughts. Mom and Dad were gone, and it was someone else's music that filled the house now, sounding tinny, contrived. It grated on my ears, and I wanted them to stop it and leave. I wanted everyone to stop whatever they were doing and leave. Mom and Dad, Grandpa George, Uncle Bernard, all of them dead within the last three years. Too much death, too many loving people taken away from me too soon.

Bodies overflowed every room, engaged in a muted cacophony of conversations and music. Waiters in OU colors of crimson and cream maneuvered their way through the crowd, balancing trays of wine and finger foods. Smiling (I hoped politely), I acknowledged well-wishers and looked around for my sister. Jeremiah and I entered the large dining room that adjoined the front room. Renovated hardwood flooring contrasted warmly with deep green, floor-to-ceiling drapes and tall, old-fashioned windows. Tall ceilings added grandness, made the room seem spacious despite the crowd. I caught sight of Angela and the stranger standing against the opposite wall from where we stood. Jeremiah paused and I leaned into him, then watched the stranger bend to place a kiss on the top of my sister's long, dark hair. He seemed about my height, which neared five feet ten inches. He looked stocky, muscular rather than fat, and his thin, dark, crudely cut hair threw his features out of balance. Thick glasses made his eyes too small for the rest of his clean-shaven, acne-scarred face. I didn't like the way his eyes shifted about, ignoring whoever was talking with him. The dark, expensive, three-piece suit he wore appeared custom-tailored, but for some reason I felt his attire did not match his personality. Maybe it was the scarring on his face. As usual I was forming a prejudice based on looks. My photographic nature, seeing everyone through the viewfinder.

His head turned and our eyes met, then he glanced away. I must have squared my shoulders because I felt Jeremiah shift. Together, we wandered over in their direction.

"Jeremiah Tyler." He sounded unusually curt. My husband's black crew cut accented his strong facial features, while his black wool sweater and wool dress slacks made him seem taller than he was and more than a little intimidating.

Jeremiah extended his right hand and I glanced at him, trying to figure out whether his curtness was due to the current circumstances or whether he might know this stranger, who seemed more than casual friends with my sister. The stranger hesitated, then gripped Jeremiah's outstretched hand.

Jeremiah turned to me. "And this is my wife and Angela's sister, Mattie."

I smiled and extended my hand, felt the sweat on the man's palm. His fingers barely touched mine before breaking contact, and I wondered whether he was nervous. And if so, whether Jeremiah was making him feel that way.

"Gary Tacque." Gary smiled suddenly and slid an arm around Angela's shoulders, pulling her close, her black designer suit, perfectly proportioned features, and model thinness accentuated by his thick, compact stature. His small green eyes darted my way, then back to Jeremiah. "Angela's told me all about you."

"Your name seems familiar. Are you from this area?" Jeremiah edged between the man and my sister, forcing Gary to drop his arm. I took Angela's hand and started to lead her away when vice-like fingers gripped my shoulder.

"Just where..." Gary's voice raked my already raw nerves. He coughed, then started again. "Stay with us." His voice sounded like a demand, his fingers dug into my flesh despite my heavy sweater. I shrugged irritably, and he let go.

"We'll be back," I threw over my shoulder.

I led my sister to the music room located across the hall. William had closed the doors to this room, so we were alone when we entered. I shut the door against the noise and the crowd, relished the ensuing silence, then turned towards Angela. Her beautiful, expressive brown eyes looked empty and lost.

"Let's have it. Who is that guy, and where'd you meet him?" Okay, maybe not the best way to ask about a new boyfriend, but we had just buried our parents. I wanted her close, not distracted by someone else.

Angela avoided eye contact. "He's a friend." She seemed really out of it. I leaned in and squinted at her eyes.

"Come on, Angela, you can come up with more than that."

Angela stared at me, and I wondered whether she had taken some sort of tranquilizer. Not that I blamed her, but the idea of her current state irked me. Angela was four years my junior, had graduated with a Masters in Sociology, and was now a social worker at the community hospital in Norman. At twenty-four she was quiet, an excellent listener, and understood other people's problems with soothing empathy. But on a normal day she was naïve to the point of clueless when it came to reading people. Her current state made her even more vulnerable. Being a photojournalist and four years older, I had more experience, had been exposed to the baser side of life. I knew her blind eye would be worse than usual, and I wanted to protect her.

"Gary Tacque." She looked at me.

"Well, yeah. He told me that. I want to know *who* he is."

She relented. "He's a representative for a drug company. I can't remember the name right off."

"Where'd you meet him?" My voice sounded as curt as Jeremiah's. I'd better quit sounding so critical. Emotions were running amok already.

Angela looked away and shrugged her shoulders. "At the hospital. He's very nice. He doesn't have many friends because of the way his face looks."

"You mean nobody knows who he is, which means he may have secrets worth knowing about." I blurted, then clamped my lips shut. Sounding accusatory wasn't going to get me very far.

The questions, however, rattled out by themselves. "So, where's he from? Does he have any family? How long has he worked for the drug company?"

Angela's chin jutted and her mouth tightened into a thin line. "Mattie, knock off the inquisition, okay? He's a nice man, and he's been at my side ever since that awful call from the State Patrol last summer about Uncle Bernard."

Our Uncle Bernard, Dad's brother and only sibling, had died in a car crash while driving back to Alabama after spending July Fourth weekend with us.

I leaned against the closed door and tried to back off. "I want to know how involved you are with him, that's all. I am your sister, and it's just the two of us now." Mom had been an only child.

Angela stepped away, opening space between us. "You're acting like you're the boss now. Since when is my life suddenly your business?"

I straightened from the door. "Since we buried Mom and Dad," I answered, trying to control a sudden burst of irritation. "You're exceptional at sensing other people's troubles, but you don't have a clue how to recognize when someone's pulling one over on you." *Damn it.* I shouldn't have said that. I opened my mouth to apologize.

"Mind your own business and leave me alone." Angela spun away and tried to step around me to get to the door.

I shifted, blocking her attempt. "Angela, wait. Please. I'm sorry."

I reached for her, but she turned with such an angry expression that I dropped my hands. Her present demeanor was unlike her. Well, so was mine. I crossed the room to one of two seven foot Steinway grand pianos located near a set of massive French double doors.

I sank down onto the bench Dad had used for years and remembered the childhood piano lessons I had fought. Why had I been so insistent about not learning something my father cared so passionately about? Why had I refused to follow in his footsteps?

Angela laid a hand on the doorknob and threw a look over her shoulder. Possibly she saw the pain and confusion in my face, because instead of opening the door, she turned and drifted over to the other piano and sat down. I watched her lift the lid covering the keys. A slow, single melody line drifted from strings hidden under the massive lid of the seven-foot grand.

"I'm sorry." I repeated, feeling like I was apologizing to my father as much as I was trying to defuse things with my sister. "I just want to know who this guy is. It's…you and me now. I…I guess I got mad because he didn't bother to introduce himself at the car." My gaze dropped to the exquisite Persian rug that carpeted most of the floor. The soft pile had provided cushioning whenever the two of us slept under the instruments. We had been young, small, innocent.

The wandering melody broke off. "Do you remember how we used to camp out underneath these?" Angela's voice broke into my thoughts. "It was so cool, lying under there whenever Dad was practicing. Or when the two of them were in here working on a program.

I wonder how they ever got anything done, the way we giggled and carried on."

"I wish you had pursued your music." I looked up at her, wishing with a fresh wave of despair that I hadn't been so stubborn about lessons. "I loved listening to you play, too." She and Dad had worked on two-piano works together during her years in high school. She had been offered full scholarships by several universities, and partial scholarships from two conservatories.

"After I saw how much the therapists helped Jeremiah's brother, I wanted to try to help people instead." And because of her decision Angela had stopped playing altogether, grown her nails out, and started dressing like a New York fashion model.

Jeremiah's younger brother, David Mud Rain Tyler, had Down's Syndrome. He only answered to Mud Rain, had recently turned fourteen. When I first met Jeremiah eight years ago, Mud Rain had been six years old, non-verbal and difficult to control. Jeremiah had taken him off the Reservation and tried several centers that focused on kids with special needs.

Reluctantly, I silently admitted that Angela had been the one who made the difference. Mud Rain responded to her gentle firmness with astounding progress. I admired her for choosing to work with kids with special needs, but the selfish side of me wished she had pursued her musical talent.

"But you're so good," I said, trying to bridge the uncharacteristic gap that yawned between us. "Can't you find time to pick it up again?"

Angela's mouth turned downward. "Quit trying to make everything my fault. I'm tired of you thinking you're always right."

I frowned, realized my expression matched hers, tried to work the corners of my mouth upward, but they quivered instead. We used to email each other daily. Thinking back on things, I realized our communication had dropped off since Uncle Bernard's death last summer. Angela and I used to talk about anything (and I do mean *anything*).

"Nobody makes a good first impression with you, Mattie. You're too busy looking at them the way they would look through a camera lens. In case you forget, I didn't like Jeremiah when you brought him home the first time." Her abrupt change in subject jerked me back to my bluntness about the new man in her life.

She stood and wandered over to where I sat. Leaning her elbows on the closed lid of Dad's piano, she began tracing imaginary patterns with the bitten end of a fingernail. "I didn't like him because I knew he was moving and you were going to go with him."

I glanced away to hide the tears that stung my eyes. Yeah, I remembered that conversation. When a job opportunity opened in Colorado Springs instead of somewhere in Oklahoma, we cried together over how Life was ripping our world apart.

I turned back to her and tried to smile. "Okay, maybe I'm jumping to conclusions. But honestly, he acted sort of rude when he met you at the car."

Her damp chocolate brown eyes focused on her moving finger. "You're not interested in getting to know him."

I leaned on the closed lid of the keyboard and pressed the palms of my hands against my eyes. "C'mon, Angela. That's ridiculous. Jeremiah and I walked over to meet the two of you, didn't we?"

"You're just reacting to what you see. Just because he doesn't have a GQ face doesn't mean he's not a nice guy."

I raised my head and stared at her. "Is that what you really think?"

She avoided eye contact. "You're not trying to get to know him at all."

I felt like two separate conversations were going on. "Angela, you can't seriously be thinking that."

Her finger stopped and she straightened. "You're just jealous because I've finally found someone besides you to be close to. That's why you don't like Gary."

I stood, my legs knocking against the heavy bench. "Hey, I just want to know more about him. Excuse me for being interested," I retorted.

"He's good company. We get along. Like Mom and Dad do…did." Angela released a long, ragged sigh.

"Angela, you're not even listening to me!" I threw up my hands and turned my back on her. Through the glass of the French doors thrashing branches bent and swayed as invisible, gale-force fingers dragged at them. Tears stung my eyes, trickled down my cheeks. Maybe my reaction had to do with the fact the man had been seeing my sister for a while, and this was the first I had heard about it.

"So why haven't you called or emailed me about him?" I didn't turn around, didn't want Angela to see how upset I was.

When she answered her voice sounded shaky. "You're always busy, and Gary is always around when I think about calling, and we get distracted doing something else. I'm away from my computer most of the day now. It would help if we could text." She stopped. I knew what she was going to say next.

"Well, I'm sorry, but I'm not buying another expensive phone to lose or get dropped in a puddle. I'm behind the wheel most of the day anyway."

"I was going to have you meet him over Christmas, but you didn't make it down."

Guilt poked me in the chest. She didn't have to bring that up. I rubbed my face with my hands, stared out the window again. Low clouds looking like Marley's ghosts raced across the late afternoon sky.

"Did you get the job?" Angela asked from behind me.

"No. Jason got it." Not only had I not come down to see family for Christmas, but the job opening I had been hoping to get with the photo shoot had not gone my way.

"You could've emailed me about him. My computer is always with me," I threw over my shoulder.

Angela didn't offer any comment.

"What…" I trailed off, balking at having to use past tense. "What…did…Mom and Dad think of Gary?"

A long silence followed before Angela replied. "He…hadn't actually met Mom or Dad yet."

Alarm bells began ringing in my head, and I whipped around. Too late I realized I was scowling.

Angela glared back. "What? He's always busy, and I moved to an apartment in Norman so I could be closer to the hospital. Sometimes I don't get off work until late. I haven't been living with Mom and Dad since last summer. Whenever I drive up to Shawnee to say hi, I always ask him to come along. He's tried to come up after his appointments, but they run too late."

"You didn't tell me you had moved. Neither did Mom and Dad." I stopped. Belatedly I realized I had been short on the phone with my parents since Christmas. I hadn't wanted to hear their ready acceptance and support of my failure to get the position.

Angela's expression bordered on hostile. "My computer crashed after I got into the apartment. I haven't gotten it fixed yet. Gary said I must've downloaded a virus from the Internet when I was setting it up."

"You could've called me, damn it." I ignored inner warnings and let emotions take control. "Or did he keep you too busy to do that, either?"

"You know what? You're being really bitchy about all of this. I've been busy. Gary's been busy. Don't get on *my* case for not calling *you*, when *you're* the one who couldn't spare enough time to come home for *Christmas*."

The music room door swung open and Gary's head popped around the edge. I opened my mouth to tell him to butt out, stalled when I tried to think of a different way of putting it, and lost the opportunity altogether.

"Angela, there you are, sweet pea. I've been worried about you." He stepped into the room. An inexplicable sense of protectiveness washed over me, and I stepped in front of my sister.

"What could you possibly be worried about? She's here with me, in our house." My voice echoed, sharp and uninviting, around the acoustically live room.

"A lot has happened since you last saw your sister. I've been with her. I know how all of this is affecting her." He sounded so patronizing I wondered how on earth my sister could possibly be attracted to the man.

Angela walked over to stand beside him. Her action seemed like a choice of sides. Disconcerting, to say the least.

"Nice talking with you." The tone of her voice said otherwise. I stared in numbed silence as she and Gary disappeared around the door, the polished cherry wood barrier swinging shut with a disturbingly metaphorical click.

Chapter Two

Six months later.

Tuesday morning, the third week of June, I was exiting the ladies room on the second floor of the Colorado Springs newspaper building when all hell broke loose.

"Mattie! Get moving! We've got a nut going crazy over at the south mall!" Jason Matthew's voice cut over the din. Reporters and photographers crowded towards the doors to the stairwells, crash bars clanking like a railcar on tracks. I darted to my cubicle, located across from Jason's, but he was already gone. The second floor office space housed cubicles around the perimeter of a circular Command Center, where senior editors and copyists did their work, and where the police scanners were. I ran into the CC to find out what Jason was talking about.

"...repeat, shots fired ..."

My ears tuned out the rest as two words rang in my head.

Shots fired.

I glanced around the now empty newsroom, then towards the door that led to the stairs. My camera equipment waited in my car. Photos from a crisis like this could launch me into a full-time position. I told my feet to get moving.

After five agonizing seconds, I moved not to the stairs but over to the other scanner located in the opposite end of the Command Center. Its frequency picked up county sheriff traffic. The radio squawked.

"...multi-vehicle accident with injuries at exit..."

"Tyler!"

I swung to face the Editor-in-Chief, Mel something. His last name was impossible to pronounce, and I could never remember it.

"What's that about a TC?" His voice rang like a baseball umpire across the room. He must have been on break. He also had ears like a bat.

"I'll check it out." And I was out the door and down the stairs before he could reply.

Multi-vehicle carnage caused by a jackknifed semi littered the southbound highway just north of the city. I'm sure Mel would be calling in more reporters to cover the mess, but for now I was the only newsperson on scene, arriving with the first wave of rescue teams. Leaving my equipment in the car, I began running among the mangled metal, checking vehicles, the small groups of victims that were forming here and there, relaying urgent messages. Units from Monument, Larkspur, and even Castle Rock arrived. Miraculously, there were no fatalities, but several were critically injured. Screaming sirens mixed with the chaotic, thumping blades of Flight for Life helicopters. Several hours passed before I got a few shots of twisted metal, IV bags and tubing, stretchers, intensely concentrated first responders, and flashing light bars.

I didn't make it back to the office until long after dark. I found Jason sitting in his cubicle, staring at the computer screen, his thick dark hair disheveled, his jeans and short-sleeved blue shirt looking like they'd been left in the middle of Academy Boulevard. Sharp contrast to his normally overly neat, almost OCD habits. Jason was in his early twenties and already possessed abilities far beyond what I struggled to obtain through two college degrees.

I rolled my chair over next to his and sat down. "I heard about the thirteen dead shoppers at the mall." Stains covered my jeans and my short-sleeved red shirt.

Jason glanced at my clothes, then at me. "I didn't see you at the scene."

"I ended up covering the accident on I-twenty-five." I looked away because I didn't want his astute eyes to see what I had not said.

Jason's attention flickered back to his computer screen and he brushed the back of his hand over his eyes. His screen saver, a picture of an enormous solitary red rock against a brilliant wash of green foliage and blue sky, represented one of his shots from Garden of the Gods Park on the west side of the city.

"Hey." I leaned forward and gently nudged his elbow. "What's on your mind?"

Instead of answering, Jason moved his hand to the mouse. With a click, a close-up image appeared. The stark brutality of the scene made my blood run cold.

A police officer knelt beside a woman's body just outside the entrance of a Bed & Bath storefront. Blood pooled on the floor around him. His left elbow balanced on his knee, both hands aimed his handgun on a target beyond the frame. The expression on the officer's face spoke volumes.

I cleared my voice and said with difficulty, "Did you use your four hundred?" I hoped so, because that would mean Jason had been further away than the shot implied. Still, he had somehow gotten into the building during the crisis.

Jason nodded.

"Hell of a picture." I looked at him. He stared back, his clear blue eyes hard.

"Helluva price, Mattie." He turned his attention back to the picture. "I watched her go down. There was chaos all around me, gunshots coming from everywhere, shouting, women screaming, police yelling, some of them I think were yelling at me. And with all of that going on, I focused on getting a fucking picture." He wiped the back of his hand across his face again. "I didn't think about what I saw. I didn't think I had just seen this woman die. I didn't think of the danger I put myself in, or whether I was screwing things up for the police trying to get a handle on the situation. All I thought about was getting the picture." He turned to me, his face wet despite the fact that his voice was steady as a rock. "What kind of person does that make me?"

I didn't know what to say.

~ * ~

Jeremiah's schedule at the National Weather Service Forecast Office in Boulder ("Boulder FO," for short) altered between days and nights, as did all the lead forecasters. He was currently finishing up a nightshift rotation, which meant we basically didn't see each other because of our opposing sleep schedules. I kept busy with follow up stories on the mall massacre, traffic accidents, and some flash flooding in Manitou Springs due to the Waldo Canyon burn scar from a recent, massive wildfire. Saturday morning I finally got a break from work and was rummaging through some photo albums in the spare bedroom when someone rapped sharply on our apartment door. Jeremiah was catching a few hours' sleep. Worried the noise might wake him, I hurried over and opened the door without checking the peephole first. I froze, felt my mouth fall open, and blinked several times in disbelief.

"Hello." Gary Tacque, now my very unwelcome brother-in-law, spread his lips in more of a leer than a smile. I tried to smile back. What I really wanted to do was slam the door in his face.

Gary and Angela eloped two weeks after the funeral. You better believe I over-reacted, but damn it, Angela was the only family I had now. There were no grandparents, uncles, aunts, or cousins. At the time I was so mad I didn't care whether I ever saw or spoke to her again. Colorado Springs is a full day's drive from Norman, Oklahoma. The distance cemented the communication breach caused by our argument after the funeral and her elopement.

With effort, I focused my attention back to the man standing on my doorstep, watched his eyes take in the sight of me in an old Oklahoma Sooners T-shirt and a pair of running shorts. I wanted to hit him. Instead, I stepped aside.

"Jeremiah's asleep, so please keep your voice down." I closed the door and worked hard to keep my voice civil. "What are you doing here?"

His small green eyes, made smaller by the thickness of his glasses, stared intently at me. His disheveled white polo shirt and jeans suggested he had been awake most of the night.

"Is Angela with you?" I asked, not waiting for him to reply to my first question.

"Naw, I came up for a business trip." He walked over to our brown cloth couch and sank into the thick cushions. Photographs I had done of Garden of the Gods, Pikes Peak, and the Manitou Incline, hung in frames on the walls. A small fireplace occupied one corner, and several valuable pieces of American Indian artwork and carvings from the Southern Ute Reservation occupied the mantel.

"Where's that ass—sorry, I mean that husband of yours?"

His blatant abrasiveness contrasted sharply with his overly sweet disposition towards my sister, another reason why I did not like the man. "He's asleep, Gary, like I told you. If you can't be civil, then there's the door." I dropped the pretense. "What do you want?"

"Just stopped by to say hello." He looked around. Jeremiah and I lived in a ground floor apartment containing two bedrooms, two baths, a sitting room, and a small kitchen. I took a seat in an old gold velvet cane chair I had picked up at a yard sale, curled my legs underneath me, and wondered why Gary was sitting in my living room. Suspicion shot up and started making snide remarks in my ear. I wouldn't be exactly upset about finding out things weren't working out between the two of them.

"What sort of business trip?" I prompted, not really caring but trying to find a way to get him to tell me how Angela was doing.

"I got sent up here for a drug rep conference at the Broad-moor."

That would be the famous hotel located at the base of Chey-enne Mountain. My eyebrows rose. "How was your flight?" He looked like hell, and I wondered whether it had been a last-minute trip.

His green eyes narrowed and he glanced away. "I offered to save the company the cost of a plane ticket and drove up instead."

"And Angela didn't want to come along?" I made no effort to hide the suspicion in my voice.

He shifted uncomfortably. "No. Actually, she doesn't want any-thing to do with you, not after the way you acted when we told you our news."

I squirmed in my chair, then stood and strode into our tiny kitchen. Being in the same room with the man was proving more challenging by the minute. I turned and faced him from behind the breakfast counter.

"I've left several messages trying to apologize. I don't remem-ber Angela ever being the type of person to carry a grudge." Tears filled my eyes. We had been inseparable, until Gary had come along. I wondered for the millionth time whether my reaction was because he had usurped my position as Angela's guardian, friend, and confi-dant. After all, now that she had a husband, Angela would confide in him rather than call me. I tried to convince myself our communica-tion breach was due to distance and busy schedules.

"How long will you be in town?" I almost choked on my ef-fort to remain civil.

"Most of the weekend." He stood, ambled over to the counter, set his muscular, stocky frame down on one of the metal barstools. I regretted coming into the kitchen because I'd backed myself into playing hostess after all. I looked at the clock on the microwave. Ten-thirty, which seemed too early to offer something for lunch.

"Have you had breakfast?"

"Coffee will do." He looked around the apartment again. I pulled out instant coffee and a cup.

"Mind if I look around?" Without waiting for an answer, he popped off the stool and started down the short hall towards the bedrooms. Shocked, I hurried after him, but didn't close the gap between us in time to prevent him from poking his head in the spare bedroom, which was cluttered and not ready for guest inspection. I thought he was done, but he swung to the second bedroom, opened the door and stepped inside. Furious, I followed him, putting my finger to my lips because Jeremiah was asleep. Gary ignored me and looked in the closet, then the bathroom. He came out and shut the door again with a soft click.

"I would think you guys would be in a house after seven years," he remarked, making no effort to keep his voice down.

"Just what the hell do you think you're doing?" I hissed.

"Going anywhere today?" he asked as I stalked to the living room.

If he wasn't going to answer any of my questions, then by God, I wasn't going to answer any of his. Standing in the center of the living room, I spun around to face him. "What's Angela doing while you're on this business trip?"

"Hanging around the house." He was being vague on purpose. He stepped around me towards the door. "Well, I need to get over to the hotel and clean up. The first meeting starts in an hour. Tell your husband he should find something better than some dead-end nightshift job."

My hands curled into rigid fists. I waited outside while he climbed into his empty, expensive red truck. As soon as he was out of the parking lot I ducked back inside and made a beeline for the phone on the kitchen counter, punched in Angela's home number. Gary's voice answered with the familiar message.

At times like this, I really despise caller ID.

"Hey, Angela, pick up if you're home," I demanded into the answering machine. "Gary just stopped by."

Nothing.

I tried her cell but got her voicemail. Exasperated beyond reason I shuffled over to the brown couch. Except for Mom and Dad's estate lawyer, I hadn't talked with anyone in Oklahoma since the funeral, although Jeremiah kept in daily contact with Becky and Bill Parsons, the family who was watching Mud Rain until we had arrangements finished for the care he would need here. Maybe I should call Becky and say hello, and ask whether she or her husband Bill had seen or talked to Angela lately. I dialed their home number, but got an out-of-order signal. Wondering if Norman was having weather problems, I tried Becky's cell but got her voicemail. I hate talking to machines so I didn't leave a message. I tossed the handset towards the opposite end of the couch, then sat and stared into space.

Jeremiah came yawning out of the bedroom shortly after one.

"Did you get enough sleep?" I asked from the couch, where I had been looking at a photo album of Angela with Mom, Dad, and me at her graduate degree celebration party last year.

For an answer, he came over, lifted the album from my lap and dropped it onto the carpet beside a box of loose pictures. Then he lowered himself onto the couch, pinning me firmly beneath him. His intentions were pretty unmistakable from the feel of things. He smelled faintly of Irish Spring and hot water. His black eyes glinted.

"I guess we're not driving to Limon today?" I tried to breathe under his weight.

For an answer, he lowered his head and nuzzled my throat, his short, thick black crewcut brushing along my jaw line.

A long time later I was still pinned into the couch and had not the least inclination to change things. Jeremiah rolled against the back cushions, the lean sinew of his arms and chest prominent.

"Who was here earlier?"

"Gary stopped by." I felt his muscles tense like a finely honed bow.

"Here?" His hand idly massaged my abdomen, then drifted up to my breast. I started melting all over again. My eyes closed, and I purred under his gentle strength.

"He said he was in town for a drug rep conference at the Broadmoor. He looked like he'd been driving all night," I finally managed to tell him.

"Odd."

I heaved a contented sigh, then opened my eyes when Jeremiah groaned and lifted himself off the couch. He pulled on the boxer shorts he had slept in, then padded over to the sliding glass doors and peered through the closed curtains. I pulled the afghan from the back of the couch and snuggled underneath its warmth.

"Lots of CBs." He was referring to the cumulonimbus clouds that created thunderheads. He turned back around. "We should stay here. By the looks of the Peak, we may get some local activity."

I mumbled an agreement as my eyes drifted closed, thoughts floating in pleasant nothingness, muscles so relaxed I didn't think I could stand up. My stomach gave a faint growl. Jeremiah's long, strong body dropped back down upon mine, and I grunted under his weight.

"Or, we could ignore the weather," he breathed against my ear.

I tried to push him off and got efficiently immobilized beneath the blanket.

"I'm hungry…for some *food*," I protested when he pressed against me. He chuckled, then relinquished and rolled onto the floor.

"Okay. Let me call Becky and say hello to Mud Rain."

I rolled onto my side and listened to the one-sided conversation while he sat on one of the kitchen barstools. When he finished, he set the handset down on the counter.

"Oklahoma is in the epicenter of a major storm system. Lucky I got through." He moved back to the couch and sat down, pinning my legs beneath his muscular thighs. "Becky said they started therapeutic riding lessons with Mud Rain. She sees a marked improvement in his coordination and verbal skills."

I met his eyes. "Are you having second thoughts about moving him out here?"

Jeremiah broke eye contact and stared at the curtains glowing with afternoon sunshine. "He seems to have adjusted well to living with the Parsons." He glanced at me. I caught a glint of mischief in his eyes and knew he was no longer thinking about his brother. He slid a hand beneath the blanket to my left knee and squeezed, then inched his way along my thigh.

"Stop it," I giggled, trying to pull my legs from beneath him.

His fingers paused. "Gary said he was here for a conference?" He asked, throwing me with his sudden change in subject.

"Yeah. He just showed up." I squirmed. "He wouldn't tell me what Angela was doing, or why he didn't bring her along."

"When did his flight arrive?"

I gave up trying to get him off my legs. "According to him, he drove up."

"He drove?" Jeremiah's question held the same skepticism I had felt.

"Yeah. I asked him why he hadn't flown up. He mumbled something about saving the company money." I squirmed again. "Would you please move?"

Jeremiah stood. I glanced at his profile, saw concentration etched into his strong features and high cheekbones.

"You're thinking the same thing that I am," I said. "That he was lying about why he drove all the way up here."

"Perhaps we should catch a flight to Will Rogers and check on Angela."

Jeremiah's comment made me sit up. I looked around for my T-shirt and shorts, put them on. "What are you thinking?" I stood close to him. Using both hands, I shoved my short black hair out of my eyes so I could see his expression better. My husband worked long hours, devoted his free time to weather jaunts with me and trips to the Southern Ute Reservation in the southwest corner of the state. That he would consider a sudden trip to Norman meant something. I just wasn't sure what.

Jeremiah looked away. "You phoned Angela after he left?"

"I tried. No answer, as usual." Uneasiness crept around me. "You're sounding like Angela might be in some kind of trouble."

He swung his eyes to me. "Why this sudden visit from Gary?"

"I don't know. There's no reason why I shouldn't believe Gary's explanation for his visit." I paused. But I didn't believe my brother-in-law's story.

"His behavior does not follow his stripe."

Occasionally, Jeremiah's verbal economy borders on the obtuse.

"You're not helping, you know. Tell me what you're thinking." I reached a hand out and grasped his arm. "Please."

Jeremiah gave me a long, searching stare, then broke eye contact and shrugged.

"C'mon, Jeremiah. Something's got you worried. What is it?" I pressed against him, trying to trap him into telling me what was on his mind. "Tell me what's got you worried."

Instead of answering, Jeremiah moved away and peered through the curtains again. "Come here. Look at the updraft on those anvils."

I frowned. "You're changing the subject."

His expression remained unreadable. "Yes, I am."

And I knew from experience Jeremiah would not relent. So I stepped beside him and looked through the sliding glass door. The sky had towering cumulonimbus piles that flattened out sharply at the tops. Angry blackness bore down the length of the Front Range.

"That looks like hail," I mused, wishing I knew how to get my husband back onto the subject of my brother-in-law.

"Yes."

An eerie, greenish twilight enveloped us. Thunder rumbled in disconnected conversation with jagged lightning bolts as clouds advanced along the mountain range. The greenish belly of the clouds turned black, lightning sizzled, and thunder became drowned out as golf-ball hail pounded the ground and buildings.

"Damn." Jeremiah muttered with a sigh.

"There goes the windshield." I winced as hailstones punched holes through the red Jeep Jeremiah used to drive to Boulder. Since I stored all of my camera equipment in my Subaru Forester, I kept it parked beneath the carport.

The temperature dropped twenty degrees in as many minutes. The storm moved away, the hail turned to rain which slowed to a trickle. I slid into a pair of sweats, heated some tomato soup, and turned on the gas fireplace. Jeremiah called a friend who owned a mobile windshield replacement service.

When the windshield guy arrived, Jeremiah walked out to the parking lot to meet him. They stood talking for a while, probably about the storm. I tried Angela's number again without success, then glanced at my watch. Jeremiah would have to leave soon, since his shift started at midnight.

"Did you get enough sleep to make it through tonight?" I asked when Jeremiah, dressed in jeans and a black short-sleeved Polo shirt, appeared later from our bedroom. He came over to the counter where I sat and bent his head to mine.

"Enough sleep, yes. Enough of you, well...."

"Oh, cut it out." I batted at his face. "You're sounding like a bad cliché."

He chuckled, gave me a slow, intense kiss, and then picked up his black leather jacket.

I followed him. "I hope the game doesn't get rained out tomorrow."

He slid behind the wheel of the Jeep, and I leaned in and gave him a long kiss. "Be careful, okay?"

He smiled at me, the look in his eyes creating knots in my stomach. I backed up and watched him swing the Jeep out of the parking lot, then around the corner of the building.

Chapter Three

Pink hues of dawn Sunday morning brushed the snow-capped summit of Pikes Peak. I stared through the west bedroom window and watched the crest lighten to a soft rosy glow, then re-dress with glaring brilliance as sunrays lit the tip and spread downward.

Excitement had thwarted my attempts to sleep late. I loved going to Coors Field with Jeremiah. Neither of us kept up with stats. It was the atmosphere. The happy, cheering (most of the time, anyway) crowd, the succulent odors of brats and popcorn, the crack of the bat when wood met leather, not to mention the opportunity to spend uninterrupted time with my husband.

I glanced at the bedside clock. Five-forty-five. It wouldn't make sense to head up to Denver much before ten because the game didn't start until one. I had five hours to kill.

What was I going to do for five hours?

I paced, did laundry, paced, vacuumed, ate breakfast, showered, then dressed in green hiking shorts and a white short-sleeved cotton button-down shirt. I stared at the new hiking boots I had recently bought after my old ones got ruined during a tornado-chasing jaunt with Jeremiah. Spotting my old, worn, sneakers, I decided to wear them instead. I'd be sitting all afternoon anyway. Per usual, I didn't bother with make-up or jewelry. I had naturally black eyelashes which accented my green eyes, my only attribute, in my opinion. Unlike Angela, my facial features were a mix of too large and too small which no amount of cosmetics would hide, and which explained why I stayed behind the camera lens instead of in front of one.

At nine, I couldn't stand it anymore. If I left now, I might miss most of the incoming game traffic and get a good parking place. My press pass was with my equipment and I knew several of the gate attendants, which meant someone would let me in. I re-checked that the tickets were tucked into my belt pack, then packed Jeremiah's and my overnight bags. We could drive east on I-Seventy after the game, spend the night in Limon, and follow a line of weather cells projected for tomorrow afternoon. With any luck, I might get shots of a few funnel clouds.

Even with written directions, I get lost every time I drive to Coors Field. For that matter, I get lost every time I try to navigate my way around Denver, which is why Jeremiah always drives. This morning, by some miracle, I made it to the parking complex after only two wrong turns, paid the fee, and followed the guys waving the bright orange batons.

Tailgate groups gathered around parked cars. Sunshine and rich cerulean hues filled the sky, promising a beautiful day for baseball. I climbed out, then looked at the blue tub in the back of my Subaru. I kept my three Nikon digital cameras, monopod and tripod, portable printer, computer, and a carrying case of lenses in the back of my car at all times. The worst mistake a photojournalist can make is not having one's camera when an opportunity presents itself. However, taking my digital equipment meant lugging a large bag full of lenses and equipment. Jeremiah and I were on vacation starting today, so I wasn't covering the game. So instead of reaching into the blue tub, I reached into the backseat. Today I would use my old 35mm Canon Rebel EOS, the camera I had grown up on, the one my father gave me for my twelfth birthday.

I like using film. The shots you take are the ones you get stuck with. No hiding behind the delete button. Over the years, me and my Canon have captured Time on a frame.

Mom and Dad. Angela. Normally, I would have been on the phone with them throughout the day, telling them about the game despite the fact they could follow it perfectly well on television. Now, the family photo albums I had created over the years held priceless pictures of the four of us.

I shook my head, trying to rid my mind of depressing thoughts, and considered pulling a sweatshirt out of my overnight bag.

No. If clouds rolled in and I got cold, I could buy myself a new Rockies sweatshirt from one of the venders along the concourse. Feeling my mood lightening with that thought, I wove through the parked cars towards the ball park entrance.

Al was at the far end east gate and okayed me to go in. I found our seats in the section just below the concourse, which provided a fabulous view between home and first base. I sat down and checked my watch. Ten forty-five. Jeremiah should be showing up soon. Animated faces milled about as excited fans created a low cacophonic rumble. The loud speakers boomed with energetic music, the announcer coming on now and again to call out another raffle winner, updates, and of course lost children and illegally parked cars. The cheerful aromas of grilled bratwurst and popcorn made my stomach growl. I looked around the stadium, then peered down towards the various camera crews on site for the game. Removing the zoom lens from my belt pack and twisting it onto my camera, I laid the short lens in my lap and stared through the viewfinder. A familiar figure came into focus.

Jason Matthews. We had become casual friends over the last couple of years, swapping jokes and weekend stories. When digital cameras first became the rage he had incessantly gotten on my case for "chimping"—grinning at the LCD screen at the shot I'd just taken and missing out on subsequent action. I was mostly over that temptation now, although he still came back from news scenes with more photos than I did.

I dug out my cell phone and called him, watched him through my zoom lens as he dug out his cell phone and answered.

"Hey," he greeted. "What's up?"

"I'm up here in the stands getting ready to watch the game," I told him.

"You know they're going to lose today, right?" He jabbed as he turned to scan the crowd. I waved, but he didn't see me.

I laughed. "Scores don't matter. It's a beautiful day. How are you feeling?"

"Mel told me to get my ass back to work, so I guess I'm doing okay. Are you on vacation yet?"

"Starting today, so don't expect to hear from me for the next week. Jeremiah and I are leaving town," I grinned.

"Have fun, and don't run through any tornadoes."

I laughed again and said good-bye, then scanned the crowd through the viewfinder on my camera. Brilliant sunshine beat down on the baseball cap I wore, warming the cloth of my green hiking shorts, relaxing my muscles. My head buzzed from lack of sleep, and the surrounding people smeared into washes of primary colors. My head jerked and I blinked, focusing blurred colors into faces, and found myself staring at two adult Asian men paused on the stairway down a section. A Rockies pitcher climbed onto the mound between them and began warming up. The two men faced each other, their profiles creating a strange quirk in depth perception with the pitcher who was winding up to throw. I raised my camera, focused, snapped a picture. It was a one-time shot, because both heads turned my way, then the two men melted into the stands.

I lowered the camera and wished Jeremiah would hurry up. Twisting in my seat, I spotted a familiar figure up a ways to my left. He wore a black Rockies baseball cap and aviator sunglasses and stood on the main concourse. The crowd shifted and eddied around him, blocking full view, but I caught his short, black hair, and his tall, athletic build. Something about his appearance bothered me and it took longer than normal for me to process the fact he was not wearing the same clothes he'd had on last night.

"Jeremiah!" My shout was lost in the crowd. He turned towards me and I realized he wasn't my husband, which answered the question about his clothes. The similarity intrigued me, though, and I lifted the camera and focused on him. His hands rested on the railing as he stared in my direction, and I snapped off two pictures.

I love taking candids. Film freezes Time onto a frame, which is the number one reason why I became a photographer.

Maybe I should call Jeremiah to see where he was. I retrieved my cell phone, punched Jeremiah's number, got his voicemail. I snapped the phone shut and slipped it into my belt pack, then searched the undulating crowd. I stood and stretched, turned to study the fans milling along the concourse. As my eyes wandered back to the stands I caught sight of a small red-haired boy, no more than four years old, blissfully asleep on his father's lap (I assumed the relationship. Both had the same red hair and basic facial features). I raised my camera and focused on the father and son, directing the viewer towards both sets of eyes. I zoomed closer to the gently closed, small young lids, their feathery red lashes brushing faintly pink cheeks. The father's azure blue eyes gazed with content yet subtle watchfulness. Silhouetting both faces against a background of blurred colors highlighted by the bright sun, I snapped a shot, then zoomed out to watch whether another shot might present itself. The small chest heaved as the sleeping boy sighed, his head drifting in slow motion towards me until his cheek rested against the pocket of his father's denim shirt. I zoomed in on the face against the button-down flap of denim, watched the father's chest rise, then snapped the last frame. The automatic film winder whirred softly and the camera clicked, wound, and clicked again before lapsing into silence.

"You there. Are you a professional photographer?"

I started at the question, asked from behind me by a deepish male voice with a distinct British accent. I twisted around. The man whom I had mistaken for Jeremiah stood on the stairs by the empty seat meant for my husband. He removed his sunglasses and his slate-gray eyes glared at me. As I opened my mouth to answer, I wondered whether his accent was affected in order to impress me or whether he was really British. And probably because I was so tired, my mind wandered to my parents' Oklahoma drawl, then to Uncle Bernard's Alabama twang.

I realized the stranger was still staring at me, obviously waiting for an answer. Problem was, I'd forgotten his question.

"I'm sorry?"

"Are you a professional photographer?" He looked annoyed.

"Yes. I freelance." I felt uncomfortable under his scrutiny. Fans filled the seats in our row, so I couldn't move away. I sat down instead and faced the field in an effort to break the tension.

"You took my picture earlier." He didn't sound pleased. Before I could think how to respond, he complicated things by folding himself into Jeremiah's empty seat.

"Looking for *contraughvessy*, are you?"

I stared at him. The muscles around his eyes squinted, then his lips curled into a smile and he proffered a tanned hand.

"Name's Hawk."

I hesitated, then decided he was trying to put me at ease, so I shook his hand. His fingers were firm and held on when I tried to release. "And yours would be…?" His eyes turned hard, and my unease spiked.

"Mattie."

He released my hand, settled into the plastic seat, and propped a black Nike sneaker across the left knee of his black jeans. He wore a gray long-sleeved Polo, which I thought would get hot and uncomfortable sooner than later. After several minutes of awkward silence, I decided to try to clarify things.

"Sorry, I didn't understand your earlier question."

"About looking for *contraughvessy*?" His directed his attention towards the field.

"That would be the one."

His eyebrows furrowed as he thought. "Uproar," he said after a minute.

I leaned away from him. "You mean controversy? About

what?"

He swung his attention back to me. "I'm not keen on having my mug in a daily, that's what." The tone of his voice made me stiffen.

"I understand." Before I could continue, he cut me off.

"Find someone else's picture to post." He put his sunglasses back on, dropped his foot and stood. "Enjoy the game."

I waved and tried a half-smile as he turned away. "You, too."

I watched him retreat up the stairs, then glanced around the concourse. Jeremiah should be here by now. What was taking him so long? I stood, climbed the stairs. Time for a bathroom break. I also wanted to change out my film, and didn't want to do that in the strong mid-day sun.

Pedestrian traffic clogged the wide walkway and the line into the women's bathroom taxed my stretched bladder. At last, I made it to a stall. I took care of nature, then changed film rolls, tucking the used one into the left front pocket of my hiking shorts. I removed my sunglasses and splashed cold water on my face, glancing in the mirror as I washed my hands. Dark purple craters dug canals under my eyes. Ugh. I needed a nap. I finished washing my hands and wiped them on my shorts, then adjusted the camera strap around the collar of my shirt and the belt pack around my waist before I walked out of the restroom. I thought about a hot dog and a Coke, decided to wait until Jeremiah got here, so instead wove my way through the crowd towards the stairs that led to our seats. My cell phone started ringing with Jeremiah's jingle. I dug the phone out of my belt pack.

"Hi there. Where are you?"

"Kansas."

I grinned. "Very funny. It's about time you got here. What took you so long?" I peered up at the sky. Thick white clouds peeped over the west-side stands, signaling the development of storm cells that would move over the stands as the day progressed. I hoped we weren't in for a rain delay.

"I got a call this morning concerning a position in Battlestar Norman. I told them I would leave immediately from the station." Jeremiah's voice sounded strained. I listened across satellite airways and felt my heart thud. A job opening in the OU Norman campus weather building would be wonderful.

Frowning, I slowed. If he had just gotten a call about a position at Battlestar Norman, why did his voice sound so tense? I knew for a fact there hadn't been any postings for over a year. Becky Parsons had told me so.

"You're kidding, right?" I asked him. "Look, do you want me to go ahead and get us some hot dogs? The lines are long and I'll bet you're hungry."

"Get yourself something to eat."

"What time will you be here?" Relief washed through me. It wasn't like Jeremiah to kid around like this. He wasn't the type who teased.

"I just passed Goodland." His words started to sink in.

"What do you mean you just passed Goodland?" He was pulling one over on me. He had to be. "You mean Goodland, as in Goodland, *Kansas?*"

Silence.

"Are you telling me that you're in fucking Kansas?" I demanded, stopping so abruptly that I got jostled roughly by the passing crowd. I moved to the railing.

"I just passed Goodland." His voice was low, almost a whisper.

Pedestrians brushed past me on the concourse. "Just what the hell are you doing in Kansas?"

"I got a call from the Storm Prediction Center in Norman."

"You told me that already! Why didn't you call me? I could've met you in Limon!" Goodland was over three hours east of Denver. No way would I be able to catch up with him now. "Who called you about it?" I could not believe what I was hearing.

If I had been on top of things, I would have caught Jeremiah's hesitation before he answered.

"Becky. She overheard that Freddie is leaving at the end of next month. She faxed me the information and set up an interview."

An opening at Battlestar Norman. If Jeremiah got the position, I'd have no second thoughts about leaving Colorado Springs. I missed Oklahoma even with the irritating constant prairie wind, the winter ice storms, and the spring tornadoes. Moving back would give me the chance to mend things with Angela. If I left now, I'd be three hours behind him. While Gary was in the Springs, I would have some uninterrupted time to work things out with my sister.

"What time is your interview?" I asked as I retraced my steps along the concourse.

"Tomorrow morning, ten o'clock."

"Well, I'm leaving now, so pull over and wait for me. I can't believe you took off on your own. What's with you?" Jeremiah had not gotten much sleep yesterday. As of this morning, he had just finished his midnight rotation and was set to go back to day shift after our vacation. "Pull over at the next exit and sleep 'til I get there. We'll still get into Norman before midnight."

"No." He sounded curt. "Stay and watch the game, then head back to the Springs. I will call you after I finish the interview."

I yelled into my flip phone. "Like hell, Jeremiah. What's gotten into you?"

I heard him sigh. "Mattie, stay there. Go home after the game. I will be in touch." He cut the connection.

I slapped my phone shut and shoved it into my belt pack. Not only was our Sunday afternoon wrecked, I was also missing out on a trip to Oklahoma.

Norman. Jeremiah and I had met there, at the University of Oklahoma, during my senior year as a mass communications major. Jeremiah, a meteorologist seven years my senior, had been working at the weather prediction center on campus. Six months after we met, I landed an internship at the newspaper in Colorado Springs, and Jeremiah accepted a forecaster position at the Boulder FO. We had married in Shawnee, then moved to Colorado. Over the last seven years we had driven to Oklahoma and to the Southern Ute Reservation in southwest Colorado so often we had names for our favorite mile markers.

So why was Jeremiah taking off on his own to Oklahoma this time? His actions were way out of character. There was no reason for him not to pull over and get some sleep while I hopped onto the interstate and drove out to meet him. Why was he being so stubborn?

My cell rang again from inside my belt pack. It wasn't Jeremiah's ring tone. I debated whether or not to answer it because I didn't have the patience to be nice to anyone right now. If the caller got an earful, that was just too bad.

"Hello?" I almost shouted as I neared the east gates.

"Hello, this is Denver Hospital. I'm calling for Mattie Tyler." The voice on the other end sounded hurried, breathless.

I moved to the side of the incoming crowd and grabbed a railing. Cold fingers of fear crept round my heart. Six months ago I received a similar, devastating phone call that started just like this one.

I shut out the memory. I had just gotten off the phone with Jeremiah, so they couldn't be calling about him. The woman on the other end was giving her name, which went in one ear and out the other.

"We have a patient by the name of Angela Tacque here in the ER, and she begged us to call you before she crashed and we had to intubate her. An ambulance brought her in from Limon, and we're admitting her to the Intensive Care Unit. She was insisting that you're her sister."

Reality reeled into another dimension, my knees buckled, and I sank onto a metal bench near the entrance. "My *sister*? Where…where is she? What's happened?" I could hardly get the words around the sudden constriction in my throat.

"We're not sure yet. I've been trying to reach her husband, but he's not answering his cell phone. I've left several messages for him to return my calls. All I can tell you over the phone is that her condition is critical, and they're trying to stabilize her enough to get her to ICU." The voice rushed on. "She's on life support. Ms. Tyler, since I have you on the phone, will you give permission for us to continue treatment?"

"Of…of course." Shock rendered me speechless.

"Just a minute, I need to get another person in on this call." The line went silent, then a male voice clicked on, identifying himself as one of the emergency room doctors. I completely missed his name, too.

"Will you confirm your sister's birthday and social security number?"

I could confirm the first, had no idea what the second was. Her birthday seemed sufficient. I repeated my consent, and they started to ring off.

"Wait!" I shouted. "Are you sure you've got the right person? I mean, my sister lives in Oklahoma! What was she doing in Limon? What do you mean her condition is critical?"

There was a pause. "We ought to have her in ICU within the hour. You better come as soon as possible." The line clicked dead. I stared at my phone in disbelief.

It simply could NOT be true. Please God, not another accident.

I did not have Gary's cell phone number. I sat there, too stunned to think. The crack of a bat reached my ears, then the collective roar of the stadium crowd. The game must be starting. I stumbled over to one of the food venders and asked whether they had a phone book. The lady behind the counter gave me a sour look and shook her head. I turned away and leaned against the cold stadium concrete wall.

Information. I needed to get hold of Gary.

I tried the 411 number on my cell. Got a recording. I tried zero. Got another recording. Called the newspaper main desk number next.

"This is Kim, how can I help you." Kim sounded bored. At least someone was at the desk today.

"Hey, Kim, it's Mattie. Will you do me a favor and look up the number for the Broadmoor?"

"This is why you need a smart phone, Mattie."

I rolled my eyes and hoped she wouldn't start in on me again about my choice of telecommunications. I heard a faint thump and guessed she had plopped the phone book down on the desk.

"I thought Mel gave you an ultimatum. Upgrade your phone or find a new job."

"Kim, that really isn't any of your business. Just look up the number for me." I had difficulty keeping my irritation in check.

"Here it is." She read it off. Without taking time to thank her, I cut the call and punched in the number. A pleasant female voice greeted me on the other end. I told the woman I needed to contact Gary Tacque, a participant attending a drug company conference being held there. An emergency concerning his wife. I got put on hold. Surely, Gary would be able to shed some light on what was going on. I leaned against the wall for support and waited through some advertisement crap droning in my ear.

The blood drained right out of my face when the woman came back on the line.

"I'm very sorry, ma'am, but there is no drug company conference being held here this weekend. I've checked the schedules of every room, as well as the International Center."

I managed to thank her, then dropped my arm to my side.

Gary had been lying. A terrible suspicion trickled into my thoughts.

Had Angela *left* Gary? Had she been in an accident while on her way to Colorado? Had Gary been chasing her down when he showed up at our apartment yesterday?

I punched in Jeremiah's cell number but got his voicemail. I left a message to call me immediately, then pushed off the wall and made my way through the crowd towards the east gates. I needed to get to the hospital.

My legs felt like rubber bands as I tried to hurry against the pedestrian flow through the gates, across the boulevard, into the parking area. My fingers trembled when I retrieved my key fob and unlocked the Subaru. I slid behind the wheel, tossed my stuff onto the passenger seat, and tried to get the key into the ignition. It took three attempts before the key slid in and I got the engine started. Belatedly I realized I could have used the key fob to start the damned engine. I sat immobile, trying to pull myself together enough to drive. Tears blurred my vision as I drove out of the parking lot and headed along the roadway.

If the patient really was Angela, then what in the world was she doing in Colorado? According to Gary, she was in Norman.

But Gary had lied about what brought him to Colorado Springs, so it followed that he might be lying about Angela's whereabouts. If Angela had left him, Gary would never admit that to me.

So, if Angela had been on her way to Colorado, why hadn't she called me?

I swore at the wedge Gary had shoved between my sister and me. Deep down I knew it wasn't really his fault, but laying the blame on him sure helped me feel better.

I swiped a hand across my face and began looking for a gas station to ask directions. I spotted a 7-Eleven, pulled into the parking lot, and ran into the store.

"Can you tell me how to get to Denver Hospital?" I panted.

The store clerk couldn't answer my question, and I realized I had the number on my cell phone. I scrolled until I found the number with the Denver area code. A woman answered, and I cut in before she could say anything more than "hello".

"I need directions to your hospital."

"Where are you calling from?" She asked.

A reasonable question, but I wasn't thinking reasonably. "I don't know!" I almost screeched. "Wait, hang on a second." I called out to the employee standing behind the cash register. "Where is this place?"

He told me the nearest intersection, and I relayed it to the voice on the phone. After a pause, she gave me the information, which I repeated to myself like a mantra as I exited the convenience store and slid into my car.

Of course I got lost. At one point I realized I was traveling the wrong way on a one-way, and pulled into a vacant parking lot. My legs shook so hard I had trouble maintaining pressure on the brake. I leaned my head against the steering wheel, curled my trembling arms against my chest, and tried to coax thoughts into something useful. When I raised my head, I saw that I was facing a broad street with bi-directional traffic. Signal lights and signs slid by in a blur. After what seemed years I spotted a tall rectangular building with **DEN-VER HOSPITAL** across the top. I followed the building, oblivious to the directions I had been given, but couldn't figure out how to get there. In the end I parked in an empty lot and ran the rest of the way.

Chapter Four

Downtown Denver sidewalks were deserted. Squat old buildings with barred windows and door fronts appeared vaguely threatening rather than simply closed. I kept the tall hospital building in sight and found the front entrance. If I had been thinking, I would have paid attention to the street names and numbers so I could find my car later.

The receptionist at the information desk told me which floor the adult ICU was on, and I headed across the atrium for the elevators. Sunshine streamed through skylights, shone on broad, leafy plants and a three-tier water fountain, did nothing for the feeling of doom that hovered over me. I thought fleetingly that the same sunshine was lighting up happy, animated faces at the ballpark.

I paced between the four elevator doors, willing one of them to open. I was ready to head for the stairs when one arrived. I punched number six and hoped it didn't stop on every floor.

It stopped once, which in my agitated state was once too many. The round lit numbers over the door pinged steadily until they reached five. The doors dinged open and an older man dressed in green scrubs and carrying an old-fashioned doctor's case stepped in, followed by two female employees dressed in printed uniforms. Irrational anger surged through me at the delay. After way too long, the doors closed and the elevator inched to the next floor. I strode to the directional arrows on the opposite wall, learned that ICU was to the right, and rounded the corner, hoping there weren't visiting restrictions. I didn't care. I was going to see my sister, even if it took creating a scene to do so.

The doors to the unit were open, and I walked into a hushed atmosphere. A crescent-shaped nursing station spanned most of the room. Individual glass-fronted private rooms lined the walls. A middle-aged woman in lavender scrubs glanced up from where she sat in front of a desk computer. Gray hair sprang from a disintegrating bun on the crown of her head. She had a stethoscope around her neck and pockets full of pens and other paraphernalia.

"Can I help you?" Her tired smile matched her tired blue eyes.

I glanced at her nametag.

"Hi, Margaret. My name is Mattie Tyler. Someone from ER called a little while ago and told me that my sister, Angela Tacque, was being admitted to your unit."

Margaret's expression grew serious and she stood. "Follow me."

She rounded the end of the desk, but instead of leading me into one of the rooms, she strode through the doors of the unit and into a nearby waiting room. She closed the door behind me.

"Sit down, honey," she instructed, indicating one of two brown leather easy chairs. She pulled a chair over, sat down in front of me, leaned forward to rest her forearms on her knees, and pressed her hands together.

"When did you last see your sister?"

Her question startled me. "Well, I was…I mean my husband and I were in Oklahoma in January. For our parents' funeral."

Margaret's eyes studied mine. "How did she look?"

My eyebrows raised. "Well, fine, I guess. Normal anyway. What's going on?"

Margaret ignored my question. "Does Angela have any chronic health issues that you know of?"

I wanted answers. "Margaret, quit asking questions and start answering some of mine. Please. What is going on, and how serious is Angela's condition?"

Margaret lowered her head and remained silent for several long seconds. Then she lifted her face. "She appears to be dying."

My heart thumped hard against my chest and I found it impossible to believe her. "What?"

"She's dying," Margaret repeated, leaning against her chair. "Not having a history or any kind of medical background on her, we can't pin down a diagnosis without running a battery of tests. Without a diagnosis, we can only treat her symptoms, rather than the cause."

I lifted my hands. "Whoa, diagnosis? I thought she was in an accident!"

She frowned. "Who told you she was in an accident?"

I lowered my hands and pressed them against the arms of the chair. "The lady in the ER said that Angela crashed."

Margaret shook her head. "No, what she meant was that Angela's vital signs bottomed out. She almost arrested on them."

My slumped against the easy chair, tears watering my eyes. "But…but if she wasn't in an accident, then what's wrong with her?"

Margaret looked at me, her expression neutral. "It looks as though Angela's suffering from severe anorexia, complicated by an inability for her blood to clot."

My mouth dropped open and my mind froze, then the room began to spin.

Margaret jumped up and leaned over me. "Head between your knees, honey, and breathe."

Sweat broke out on my forehead and began to stream down my face. Her firm but gentle hand massaged the back of my neck. I gulped air and told myself fainting was for sissies. After what seemed like ages things began to settle and the floor slid into focus.

"Better?" Margaret asked.

I nodded, still staring at the floor.

"Good. I'm going to get you something to drink and a cold cloth. I'll be right back. If you start feeling faint again, pull that cord beside you."

I raised my head enough to see a long white cord dangling from a metal panel switch. Above it **EMERGENCY** was stamped in large black letters.

I started to sweat again and lowered my head. I watched her white rubber-soled shoes walk away, then a triangle of light widened on the carpeted floor when she opened the door to the waiting room. Voices came from outside the door, and I heard her ask whoever it was to use another room. A few minutes later she was back with a Styrofoam cup.

"Here, honey, drink this."

I straightened and leaned back. Margaret pulled a lever, and the chair reclined. I took the cup. Orange Juice.

Angela's favorite. Mine had always been tomato. I wasn't sweating anymore, but I felt cold. Not from the temperature in the room, either. It came from deep, deep inside. Margaret handed me a cold wet washcloth, which I used to wipe my face.

"We don't have any history on your sister, so I need to ask you some questions."

I took a sip and nodded, pressing the wet cloth to the back of my neck.

She resumed her seat. "Has she ever been diagnosed with depression, or been suicidal?"

I choked, leaned forward, tried to catch my breath. "Wh—what? No! Whatever would give you an idea like that?"

Instead of answering my question, Margaret asked another. "Has she been on any anti-depressants or anti-coagulants that you know of?"

"Would you get off this depression crap?" I demanded, pulling the cloth from the back of my neck. "Angela has never been depressed in her life!"

Margaret studied me for several silent moments. "Mattie, I know that you might not want to think of your sister like this, but I need you to try to see beyond the person who is your sister and look at her just as a person for a moment." Her expression held empathy, yet somehow I got the feeling she wasn't emotionally involved. I wondered whether maintaining distance from patients and their families was a professional necessity.

I emptied the cup and set it down and the cloth on an end table. The subdued glow of the table lamp did nothing to soften Margaret's news.

"Have you gotten in touch with her husband?" I asked.

"We haven't been able to contact him. I've left messages on his cell phone. Fortunately, ER got hold of you. I haven't found any other numbers or contacts in her purse."

"Well, he showed up at our apartment and said that Angela was in Oklahoma. She didn't call me about coming up for a visit, and she hasn't told me that she's been sick. Why didn't she let me know she was coming to Colorado? How did she get to your ER?" I couldn't remember what the ER person had said in our brief conversation.

Margaret held a hand up, and I stopped. "An ambulance crew responded to a nine-one-one call and found her along the interstate just east of Limon," she explained. "When they got there, your sister was awake but rambling. They decided to bring her here instead of the county hospital. She had just arrived when she crashed. Her vital signs, that is."

I scooted to the end of the recliner and stood. "I want to see her."

Margaret stood with me, her expression sober. "It's going to be a shock."

My mouth tightened. "I want to see her anyway."

Margaret nodded and led the way through the unit doors, passing a small group consisting of a woman and three children, all of them in tears. We walked to the glass-enclosed room on the furthest end from the ICU entrance, but the closest room to the nurses' station. Rapid, regular high-pitched chirps and soft mechanical wheezes sighed from behind the closed curtains. I inhaled a steadying breath and stepped around.

At first I felt relief, because the woman in the bed did not look anything like Angela. Wispy, dull brown hair straggled around a skeletally thin head and face. Bits of a pasty looking chest and bony shoulder peeked from beneath white linens. Prominent purple veins snaked along the back of the woman's bony hand. Multiple strands of IV tubing rose from her exposed collarbone to several bags hanging on ceiling hooks, while telemetry wires dangled from an overhead monitor. Green spikes registered her rapid heart rate. A short, square machine wheezed and sighed at the bedside, rhythmically moving the opaque, corrugated plastic tubing that connected to another tube protruding from one corner of her mouth. My eyes traveled to the woman's face, and I leaned closer as I spotted something familiar. A scar, normally hidden by her hairline, stood out in stark whiteness against the gray color of her skin.

A scar Angela had gotten from a laceration when we were kids playing in our massive backyard. Down among the trees we had discovered a large piece of corrugated tin that had been blown from someone's property during a spring storm. We thought it a grand idea to haul it back to the sophisticated play area Dad had installed for us, and use the crossbars on the swing set to make a slide out of it. We had been climbing all over the thing when Angela had fallen, slicing open the side of her face on the sharp metal edges. While Mom whisked Angela to the ER, Dad had tried to soothe my hysteria at the sight of all her blood. The original ragged scar required a couple of cosmetic surgeries to reduce it to the thin line she had now.

I covered my mouth with my hand to muffle a choking sob.

"Is she your sister?" Margaret's voice asked from behind me.

I nodded, my eyes now focusing on the unmistakable signs of approaching death. Bloody drainage leaked from the corners of her closed eyelids, from her nose, crusted around her semi-parted lips. Margaret stepped around me, pulled a pair of latex gloves from a box on a shelf at the head of the bed, put them on, then took a damp white washcloth from the bed railing and gently cleaned her face.

"She started bleeding like this shortly after we got her in here. Stat blood work showed that her clotting time is way off. We're typing her for several units of platelets and whole blood, but without knowing what has caused her clotting problems, we're treating blind." She tossed the blood-smeared cloth into a tall red plastic bag with the word **BIO-HAZARD** in large black letters. Then she peeled off the gloves and threw them into a second red bag. I motioned with a hand towards the tube in her mouth, unable to form words into a query.

Margaret understood my gesture. "We had to intubate her. She stopped breathing, and the ER doctor inserted a tube to get air into her lungs. She's not breathing on her own."

I shook my head and tried to force words around the lump clogging my throat. "Angela would never...she...she would *never* do something like this to herself."

Margaret nodded towards the door. I followed her back through the curtains and out to the nurses' station. I'm sure other nurses and hospital personnel were present, but I was in a fog. All I saw was Margaret's haphazard bun threatening to tumble loose from the top of her head. As she led me around the main desk to a small conference room, I tried to order my disjointed thoughts.

"Has your sister ever been diagnosed with a blood disorder, like clotting problems, something like that?" She asked after shutting the door and motioning for me to take a seat in a hard, plastic, straight-back chair. She sat beside me.

I shook my head.

She leaned towards me and pressed her hands together. "I know I asked this earlier, but I need to know whether she has a history of depression, either chronic or acute, and whether she's ever had any suicidal tendencies."

I shook my head again. "No...I mean, I don't think so." I stared straight into her tired blue eyes. "Angela got a job at the hospital in Norman, in Social Services. If she started having emotional problems, it's only been in the last six months or so."

"When is the last time you talked to her?"

I cringed. "In...February." I leaned my elbows on the oblong brown Formica table and held my face in my hands. "I...I got mad at her because she and her husband eloped without telling me. We lost our parents in January. Angela and I were really close, before Gary—he's her husband—came along. I didn't like him." I leaned back, avoiding Margaret's eyes. "I know, it's her life, not mine. I shouldn't have gotten mad at her for eloping instead of going through the rigmarole of a wedding. I was being selfish. And then we just quit calling each other." I looked at her. "How long do you think she's been sick?"

Margaret shrugged. "It's hard to say without medical records. She could have been anorexic for a while."

"But she was healthy and active six months ago," I insisted, leaning forward.

"It doesn't take long to wreck your system when you go on a starvation diet," Margaret replied with patience.

I sat for several minutes, thinking. "What would make her blood clotting go haywire like that?"

"If she has a history of clots, she might have been started on Coumadin. Overdosing on aspirin will do it, but it would have to be a major overdose for her to get this bad." She hesitated, then added, "Rat poison is another possibility."

"Won't the treatment be the same?"

"At this point, we're trying to cover all bases. What's your blood type?"

I told her. Mine was different than Angela's.

Margaret shook her head. "That's too bad. The blood bank is really low on Angela's blood type."

I squeezed my eyes against the image of my sister and choked out my next words. "Can you…can you turn things around?"

Margaret laid a gentle hand on my arm. "Chances of recovery in her present condition are very, very slim. I hate to paint such a negative picture, but I feel it's only fair to be completely honest with you. Lab-work shows her organs are shutting down. Once we get the transfusions started, things might get better."

My next words were even harder. "Is…is she in any pain?"

Margaret shook her head. "She has not recovered consciousness since she came in to the unit. She's not responding to either verbal or painful stimuli. The doctor has ordered a CT scan and an EEG. He's worried that she might have some cerebral bleeding. She's not light enough to be feeling any pain."

I had been doing okay until now. I stared at her, appreciating her honesty and hating it at the same time. I leaned over and tried to control the sudden onslaught of sobs, tried not disturb the hush of the room. Margaret rubbed her hand up and down my back. I couldn't stop or even slow down the emotional tidal wave.

"Do you have numbers of friends and other relatives? I can start making some calls," she offered. Her question gave me direction.

"Let me do some calling around...I...I want to call the hospital where she worked. And we have f-friends, but I don't have all the n-numbers with me," I managed in shaky tones.

"We'll keep trying to reach her husband." Margaret stood and led the way through a door. We walked back to the waiting room. A young woman and two toddlers were watching a kids program on the television. Margaret asked them to give me some privacy, then closed the door and turned off the TV.

"Come and get me if you need anything. I'm here until seven tonight." She paused, frowning. "I really hate to bring this up, especially at a time like this...but sometime before you go you'll need to go down to the business office and hash out an arrangement concerning payment or insurance information. When I looked through Angela's wallet, I didn't find an insurance card."

"Can I have Angela's purse? She might have some numbers I can use to contact people about this."

Margaret nodded and disappeared though the door. I paced the little room until she returned with Angela's handbag.

"Margaret?" She had opened the door and turned when I called her name. Light from the hallway created a halo around her straggled hair. It took several moments before I had enough to courage to ask the next question.

"How...how long do you think she has?"

She leaned against the door to keep it open. Her calm, professional expression did not change when she answered. "It's hard to tell. Maybe a couple of days, not longer than a week if we can't get her clotting factor stabilized. I'm sorry."

I nodded, then sank into the brown recliner and tried to think whom to call first. Angela's image kept crowding in, paralyzing my efforts to do anything. I pulled my cell phone from my belt pack and tried Jeremiah. When I got his voice mail again, I almost threw my phone against the wall.

Oh, Angela, I silently wailed, *what happened?* I couldn't control the suspicions that began to grow. Why did Gary lie about her whereabouts? Why did he lie about the reason he came to the Springs? Had he been trying to protect me from whatever had happened to Angela? Was he protecting Angela, thinking I would react the same way I had when they told me about their elopement?

Did he have something do to with her current condition?

Why hadn't Angela called to tell me she was so sick? Why hadn't she called when she started driving to Colorado?

I found Angela's wallet and pulled out one of her business cards. That sounded as good a place to start as any. I began punching numbers into my cell phone.

"Norman Regional Hospital. How may I direct your call?" The female voice spoke with a heavy rural accent.

"I need to talk to someone in Social Services."

"I'm sorry, ma'am, no one is here today since it's a Sunday. But I can give you the number for the person on call. Hold just a minute, please." Radio music came over the line. The line clicked, and the lady came back on with the information. I thanked her, ended the call, then sat and stared at the beige paint on the walls. I needed answers. Angela's boss wouldn't be in the office until tomorrow. Control struggled with the strong urge to scream.

My sister would never starve herself, or try to commit suicide. Despite what might appear to the nursing staff to be anorexia and a suicide attempt, I knew my sister.

The image of Angela's shrunken body pressed before my eyes. What was wrong with her? Was there anything the doctors could do to turn things around? I squeezed my eyes shut and swiped at tears with cold, shaking hands.

I tried Jeremiah's cell for what seemed the millionth time, and for the millionth time got his voicemail.

Why wasn't he answering his phone? I needed him to turn around and get his butt back to Denver. Interviews could wait, damn it. I didn't have Gary's cell number, not that I would be able to carry on a coherent conversation with him anyway. Angela probably had it in her wallet somewhere. I rummaged through the rest of her things and came up with a bunch of loose change, wadded up Kleenex, and some mangled soda straws, but no cell phone or address book. I searched for Becky Parsons' number in my contacts list, but got another voice mail.

What day was it? Oh, yeah. Sunday. Duh. She and Bill were probably involved with church functions. The only other person I could think of to call was Irma Greenbeck, but I didn't have her number with me, and I couldn't Google the information on my ancient flip phone. Should I drive all the way back to Colorado Springs for the information or should I wait here and keep trying the numbers I already had?

In the end, I decided to return to my car and retrieve my overnight bag. I would ask Margaret about bringing in a cot so I could sleep in the room with Angela.

I walked back to the nurse's station and looked for Margaret, but she wasn't in sight. I felt horrible, but I could not bring myself to go back and be with my sister yet. I needed time to adjust to the way she looked. Margaret appeared from around the curtains of the cubicle Angela occupied. Fortunately, when I described the parking lot where I had left my car, she knew the location and drew a map for me. As I walked to the elevators, I wondered how she managed to deal with death and tragedy on a daily basis without losing her mind.

Dark, heavy clouds encroached upon the pristine afternoon as storm cells piled high into the upper atmosphere. Ominous rumbling echoed around the tall downtown buildings. A cool wind stirred, carrying with it the scent of rain. I stood there for several minutes, staring at the broad avenue in front of the hospital and wondering where all the people were. Surrounding structures threw premature shadows over parked cars and swaying trees. I started down the sidewalk, referring to Margaret's map as I walked.

The low grinding sound and pungent smell of diesel hailed the approach of a city bus. I glanced back to see it lumbering along in the closest lane. Thunder rumbled again, louder than earlier. My thoughts focused inward as I walked.

Why oh why had I not called every friend in Shawnee after losing communication with my sister? I should have called the Parsons and asked them to talk to Angela when I couldn't get hold of her. Better still, I should have beat it down to Norman and talked to her myself.

Gary's face came to mind and anger steamed through every pore. That lying, low-life, creepy bastard. All I could think was that he had something to do with Angela's condition.

My feet slowed, then stopped all together and I stared at the concrete sidewalk as a thought slowly unwound, like film from a spool. My chest constricted until I couldn't breathe.

No, no, no. This was real life, not some TV show. There had to be another explanation, I told myself, trying to block the thought. But my revelation made sense, connected all recent events, explained the breach in communication between Angela and myself.

No sixth sense warned me of imminent danger, no sudden sound caught my attention. I was jerked from my preoccupation when a pair of rough, powerful hands seized my arms from behind. A man snarled in my ear as he tripped my feet, then shoved me so hard that my head snapped backwards, propelling me off the sidewalk into the path of the oncoming bus.

Chapter Five

The front of the bus loomed like a garish metal monster. I was too close for the driver to swerve in time to miss me. A fragmented image of splattering blood and body parts flashed before my eyes. Please don't let there be children around, I prayed.

I crashed onto the unforgiving surface of the boulevard, cracking the side of my head hard as I tumbled and rolled. The turbulence from the bus whipped around me, assaulting my nostrils with the odors of tires, diesel, and asphalt. Pain knifed through my head and body.

Scattered shouts, blaring horns, and shrieking tires punctuated the air. I realized vaguely I was still alive, and if I wanted to stay that way, I needed to get myself out of the middle of the boulevard.

No go. I couldn't organize whirling brain cells enough to move muscles.

Just as I figured I had only postponed death, hands snaked under my arms, hauled me up, and dragged me across the remainder of the boulevard.

"On your feet! *Quickly!*" The man's voice was low, hissing, and British. With a startled gasp I realized he was the same man whom I'd mistaken for Jeremiah at the ball park. His strong arm coiled around my waist and began dragging me along the sidewalk. Thoughts of a probable concussion swam around the sharp jabs in my head. Great. Lying down seemed infinitely wiser. I tried to push his arm away.

"Take...me...to the...ER." I winced because talking aggravated the pain in my head. He held me close against his side. I tried waving my left hand to catch his attention.

"Quit fighting," he ordered.

"L-let g-go." My thinking slowed and my tongue thickened. "I n-need to g-go to the ER...p-please."

Ignoring my pleas, he pushed on. Our movement triggered vague waves of nausea, and I broke out in a damp, shivering sweat.

"I-I need to lie d-down. I'm f-feeling sick." If I threw up all over the idiot, it would be his own fault. I squeezed my eyes shut and concentrated on keeping stomach contents on the inside.

We crossed two intersections, then abruptly turned a corner. I risked opening my eyes and saw tall concrete walls and dim shadows instead of glass sliding doors leading to an emergency room. No pedestrians, no cars. Warning bells began mixing with the pain in my head.

"I need to get to an ER." I tried again. "I…think I have a…concussion."

"You're going to have more than a bloody concussion when I'm done with you, if you don't give me some bloody fucking answers." He grabbed a fistful of my short hair, spun me around, and pinned me against the cold concrete, his free hand catching my left wrist and cruelly twisting my arm almost to my shoulder blade. I cried out in pain. Terror blew through every fiber.

"Narrow miss that time. Almost got yourself splattered on the front of that lorry, didn't you? Why did you run from Lee?" His low, angry words hissed in my ear.

"I-I g-got p-pushed." I choked as he crushed my chest against the cold concrete. Pain scorched through my left arm and shoulder.

"Bloody liar. I saw you take off from the ballpark. Who told you I'd be at the game today? Who were you planning on giving that picture to? Which bloody ragmag do you work for?" His strong accent made nonsense of his words. He wrenched my arm and I choked on a cry.

"Answer me!"

"I d-don't know!" I stammered. "I don't k-know what you're t-talking about! P-please! You're b-breaking my arm!"

"Damned straight I'll break it, if you don't start cooperating." The sudden drop in his tone shot ice through my limbs. My mouth took off on its own.

"I g-got a c-call from Denver Hospital while I was at the game. The l-lady said my s-s-sister's in ICU. They f-found her in Limon. She said she was c-critical. She said I n-n-needed to get to the h-hospital as soon as p-possible."

"Why did you take my picture?" His body pressed against my ribcage until I couldn't breathe. Hysteria thrashed my insides in an uncontrollable windstorm.

"I-I thought you were my husband. I thought you were Jeremiah. When I used my camera to get a closer look, I saw that you weren't him. B-but…" I broke off, too terrified to continue.

My arm felt like it was tearing right out of the socket. Black spots danced around my blurred vision.

"But what?" He snarled in my ear.

My voice deteriorated to a harsh squeak. "But I l-like taking candids, and I l-liked the way th-the f-frame looked, so I-I…." I couldn't finish.

Awful, silent seconds passed.

I felt him relax, and I began to tremble violently. When he let go and stepped away, my left arm slid down to my side like a slab of dead meat. My knees buckled and I sank to the cold, hard concrete floor, huddling my right side against the chilly wall. Pain throbbed everywhere.

Clothing rustled, and I sensed the man kneel down. Coarse tremors shook me, my teeth chattered. I coughed and couldn't slow down my ragged, panicked breathing.

"Look at me."

I didn't want to. I squeezed my eyes tightly closed and begged God to grant that childhood belief, that if I couldn't see him, then he couldn't see me.

Steel fingers gripped my shoulders and twisted me around until my back pressed against the wall. My left arm hung at my side, his grip digging like talons into my shoulder.

"Look at me," he repeated.

I opened my eyes and tried to focus on the face in front of me. Shock and head injury refused to line up eyeballs.

"Why would Lee be over here, meeting with you? What threat did that ragmag send across the waves?"

I stared into the cold shadows that held his eyes, tried to fight terror with a modicum of anger.

"I…I don't know what the hell you're talking about. Go away, you fucking Brit."

He squatted in silence for several minutes. I closed my eyes. My legs and feet started to tingle from being bent awkwardly beneath me.

"Where's your mobile?"

Using my right hand, I fumbled with the zipper on my belt pack, but my fingers were too cold and numb to get the thing to work. His fingers brushed mine away, pulled the zipper, then rummaged through the contents. I opened my eyes and watched as he flipped my phone open.

"What's the number?"

I struggled to figure out what he wanted. "You mean for the hospital?"

I assumed his cold stare meant yes.

"The area code is three-oh-three. I don't know the number."

Evidently he found it. As he raised the phone to his ear, his attention turned back to me. "What's your sister's name?"

I told him. Somewhere along the way he had lost his ball cap and sunglasses. I didn't try to get a better look at his features. If I got out of this alive, that would be enough. I raised my right hand and gently massaged my left shoulder and arm, but only managed to make things worse. I gave up and dropped my hand to my lap. His eyes met mine when he spoke. I closed mine again and wished he would go away.

"Yes, I'm on holiday, and I've a friend who's in hospital. I'd like to send flowers. Her name is Angela Tacque." His manners were impeccable. "Yes, that would be the one...in ICU is she? Might I send flowers anyway? Yes, thank you...You've been most helpful." He closed the phone and tucked it into a pocket of his jeans. "Where's your camera?"

"I left it in my car." I kept my eyes closed, hoping he might still disappear.

"As you didn't have the incriminating evidence on you, why did you avoid Lee?"

My eyes snapped open, and I tried to glare at the unfocused blob in front of me. "I don't know anyone named Lee. I was too busy trying to figure out what my brother-in-law has done to my sister, and I was walking back to the car to get my overnight case." I wriggled my feet out from underneath me and unbent my legs. Sharp tingles jabbed my thighs and calves as circulation got going again. I straightened against the wall and stretched my legs, then wiggled my toes in my sneakers. At least they still worked.

I waited for his next accusation, but he fell silent. I should have tried looking around to see where we were, but the pain in my head felt better when I closed my eyes. Besides, looking at the backs of my eyelids felt infinitely safer than looking at him.

Nausea surged, vile and vicious. Sweat broke out on my forehead and started trickling down my face.

"You've gone green." He grasped my shoulders and steered me onto the cold floor. I started to shiver. When I heard some metallic clicking, I blinked my eyes open with automatic curiosity.

The man had a gun in his hand, one of those semi-automatic things like the police carry nowadays, and was screwing a long cylinder onto the end. He glanced down, saw me watching. He reached behind him and tucked the weapon underneath the back of his shirt.

"I shouldn't have seen that." I squeezed my eyes shut and mourned the cold fact that I couldn't become invisible.

"No, you shouldn't have." His words echoed through my head, their threat clear.

Shadows encroached, and I thought about Angela. I needed to be at the hospital. As gray slid into black, I wondered whether I'd be alive long enough to wake up again.

~ * ~

I awoke to chilly twilight, cold concrete, and complete disorientation. The left side of my head ached miserably. Muscles complained when I lifted my left arm to my head, and I found a large lump just behind my left temple. I was lying on my right side. If I shifted my eyes slowly, my vision remained steady. I looked around, trying to get a bearing on where I was, but couldn't see anything other than some scattered newspapers lying nearby. The dull throb in my head accelerated to a heavy pounding when I tried to sit up. Vague memories of terror hovered close to the surface.

"You're awake."

Movement in the corner of my eye caught my attention, and a shadow shifted into the form of a man. I jolted so badly, my head thumped against the concrete floor. Memory slammed back, and my heart galloped around my chest when he bent close, grasped my arms, and eased me into a sitting position. I leaned against the concrete wall and knew my expression reflected my panic. I decided not to ask why I was still alive.

"Why are you still here?" I asked instead.

"You passed out before I could get directions to your car." He squatted on his heels in front of me.

"Since you obviously found a way to follow me from the ballpark, then you should already know where I parked." I bent my knees and struggled upwards until I stood. My head began a wicked spin and I leaned against the wall for support.

That's when all the other injuries made themselves known. Pain hit from everywhere. Arms, legs, and torso felt stiff as rigor mortis. I would believe I was dead, except for the fact I was still breathing. I groaned and closed my eyes against screeching nerve endings. Maybe I would have been better off plastered against the bus grill.

"You've quite a knot on your noggin."

"I wish you'd speak plain English," I muttered, wishing I could somehow fall off the careening mental merry-go-round.

"You hit your head."

I opened my eyes to look at him. He stood next to me, more like a blurred shadow than a person.

He glanced down at his wristwatch. "Half past seven. You've been out all afternoon. I thought you might have gone and slipped into a coma."

"You should have taken me to the ER, like I asked you to." I prayed he wouldn't notice the way my voice shook.

"They wouldn't have improved things."

I spent two fuzzy days with Jeremiah after the Elephant Rock bike ride three weeks ago. I'd been cruising downhill close to thirty miles an hour when I hit a pothole, lost control, and ended up on my head in a large ditch. The ER staff had checked me in, checked me over, then checked me out in the care of my husband, with instructions to bring me back if I went to sleep and didn't wake up. Upon reflection, I supposed the man had done what the ER doctor would have instructed anyway.

"I'm awake now, so go away." I swiveled my eyes past him, wishing someone would walk by so I could grab an arm and get away from this nut. I pushed myself from the wall with the intention of walking past him. My gut started to roll again and various aches converged into one overwhelmingly wave of agony. Sweat streamed down my forehead. I needed to lie down before I fainted, but I refused to listen to common sense. I swayed, reached a hand to the wall for support, decided a face plant wouldn't hurt any worse than my other injuries.

The man stepped close.

"Right bundle of cheer you are." He grasped my arms. "You're in no bloody shape to go anywhere."

His touch created another jolt of panic, and I closed my eyes. "I'm fine. And I definitely don't need your help." The wicked spinning did not relent. "Where is everyone? Why hasn't someone called the police on you for loitering?"

Why was I still with this guy?

"A bit of rubbish and a few dailies go a long way. We're a couple of bums taking an afternoon snooze. Some lady even dropped me a fiver." His strange change of mood made me nervous.

"I need to get back to Angela." I tried to sound assertive in a way that would convince him to let me go.

"Right." His arm snaked around my waist like a python before squeezing its prey.

"Let go and leave me alone!" I couldn't hide the fear that shot through me.

Instead, he tucked my limp left arm beneath his armpit and started out of the empty shadows.

Panic seized me. The last thing I wanted was to be forced to go anywhere with the man. "Look, my car is in an empty lot. Take the keys and just take the car. It's got all my camera equipment."

He hauled me along the sidewalk. Occasional vehicles rolled past. No one was around, not even a pet owner walking their dog in the cool evening hours.

Damn it all, where are people when you need them?

Cool air swirled around us as twilight deepened. Street lamps threw oval glows that did not illuminate his face. I took a deep fortifying breath.

"Who is Lee?" I asked, although I didn't really care about an answer. Asking questions might kick my brain into gear.

He snorted. "Don't expect me to believe you don't know. You ran from the ballpark to meet the chap."

"I wasn't meeting anyone. I was trying to get to the hospital." Talking was making the pain in my head worse.

"And took your bloody time getting there. Pre-mapped your route, did you?"

I wanted to hit him. "I was lost. I can never find my way around downtown Denver." Conversation wasn't helping. My head and stomach clashed with miserable results. I started dragging my feet, hoping he would stop.

His grip tightened. "Keep moving. We're easy targets out here."

We turned right at an intersection, and I spotted my red Subaru alone in a pool of light thrown by one of the parking lot lamps. Maybe I should try screaming.

"Don't be stupid," he snapped when my ribcage expanded

against his arm.

I blew out a ragged breath. "I am NOT getting in that car with you. If you followed me to get your hands on the camera, then go get it. Then go find Lee, whoever the hell he is. I need to head back to Denver Hospital and protect my sister. I've got to find out what Gary..." I broke off.

"What about Gary? Is he the brother-in-law? You mentioned something about him." His astute comment unnerved me.

"I didn't mention anything about him." Who was this nut? And was he still carrying a loaded weapon in his back pocket? Was he going to use it on me in the vacant parking lot?

Thoughts of hired killers whirled around, bringing the threat of renewed panic. Was that the reason he hadn't wanted his picture taken? Was he some hired gun? Why had he followed me from the ballpark?

Gary would know which hospital Angela was in. Margaret said the ER had left messages on his cell. He could have called this guy with the information and told him to get rid of me. Maybe this psycho had pushed me in front of the bus. Maybe there had been too many witnesses. Maybe he realized when I missed getting hit I might have seen him and would have a description to report.

Maybe, I thought with a cringe, I was going nuts.

We reached the parking lot, and my keys appeared in his left hand. He pointed the key fob towards the car, then hesitated.

I took the opportunity to try one more time. "Please," I whispered, "Take the car. Leave me here."

"Quiet." He had tensed. I heard the automatic starter crank and opened my mouth to scream when the man swung me off my feet and slammed us to the pavement. My head smacked against the tarmac, jettisoning my headache from a throb into a full-throated jackhammer.

K-A-A-B-O-O-O-M.

The deafening explosion ripped the quiet night and rocked the ground beneath me. Sounds of screeching metal and roaring assaulted my ears as white-hot flames threatened to sear clothes and skin from both of us. The man rolled, taking me with him, until we were clear. Heavy black smoke billowed upwards.

"Keep moving." He rolled again. I felt cool pavement underneath me and tried to stop. He slid over me, then dragged me around a corner and down a concrete slab into what seemed to be a culvert.

"You…blew up…my car." I could barely put words together. "I'm…not going a-anywhere with you…you…b-bastard…you… blew up my car!"

"Not bloody likely," he snapped as he hauled me to my feet. "We need to stay out of sight and get back to the garage." He held me upright when my knees sagged.

"I'm not going anywhere with you." I tried to fight as he dragged me along the dry rounded bottom of the culvert. I kicked at him, but he clamped his free hand around the side of my neck and twisted my torso until I couldn't use my legs for anything but shaky support. Pain rocketed through me.

"You bastard," I groaned, wishing I could shout loud enough for someone to hear. We stumbled around corners and down empty alleys. Faint sirens pealed through the air. He curled around yet another building, then pressed me against a cold brick wall. Darkness hid us. When I tried to scream his hand gripped my mouth.

"Keep quiet." He peered around the corner of the building and his left hand slipped behind his back. The memory of his gun generated another memory, and a gut-wrenching childhood nightmare threatened to surface.

"I need some straight answers." His attention remained on whatever lay beyond the shadows of the building. "Was Lee your contact?" He loosened his hand enough for me to reply. If my head hadn't been feeling like it was about to split open, I would have started cussing the man.

"How many times do I have to say…?"

"A simple 'yes' or 'no' will suffice," he interrupted.

"No."

"Did he meet you at or near your car?"

I tried to shift. The rough bricks dug through the back of my thin button-down shirt. "No."

He either didn't notice or chose to ignore my discomfort. "Did you meet or notice anyone else…?"

"Look," I cut in, "I was concentrating on getting to the hospital. I don't remember seeing anyone. That doesn't mean no one was around."

He glanced at me, then around the corner of the building again. "What about your brother-in-law?"

I swallowed. My breath fanned against his hovering palm. His left hand was still behind his back. "What about him?" I hedged.

It seemed as though the man was avoiding eye contact. "You've implied he might be connected with whatever is wrong with your sister. Does he have reason to be after you, too?"

His words made real the fear I had tried to convince myself was just imaginary. He made it sound as though he wasn't involved, but I didn't believe him. The coincidence was too ironic, my current situation too dangerously close to Angela's.

"Not if he hired you to get rid of me," I told him.

His head whipped round, bringing our eyes scant inches apart. Even in the darkness I could see his pale, almost iridescent gray irises.

"I beg your pardon?" His uniquely British inflection scattered any doubt of his citizenship.

I squirmed, trying to get him to ease off, and got pressed harder against the wall.

"You heard me." I fought to think while gongs rang in space my brain normally occupied. "Did Gary hire you to get rid of me?"

His eyes narrowed. "Bloody serious knock you've..."

"A simple 'yes' or 'no' will suffice," I cut in, trying to imitate the same irritation in his earlier remark.

He stared at me for long moments, then released a careful sigh. "Are you implying that I am in that line of work?"

"Well, you're certainly acting like it," I snapped.

"You need to start giving me some answers about what you know." His tone matched mine.

I drew a breath and tried to maintain a steady voice. "Well I don't have any answers to give. Now let me go and get on with your life."

He neither answered nor acquiesced. He shifted and his left hand reappeared. It was empty. When he leaned away, I almost sprawled onto my face. He slipped an arm underneath my knees and with terrifying strength lifted me off my feet and cradled me firmly against him.

"Put me down...!" I struggled, using my right hand in an effort to wrench myself loose.

"Keep still, or I'll toss you over my shoulder, knotty noggin and all," he growled.

He moved in short increments, staying in shadows as much as possible. I hated the feel of his shoulder under my cheek, my chest pressed hard against his. Nausea and pain were getting worse. I curled my arms, fought to keep down stomach contents, and closed my eyes against irrepressible tears.

My sister lay critically ill just blocks away. My car had just been blown to smithereens. And now I was being kidnapped by an unknown man to God only knew where. It would take a while before authorities discovered I owned the demolished Subaru. The fact it was in an empty lot in the middle of Denver would not help when police began to investigate my whereabouts.

How long would it take before CSI determined no one had been killed in the explosion? Even if they eventually connected me with Angela, they would get nowhere. I had told Margaret only that I was going to my car and would be back soon. I had no way of contacting Jeremiah, and if and when authorities finally did, he would have no clue where I was.

No clue at all.

Chapter Six

The man set me down when my gut started to spasm. I got a vague impression of familiar concrete walls and floor before rebelling stomach won with brutal force. Sinking to my hands and knees, I heaved. I hadn't eaten since early morning, so nothing came up. Muscles trembled and icy waves washed over me. Things took a while to calm down, and when they did, I wasn't sure which way was up.

The man knelt close. "Don't you dare kick off on me."

His head bent over mine. I was sick and tired of him but had no fight left at all. My teeth chattered with such violence, I could hardly get the words out. "M-maybe you sh-should just sh-shoot me and g-get it over with."

He grunted. "You get points for a sense of humor."

I didn't have the energy to tell him I wasn't joking.

He shifted beside me and roughly pulled my limp arms. "We need to get to my car."

We needed to stay here, I thought, wherever 'here' was, since it was quiet, dark, stationary, and away from burning vehicles and moving busses. I didn't want to go anywhere. I didn't want to stand up. Doubled-over on my knees already took more strength than I had left.

"I...I don't think m-moving me is a good idea right now." I felt like any shift at all would acutely worsen everything.

Surprisingly, he relented and carefully tilted me over onto my side. Steel-like fingers slid down my face and pressed the underside of my jaw. If he was trying to count my pulse, good luck. It was probably off the charts.

"Right." He slid his arms underneath my shoulders and knees. I cringed when he lifted me again, tried and failed to stifle a moan. He moved around the bends of what I guessed was a public parking garage, then walked down a couple of ramps into the bowels of the structure.

"Setting you down now." He lowered me to the concrete floor. Clothing rustled, I heard the jingle of keys, then the soft click of car doors unlocking, and felt any hope of rescue leak out with the tears that dampened my face.

He lifted me again and dumped me into the back seat of a vehicle. More rustling followed, and a thick blanket settled over me. I curled as tightly as I could underneath the fabric, trying to generate some warmth in my freezing limbs.

More sounds of opening and closing car doors, then the engine purred to life and we started moving. We turned corners and climbed ramps, stopped at intervals. Eventually, I felt the car surge with powerful acceleration and guessed he had made it to the interstate. I opened my eyes. Passing streetlights beyond the tinted windows aggravated my stomach and my head. I shut my eyes again and felt cold, cold, cold.

I lost track of time. I wasn't aware when I drifted off, but had the sense of waking up whenever I heard his voice. His intermittent questions merged into the images drifting around my bruised brain. He drove me to Coors Field and I got out and started looking for Jeremiah. A black bus rambled along in the nearest lane and I thought I glimpsed my husband's face in the window. I tried shouting to catch his attention when the bus exploded, throwing me backwards. Cars and trucks flew in all directions, crashing onto the sidewalk around me, becoming insurmountable obstacles as I crawled and clawed my way towards the burning bus. Terrified, I searched the windows for Jeremiah's face, spotted him near the back, but he wasn't moving. I screamed for him to jump out, but he just sat there, staring at me with unseeing eyes. Other figures floated around him. Thin, holocaust faces filled the windows, and I realized that each of them was Angela. In desperation I swung round. The stranger stood behind me, ignoring the carnage as he carefully screwed a long cylinder onto the end of the gun he held. I opened my mouth to scream, but fingers grabbed my throat from behind and Gary's voice snarled in my ear. The man lifted his eyes and looked straight through me. He raised the weapon until I was staring down the round, lethal hole. I choked and dug at the vice-like fingers around my throat. The fingers squeezed and I couldn't breathe, couldn't shout for help, couldn't do anything but stare at the loaded weapon aimed mere inches from my forehead....

I became aware that the car was slowing. Gravel crunched under the tires when we pulled off the paved road and stopped. A car door opened, then shut again. I heard the click of automatic locks and wondered where we were. I mentally ordered my arms and legs to move, open a car door, run for help.

I couldn't even lift a hand to wipe my dripping nose.

After several minutes the man returned, started the engine, pulled slowly across more gravel, then stopped again. More car door sounds, then his hands slipped under my shoulders.

"Here we go." When he lifted me from the car seat my stomach twisted into hard, terrified knots. He got me through a doorway and settled down onto a bedspread before I began to heave again. I heard the solid clank of a motel door closing, and then he was pulling a trashcan to the side of the bed and holding my head over the side. Nothing came up, but my abdomen hurt like hell when the spasms finally passed. I lay on my side with my eyes closed and felt too awful to care what he had in mind.

The backs of my eyelids lightened.

"Mattie, open your eyes."

I obeyed. Two blurred beams of bright light flickered in front of me. I squinted and buried my face in the pillow to shut out the brilliance. Pain rocketed through my skull.

"D-don't…don't do that again," I moaned into the moldy-smelling linen.

His fingers inspected my skull and my neck. "I don't feel any new injuries."

I didn't bother to tell him that re-bashing the old one had been more than enough.

"Still nauseated?"

I gave a tiny nod, wondering why in the world he would even care. I should be dead by now. His actions were not making sense, which increased rather than assuaged my fear of him.

"How's your vision?"

My answer came out muffled because I preferred a smelly pillow to looking at him. "There's at least two of you at the m-moment. I didn't like b-being around one."

He released a long sigh. "You should probably be in hospital."

I turned my head and tried to glare at the man. "No shit, Sherlock. I should have gone to the ER after the bus incident." I closed my eyes again and steeled myself for my next question. "Where are we?"

"In a cheap motel near Limon."

I didn't want to ask why. Besides, ordering the thought into words took too much effort. He pulled the blankets from the other bed and tucked them around me, then sat beside me for what seemed like a long time. Each time I started to drift off, he nudged me into answering some inane question. After a while the tremors eased and warmth began seeping into my limbs.

I heard movement around the room. The door opened and closed a few times. I felt the mattress sag when he sat on the edge of the bed again and kept my eyes squeezed shut as I trembled beneath the blankets. "Why...why did you blow up my car?" I couldn't keep my voice steady.

I heard him release an irritated sigh. "You've been dreaming again. You were muttering something about Jeremiah and Angela a bit ago."

Cold shivers coursed through me. "But...but why did you blow up my car?"

"What would I gain by torching your car?" He countered.

Why couldn't he just give me a straight answer?

"Did you blow up my car?" I tried again.

I felt him shift on the bed. "No, I bloody well did not. Now open your eyes."

"Well if you didn't, then who did?"

Silence.

"Excellent question," he murmured after a long pause, then added in a voice so low I almost didn't understand his words. "And which of us were they after?"

I opened my eyes and tried to focus on the dark blur hovering over me. "You happened to be nearby when I got pushed in front of that bus, and then my car just happens to blow up when you're right beside it. According to you, you've had nothing to do with either."

His gray eyes locked on mine. "Are you still on about me being in with your brother-in-law?" He sounded agitated. I needed to stop.

"Yeah, I am," I said anyway.

He planted a hand on either side of my head and leaned down. "Mattie, if I had planted the car bomb, I would have let you die in the explosion. If I pushed you into the path of that bloody lorry, why did I take a flying leap and pull you out?" His proximity and his use of my name created a terrifyingly intimate connection between us.

"H-how would I know?" I stammered. "Too many witnesses?"

He bent until his scowling face filling my vision. "If I intended to take you out, you'd have copped it by now. No trail, no questions."

I tried to break eye contact, but couldn't. Tears slid down the sides of my face and trickled into my ears. I closed my eyes, shutting him out.

"Open your eyes."

I obeyed. No pain rocketed this time when he shined the penlight into each of them.

"How's that stomach of yours?"

I nodded, wondering again why he seemed to care about my state of health.

He sighed. "Your pupils are reacting better. Good signs. Bedtime."

I stamped down a surge of panic when he reached over and pulled off my sneakers, then coiled his hands around my waist and unsnapped my belt pack. I curled my knees tight against my chest. The man crossed the room to the door, secured the bar lock, and flipped the wall switch, then lay down on the other bed.

My eyes adjusted to the darkness, and I watched him drift off. His muscles twitched faintly a couple of times before his breathing evened out. I thought about creeping to the door and making a break for it, then reluctantly admitted the utter stupidity of the idea. I stared at the long length of his body, then glanced towards his face. I swallowed when my eyes came to rest on an object just visible under the pillow he was using.

The square black shape of a gun butt rested against the palm of his left hand. The childhood memory, full of blood and violent death, threatened to surface again, but I managed to shut it out.

~ * ~

When I awoke the next morning, the man's head was bent over a stack of unfolded maps on the opposite bed. His face lifted when I sat up and gingerly swung my legs over the side.

"Rise and shine." He was trying to drawl in what sounded like a Texas accent.

I glared at him. "You sound like a Brit trying to sound like a Texan."

"Not a cock riser, are you?"

My eyes widened in shock. He grinned. "Not the term you Yanks use for male chickens?"

"Never mind." I waved him off and tried to stand. He rose and gripped my arm when I swayed. I realized with a surge of angry embarrassment that I was going to need help.

"Off to the loo then?" He guided me around the end of the bed towards the tiny bathroom. Thankfully, he didn't try escorting me into the toilet. I needed his support more than I wanted to admit on the short trek back to the bed.

"Hungry?" he asked after I lay down. His mood swings terrified me, and I didn't want to think what was making him so cheerful. I felt sweaty, smelly, and unsociable. I made no effort to be civil.

"No." My head throbbed around my left temple instead of all over. Lying down did not improve things. I sat up again. Couldn't remember the last time I had tried Jeremiah's cell. Whenever it was, I needed to try again.

"Right then. We'll worry about that later. Now, what's wrong with Angela?"

His abrupt change of subject caught me off-guard and I blurted the answer. "I think she's dying."

His eyebrows rose a fraction. "Sticky wicket."

I frowned. "It's none of your business, and I don't appreciate you making fun of me."

"It most certainly is, and I am not poking fun. Continue." He sat on the edge of his bed and faced me. Our knees lined up almost exactly opposite each other. I glanced around the room, searching for an escape. Heavy-duty lengths of chain anchored the television and tables to the floor. I wondered whether it was meant to prevent theft of said items, or to prevent them from being thrown. Maybe both. The worn gold-colored indoor-outdoor carpet sported enough stains and burn holes to be considered part of the design. Dingy walls and stained ceiling did not improve things. Thread-bare curtains let in more light than they kept out.

In other words, a perfect place for a murder. My skin crawled.

The man let the silence linger. I stirred and looked at him, trying to remember his name.

"Who are you again?"

"Hawk." He leaned forward. "And you would do well to co-operate and answer my questions."

I swallowed. "I got a call from someone in the ER this morning. Well, I guess it would be yesterday morning now. An ambulance picked my sister up in Limon, and then she crashed, and they had to put her on a respirator." I paused.

Hawk did not move or break eye contact.

I waited a few moments, giving myself time to build the courage to continue. "When I saw her, at first I thought they had made a mistake. But then I recognized a scar Angela got when we were kids." I swung my eyes up to his. "Six months ago Angela was healthy, active, and just fine. When I saw her in that hospital bed she was so thin I could see every bone. I don't know what's happened to her."

"What did the doctors say?" he prompted, leaning on one hand and crossing one knee over the other, his casual position belying his earlier threat.

"Well, the nurse started asking me whether Angela had a history of depression or..." I hesitated. "Or of being suicidal. I couldn't believe she was asking stuff like that. Angela has never been depressed, much less..." I could not bring myself to repeat the word. "...the other. So...so I started thinking that maybe her husband might have something to do with what's happened." I looked away again. "But that's really a stupid thing to think. She must have gotten sick and they just didn't want to tell me about it." That had to be the reason.

"But you don't believe that."

I reluctantly met his eyes. "There's absolutely no indication Gary had anything to do with Angela's condition. But there are discrepancies."

He didn't move. "Such as...?"

I didn't want to continue. I didn't want to give him any (more) ideas on possible methods to get rid of me.

"Mattie, I have any number of ways to persuade you to continue." His voice sounded calm, his words sent chills racing through me.

"Well, for one thing, why didn't she call to tell us she was driving up, especially as sick as she is? And why didn't Gary come with her? He showed up on Saturday at our apartment. He said he was in town for a drug conference, but when I tried to reach him at the Broadmoor, the lady said there weren't any drug rep conferences being held. And he lied about where Angela was, although maybe she left after he started driving to Colorado, I don't know." I fell silent.

"How long have they been married?" His insistent questions

unraveled my thin control.

"S-since F-february," I stuttered, my voice shaking.

Silence hovered again. My tongue was sticking to the roof of my mouth, and I could smell the faint stench of bile. I thought about a glass of water, but didn't want to ask Hawk for one. No toothbrush, either. That got blown up along with everything else in my car, including my 35mm camera and all of my professional equipment.

None of this helped my efforts to remain calm.

Hawk rose and wandered over to the window. He turned and leaned against the sill, crossed his ankles and folded his arms over his chest. Well-defined upper body and shoulder muscles filled the material of his long-sleeved shirt. I shuddered at the memory of his strength.

"Chilled?" He asked.

I shook my head. My left shoulder tingled with residual soreness.

"Mattie, where is your husband?"

I leaned my elbows on my knees, propped my forehead in my hands, and wished with all my heart that I didn't have to reveal more personal information.

"From your silence, I should guess you are not quite sure," he murmured.

Shocked that he had guessed the truth, I jerked my head up to meet his stare. Bemused, he glanced through the curtains, then turned to me again. "Have you contacted your parents regarding Angela? Other relatives?"

I hesitated, staring at the mottled carpet. A dark shadow running along the bottom of the bedside table looked suspiciously like mold. "Boy, you do know how to pick the resorts," I sighed, trying to stall.

Hawk did not move or comment. I ran a hand through my grimy hair and wished for a shower. There was no way I would chance getting naked in a motel with only a flimsy door separating me from Hawk. Uh-uh, I repeated to myself. Besides, they probably didn't have any hot water in this dump anyway.

"Mattie, answer the question."

I glanced up, recalled with a twist in my gut his cruel strength. I did not want to be subjected to another of his interrogations.

I rubbed my left shoulder, trying to ease the ache. "Sorry, what did you say?"

"Have you notified your parents? Other relatives?"

I mustered up the courage and told him about the accident that killed Mom and Dad and the subsequent breakdown in communication between my sister and me.

"Are there other relatives?"

"Dad had a brother who died about three years ago. Mom was an only child. Not that any of this is your business." The ache in my left shoulder spiked, sending spidery threads of pain down my arm.

His next question almost stopped my heart.

"Is there an inheritance?"

I moved my hand from my shoulder to rub my face and felt the grime roll beneath my palm. I felt as grungy as the motel room. "Yeah," I answered after yet another long silence. My headache was getting worse, and my vision had started to blur. I tried to focus on the figure across the room.

"Let me get you some water." Hawk straightened from the window and crossed to the bathroom located behind me. A faucet squeaked, then the spigot spit and coughed. Yep, probably no hot water. Probably not even enough water pressure to sustain a decent shower.

I heard Hawk rinse a cup out several times, then let it fill. He reappeared, holding a Styrofoam cup, which he held out to me.

"Fresh from the source…with a bit of mouth rinse to counteract the rusty taste." He was being nice again, which made him seem all the more dangerous. I hesitated taking the cup he held out.

"Drink it."

My mouth felt like a wad of cotton; I took the cup and emptied the contents.

"Better?"

I nodded.

"Hungry yet?"

I shook my head, wondering where he was going with this new line of questions.

"So your parents' estate solicitors contacted you two fortnights past?"

His sudden change in subject, not to mention his syntax, confused me. I set the empty cup down on the table. The water had been a little brown, a sure sign of rusted pipes. Ugh.

Realization oozed through injured brain cells as I worked out his meaning. I lifted my eyes to his. "How did you know that my parents' lawyer came to our apartment a couple of weeks ago?"

He waved off my question. "How much inheritance?"

His blunt question made me cringe. Studying the Styrofoam cup, I tried to come up with a way to avoid answering. My life depended on keeping those details to myself.

Angela and I had always known the financial arrangements upon our parents' deaths. Mom and Dad had reared us as though our bank accounts were like everyone else's. Neither of us planned our future around what we'd eventually inherit. I didn't want to think down that road, but that was the only explanation that gave answers to all of the questions surrounding Angela's condition.

Both Angela and I were billionaires. Heiresses to the enormous Lamont fortune inherited and enlarged over several generations on my father's side. Upon her death, Angela's trust fund would automatically go to Gary. Neither Angela nor I could access our trust funds until we turned thirty. I was two years away. Angela, six. Gary was about Jeremiah's age, which was seven years' my senior. That meant Gary would be able to access Angela's multi-billion dollar trust fund immediately upon her death, provided the insurance company didn't balk at the fact she'd died less than a year after becoming his wife.

"Enough," I hedged.

"And when, precisely, did Gary knock up your apartment?"

His British colloquialism threw me again, and I had to guess what he was asking, because I hadn't the energy to ask him to clarify. "Saturday morning. He looked like he'd been driving all night. He could've left as late as possible so he wouldn't leave Angela alone." I stopped, seeing the glaring inconsistencies. So why lie about the drug conference? Why didn't he just admit he drove up to tell me about Angela? In her condition, he would have left her with someone.

Why, why, why? I needed some answers, damn it, not all these questions.

A gentle wave of dizziness washed over me. I stilled and waited for the sensation to pass.

"Feeling all right there?" Hawk prompted.

"Not really," I admitted.

"Perhaps you should lie down."

I nodded in reluctant agreement and sank back down onto my right side. Spots danced around the gray of my eyelids. I wondered what was creating them. They didn't seem to have any pattern or regularity.

"Mattie." Hawk sounded close. I opened my eyes and tried to focus on the figure now sitting on the side of my bed. Damned concussion.

"Did Gary speak with Jeremiah when he popped up at your apartment?"

I yawned. "He was asleep when Gary showed up." A mellow sensation floated through me. I thought about what I'd said, decided to add some more. "He waltzed right back to our bedroom and opened the door. I wanted to throttle the nosy creep."

"Are you quite certain your husband was asleep?"

I shrugged. "I think he was." The pillow nestled my head in a cloud of soft feathers. My headache was much better. It had been a good idea to lie down.

"If your brother-in-law was responsible for your sister's illness, why didn't she contact a local hospital or authorities?"

I frowned. "Good question," I told him. "To tell you the truth, I don't know. She really was too sick to make a trip all the way up here."

"And you never received message or voicemail from her?" His voice sounded strangely distant. Good. The further away, the better. I really didn't like him.

"No." I felt my muscles relax more. "I really don't understand why she would try to make a twelve-hour drive in her condition and not call and let me know."

Silence ensued. I felt as though I were floating. A gentle buzz filled my head.

"How are you feeling?" His voice had softened.

I smiled. "Better, especially now that you're further away. I don't like you at all, you know."

"Mattie, who stands to inherit upon your death?"

What a strange thing to ask. Really, the man had the most unusual way of carrying on a conversation. Must be because he's British. I decided to tell him.

"You know, you have a weird way of talking to people."

"Answer the question, Mattie. Who inherits your family money should you die, say, in an accident?"

"There for a while I couldn't understand a word you were saying." I rambled on. "But that's getting better. Maybe I'm getting used to your accent."

"Concentrate on the question, Mattie." Hawk sounded very patient, very soothing. Why had I been so afraid of him?

"Mattie, stay with me just a little longer, then you can sleep." I think I nodded. "Okay."

"Who inherits your money should you die suddenly?"

He must really want an answer to that one. "Angela." My voice sounded just as far away as Hawk's.

"Not your husband?" He seemed surprised.

I shook my head very carefully. I didn't want to lose the comfortable buzzing sensation that floated around the inside of my skull, padding injured brain cells.

"He signed an…adiffat…affidavit." The words rolled around, mixing up letters. "He flatly…" I liked that word. It felt good. I said it again. "Flatly, flatly…Fl-a-a-t-ly…"

"Flatly what?"

"Well, he refused to be included in our family financial arrangements." I smiled at the memory. "He wanted to make sure Mom and Dad knew he wasn't interested in me because of my trust fund."

Fingers tucked blankets around me, and I felt warm and cozy…and buzzed, like I'd had one too many glasses of wine. I only drink occasionally anyway, so it doesn't take much to put me under the table. I barely heard Hawk's next question.

"And under current arrangements, should Angela die and then in a freak accident you happen to be killed, who inherits your trust fund?"

I was floating away into a soft, soft cloud. No pain, no worries. I breathed out the answer as warmth wrapped around me.

"Gary."

Chapter Seven

I sat on the edge of the bed and thought how much safer and better off I would have been if Hawk had been gone when I woke up. I'd slept over six hours, plenty of time for the man to be far, far away.

"There is no way I'm stripping stark naked and standing in that damned shower with you anywhere in the vicinity," I snapped. My head still hurt. Road rash and bruises made themselves known, stinging, aching, and stiff with the slightest movement. I could sit, but that was about the scope of my activity without assistance. My hair and body stank so badly, I wondered how Hawk could stand to be in the same room with me.

"Mattie, if I were interested in sex, no amount of clothes would protect you." His bluntness made my skin crawl. I glared at the man leaning against the window and hoped he would stay there.

"If you're trying to reassure me, you're doing a shitty job of it. Besides, I doubt they have hot water in this resort you picked out, and I'm not standing under a cold shower."

"I washed earlier. The pressure could be better, but the water was hot enough." He straightened and uncrossed his arms. "The sooner you get this over with, the sooner you can eat."

I grit my teeth and willed myself to remain calm when he crossed the room and grasped my arm. Wobbling despite his assistance, I stumbled to the tiny bathroom. Panic hit hard when he reached for the buttons on my shirt and I slapped his hand away.

"Leave it alone. I can manage. I can't walk straight, but I can damn well undr…" The words clogged my throat. "Anyway, I can do it, thank you."

Hawk sat me down on the uncovered toilet and then closed the door behind him.

"If you get into trouble, I'm just out here," he called through the too-thin door.

I fumbled with the buttons, then hesitated long minutes before I actually took anything off. By the time I was naked, my head swam with fatigue. I wasn't about to let Hawk through that door, so I concentrated on getting myself into the tub.

He was right about the water pressure, but at least I didn't freeze. I sat down in the tub and waited until I got thoroughly wet. Travel size shampoo and a bar of soap occupied a corner, evidence Hawk had done some shopping while I slept. I lathered and soaped twice, wincing and gasping through the stinging road rash. I thought about staying in the shower until Hawk died of old age, then reluctantly turned off the faucets. With my hands on the (mildew-crusted) tile wall, I stood and reached for a towel. The flimsy white square wasn't big enough to go around once. I reached for my clothes, which I'd dropped on the floor.

"Hey! I want my clothes back!" I demanded, leaning against the wall and trying not to panic when I realized said articles were missing.

Hawk took my outburst as his cue to open the door. I was sure I had locked the damned thing. A folded white sheet appeared.

"Use this. It's fresh from the dryer. I've taken your clothes to the laundry," he said from the other side of the open door.

I clamped my mouth shut, took the sheet, and slammed the door shut. Wrapping the sheet around until I felt like a mummy, I sat down on the toilet and waited.

After about twenty minutes on the toilet seat, I stood up and put my ear against the flimsy bathroom door. Things seemed awfully quiet on the other side. Maybe he had left. I opened the door, my heart thumping harder than necessary.

The room was empty. I wobbled to the side of the bed, sat down. I tried to focus on the phone, but could only see a vague black blob. My recent activity had made my headache worse, and now pain knifed viscously through my skull, slicing to bits my efforts to think. I leaned onto my right side and closed my eyes. Bruised and skinned muscles throbbed. If I lay here quietly for a few minutes, maybe the throbbing would quit and my eyesight would clear enough for me to use the phone....

"Mattie."

My eyes snapped open at the close proximity of Hawk's voice. His face loomed inches from mine. I shot into a sitting position so fast, we clunked heads. Hawk muttered an oath and staggered back a step.

"*Shit.*" I rubbed my scalp where we had connected and gave myself a mental slap on the face for being stupid enough to fall asleep.

Hawk held out my folded clothes and a Wal-Mart shopping bag. I glanced at him, then took my clothes, which were still warm from the dryer. I ignored the bag and started to rise, but he stopped me with a hand on my shoulder, his tensile fingers curling into my bare skin.

"These are for you, too. I did some shopping."

"Can I get dressed first?" I shot back, trying to sound irritated, unable to control the tremor his contact created. If I had stayed awake, I would be safe and sound *and* dressed by now. Damned, stupid concussion.

"Change into these." He lifted the white plastic bag. All kinds of repulsive possibilities slid through my brain. I took the bag from him and peered inside.

Toothbrush, toothpaste, mouthwash, hairspray, hairbrush, miniature dryer, deodorant, and disposable razors all lay tucked on top of some folded clothes.

I met his eyes, aware my nervousness was probably plainly visible. "Okay, this was thoughtful." His nice streak had to have an ulterior motive. I just couldn't figure out what it was. "Thanks," I added after a pause.

"Weather's turned too cool for short sleeves and shorts." His unreadable expression did not help allay my suspicions.

I shrugged off his hand and stood. Clutching my clothes and the bag, I padded carefully around the bed and back into the bathroom, shut and locked the door, then set the bag on the floor. Clean underclothes felt warm and fresh. I debated the wisdom of ignoring his request to change into the clothes he had bought, knew without a doubt his ability to wrestle me to the floor and force me to obey his instructions, and with a reluctant sigh pulled from the Wal-Mart bag a pair of blue jeans, a black hooded fleece pullover, and a black baseball cap. I slipped into my short-sleeved shirt, then carefully slid my legs into the jeans, wincing when the road rash scraped against the denim. They were a perfect fit and were warm and soft, too, as was the hoody, and I suspected he had washed them with my clothes. He must have used his British accent to swoon the motel laundry lady. I put on socks and laced up my sneakers, then stuffed my shorts into the bag.

I thought over his possible motives for the clothes. They would be warmer than what I'd had on, and they did cover up the extensive bruises on my arms and legs.

They also changed my appearance, in case anyone reported me missing.

The thought sent a shiver through me. I left the baseball cap in the bag, then opened the bathroom door and slid my hands through the warmer of the sweatshirt.

Hawk was on the far bed, studying his pile of maps again. The succulent odor of fast food hit my nostrils, and I realized I was starving. My stomach emitted a loud rolling rumble. Hawk lifted his head, and I thought I saw a hint of a sly grin flit across his mouth.

"Thought you might be hungry."

I walked to a table across the room from where Hawk sat and took a seat in the metal chair. Hawk picked up the McDonalds bag on the bedside table, then stood and walked over to where I sat. He set the bag on the table, then brought over two large Cokes and held one out. I took it and drank, felt the carbonation tickle my taste buds, and set the Coke down. To my intense disappointment, Hawk pulled a second chair close and sat down opposite me. I dug into the bag, found a large order of fries.

"How do the clothes fit?" He asked as he reached into the bag and pulled out a wrapped hamburger. His accent seemed less confusing, but I was concentrating on the food too much to wonder why.

"They fit fine, thanks." I popped the fry into my mouth, dug into the bag, pulled out a Big Mac.

"How's your noggin?"

"Better," I lied.

"Ever dabbled in a bit of extortion?" His question came out as casually as though he'd asked about the weather.

Stunned, I paused in mid-bite and stared at him. "What?" I mumbled around the hamburger.

He leaned against the back of his chair and crossed one leg over the other. "Ever dabbled in a bit of extortion," he repeated. "You know, a bit of extra money under the table. That sort of thing."

My hamburger drifted down towards my lap. "Are you nuts? No!" I stared at him. "Why?"

"You're a photojournalist. You've admitted you enjoy taking candids." The predatory look in his expression belied his relaxed slouch.

Disturbed by the sudden turn of the conversation, I set the

hamburger on the table. "Are you being serious?"

His eyes remained steadily on mine. "Quite."

I swallowed with difficulty. "Hawk, I have *never, ever* considered something like that. It's...it's despicable."

"You've the means and access." He popped the remaining bit of hamburger into his mouth, then sat there watching me as he chewed.

"I also have morals," I said carefully. The intensity in his eyes reminded me of a cougar waiting to spring.

"You can't tell me you've never snapped a shot of a familiar face, say at a ball game, with someone they shouldn't be with? Perhaps your boss with a girl other than his wife?"

I sat and stared at the man, wondering what planet his brain had just landed on. "Is this a British thing, or do you normally ask ridiculous questions out of the blue?"

He started to reply, but paused when my expression turned inward. Something about his last statement was triggering a memory...almost there...almost....

"My film!" I gasped as the fog cleared. I stood and wobbled to the bathroom, wishing the food would help me feel better and steady my balance. I retrieved the Wal-Mart bag and stumbled to the bed I'd slept in.

Hawk moved to the opposite bed and sat down. Irritated, I took my shorts from the bag and dropped the bag onto the floor, then rummaged through the pockets.

No film. I looked up at Hawk.

"Did you find a roll of film in any of the pockets of my shorts when you took them to the laundry?"

"Film?" He echoed. He'd brought his drink with him. He took a sip, and I swore I could see tension around his eyes. I felt like he was up to something, and the feeling made me acutely uncomfortable.

"Yes. Thirty-five millimeter. I use it for my hobby shots, and it was the camera I was using at the game Sunday. I changed rolls in the bathroom and put the old roll in my pocket." I rummaged through all the pockets again. "At least, I think I did."

He held his Coke out and stared at the plastic cup, then snapped his eyes to mine. "Why the bathroom?"

I wanted to put distance between us, but standing up and walking back over to the table would be too obvious. I didn't want to scoot back on the bed, so I tried to create a gap between us by leaning away.

"I didn't want to risk changing rolls in the sun. Old habit." I dropped the shorts onto the floor next to the bag. "Damn!" I remembered my belt pack and looked around, but didn't see it on any of the furniture. I swung my legs up and across the bed, then stood on the opposite side, away from Hawk. The movement made my headache worse.

"Have you seen my belt pack? Maybe I put it in there."

Hawk's attention returned to the cup he was holding. He sucked his drink empty and tossed the cup into the trashcan that sat on the floor between the beds. "Were there important pictures on the roll?"

I shot him what I hoped was an irritated glare for ignoring my question. "Well, according to you, yeah. Your picture was on there. But there were some of the Garden of the Gods. I don't want to lose those."

"What about ones of the ball game?"

Fog blurred my thoughts again, and I frowned. "I think so." I wanted to pace, but didn't trust my balance enough to risk it. "Damn it. I must've lost it somewhere between the ballpark and the hospital." I frowned at him. "Or when you dragged me off."

My hamburger sat on the table, still warm, still edible, but suddenly unappealing. I looked around for another trashcan, saw only the one between the beds, I walked over and threw the rest of the burger away. I hesitated, then sat down on the empty bed and faced Hawk. He sat there, silent as a statue, watching.

"Where is my belt pack? I asked. "My film might be in there. And I need to call Jeremiah, then contact the hospital and check up on Angela."

Hardness glinted around his eyes, and in a flash I was facing the man who had pinned me against the wall yesterday. I barely avoided cringing, started to rise, but his hand rose in a clear warning. I stilled.

"Jeremiah. As I recall, he would be your husband."

I nodded. "I need to let him know what's going on with my sister." I tried to keep my voice steady. "And I need to be in touch with the hospital about Angela."

Hawk's strangely iridescent gray eyes watched me, and the room grew uncomfortably cold. Or maybe it was just me, since all of my blood now seemed to be pooling somewhere around my toes.

"And where would he be at this time of day?" His voice was low, hard.

"He's on his way..." I changed in mid-answer. "He's on his way to Boulder by now...for work."

Without a word, Hawk pulled my cell phone from his jeans pocket, flipped it open, then punched the keypad. I stared at him, then at my phone in his hand, remembering that he used it to call the hospital yesterday.

He leaned forward and turned the screen for me to see. "Nothing from Jeremiah's number."

I stared at the screen, not believing my husband had not tried to contact me. Surely, by now he would be in Oklahoma. He would have tried calling to tell me how his interview had gone.

Hawk voiced my thoughts. "If he were following his normal routine, he would have realized something's amiss and ought to have been trying to reach you on your mobile."

I raised my eyes and briefly met his, then looked away and folded my arms across my chest. My hands felt like icicles.

Hawk's voice matched the coldness of his stare. "I'll ask you again. Where is he?"

I sure as hell wasn't going to tell him I had no idea where my husband was, why he had not been trying to call me, and that I had not talked to him in over twenty-four hours. "In Boulder," I lied, then pressed my lips together.

Hawk leaned in, bringing his face uncomfortably close to mine, forcing eye contact. "You're lying."

I felt the color drain from my already pale face and looked away. "You don't need to know."

He swung over and sat down, using his legs to trap mine against the bedside table. I began to tremble. I wanted to scream, to jump up and run away, but I knew either action would elicit a dangerous reaction from him.

"Try again." When he leaned into me, I buckled.

"In...in Oklahoma. He should have left a message by now to let me know he's gotten there safe."

Instead of backing off, Hawk reached across and lifted the phone receiver. "What's his mobile?"

I felt his strength, felt my heart jerk around my chest "Why are you so interested in my husband's whereabouts all of a sudden?"

"Answer the question." He stared at me, waiting. I refused to look at him, but gave him Jeremiah's number.

Hawk punched in the sequence, held the receiver to his ear. An angry look crossed his face, and he disconnected the call.

"His mobile is off. What did the two of you discuss last?" he snarled.

I ignored his question, concentrated on keeping my voice steady. "He's probably at the Norman Weather Center. He may have turned off his cell for his interview and forgot to turn it back on."

I watched him scroll down the list of contacts on my cell until he found the number of the OU Prediction Center. He punched in the numbers on the motel phone, then brought the receiver close to both of our ears.

"Need I remind you against trying something stupid," he warned, his hand gripping the nape of my neck. The line clicked.

"Storm Prediction Center," a faint female voice greeted.

I had to clear my throat twice before any words came out. "I'm trying to reach Jeremiah Tyler. He's there for an interview to-day." Tremors shot through me, and I longed to scream for help. Hawk's fingers tightened.

I'd have preferred being embraced by the jaws of a great white shark.

"Would he be a visitor, student, or employee?"

"V-visitor." My voice shook.

"Just a minute. Let me check the sign-in log." I got put on hold. My eyes flickered to the window, and I longed for a set of wings.

"Ma'am," the receptionist said, picking up the line, "No one by that name has signed in."

My gaze riveted to the curtains. Hawk leaned his head into mine, his breath fanning the side of my neck.

"Are you sure? He was supposed to be interviewed for a lead forecaster position." The woman had to be wrong. "He had an in-terview this morning. Ten o'clock, I think. I haven't been able to reach him on his cell, and it's an…" I broke off when I felt Hawk tense. "…it's really important," I ended lamely.

"Just a minute. I'll see if any of the forecasters on duty know anything about it."

Once again I got put on hold. The silence punctuated new fear, and I momentarily forgot about Hawk and his threats.

What if Jeremiah had been in an accident? What if he had never made it to the interview, but was lying comatose in a hospital bed somewhere in the middle of Kansas?

What if he was lying dead in some morgue?

After what seemed an eternity, the line clicked. "Ma'am, I talked to one of the lead forecasters, and he said that no interviews were scheduled for today. He also said that there are no interviews scheduled for the entire week."

Numbness oozed through me. "That can't be right. Who did you talk to?"

"The supervisor." The lady was beginning to sound annoyed.

"Well, he must have his facts wrong. My husband wouldn't tell me he was driving twelve hours for an interview if there wasn't one," I argued, ignoring Hawk's warning squeeze.

"Well, *ma'am*," the snooty voice replied, "I can't tell you why your husband told you he had an interview. I can only tell you that there are no interviews scheduled for the entire week, including today."

"Isn't there someone else I can talk to?" My voice cracked. I needed to talk to Jeremiah. He was my only hope of getting out of whatever I had stumbled into.

"No one is available at the moment. You may leave a message if you like."

I opened my mouth to tell Miss Snooty to get her supervisor on the line when Hawk disconnected the call. I stared blindly at the window. Panic oozed through widening cracks in my self-control.

"Didn't Jeremiah say he was going to Oklahoma for an interview? Did I hear him right?" My voice trailed off. I tried to remember our conversation yesterday morning. Only yesterday? It seemed years ago. "Where is he?" I couldn't stop the words. They came out high, thin.

Hawk's hand released my neck and slipped around my back. When he reached across with his other arm to replace the receiver, he pressed against me with terrifying intimacy. Hysteria shattered last remnants of control into a million emotional splinters. The muscles in my arms and fingers contracted with strength so fierce, pain shot through the tendons in my wrists. I stared at nothing and couldn't block the conversation from replaying over and over in my head.

No interviews scheduled for today or all week. No one signed in by that name.

My wrists started curling inward. Hawk's arms tightened around me.

"Go away." My voice deteriorated to a high squeak as I chanted, *"Go away, go away, go away…"*

Abruptly, Hawk released me and stood, and I heard him walk to the bathroom. The spigot coughed, followed by the sound of running water. I tried to stand, but my muscles locked and wouldn't move.

Jeremiah, where are you? Jeremiah, Jeremiah….

The edge of a Styrofoam cup touched my lips as Hawk's hand gripped my hair and forced my head back. I coughed down a sip of rusty, foul-tasting water.

"Down the hatch, all of it."

I obeyed because I couldn't do anything else. My forearms were clamped against my chest, my hands useless, frozen fists. I choked down the awful-tasting water, and Hawk released me. He threw the cup into the trashcan, then sat there, doing nothing. I wondered what he was waiting for.

After several minutes, a familiar wave of dizziness washed over me.

Shit.

Hawk sat beside me, waiting like a spider for the fly.

"What was that you just made me drink?" The dizziness increased, joined by a buzz that loosened my paralyzed muscles.

"Was Jeremiah meeting you at the ball game?" Hawk's question seemed far away. I nodded.

"He…he was…supposed to drive down after he got off work."

"Do you normally take candids when you're at the ballpark?"

I nodded again.

"And does Jeremiah ever tell you to take a candid of a particular person?"

I wanted to shout at him to quit asking questions but couldn't generate energy to form thought into words. I didn't like the way he kept saying the word "candid". He made it sound like something dirty.

"When did Jeremiah phone you?"

"After…after you left…." A familiar mellowing sensation oozed through me despite my attempts to fight it. My arms and legs began feeling like rubber bands. I closed my eyes and sighed, tried to generate the energy to open them again.

"Before or after the call from the hospital?"

I shrugged.

"Answer me." The bedsprings creaked. "Which phone call came first?"

My thoughts swirled, out of place, not making any sense.

"You went to the loo to change out the film…" Now he was sounding accusatory.

I shrugged again. He sure was being persistent about all of this.

"Who called when you were standing outside afterwards?"

Coming up with the answer to that one required much too much concentration. "J-Jeremiah." Another memory drifted through. "And then, almost right after he called, the ER called about Angela."

"Did you see Gary at the ballpark?"

It took me several beats before I realized he was asking about my brother-in-law. "Gary? Why are you asking about him?"

"Answer me, Mattie. When did you speak with Gary?"

"He was at the apartment. On Saturday. He was being really rude and nosy." I thought about Gary and giggled. His face reminded me of a Pug.

"You didn't talk to him at the ballpark? Perhaps you saw your husband talking with him?"

My head spun wickedly when I tried to shake it. What was it I going to tell him just now? Something funny….

"You're lying, Mattie. Were the three of you planning on splitting the money you got off those pictures? Is that why Lee pushed you into the path of the lorry?"

"What's a lorry?" The gentle, uncontrollable buzz filled my body. Fatigue trembled through my muscles.

I felt Hawk pin my hands between his. I opened my eyes and looked at his fingers. They were long, strong.

"How long have Jeremiah and Gary been in business together?"

I leaned over in slow motion until my head sank into the soft pillow. Hawk released my hands, gripped my shoulders, and pulled me back into a sitting position.

"Mattie, answer me."

I tried to focus on his eyes. "I don't think…Jeremiah likes

Gary very much."

"Your bloody inheritance isn't enough? Who's your source? Who told you I'd be at the game?"

I tried to think of answers to his rapid questions. Thoughts flitted about, defying my efforts to form them into something sensible.

"I…I don't think…."

"Where's your husband, Mattie? What was he doing while you took those pictures? Who are he and Gary supposed to contact for your bloody fucking pictures?"

The effect of the drug gripped me. The buzzing sensation intensified, and I leaned heavily against him.

"Lie still while I tidy up." He laid me down. I heard him rustling around the room, then he grasped my arms and pulled me to my feet.

"The car's in the night manager's garage. Let's take a walk."

I giggled at his pronunciation of 'garage.' Tried to imitate it. "GARE-rauwge. G-A-A-R-E-r-a-w-g-e." He began walking. I stumbled along, felt his hands tighten around my waist. I heard the motel door open, felt cool evening air brush my face. Everything was dark. My knees sagged, and I stumbled along, trying to put one foot in front of the other. After what seemed a millennium, I heard the sound of car doors unlocking. Hawk eased me onto the back seat. With a vague feeling of something being critically wrong, I lay down on the cool, soft leather.

Chapter Eight

The man was lost. He had to be. He was lost because I didn't want to think of the other reason he would stop in the middle of nowhere, on a dirt road, before the break of dawn. Indirect light from the imminent sunrise reflected off the graded dirt road and surrounding tumbleweeds, painting squatty cacti and desert grass in a wash of pale tans and greens. The milky-blue sky overhead would gradually deepen into a rich azure as the sun climbed. A cool, dry breeze ruffled through my hair.

I knew where we were because of the landmarks. The surrounding ring of ancient volcanoes, whittled down by erosion to lonely cones among frozen waves of tumbled black lava rock covered with desert grass and cactus, meant we were near Capulin Volcano National Monument. And that told me we were in northeastern New Mexico.

Hawk wasn't acting lost, which worried me. He should have had maps out, or maybe he was about to ask me where the hell we were. Instead, he seemed to be watching me as though expecting some sort of reaction. He slid from behind the wheel and walked to the back of the SUV. I stayed in the back seat and watched him.

"Any reason why you decided to park in the middle of New Mexico?" I called through the open window.

"Nice and empty. No one to interrupt," he answered casually over his shoulder.

My heart pounded against the inside of my chest. It was empty all right. Not even a visible highway for cars to pass along, though I figured the dirt road we were on intersected the state highway at some point.

"If you were trying for I-twenty-five, you've missed it by about a hundred miles." I leaned against the seat back, crossed my arms, and looked through the window at the ancient lava flows barely visible beneath the high desert vegetation.

Hawk opened the door on my side and motioned me out of the car. His eyes narrowed, reminding me of the hooded watchfulness of the predatory bird that was his namesake.

"You know where we are." He didn't sound pleased.

I nodded as I moved away in an attempt to put space between us. "Jeremiah and I take this route whenever we go to Oklahoma."

Hawk closed the distance I had just created, his eyes cold and angry. "Mattie, do not play games with me."

I motioned at the wide emptiness all around us, then shot a belligerent look at him. "I'm not the one who's playing games."

Taking hold of my elbow, he steered me to the rear of the car. I resisted, and he let go once I was standing near the rear bumper.

"Look. I need to be in Denver, with my sister. And talking to the police about locating my husband."

Hawk raised the back hatch, then reached in and removed a packet of photographs from behind the driver's seat. He held them out.

Confused, I reached for the packet, then backed away before I opened the flap and pulled out the stack of photos.

"These are from the roll of film I asked you about!" I tried to sound angry, but the words came out relieved. "Why didn't you tell me you had them?"

Hawk didn't offer an explanation, and I forced my concentration off my anxiety as I began flipping through the shots. My heart lurched with a painful twist of worry when I came upon ones I had recently taken of Garden of the Gods. Jeremiah would love this one, and I hoped to God he was okay. I stared at the rainbow that shone faintly in the left-hand corner of the shot. Another image had caught a funnel cloud produced by a severe weather cell that had moved over Pikes Peak. Jeremiah would love this one, too, I thought, then blinked, trying to distract myself from the fact I had no idea where he was or whether he might be in trouble, just like he had no idea where I was or what kind of trouble I was in. I flipped through and found the one of the Asian men and the pitcher.

Hawk walked over and tilted his head until he was peering at the picture I was looking at. "Interesting, that one." His voice sounded strange.

"Yeah," I tried to ignore the creepy feeling his voice created. "I wasn't sure how it would come out, but look at this." I held it out. "A perfect candlestick shot. The two are facing each other, and it almost looks like there's a miniature pitcher between them. I was trying for a warped sense of depth perception."

"You're very good. Looks like someone used special effects."

Hawk winked at me. Startled, I wondered what could have sparked that kind of reaction.

"Yeah, maybe, except that this is thirty-five millimeter, and the sun's reflecting off the guy's glasses on the left. But the faces do look almost exactly alike, don't they?" I set the picture aside and rummaged through the others until I located the ones of Hawk. Both were close-ups, almost identical. I held them out for him to see.

"I liked the angles of these. See? There's the slant of the stadium overhead that zigs into the line of the bill on your cap." I looked closer and realized I had caught a reflection of the field in his sunglasses. Staring at the two photographs, I mused over options.

"What are you thinking?" Hawk's question jerked me out of my preoccupation.

"What? Oh. I was wondering what the effect would be if I cropped out everything but the two shades of the sunglasses, then enlarged the shots. Might turn into a pretty cool-looking effect, having the field reflected in the shades like that. Not that it'll ever end up on the front of *Sports Illustrated*."

Reluctantly, I found the strip of negative that included his pictures and held it out with the two prints. "These are yours, I guess, after all the effort you went through. Take them before I change my mind."

He took the pictures and negatives, then reached into a pocket and removed a cigarette lighter. As I watched, he knelt down, held the photographs and negative close to the ground and flicked the lighter. A small flame curled around the photographs, and smoke rose when the thick paper started to burn. He dropped the burning pile onto the dirt, and I silently mourned the loss of the negatives, which included the one of the Asians. To distract myself, I flipped through the remaining pictures. The two shots of the father and son had gotten stuck to the back of a third picture, and it took a moment for me to separate them from each other. I tried to focus my thoughts and critique what I saw, but instead all I saw were memories of my own family. If Mom and Dad had been alive, I would have gotten a shot of the two of them. Their faces had always been so animated, so full of life.

Life. I swallowed and thought about Angela. Was she still alive? Yes, of course she was. She would recover, and then she and I would go to a Rockies ball game, and I would take a bunch of pictures of her and me and Jeremiah. I sniffed and rubbed my face against the warm sleeve of my sweatshirt.

First, I had to get myself out of the mess I was in with Hawk.

Hawk leaned into the back of the car, pulled open a side compartment. "Want something to eat?"

Ignoring him, I shuffled the pictures, then slid them back into the packet. I set them down beside him, then stepped back and crossed my arms. The tiniest crest of sun peeped over the horizon.

"Can I go now? The pictures I took of you are destroyed. There is no reason why I can't start walking towards the highway."

Hawk pulled out a couple of granola bars, then a can of V-8 juice. "Here drink that." He held the can towards me.

I shook my head. "No thanks. I'm not hungry."

"Drink it anyway." There was an edge to his voice that made my heart thump hard against my chest. Reluctantly, I accepted the can he held out, then popped the lid and took a sip of warm V-8 juice. I looked at the emptiness that surrounded us and tried to guess how far the highway was from where we were.

Hawk unwrapped a couple of granola bars. I watched the muscles along his jaw work as he ate, his eyes squinting against the brilliant light of the sunrise.

"Your press pass identifies you as a newspaper employee. When I ran the name through the motel computer, the Colorado Springs daily came up. Do you work on the side for some ragmag?"

I set the can of V8 juice down on the bumper. "What's a ragmag?"

The distant sound of an eighteen-wheeler drifted across the emptiness. I willed it to be a stock truck that was delivering cattle along the abandoned dirt road. Instead the sound gradually faded.

"Gossip column."

I turned back to the man sitting on the bumper of the Mercedes. "I don't work for the tabloids, if that's what you're asking. Why are you back on that again?"

"Because you've yet to explain how you knew I would be at the game this Sunday past." His words were low, calculating, and I slowly acknowledged the reason why he had stopped all the way out here.

My life depended on my answering him in a way he would accept as truth.

"Hawk, it was a coincidence. You look a lot like Jeremiah. Same hair color, roughly the same build. I was expecting him to show up at the game, and I thought you were him. When I looked at you through the lens I realized my mistake, but I liked the frame, so I snapped a couple off. It's habit. Then you showed up, obviously upset about the picture. Thirty-five millimeters don't have delete buttons." I paused, giving him opportunity to comment. When he didn't, I tried another tact. "You know, you've been all worked up about the coincidence of my taking your picture. Personally, I think it's a bigger coincidence that you wanted the picture bad enough to follow me all the way to the hospital. It's just a picture, after all. You've solved the problem anyway." I gestured towards the small pile of black ashes on the ground. "Finding Jeremiah and getting back to Angela are my problems, not yours. I really don't see where it's necessary to keep me with you." I took another step back and uncrossed my arms. I felt as though I were on trial. My hands slid into the warmer of the hoody, and I gripped my fingers together.

"You also took a snapshot of Lee."

"Lee?" Now what was he talking about? "Who is Lee?"

"The chap you were trying to avoid when you leaped into the path of the lorry."

I stood there and stared at the man for what must have been a full minute. His gray eyes drilled into mine. The can of V8 perched between us on the bumper. The brilliant sunrise scattered lingering shadows.

"If you did not take off from the ballpark to meet Lee at a pre-determined, well-marked location to discuss the picture you took of me…"

"What in the hell are you talking about?" I interjected.

He continued, ignoring my interruption. "…then the only other explanation is that he followed you because of the shot you took of *him*. Just how in bloody hell are you, Gary, and Jeremiah connected in with Lee?"

I grappled with his accusations. "You sound as though you know this Lee. Were the two of you supposed to meet or something?"

When he didn't answer, I stared at the surrounding emptiness and started thinking aloud. "You keep asking how I knew you'd be at the game. Does that mean no one was supposed to know where you were?"

"You're very good at this, you know. I'll grant you that." Hawk's hand slipped behind his back.

Somehow, I didn't think he meant what he said as a compliment. My eyes fell to his hands.

Or rather, the handgun that rested in the palm of his left hand. The muscles in my legs turned to water as I watched the fingers of his right hand casually screw a long cylinder onto the barrel. His actions appeared so nonchalant, he might have been doing something as inane as tying his shoe.

I looked up and met his eyes. They were cold, emotionless, waiting.

I kept my eyes on his, tried to ignore the object in his hand, but couldn't maintain the effort. My eyes drifted back to the weapon. With a vicious twist of clarity, my mind flashed back to a memory almost twenty years old. A childhood vision, one filled with the bloody mess of human remains that had been our next door neighbor. Sounds of a shotgun echoed in my head, still as terrifying now as they had been to my nine-year-old ears.

My entire body trembled so badly I gripped the side of the car to keep from collapsing onto the ground. I didn't know how much longer my legs would hold me up.

"My superior officer, Chan Lee, works out of London."

His words echoed in my head, didn't make any sense. The memory of the exploding shotgun buried his voice. I squeezed my eyes shut as I tried to block the memory of the dead body, the mistaken identity that had resulted in death.

"He's one of the Asian twins."

It had been one of our neighbor's twin sons who shot his father. All because his father had forgotten his house key and had tried opening a window to slip into the house because it was late.

"Lee's file includes a thorough background check for security purposes. The information given proves he's an only child."

My heart rate accelerated and my skin grew cold. Angela and I had been camping out in our vast backyard the night of the shooting. The neighbor's house bordered the back of our property. When a shotgun blast shattered the nighttime stillness, Angela ran to our house. Curiosity had driven me towards the screams and wailing to see what was causing the mayhem, then closer to see what the lump was on the neighbor's back porch. The powerful outdoor lights laid bare the image of the mangled, headless body, the blood, the bits of human flesh. I had stood there, silent and motionless because I couldn't get my mouth open to scream, couldn't get my feet to run.

Just like I couldn't get them to run now.

Hawk's gray eyes drilled through my green ones. "You take two pictures of me. And on the same roll of film, you have a shot of Lee with a twin brother he's not supposed to have. Bloody fucking coincidence, wouldn't you agree?"

I tried to breathe, but my chest wouldn't expand. Blood everywhere, brain matter, pieces of skull....

I stared at the gun in his left hand. Hysteria gave up on my feet and took the form of garrulity. "You think I took your picture to sell to some tabloid. That's why you're asking all those questions about extortion. You think Jeremiah and Gary are in it. And the Asian twins aren't really twins, and General Lee is after me for whatever reason I haven't figured out yet."

The dead man lying there, a bloody pulp, shot by one of his own sons. I dragged my eyes back to Hawk's. "Did the Asian twins shoot each other?"

Hawk sat motionless, his left hand still resting on his knee, the gun in his hand. He stared at me, and I gradually realized that he appeared perplexed. The cold detachment in his eyes began to thaw. He drew a breath. "You've really no idea who Lee is, have you?"

It dawned on me that his was a rhetorical question and that for once I didn't have to try to come up with an answer. My eyes locked on the gun in his hand, and the memory of the bloody carnage on our neighbor's back porch locked up my brain cells.

"Perhaps I've been a bit inaccurate in my assessment." His left hand lifted and I gripped the doorframe so hard that the metal sliced my palms. I felt blood trickle into the sleeves of my sweatshirt.

Hawk's long fingers began to unscrew the silencer. "It appears that you and I might have gone and stumbled into each other's problems. Question is, are our problems related?"

I heard his words, but didn't understand what they meant. Through glassy eyes I watched the silencer disappear into Hawk's right back pocket as the gun disappeared behind his back. I could not understand why he hadn't shot me. What had stopped him? I was a witness, regardless whether or not I answered any of his questions. And because I was a witness, I should be dead by now.

I tried to unbend my fingers from the edge of the car, managed to work them loose from the metal edge. On weak, trembling legs, I stumbled away. Away from the car, away from Hawk. Away from the awful memory of guns and what they did to humans. I couldn't run, didn't have enough strength in my legs. To be honest, I didn't make it very far from the car and the man before I staggered onto the ground. I heard footsteps behind me and tried to get my feet beneath me, but had no strength to pull myself upright.

I could not face that man again, could not face the weapon I knew he carried, could not face anymore accusations. When Hawk's fingers wrapped around my upper arm I almost fainted. I stared at the black cross-trainers on his feet, refused to look at him when he knelt down, refused to let him see past my eyes into the state of my emotional breakdown.

"It may be that your brother-in-law is the one connected with Lee and his network. If so, then they may be after the both of us." Hawk's voice was quiet, his grip on my arm firm but not painful.

I was shaking so hard my teeth rattled in my head. I couldn't understand why I wasn't dead, why he was still talking to me, why suddenly he was being nice again. My insides reeled, my vision whirled. Images of the dead father, Hawk's handgun, blood and body parts everywhere, all of them blew through my head with the violence of a tornado.

Hawk's fingers relaxed. "We need to keep moving. We're easy targets out here."

I shook my head, my insides flipping in several unpleasant directions. Any minute now, my stomach was going to heave itself inside out. I braced my palms against the ground and forced myself to swallow several times.

Hawk seemed oblivious of my mental state because he continued. "It's best we avoid whomever is planting bombs and pushing young ladies in front of lorries."

He straightened, his cross trainers shifting on the ground sounding like so many popguns. I couldn't get the image of his handgun out of my head. I refused to look at him, so I stared at the dirt on the knees of my new jeans, felt the sharp jabs of rocks along my shins, stared at the thin, bloody cuts across my palms.

His voice drifted down to my ears. "According to you, the medics found your sister in Limon. I'd like to follow-up on that, then backtrack her route, see if something connects the dots between her, your husband, your brother-in-law, and Lee."

I cleared my throat. "None of it is any of your business. Butt out and leave me alone." My words came out in a croak so hoarse that I didn't recognize my own voice.

Hawk sighed. "I'd rather not backtrack a route I've used." He seemed to be trying to explain something to me. "Time consuming, yes, but unpredictable, which gives a slight advantage when one's unsure who might be following."

I had no idea what he was talking about, but since he seemed to be ignoring me, then I would do likewise. "I'll thumb my way to Denver. I need to get back to my sister."

"Too much risk, particularly if the network is involved. I've also a fancy to know where that husband of yours has got to."

"No you don't," I mumbled, realizing with a sour twist of my stomach that he wasn't ignoring me. He was ignoring my request for freedom.

Hawk's voice floated over my head. "I think it's too big a co-incidence your brother-in-law shows up, and the next day your husband goes missing and two international assassins pop up in the vicinity."

I tried again. "Like I said, my brother-in-law is none of your business. Now, leave me alone."

But his words were sinking in. I wondered why Jeremiah had told me he was going to Oklahoma for an interview, and why I hadn't heard from him.

Hawk squatted in front of me again. "I'd like to know who was behind that car bomb. Puzzling, that one."

The scene of the car explosion superseded my childhood memories. Synapses began to fire. "A car explosion means an investigation," I murmured to myself. An investigation would mean realization I was missing. Law enforcement would be getting into the picture soon, if not already. If I could get to the highway, someone might be on the lookout for me.

The car explosion also meant Gary could not be responsible for the car bomb. If he were after my inheritance, then he would want my death to look like an accident, just like Angela's.

My knees started to hurt from the hard, rocky desert ground. When I moved to stretch my legs so I could sit, Hawk reached down and grasped my arm.

"We need to move."

I shook my head. "I'm not going anywhere with you. I swear I won't say anything about you or about what's happened. All I want to do is get back to Angela."

Hawk tugged on my arm. "As of last night, our mobiles no

longer exist. Nor do credit cards, or any other form of paper trace. I've cash, and I'll pick up a burn phone at the next petrol station."

"I'm not going anywhere with you," I repeated, starting to feel stabs of panic slicing through my chest.

Hawk peered at me. "At the moment, your best bet on staying alive is to stay with me. I've given us anonymity, which gives us a slight advantage."

"You're not getting it, are you?" I shouted in his face. "I'm not going ANYWHERE with you—HEY!!"

He jabbed his shoulder into my ribcage, then stood up.

"PUT. ME. DOWN!!" I yelled at him, though not with much effect since I was now upside down over his shoulder. "I…AM…NOT…GOING…ANY…WHERE…WITH…YOU!!" My head bumped against his broad back as he strode across the rocky terrain. When we reached the car, he set me onto my feet.

"The police are going to be after you, since you probably stole the car. You'll end up in jail for grand theft auto and kidnapping!" I jerked away and turned to run, but he caught my wrist.

"Nicking vehicles creates trails." His grip tightened and I expected him to twist my arm behind my back any second.

"I'm not going with you," I whispered, trembling, hearing my voice crack.

Hawk dropped his eyes to my hand. In an effort to hide the injuries, I balled both hands into fists.

Hawk applied pressure, forcing my hand open. "Let me see your other one." He motioned towards my hoody, where my other hand rested. I tried backing away and bumped against the side of the car. Stilling gripping my wrist, Hawk stepped in close.

"It's nothing," I shook my head frantically.

Hawk's eyes locked with mine. "Let me see your hand," he repeated.

I almost dissolved into a hysterical slobbering mess as I pulled my other hand out and turned my palm upwards. When he reached for it I closed my eyes, balled my free hand into a fist, stuffed it back into my hoody.

"Don't."

"I've salve and bandages in the back." Releasing me, he stepped to the rear of the car, and I heard clanking and the rustle of plastic and paper. He reappeared and motioned for my hands again. I slid down the side of the car until I slumped on the ground.

Squeezing my eyes shut seemed the only way to avoid watching while he treated the cuts on my palms, though I still felt his fingers against my skin.

"Whatever bloody mess your brother-in-law has created, you'd best consider your husband is likewise in it up to his neck. You're only option of staying alive is by staying with me," he murmured after he was done.

I sat there on the ground leaning against the car with my eyes still squeezed shut and shook my head. "N-n-no."

I felt his finger touch the underside of my chin. "I've no longer reason to kill you, Mattie."

"N-n-no," I whispered for what seemed the millionth time. I opened my eyes and stared straight into his. He seemed to relent because he dropped his hand, leaned back, and propped his elbows on his knees. "Right. Well then, will you at least show me which way to the bloody motorway?"

I stared at him, suspicious he was up to something despite his sudden change in tone. "Which one?"

"Whichever is nearest." He stood, opened the rear car door and retrieved a map.

I could not stand up. He squatted again, held out the map. I stared at the white bandages he had used to wrap my palms, then pointed a shaking finger at the chart. I had to clear my throat twice before any words came out.

"We're here, off of highway eighty-seven. Y-you can head west and catch I-twenty-five in Raton."

He looked down at me, his gray eyes seeing more in my face than I wanted to share.

"I'd rather like to avoid common routes."

Shrugging, I pointed a shaking finger at the map again, trying to trace the route. "Then go north on two-eighty-seven, then west on one-sixty. That'll take you through the Comanche National Grasslands. There's nothing out there."

"Isn't that one of your Indian reservations?" Hawk looked doubtful.

I shook my head. "No, actually, it's a national park. Instead of forest, its prairie grass." I took a deep breath and hoped he would leave soon.

"Are you quite sure?" He didn't seem in as much of a hurry as earlier. Damn.

I pointed towards the western horizon. "See those cone-shaped hills and the black rock formations? That's Capulin National Monument. They're part of an extinct volcano bed, which means we're near eighty-seven. The highway is a common route, so traffic will be increasing soon. If you want to avoid it, I suggest you hit one-sixty."

Hawk refolded the map, put it and the first aid supplies in the back of the car, and closed the rear hatch. I managed to scramble to my feet when he stepped around me and opened the rear door. We stood motionless watching each other for several minutes.

"Get in." He nodded towards the open rear door.

I stared at the soft gray leather of the back seat and thought I would die if I had to sit in the same car with him. I'd been wrong. He wasn't relenting. I stared at the open car door for a long, long time, trying to think of a way out. If I ran, he would catch me. I couldn't fight him, I had nothing to use as self-defense. He had drugged me twice, and there was nothing stopping him from resorting to that option a third time.

As if reading my mind Hawk grasped my arm, guided me onto the back seat, shut the door, then walked around and climbed behind the wheel.

Chapter Nine

I awoke in the back seat of the car with a clear idea of what to do, a feeling of acute guilt for not having thought of it sooner, and a cramped feeling in my gut at the prospect of yet another confrontation with Hawk.

Afternoon thunderheads piled against each other, pushing into altitudes that promised severe weather sooner than later. No dizziness hit when I sat up. Thankful my brain seemed to be returning to normal, I looked around to see where we were.

Hawk had pulled into a run-down gas station in the wasteland where New Mexico, Oklahoma, and Colorado meet. Beside the station were boarded up wooden buildings and the rusted, empty carcasses of cars almost hidden by weed-choked driveways. The surrounding stark emptiness emphasized the ghost-town silence.

I looked towards the dash and spotted a red alarm light blinking, so I waited until Hawk appeared from the wooden doorway of the gas station-slash-store. I watched him walk casually across the rough gravel. He claimed to want to help locate Jeremiah and track Angela's movements. I had a way to do both. Question was, could I muster enough courage to call his bluff?

With difficulty I pushed away memories of guns and deserted dirt roads, forced myself to focus on Angela and my need to find my husband. I closed my hand, felt the bandage Hawk had wrapped around my palms. I remembered all too clearly how I'd gotten those cuts.

I heard the automatic locks click and opened the door.

"Feeling better?" he asked when I climbed out.

I took a deep breath. "There's a telephone booth next to the station."

His eyebrows twitched, and he walked around to the side of the car and began unscrewing the gas cap. I followed. The faint throb in my head did not increase with physical movement. I swung my attention to the building and the pay phone in an old-fashioned red booth.

"I want to call the OU Prediction station again." I watched as he lifted the gas nozzle and flipped up the metal handle. His eyes drifted down to meet mine. I sighed and did a quick mental evaluation of what to tell him. God, it felt good to be thinking clearly.

"Becky Parsons and her family have been taking care of Mud Rain since Mom and Dad died. Becky is in charge of the tours they do of the building, and her son is one of the lead forecasters. She watches over Mud Rain when he's in the building. Jeremiah checks in daily with her, then talks to Mud Rain. If anyone knows where Jeremiah is, she will. I'm kicking myself for not thinking of it sooner." I was also kicking myself for not memorizing the Parsons' phone number. I had never imagined not having access to my cell phone and its list of contacts. I had no idea what Becky's cell number was, if I ran into a dead end trying to reach her at the Prediction Center.

There are definite disadvantages to relying on technology.

Hawk watched me. "Who is Mud Rain?"

The answer to that question touched upon sensitive family issues. I debated how much to tell him. "Mud Rain is Jeremiah's younger brother. He works at the campus building where Jeremiah was supposed to go for the interview. I've been thinking that maybe the interview wasn't common knowledge. I can't believe he would make something like that up. Becky would know for sure whether the lady on the phone yesterday had the right information. She should be able to clear up some of this mess."

"Why her? Why not Mud Rain?"

I should have known Hawk would push me into a better explanation. "Look, can't you just take my word for now that I need to call Becky?"

The nozzle clanked, and he withdrew the handle and replaced it into the holder. Then he picked up the gas cap and snapped it into place. His eyes lifted to mine with cold inflexibility. I sighed, hung on indecision, and broke eye contact to gaze at the darkening clouds on the horizon.

"Mud Rain has Down's Syndrome," I admitted. I wondered again why, if Jeremiah had made it to the building, he hadn't signed in. What if the receptionist was right and there hadn't been an interview? Had Jeremiah planned a reservation excursion with Mud Rain and decided not to tell me?

That didn't make any sense. Jeremiah would have no reason to hide the fact he was planning a trip.

Hawk's voice broke into my thoughts. "If there was an interview and your husband didn't show, Becky would have followed up with a call. Either he accessed the building without signing in, or he misled you about the interview. Either way, calling the weather station in Norman will not provide answers."

I didn't like the look in his eyes. "Yeah, well maybe you're forgetting that I haven't been home to check messages, and that you confiscated my cell phone. If you're not going to give me back my phone, at least let me talk to someone who can confirm whether Jeremiah showed up where he said he was planning to go!"

Hawk crossed his arms, then leaned against the car and gazed across the graveled parking lot towards the building. Light reflected off his eyes, highlighting tiny black flecks and the black circle that ringed each iris. His eyes fixed on the front of the gas station, his answer clearly in his posture.

Damn it. My eyes drifted to the peeling, gray boards of the gas station.

"Hawk," I tried again, "I need to talk to Becky. At least to tell her that Angela is in Denver Hospital!"

The man remained stubbornly silent. I stormed around the car and over to the station. An old wood plank lay across two cinderblocks and served as a bench underneath the overhang in front. I slumped down onto the makeshift bench. Hawk followed and took a seat beside me. The board creaked and sagged.

I inhaled, prayed for patience, and turned what I hoped was a calm, steady gaze towards Hawk. "I need to call Becky and tell her about Angela, and then I need to call the hospital to find out how Angela is." The phone booth was a few feet away. I started to rise.

When Hawk dropped a firm hand on my arm my calm evaporated. I pulled hard against his grip. "I need to start getting some help with this!"

"You know enough to suspect Gary…"

"…I need to tell her about Angela…" Our conversations began to overlap. I strained against him, and his fingers tightened.

"…We're not breaking silence…"

"…I need to find out whether Becky's heard from Jeremiah…."

His fingers bit painfully into my arm. "There is nothing to find out from Becky."

I glared at him. "Angela is critically ill, and Jeremiah has disappeared! I need to be calling the police!"

Hawk shook his head. "You will not contact law enforcement."

"Why not?" I shouted, trying to yank my arm free. "I am completely out of contact with everyone, and I need some help!" From the corner of my eye, distant lightning blinked downward in thin silver streaks, too far away for the thunder to reach us.

Hawk stared at me, a light wind stirring his short, curly black hair, exposing white at his temples. He released my arm and leaned forward, resting his forearms on his knees and entwining his fingers. Lines seemed to deepen around his eyes and mouth. "I work with the...British secret intelligence community."

I froze, then gaped at him. "Wait a minute. Are you telling me that you're an...an *agent*? As in James Bond double oh seven and all that MI-six stuff?"

He gave up a thin smile. "We prefer to think ourselves civil servants."

I snorted. "That's a political mouthful."

Hawk opened his mouth, then closed it again and gazed at the horizon. Minutes passed before he continued. "Two years ago, I helped plan an operation to trap a suspected member of a group known as the Charlie Network. The group has taken responsibility for several political assassinations over the years. We nabbed our bait, had an opportunity to plant one of our own into their network. Our catch would have given us names and descriptions. The car he was in exploded at the front gate of the facility we planned to use. The intercom wasn't working, and I got out to notify the guard when it blew." He fell silent.

I waited for him to continue, but the silence lengthened. I leaned back against the rough boards of the building. "Were you hurt?"

He nodded, his eyes lingering on the horizon. My gaze wandered over the same direction as lightning jumped between clouds and earth in jagged, thickening bolts. Distant thunder rumbled closer, and the light breeze around us stalled.

Hawk winced as though coming back from painful memories. "The flames got my legs and back. I've been in hospital and rehab for most of the last two years. Someone from Charlie knew which car was used to transport our chap."

"How did they find that out?" I wasn't sure I wanted to know the answer.

"From one of us."

"But…but that means someone in your organization was working for Charlie." I stopped.

His lips pressed into a thin line. "Precisely."

I thought it over. "So, since you survived the explosion, does that mean Charlie is still after you?"

He shook his head. "I died two years ago."

I waited for the punch line. "Seriously?" I finally asked.

He nodded. "A CIA agent in on the operation arranged to swap identities when I went in for surgical debridement. He suspected our organization had been compromised. As it happened, a victim of an abandoned warehouse fire was admitted about the same time. I went in to surgery as myself, but came out with the other chap's name and was taken to his room. Poor bugger died twenty-four hours later, despite the fact he was the more stable of the two of us. Max, the CIA agent, took things seriously and got me re-located to Denver. I've been underground since. Even Lee, my superior officer, doesn't know I'm alive." He threw me an exasperated look. "After two years of hiding, I pop my head up for a bit of afternoon baseball, and a bloody news photographer snaps my picture."

I flinched. "No wonder you were upset when I took your picture the other day. You wouldn't want your face in the paper, or on a blog site."

Hawk leaned against the store, his eyes flickering over the two abandoned buildings. Approaching thunder was now providing ominous rumbling commentary.

My thoughts came fast. Lee was his boss. Lee also had a twin whom, according to Hawk, no one knew about. What if Hawk hadn't known about the twin, either?

I stared at the man sitting next to me. "Did Lee know which car would be used to transport this guy you were after? When the car got blown up?"

Hawk nodded.

I chose my next words with care. "Then, is it possible that this Lee guy…your boss…might be a mole for this Charlie Network?"

"A man whom I've entrusted my life…" Hawk stopped and stared off into space.

"…almost got you killed." I finished for him.

Hawk turned his head and looked up, his gray eyes intense.

"He knows who you are now. And he will no doubt know all about Angela and Gary…and Jeremiah." He paused. "If he's been feeding security information to the network all these years, he'll want to protect his position by getting rid of you, the film, and anyone with whom you might have shared the information."

"Do you think he has something to do with my husband's disappearance?"

Hawk shook his head. "No. The timing doesn't fit. And, we haven't come across any bodies." His last words hung in the air.

My heart jumped into my throat, and I had difficulty swallowing. "Can't you call in to the CIA guy for some help?"

Hawk frowned. "I've nothing to tell him."

"Nothing to tell him?" I barked out. "That bozo boss of yours tried to kill an American!" I stared at him, searching for a reason why he wouldn't want to call in reinforcements. "Do you think Lee saw you?"

"It's likely." He was starting to sound like Jeremiah. Curt, unhelpful answers and mostly monosyllabic conversations.

I poked him in the shoulder. "Then why didn't you go after him, after you got me out of the street?"

Hawk didn't move. "When you dived into that oncoming lorry, I thought I might have a go at you. Try to get some answers, since you managed to dodge Lee."

When I scowled at him, he threw me a chagrined look. "Those were my thoughts at the time."

"So, how was it that he happened to be at the ballgame the same day you were?" I demanded.

Hawk gave me a long, penetrating stare so intense that I leaned away. I broke eye contact and looked at the ground. Answers crawled through healing mental cracks.

"You…you think someone leaked the news of your whereabouts…." I paused, waiting for him to refute. When he offered no comment, I continued. "Which is why you kept after me about how I knew you were at the game. And why you don't want to contact any law enforcement, because you'll have to spill the information that you're alive." I rested my head against the rough planked boards of the building. As if I didn't have enough problems already with my brother-in-law, all I needed was to find out a professional assassination network was mixed into the mess.

How was I going to get out of this and help Angela, and chase down my missing husband?

I turned my head towards him. "Do you think Gary is involved with this Charlie Network?"

Hawk turned his face towards the approaching storm. Thunder grumbled and growled as black clouds bore down on us. "He could have contracted one of them to get rid of you."

My gaze traveled along Hawk's frame, and I wondered what sort of scars lay underneath the clothes that he wore. He glanced at me, saw me staring. "Checkerboard of skin grafts front and back, including my arse and legs. Took a year before I could walk again, another year to rebuild muscle and strength."

"*Jesus,*" I whispered.

He shrugged and turned away. "Comes with the territory."

A dusty blue minivan pulled into the rutted gravel and rolled to a stop in front of the building. The dinged up doors opened and a family of four emerged. Obesity added years to the faces of the two children and their parents. I glanced away to avoid staring, but the woman's complaints caught my attention.

"I didn't want a big, fancy camera like this." The woman's voice drifted back as they disappeared into the store. "Sue wasted a lot of money on this thing. It's awkward, heavy, and it's making my neck cramp."

Her companion's answer came through the open window above where Hawk and I sat. "Then leave it in the car. Use your cell."

"My phone is dead, and I can't find my charger. I want one of these disposable ones."

An idea occurred, and I turned to Hawk. "Do you have any cash?" I whispered. He hesitated.

"Please." I pressed my hands together. "Thanks to a car bomb, I've lost all my equipment. This might be a chance to replace some of it."

"You don't even know what kind she has." He looked at me as though my brains had just leaked out of my head. I barely aborted the urge to kneel.

"If I find out it's not the kind I want, then no harm done. But if it is, I want to be able to make an offer."

Hawk regarded me, then looked away.

I shook my folded hands at him. *"Please."*

Shaking his head, Hawk stood and started in the direction of the Mercedes. I followed, trying to keep my pace at a walk. He opened the back, dug around one of the side compartments, and pulled out an impressive wad of bills.

"Start low. Otherwise they'll think you want it," he advised, handing me a mix of twenties and fifties.

I closed my eyes, opened them again. "Please tell me you haven't tossed my belt pack. I had my zoom lens in there."

Hawk grunted something unintelligible, reached into the car again, and handed me my belt pack. I glanced down at my dusty hoody. My shirt underneath wasn't much better. I pulled the sweatshirt off and threw it into the back seat, tucked the money into a pocket, slung my belt pack over a shoulder, then spun on my heel towards the store.

Thirty minutes later Hawk and I were once again the only ones in front of the station. I'm sure he turned apoplectic when I gave the couple three hundred more than they asked.

"You should have kept your mouth shut," Hawk accused, true to prediction, as I rummaged through the accessories bag.

"Yeah, but then I might not have gotten all this extra stuff." I was feeling enormously pleased with myself. "Besides, I could not in good conscience pay that for a brand new digital Canon Eos." An excellent hobby camera, though I would replace my professional equipment with Nikons.

Hawk glowered at me. "Bleeding heart Yank."

I ignored him, felt enormously pleased about it, felt even more pleased with myself as I removed the smaller lens and screwed on my zoom lens. Canon lenses are universal. I removed the cap, turned on the camera, and brought the viewfinder up to my eye.

I lowered my camera and pointed at the approaching storm cell. "Your car is about to be inaugurated to a Colorado hail storm."

Hawk grunted. "They believed your storm chaser story easily enough."

I flashed him a devious grin. "That wouldn't have worked with anyone who's grown up around here."

"Why not?" He seemed genuinely perplexed.

I gestured towards the Mercedes. "No hail damage. If you're from around here, and especially if you're a storm chaser, your car would never look like that. You'd have pockmarks all over that shiny black paint. Probably will anyway, by the looks of what's coming. Those CBs are spiking pretty high." I looked at the sky again.

Hawk raised his eyebrows at me. "I beg your pardon?"

"Cumulonimbus clouds. The ones that look like stacks of mashed potatoes. And see where the tops have flattened out? Those are anvils. That happens when the CBs can't rise any higher because of the altitude and cold air currents. Hail-makers, those are. And the green color along the underside of the clouds is a sure sign that hail is on the way. From the looks of things, we're in for a real doozy. Might even get some rotation out of this one."

He squinted at the approaching storm. "Sounds as though you're rather good at this."

"Naw. It's mostly what I've picked up hanging around Jeremiah and the other weather-weanies." I got distracted as lightning flashed, and focused on a spot under the cloud cover that seemed to be generating the most activity.

"A weather *what?*" Hawk's astounded question jerked my attention back to the conversation.

I mentally re-wound my last comments. "A weather-weanie. That's what the senior forecasters call each other. At work, anyway. What'd you think I said?"

Hawk shook his head and turned away. I thought I heard a chuckle. "Never mind."

The air chilled. Insect and bird sounds faltered, then quit all together. I kept the camera trained on the approaching clouds and shot several exposures before a dust devil kicked up too much debris to give decent results.

"If Jeremiah was here, we'd be out chasing that," I said above the gusting wind.

Hawk eyed the now huge black monster that spanned the entire horizon. "Jeremiah sounds certifiable."

A long electrical trunk flashed then splintered into thin, flickering fingers. Clouds dropped into a classic wall formation. I felt sorry for the family in the minivan, because they were heading straight into the middle of it. Gale-strength winds rattled the plank board walls of the old building and sent debris scuttling across the tin roof. The wind swirled with significantly colder air as large scattered drops smacked against the earth. I gathered my new camera gear and scurried into the store without waiting to see whether Hawk followed. Thunder clapped in harsh, percussive echoes, followed by hail that bounced around, falling with increasing density until quarter-sized ice drilled into the damp, muddy ground. The roar on the tin roof rendered conversation useless. I couldn't even hear the thunder.

As I stood in the doorway watching the storm, an elderly gentleman ambled over to the window that opened over the bench Hawk and I had been sitting on. The dark rectangle of the window framed his silhouette as he leaned his forearms on the sill. I raised the camera and zoomed until his creased, lined face filled the right side of the frame. The hailstorm provided a murky, grayish backdrop to his lightly shadowed profile. I snapped several, then pushed the review arrow and felt an eerie chill at the stark solitude I had captured.

Recognition dawned, and I jerked my attention up. "Joe?"

When the man turned away from the window and faced me, I couldn't believe what I saw. "Joe Healing Water!"

A white-toothed grin split the old man's face. "Wondered when you'd make the connection." He ambled towards the counter. Another hard, thunderous crack rattled the cans on the shelves as blue-white lightning flashed. The hail tapered, turned into a torrential downpour.

I followed him to the counter and sat down on a barstool. I had met him during my first visit to the Southern Ute Reservation with Jeremiah. He had been old way back then. He didn't look like he had changed a bit. A long single dark gray braid trailed well past his shoulders. Sharply chiseled cheekbones lent the impression of wisdom rather than of age. A long-sleeved red plaid shirt and old blue jeans hid the rest of him.

"What are you doing out here? I thought you were on the Reservation," I asked him.

Joe's black eyes glittered. "Moved here five years ago. Wanted some peace and quiet."

Hawk, who had been standing just inside the doorway, followed me and took a seat on the other barstool. He seemed to be inspecting Joe, and I wondered what he thought about Joe and me knowing each other. I wondered what he thought of this coincidence, since he had told me numerous times he didn't believe in them.

Joe focused his penetratingly black eyes on Hawk. "You look pretty good for a dead man."

The two men stared at each other for so long, I thought both of them had turned to stone. The semi-darkness created an eerie intimacy among the three of us. Joe spoke to me, but kept his attention on Hawk.

"What are you doing with this clown? Jeremiah assured me you were safe and sound back in the Springs."

Hawk straightened and started to slide his arms from the countertop.

Joe's expression darkened. "Keep your hands where I can see them." He jerked one of his arms, and I heard the metallic, lethal rack of a pump-action shotgun.

Hawk went rigid. It was then I noticed that both of Joe's hands were out of sight behind the counter.

"Mattie, move over here with me," he ordered curtly.

I did as he instructed. When I was behind the counter, I glanced at the shotgun he held. I also noticed the cabinets underneath only reached halfway to the countertop, which meant Joe's gun had an unobstructed view of Hawk's entire mid-section. My imagination painted a perfectly clear picture of the blood and guts that would splatter everywhere, if Joe pulled the trigger.

I glanced at Hawk, who did not break eye contact with Joe.

"Now, Mattie, how about you telling me what you're doing out here, instead of being at home." Joe sounded pissed as hell.

"It's...it's a long story." I stammered, trying to suppress the presence of the gun and the images in my head.

"I've got all day." His voice was cold as death.

I told him all of it. Taking pictures of Hawk at the ball game and his reaction, Jeremiah's strange phone call and then my inability to reach him, the call from the hospital ER and how Angela looked when I saw her, being almost run over by the bus, then kidnapped by Hawk. I saw the muscle along Hawk's jaw clench when I mentioned the events in the motel and being drugged. When I got to the point of being alone with him in the middle of New Mexico, I faltered.

"He pulled a gun on you," Joe stated rather than asked.

I didn't know how to answer him. I really didn't want to witness Hawk being blown literally to bits. I decided to avoid the subject altogether.

"I tried to get Hawk to let me talk to Becky, to see if she's talked to Jeremiah," I stammered.

"She hasn't. Jeremiah didn't want her pulled into the situation, either." He continued before I could absorb what his words implied. His eyes, steady on Hawk throughout my monologue. "From what you said outside there, sounds like your case manager set you up."

"So it would appear." Hawk remained still, his hands motionless on the scratched, thick, green glass.

"How did you come up with this nonsense about Mattie being involved?"

I glanced again at Hawk and saw the merest flicker of his eyes in my direction. The muscle in his jaw clenched again.

"I was convinced she had got a tip from a bloody ragmag to get my picture for a nice bit of pocket change."

Joe snorted. "Not very good at putting two and two together, are you?"

Hawk did not move. "I was not aware that my math skills were in doubt."

I had to admire the man for his coolness, especially under the current circumstances.

Hawk continued, his voice dead steady and devoid of emotion. "I watched Lee approach her in front of the hospital…"

"You followed her from the ballpark?" Joe's question cut him off.

Hawk gave the merest hint of a shrug. "We call it surveillance."

Joe's eyes glinted cold, hard, and black as flint. "We call it stalking in this country, son. For your information, it's also illegal."

Chapter Ten

Joe stood behind the counter, the shotgun aimed out of sight at Hawk's mid-section, his flint eyes narrowed at the man sitting at the counter. "You assumed that she was guilty, rather than looking at the one who has suddenly shown up all the way from London for no apparent reason. Mattie here is pretty easy to read. How could you possibly come up with the notion she was tied up in something illegal? Or are you just used to assuming Americans are always the guilty ones?"

Hawk's Adam's apple moved slightly as he swallowed.

Joe flicked his eyes in my direction. "Did this clown touch you, Mattie?"

His abrupt question caught me off guard, and I wasn't sure how to answer. In my description of the last twenty-four hours I left out Hawk's physical attack.

And because I hesitated, the look in Joe's eyes changed, took on the same lethal detachment I had seen in Hawk's eyes on that dirt road when he'd been screwing the silencer onto his gun.

"Joe," I gasped, "Don't shoot him. Please."

Joe released another derisive snort. He was starting to sound like a bull. His expression certainly resembled one. "You haven't buckled under that Stockholm Syndrome nonsense, have you?"

I backed up and ran both hands through my disheveled hair. "No, Joe. No, I haven't."

"We need to talk. Recent events have complicated things." Hawk's voice was very quiet.

"Not the least of which was you going after Mattie here," Joe snapped. "Sounds to me like you planned on getting rid of her in someplace nice and quiet, which was never part of our deal."

I stared at Joe as his words sank in. "Do you and Hawk know each other?" I demanded.

Joe motioned his head towards the open door. "Mattie, go outside."

"Answer me, damn it!" I shouted, then clamped my lips shut when Joe's black eyes met mine. Shaking, I stumbled for the doorway. The rain had lessened to a sprinkle, the outside air was down-right cold. I stood outside shivering, standing at the window and trying to hear what was going on. I half-expected Joe to yell at me to move away from the building, but all I heard was the low muttering of male voices. I started pacing the front of the store, trying to work out how a British operative and a Southern Ute Indian could possibly know each other, because Joe's non-answer acknowledged that they did.

Joe's voice called from the interior of the store. "You can come inside now. We've come to an agreement."

I made my way back inside, sat down on the empty stool, and rubbed my freezing arms to generate some warmth. Hawk had not moved. Joe's hands rested in his pockets. I wondered what the two men had discussed for so long.

Joe turned to me. "Jeremiah came through here Sunday after-noon. Said he was after a man who kidnapped Mud Rain. He said he'd told you he was on his way to Oklahoma for an interview, hoping that if you got pissed off and decided to follow him at least you'd be out of the way."

I stared at him, too stunned to reply.

Joe went on. "Jeremiah and Mud Rain stop here for gas when-ever they make a trip to the Rez. Sometimes I'll close up shop and go with them."

"You saw Jeremiah on Sunday?" I managed to croak.

"Isn't that what I've been saying? Are your ears for decoration only?" A large, white-toothed grin softened his words.

I was too busy trying to understand what he was telling me to take offense. "You said that Gary has Mud Rain?"

Joe's eyes flickered to Hawk, then back to me. "That's not what I said, but you're right. Jeremiah got a call from Angela Sunday morning. She was trying to get Mud Rain to him, but her strength ran out and she had to pull over in Limon. He was on his way to Limon when he received a call from Gary saying that he had Mud Rain and was heading for the Rez."

Joe shifted his attention back to Hawk. His smile vanished. "You were supposed to monitor her actions, not kidnap her." He shook his head. "Leave it to a damned foreigner to screw things up."

"Your advice?" Hawk asked.

Joe's eyes drilled through him. "Jeremiah's headed northwest, towards Walsenberg. Do you have another handgun other than the one you're carrying?"

I looked at Hawk, who answered Joe's question with a curt nod. "Of course."

Joe looked at me, then back to Hawk. "Teach this lady how to use one. My specialty is rifles, and you'll teach her faster than I would be able to."

"NO!" The word slipped out, well more like shouted out, before I could stop myself. I turned to Joe. "No, Joe, no way."

"You thinkin' camera shots will save you and Jeremiah?" Joe could be just as bull-headed as my husband. Just as bull-headed as Hawk, for that matter.

"NO, Joe! I'm not going anywhere near a gun!" I pointed at Hawk. "Especially if it involves him!"

"It's a problem you'd better get over pretty quick." His face turned stony again. I couldn't believe that he was siding with Hawk.

I jabbed a finger in Hawk's direction. "That man kidnapped, almost shot me, and now you want him to teach me how to shoot a gun? Have you gone nuts?"

Hawk rose and turned towards the door. Joe motioned for me to follow. "Go on, face up. Jeremiah's going to need more help than just that bozo."

I glared at Joe Healing Water and saw I was not going to win this argument.

"Go on. Get going." Joe nodded towards Hawk.

Exasperated, I spun on my heel and followed the man to his car. The sky remained black, promising the arrival of more violent weather. We wouldn't be going anywhere for a while, possibly not before morning. Water dripped and trickled along deep ruts in the dirt and gravel, gouging through the inch or so of ice that had fallen. I shivered, though whether it was from cold air or cold memories I wasn't sure. When we reached the now pock-marked car, I reached in and retrieved my hoody and shrugged it on, thankful for the warmth. I adjusted my belt pack, clipped it on around the thickness of the hoody.

Hawk opened the rear hatch, lifted the gray carpet, and twisted a heavy metal ring. When he pulled, the entire floor lifted to expose a large, deep storage compartment. I clamped my hand over my mouth when I saw what the storage area contained.

Hawk explained. "A pump-action shotgun, a bolt-action three-oh-eight rifle with scope, an AR, two semi-automatic handguns, ammunition for all. Underneath, camouflage gear, ghillie netting, and two flak jackets." He leaned into the car and picked up the smaller of the two handguns.

"This is a forty caliber semi-automatic Glock. It'll be a good one for you to learn on." He ejected the magazine, then pulled the slide and ejected the round from the chamber. He reached into the large container and retrieved a small compact box that probably held ammunition. When he slid the Glock's magazine into his left back pocket, and I saw the outline of the gun at the small of his back underneath his shirt.

Memories of the deserted dirt road slammed me between the eyes. I spun around and stalked away. I heard Hawk slam the back hatch and figured he was on my heels.

When I got back inside, Joe was sitting on a stool behind the counter.

"Joe, I shoot film, not bullets. I don't want anything to do with a gun. I want to find Jeremiah and Mud Rain." I paced back and forth in front of the counter, waiting for him to give me an earful, waiting for Hawk to arrive and give me another earful.

Joe watched me from where he sat. Hawk walked in and without a word took a seat on one of the empty stools. I reached around him and snatched the camera from where I had left it on the scratched, worn surface of the counter. I tried to ignore the two men by aiming the lens through the open front door at the stormy horizon.

"Watch how you point that."

I spun around. "What?!"

Joe's attention went from me to the gun Hawk had set on the countertop. I noticed the barrel pointed away from all three of us. He continued. "Doesn't matter whether it's loaded or not."

"Well, I'm not planning on picking it up, so it's nothing you'll have to worry about." I turned my back on him, but not before I thought I saw him glance at Hawk with a hard expression.

"Hey!" I exclaimed, as Hawk plucked the camera from my hands.

He scowled at me. "Cooperate, and I'll give it back."

I glared at him, didn't accomplish a thing, and jerked around to glare through the doorway again. Lightning flickered, bright against a premature twilight. Thunder rumbled from the southwest in strange harmony with the retreating storm to the north.

"There's a barn out behind the store," Joe said into the tense silence that had fallen between the three of us. "Pull your car into it, if you like. There's nothing in there but hay, owls, and mice."

A convenient way to hide Hawk's car, I thought. Joe definitely sounded like he was on Hawk's side now, instead of mine.

Men. Always backing each other up.

"You can stack some of the hay bales and make a practice range." Joe told Hawk.

Yep, he'd changed sides. I felt more than a little betrayed.

"Excellent idea." Hawk stood and I watched him stride through the door and across the gravel to the Mercedes. My camera dangled from the strap in one hand, the gun tightly gripped in his other.

I still had my back to Joe. I heard him shuffle from behind the counter until he appeared in my peripheral vision.

"C'mon, Mattie." He headed to the rear entrance of the store.

A large, plank-board and tin-roof structure stood behind the station. Large gaps in the roof let in more rain than it kept out. Holes and rotting gray boards riddled the sides. Open haylofts ran down the length of the barn on both sides, supporting shadowy brown bales that reached high into dark wooden rafters. Thick webs of dust clung to beams and corners. Soft, irregular rustlings disturbed the silence. I guessed the inside of the barn ran at least thirty yards deep, probably twenty yards side to side. Joe walked over to one side and flipped an old, dusty switch. Single, bare light bulbs hanging at the door of each stall blinked on, throwing yellow but sufficient light down the length of the barn.

Hawk drove the Mercedes through the yawning black hole where doors should have been, then backed it into what was left of an old stall. I wondered how wise it was to hide Hawk's car in here. Then again, the building had withstood the last storm, so I figured it would probably survive at least one more.

I thought about what Joe had told us. Gary had Mud Rain with him, and Jeremiah was tracking Gary. Jeremiah had lied to me to keep me out of the way.

If Angela had Mud Rain with her, where had Gary found him? And what was he planning to do with him and Jeremiah?

After parking the car, Hawk walked to the far end of the enclosure and began shifting some scattered hay bales to the center of the back wall.

"Mattie, hunt around for some old tins." He instructed as he disappeared into the long shadows.

I crossed my arms and didn't move. "No."

Joe sighed, disappeared into various corners, and eventually reappeared with a couple of Pepsi cans.

Hawk stuck an assortment of trash into the stacked hay bales, then retreated a couple of steps and surveyed the result. An old Folgers coffee tin, a couple of bare soup cans, a large Bush's Baked Beans can, and soda containers made up the targets. Joe added the cans he had found. Then both of them turned and walked to the middle of the barn.

I stayed where I was. Thunder rumbled outside.

"I'll be fixing dinner." Joe's mellow voice echoed down the enclosed length.

"You'll be staying here," I objected, feeling my heart jerk in my chest at the thought of being alone again with Hawk.

I watched Hawk walk over to him. "Thanks, Joe, but no need. We'll buy some tins in the store."

"Good luck." Joe turned and disappeared into the blackness outside. My eyes followed his shadowy form through the back door of the store and I wondered which of us he had been talking to.

Hawk walked into the stall adjacent to the Mercedes and reappeared a moment later hauling another bale of hay, which he dropped in the middle of the floor, sending up puffs of dust and dirt. He waved me over with his free hand, his other holding the weapon. A lingering fear of him crept through me as memory flashed to the scene along that deserted dirt road just this morning. I couldn't help it. An undercurrent of menace pulsated around the man. I didn't like who he was. Or what he was, either.

I crossed my arms tightly over my chest. "No, Hawk. I'm not going to do this. I don't care what Joe or you think."

He dropped his hand. Maybe he was seeing the resolve in my expression and was finally accepting the fact I was not going to cooperate on this. Well, not that I had cooperated on anything since he dragged me out of the middle of the boulevard.

"How's your noggin'?" He asked across the distance between us.

I shrugged, warning bells clanging in my head. He was being nice again. That had to mean that he was up to something. "It still hurts. I get dizzy if I move too fast."

"Then we'll practice from a sitting position." He patted the hay bale. "Over here. Don't make me come fetch you. I'll toss you over my shoulder again."

His voice sounded light enough, but I knew he would do exactly what he threatened if I didn't follow directions. I glanced away, looked at the stacked hay bales, then squinted at the corners, looking for a way out. If there was another door somewhere, I could make it outside without having to dodge around him.

Hawk's hand closed around my upper arm, and I released a startled yelp and whipped my head around. The man had closed the distance between us without a sound.

He drew me over to the hay bale. "Sit down."

Hawk straddled it behind me, his long legs pressed against mine. When he gripped my upper arms and pulled my back against his chest, I thought I might lose the little control I maintained over a growing hysteria right then and there.

"Lesson one." His arms circled round me, bringing the gun into sight. He pointed out the trigger safety and the small button that released the magazine. I tried to ignore what he was telling me.

"This is a double-action semi-automatic model. After you've loaded the magazine, you'll need to rack the slide to load the first cartridge. After that, the gun will automatically re-load, and all you need to do is squeeze the trigger. The slide will lock open after the last round." His breath brushed my hair and I shuddered.

"I don't want to do this, Hawk." I tried to ease myself away from him. A sudden, overwhelming need for my husband's protection hit me. I needed him here, now, in this place. I knew he was capable of killing, but he had never given me the impression of being cold-blooded. He hunted animals, not humans.

I got a far different impression from the man sitting behind me, and I didn't like it. Not one bit.

Hawk's arms tightened around me as his right hand closed mine around the butt of the gun. His left guided my left around the butt and overlapped my right.

"Steady the gun in both hands. Move your arms up and down from your shoulders. Swivel from your waist. Always keep your shoulders square with your target." His voice was soft, his head beside mine as he lifted my arms up. He brought the gun up to eye level. I noticed the sights along the barrel and at the point of the muzzle, and my trembling worsened. I didn't know which I hated worst, Hawk's intolerable proximity or the feel of the weapon.

"I really don't want to do this."

Of course he ignored my remark. "Keep both eyes open. Line up your front sight between the notches of the back one. Remember to line up the sights slightly higher than your target."

I shut my eyes and tried to block the feel of the gun, his incessant instructions, the discomfort of the plastic grip against the bandages protecting the cuts across my palms. Hawk guided the direction of the gun to each of the targets, showing me how to move from the waist, keeping my shoulders in line with whatever I was aiming at.

"Right. Let's try some ammo."

Let's not, I thought, rolling my eyes at the idea. I felt him retrieve the magazine from his back pocket. I hoped he would stand at that point, but his arms came back around to loosely encircle me again. He took the gun from my hand, checked the chamber, then slid the magazine into the base. He pushed the release button and the magazine dropped back out again.

"Your turn." He handed the gun to me. "Always check the chamber."

I shuddered, but copied his actions with fair success. Next he slid the magazine in, then pulled the slide to load the chamber.

I almost lost it when the black metal snapped into place. The sound echoed through the empty barn and the room spun as bile rose to the base of my throat. I swallowed with difficulty and watched Hawk drop the magazine, then carefully eject the loaded round. A copper-encased bullet flipped out onto the dirt floor.

"Pick it up."

I did as I was told, my fingers closing around the object whose sole use in this world was to end a life. Hawk's fingers closed around mine. He hesitated, then took the bullet and tucked it into his pocket.

"Your turn. This time leave the chamber loaded."

The loaded gun felt like some horrible monster, and I closed my eyes against memories of my narrow escape from the lethal end of one this morning. Hawk's long fingers wrapped around mine before I had a chance to set the damned thing down.

"Remember, trigger finger stays outside the trigger guard until you're ready to shoot." He folded himself more snugly against me. His arms brought mine up until the sights lined up with the coffee tin sitting in the middle of the stacked bales. I watched the gun barrel waver. He hugged me tighter, steadying my hands. I couldn't suppress the image of the gun in his hand, his horrid demeanor of utter calm, the impression I had that killing meant nothing more to him than reading a newspaper. Thunder echoed close. Lightning flickered through the skeletal remains of the old building.

"Sight slightly above the target," he whispered. "Inhale, then exhale slowly."

He held me motionless for what seemed like years. Another bolt of lightning flashed. Thunder followed much sooner this time, as heavy drops of rain smacked against the tin roof.

"I thought these things had hammers." I was looking for anything to distract him from making me fire the gun.

"It's hidden inside the slide." His finger guided mine into the trigger guard and squeezed.

The report of the gun echoed brutally around the empty space as the gun kicked against my hand.

Hawk guided my hands upward. "Try again."

"*No!*" My voice shook, and the word got stuck in my throat. I tried to wriggle away from Hawk, but his arms and legs tightened. I still had my finger on the trigger and when I tried to move, my fingers reflexively contracted.

The gun fired again.

I jumped at the sound and ducked my head, my ears ringing viciously from the explosive report. My finger jerked, and another shot rattled the old barn before Hawk's finger curled underneath mine, guiding it away from the trigger.

"I can't do this. Let go!" Panic shook my voice. Thunder cracked as the rain increased.

"Calm down." Hawk squeezed until I quit squirming.

Trying to catch my breath, I lost control with the terror surging through me. "I shoot with a camera. I've had enough of this thing." My voice was shaking as badly as the rest of me.

Hawk's muscles tightened. "You control the gun. The gun doesn't do a thing on its own."

"Except kill people," I snapped. "Pictures don't kill people."

Hawk pressed his head against mine. "Guns don't kill people, either. People kill people."

You kill people, I almost shouted, but changed the words just in time. "Guns kill people. Don't split hairs." I lurched against him, fear creating painful pressure in my already constricted chest. "I don't want to have anything to do with it! Now let go!"

Lightning flashed, and thunder cracked with ozone-sizzling impact. Rain turned to hail that drilled against the high tin roof. Tiny white balls of ice fell through holes, pelting the dirt, splashing into scattered puddles.

Then, with a flicker, the lights blinked out.

Hawk held me still in the darkness. Rain and hail rattled what was left of the tin roof.

"We can't do this in the dark," I retorted, using my elbows roughly against his chest in an effort to extricate myself from what now seemed uncomfortably like an embrace.

Hawk ignored me. "It does present a bit of a problem." He took the gun from my hand, ejected the magazine, emptied the chamber. I felt him shift, his left arm releasing me as he laid the weapon somewhere behind him. His arms encircled me again before I could squirm my way free, his strong hands folding mine tightly against his forearms, trapping my elbows beneath his. Blue-white lightning flashed as thunder exploded again.

"Let go, Hawk," I demanded, hoping I sounded angry instead of scared to death.

Lightning created flashing black shadows as thunder cracked again.

"You do smell good..." He trailed off, his nose buried in my short, windblown and very dirty hair.

I tried to keep my voice calm, matter-of-fact. "I smell like day old deodorant and the back of a damned car. Now let go. Please."

Through the heavy downpour outside, the distant rumble of a gas generator reached my ears. The lights flickered, then gradually lit up, not to full power, but at least enough to see. As pale yellow light spread through the room, Hawk loosened his grip, his left hand reaching behind him.

"Right then. Let's get back to business." His hand reappeared with the gun, his voice so mild I wondered whether he had scared me on purpose because he enjoyed that sort of thing.

"Like hell. I'm done with lessons and with sitting here feeding whatever fantasies you may be suffering from!" I elbowed him hard in the ribs. Hawk gasped with pain and for a split second his arms dropped. I threw both my arms against his and almost made it off the bale of hay, but his arms snaked around me, collapsing my rib-cage inward. I choked on a groan.

"I'm trying to teach you how to defend yourself."

No, he wasn't. He was wearing me down, chipping away until I ended up nothing more than a puppet. I felt his chest expand as he drew a slow, deep breath. My muscles quivered beneath his.

"Let's try this again." He brought the gun up.

My teeth chattered so violently, I almost bit my tongue. I jolted hard when his fingers curled around my right wrist and lifted my arm.

"Remember, finger on the trigger only when you're ready to shoot."

I struggled to sit upright, could not hold the weapon steady. My fingers felt like so many icicles against his. I watched with a sort of detached fascination as he held my hands against the gun, the cuts on my palms stinging despite the bandages. The weapon came up and leveled with the targets. I shut my eyes, tried to block everything from my mind.

"It's generally easier to see the target with your eyes open," Hawk murmured in my ear.

I forced my eyelids open and squinted at the blurred stacks of hay bales. My finger shook as it curled around the trigger, felt slight resistance, squeezed past the break.

The gun jolted in my hands, and my ears rang with the report. The coffee tin jerked on the haystack.

"Very good," Hawk murmured. With his hands over mine to steady the gun, I shot the remaining rounds. After the last one the slide locked, and with shaking fingers I ejected the magazine. Hawk took the weapon, then rose and walked to the car.

I stood, my legs feeling like rubber, the room starting to spin. I hoped I didn't appear as unsteady as I felt.

Fortunately, Hawk didn't seem to notice. "We need to find something for you to carry this in." His voice drifted across the space between us.

I kept quiet, thought about Joe's comment about the Stockholm Syndrome, and wondered how anyone could possibly feel anything but revulsion for someone like the man standing next to the car.

He opened the driver's door, then turned to me. "Where is that waist pack of yours?"

I was wearing it. Hawk noticed. "Right." I watched him close the distance, wanting to run but unable to move my feet. He stopped in front of me, our bodies close, and reached for the zipper on my belt pack. He slipped the gun inside, then zipped everything shut. I avoided eye contact when he backed away several paces. Wishing my legs felt stronger, I turned and started towards the yawning gap at the front of the barn.

Wisps of clouds skirted across the black sky, distant thunder whispered. Wet grass and cacti dampened my sneakers as I walked through the darkness towards the back of the station. Hawk's presence loomed behind me, silent and ominous. When I reached the little store, Hawk dropped a hand on my shoulder. I lurched to a stop, didn't turn around until his fingers applied pressure. I looked past his dark silhouette and wished with all my heart that my husband were here to beat the living crap out of him. I could not fathom how Joe was so willing to trust this man, and wondered again how the two could possibly know one another.

"Your brother-in-law will use Mud Rain as a hostage to control your husband's actions." Hawk's dark shadow wavered like a ghost against the surrounding blackness. I thought about my American Indian husband who attended tribal rituals, hunted alone in the back country each fall, listened more than he talked. My next words came out by themselves.

"Jeremiah will kill him, if he's hurt that boy."

Hawk lifted his hand from my shoulder and reached around me to open the door. "Jeremiah will have to be careful. Your brother-in-law has a lot at stake."

His words hung in the darkness, and whispers of violence and death filled the night air around me.

Chapter Eleven

Joe Healing Water lived in a square mud-brick adobe hut next to the station. An old wood stove in the middle of the room provided heat and a cooking surface. When I crossed the room to peek through the back screen door, I saw an orange-handled water spigot near the outside wall. About ten yards down a dirt path stood a small wooden outhouse that no doubt provided shelter for an impressive collection of spiders and other creepy-crawlies.

I looked around the impeccably kept room. Small windows in each wall offered enough cross-ventilation to keep the inside cool during the summer. A single bed and small nightstand stood in one corner. A military locker rested at the foot of the bed. Other furniture consisted of a lighted hurricane lantern set on a heavy log picnic table near the wood stove, an old wardrobe closet, and a large cupboard against the opposite wall.

Succulent odors of food filled the little room. My stomach felt like a lead pit, but I tried to ignore the feeling and appreciate Joe's effort. Hawk took a seat on one of the heavy log benches and motioned for me to sit beside him. I sat down on the edge of the bench and did my best to drum up an appetite. Steaks, canned corn and boiled potatoes filled three tin camping plates. Joe disappeared into the darkness between the two buildings and returned carrying three beers. I took a sip, hoping the familiar taste would unlock the increasingly uncomfortable digestive knots. Joe sat down opposite us and picked up his fork.

"Dig in," he grinned. "Don't wait for me."

"Thank-you," Hawk said around a bite.

I took up knife and fork and spent a good amount of time cutting everything up, but just the thought of sticking something in my mouth increased the discomfort in my gut. I set the utensils down and shivered. The cold feeling was getting worse. I could feel it clear through to the marrow of my bones.

I stood. "I'll be back." I didn't catch the look Joe shot my way as I headed for the back door. I hoped the two men would think I needed a bathroom break.

The faint clinking of stainless steel dinnerware followed me through the screened door. I leaned against the rough adobe wall and tried to stop shivering. My brain felt heavy and dark, as though someone had switched off the electrical circuits. Sliding down the cool mud wall until I was sitting on the rough wood planks, I closed my eyes and tried to tune in the night sounds but couldn't concentrate because of my course shivering. I hugged my arms around my chest and longed for Jeremiah to come walking out of the darkness.

Instead, Joe Healing Water walked out the back door. I heard the faint creak of aging joints when he stooped down and took a seat beside me.

"How are you holding up?" Joe's voice blended with the surrounding quiet, rather than disrupting it.

I shrugged and looked away.

He lifted his face skyward and closed his eyes for several minutes. Gentle insect sounds surrounded us. "How did shooting lesson go?"

"I didn't shoot myself in the foot." I rubbed my face with my hands and wished Jeremiah, Mud Rain, Angela, and I all were in Shawnee, at Mom and Dad's house, listening to them work on a recital program.

Reality created a choke hold on my throat. I dropped my hands and turned to Joe, and tried to make him see reason.

"I need to notify the police. He kidnapped me for no reason. I don't care what you might think or how in the hell the two of you know each other. He's a violent psychopath and a trained killer. The police need to lock him up and throw away the key. I need to tell them about what's going on with Jeremiah and Mud Rain. And I need to get back to the hospital."

The utter darkness around us made his already black eyes almost invisible. I felt like I was looking at a ghost.

"Did that clown come on to you?" His blatant lack of reaction over what I'd just told him made me mad.

Really mad.

"Of course he did," I snapped, turning my face away. "He's a Brit, an operative, and male. He's delusional and probably thought I'd swoon like those double-oh-seven Bond chicks." I hugged my arms around my chest again. I took a deep breath, trying to break through the numbness that gripped me. I wondered what Hawk was doing inside. I didn't want him joining us. I didn't want to be within a mile of the man.

I felt Joe's black eyes on me. "His manners could use some polishing." His words floated on the night air.

I blew out a breath. "No shit." I started to rise, but Joe laid a surprisingly strong hand on my arm. The full moon threw spectral paleness around the man, creating stark shadows and crevices, and not a hint of a smile. He turned his face towards the vast darkness beyond the porch. "There are *nï-mï-tï-kï-ddï-ï* about. Most of us soldier types aren't real civilized, but that differs from harboring evil."

I couldn't believe what I was hearing. "*Civilized?!* Haven't you heard a word I've been saying? The man *kidnapped* me, threatened …"

Joe cut in. "You have no wheels, no help, no weapons. By the time law enforcement hashes out who should start looking into all of this, Jeremiah and Mud Rain will be dead."

Feeling alone and betrayed, I stared at Joe's hand on my arm. I needed to get back to the hospital to my sister, and Joe was creating as big an obstacle as Hawk.

I'd known Joe Healing Water almost as long as Jeremiah, but that amounted to less than a decade. I frowned at him. "Why are you insisting that I stay with him? Why in the world would he help me find Jeremiah?"

Joe Healing Water's black eyes looked through my own. "Whatever you may be feeling at the moment, you need to trust me. And that Brit clown. He may have gotten off to a bad start, but he is your best hope of reaching Jeremiah and Mud Rain before Gary kills both of them." He dropped his aged hand from my arm, grunted as he got slowly to his feet, and opened the screen door. "C'mon. Your food is cold."

Getting to my feet, I reluctantly followed him back into the adobe, acutely aware that he had not answered my questions.

Hawk still sat at the table, his elbows on the surface, his spotless plate in front of him. I hesitated, then sat down beside him. The food on my plate was not completely cold, and I tried to eat the bites I had cut up earlier. I only managed a few before I gave up and pushed my plate away.

"Excellent meal." Hawk stood and picked up all three plates, then disappeared through the screened back door. I heard water from the spigot and rolled my eyes at his impeccable manners. I wondered whether he had heard our conversation. I had forgotten about keeping my voice down.

Joe waited until Hawk resumed his seat, then turned his black eyes my way. "Are you a crack shot now?"

I winced in the soft light. "Of course not." I wondered why he was even bringing the subject up. "You were there when Jeremiah tried showing me how to use his handgun, remember? It was shortly after I met him."

Hawk glanced my way and leaned his elbows on the rough tabletop. "And what, exactly, happened?"

I grimaced at the memory. "I sort of...well, I fainted."

"Really." Hawk's British accent gave the word unique inflection; his eyebrows disappeared into his hairline.

I glowered at Joe for embarrassing me like this. "No, I faked it. I decided to drop straight down to the ground and bruise my shoulder just for the hell of it."

Hawk stared at me, then turned his attention to Joe. "In answer to your question, she's got the basics. In an emergency, if she keeps her cool, she shouldn't be hazardous."

Joe studied me for several very quiet moments, then returned his gaze to the man sitting beside me. "If you intend to follow Jeremiah, you'll need reliable backup."

"Joe, this isn't any of his business." I remembered what he said on the porch about involving law enforcement. "We need to call the police," I said anyway.

Joe watched Hawk. "What resources do you have available?"

I struggled to keep my mouth shut, lost the battle with better judgement, and jumped up from the bench. "Joe Healing Water, listen to me!"

"Sit down." Joe's voice cut over mine, his black eyes as hard and coldly unemotional as Hawk's.

I sat down.

"I'll never be able to live with the guilt if I let you go chasing after Jeremiah on your own. Now sit there and keep quiet." He turned his attention back to Hawk. "Resources?" he repeated.

Hawk studied the old man for several minutes, then shook his head. "None without risk. Right now, invisibility's my first priority. I can't take any chances until I've figured out whom to trust."

"How good is the Charlie Network?"

Nothing wrong with Joe's ears or his memory, I mused.

Hawk sat silent for so long, I didn't think he was going to answer. "They've an international reputation. To our knowledge, they've no failed missions," he admitted after a while. "Up until now, none of their targets have survived."

Joe grinned slyly. "Except you."

Hawk's gray eyes drilled into Joe's black ones. "Yes, and I hesitate to risk that advantage until absolutely necessary."

Joe shifted on the bench. "Their intel is sophisticated?"

Hawk nodded. "Absolutely. Their intel and arms support rival any of our agencies." He paused.

"I'm listening," Joe prompted.

"I believe I've the reason why Lee went after her. And who torched her car," Hawk said, his voice neutral. "It is possible that her brother-in-law contracted someone else in the Charlie Network to insure the success of taking out her and her husband. That would explain why Lee was in Denver, why he tailed her, and who was responsible for the car bomb. His twin may likewise be involved." Hawk turned to me. "Hence the communication silence. We've had luck so far. However, one mistake will put Lee and the network onto our trail. They are patient, and they are no doubt listening to air waves, land lines, and cyberspace, just waiting for a key word to pin down our location."

I wasn't ready to believe him. "How do you know Lee and his twin are even still around?"

"Because not only did you snap their picture, you are an eye witness."

I swallowed.

"You don't have access to a coded line?" asked Joe.

Hawk sent the old man an appraising look. "You've a history." His voice was so low it took a moment before I understood his words. I had no clue what he meant. I looked at Joe, who seemed amused, but he did not offer an explanation.

Hawk continued. "Under normal circumstances, yes. But at this point, I can't risk compromising my position."

Joe winked at me and his white teeth gleamed as his sly grin returned. I swore I thought I caught a twinkle in his eye. "I have something that might interest you," he said to Hawk.

Joe stood and ambled over to the footlocker. He undid the clasps and lifted the lid, then laid aside several stacks of clothes. His hands dipped into the contents, pulled out a small object that I couldn't see from where I sat. He walked back to the table and laid the object in front of Hawk.

It was a satellite phone. He opened his other hand to show a second one.

"I use these when I go hunting. My grandson insists on checking up on me when I'm in the middle of nowhere. Damned thing chases off the wildlife because I forget to turn it off." He paused and gave Hawk a keen look. "Any trace will pull up my grandson's name. I'll keep this one open, in case you need help close by."

Hawk picked up the phone as though it was something fragile, then looked up at Joe. "This would be rather helpful." His reaction was as close to speechless as I reckoned I'd ever see from him.

Joe turned around and ambled back to the footlocker. "I've got something else you might be interested in." He retrieved a long, slender object wrapped in an old oilcloth. Hawk's attention sharpened and he stood when Joe unwrapped what turned out to be an odd-looking gun.

"Is that what I think it is?" He slipped the phone into his jeans pocket, then walked over to where Joe stood. Gently, almost reverently, he reached out and grasped the weapon.

"Depends on what you think it is." Joe was enjoying himself. I noticed the heightened look of respect Hawk sent towards the old man and stood up, then took a couple of steps towards the two men so that I could see better what Hawk was holding.

The weapon resembled a semi-automatic pistol that had been adapted to mate with a disproportionately long clip attached to a thick, bulky barrel. The whole thing ended with a stainless steel cylinder that had been screwed on. A loop of thick metal wire, looking more like a giant unbent paperclip than a gun part, jutted from the butt.

"What is that?" I asked as Hawk turned the weapon over.

"An M-three grease gun, complete with a Sionics suppressor." He studied the old Ute. "You saw action in Korea. Or Indochina."

Joe's face broke into a sly smile. "I'm old but not that old. No one knew where I was."

"No one on the receiving end of this knew where you were, either." Hawk handed the weapon back. The black metal gleamed despite its age. Joe re-wrapped the weapon and tucked it back into the trunk. When he had replaced the neatly folded clothes, he shut the lid, then crossed to the corner between the bed and the wall and picked up a rifle resting in the corner. This one looked more like a typical hunting weapon, with the exception of the magazine that jutted from just forward of the trigger and the thick cylinder on the end of the barrel.

Joe handed Hawk the rifle. "Use this for hunting."

Hawk inspected it, then walked to the opened front door and held the rifle up to peer through the scope. A chuckle whispered through his lips. "A night scope with the silencer. You don't give the game a fair chance."

Joe shrugged. "They run faster than I do now. See better, too. And what the game warden doesn't hear, he doesn't miss." He gestured towards the rifle. "It's cleaned and zeroed."

Hawk cradled the rifle in the crook of his left elbow and studied Joe, an unspoken, telepathic communication clearly going on between them. "All I have is emergency gear. My regular equipment is out of reach," he murmured into the silence.

Joe nodded. "I guessed as much. I can also tell you that you're dealing with someone more dangerous than anyone you might suspect to be connected with this Charlie Network you've been going on about. Carrot Eater is your worst nightmare. You'll want to be careful."

I wondered whether I had nodded off and missed something, and raised a hand. "Wait a minute," I told Joe. "Who is Carrot Eater?"

Joe's black eyes cut to me. "Carrot Eater is the man you know as Gary Tacque."

I watched Joe amble over to a set of cupboards along one of the walls. Hawk strode to the table, propping the rifle beside him as he sat down, then watched the old man's movements with steady eyes.

Joe opened the cupboard and pulled out a dented camping coffeepot. "Want some coffee?"

I stood in the middle of the room, frustration engulfing my chest. "No, Joe. I want you to start explaining why you've waited so long to tell me all of this."

Instead of answering, he took the coffeepot and disappeared out the back door. I started to follow him but Hawk moved fast to his feet and gripped my shoulder, aborting my intent. I heard the sound of running water; then Joe returned and set the full pot on top of the wood stove. He went through the motions of getting the coffee started.

"Joe, I want some answers, damn it." I was almost sputtering.

Joe sighed and looked at Hawk. "You'll find this one's not very patient."

I wanted to throttle both of them. "You need to tell me what you know!"

"You need to keep quiet," Joe cut in. "I may not be able to stop you from chasing after Jeremiah, but I sure won't send you out there without briefing Bozo here first." He pulled out three white ceramic mugs from the cupboard and brought them over to the table. Then he ambled back and picked up a gray rag from the floor beside the stove. Using it as a potholder, he carried the steaming coffeepot over. Thick black liquid poured into the three cups. The stuff looked like it would stand alone. Joe sat down opposite Hawk and looked at me. "I'm not saying a word until you show some manners."

I resumed my seat beside Hawk, who rested both forearms on the table and wrapped the cup with his hands. I leaned forward.

"How do you know Gary? How do you know he's this Carrot Eater guy?"

Joe's black eyes regarded us in silence. I looked down at my cup sitting on the table, hooked two fingers through the handle, but my hand was shaking too hard to pick it up. I let it go and stuck both hands in my lap. I practically bit my tongue when Joe picked up the cup in front of him. His wrinkled fingers curled around the ceramic as he blew across the steaming surface. The silence around us was absolute.

Next to this guy, Jeremiah was a fountain of information. I was ready to scream at him when he looked up.

"Carrot Eater, aka Jay Wild Horse Houser, grew up on the far northeast corner of the Ute Mountain Ute Rez."

"The Ute Mountain Ute Reservation?" I interrupted. "That's different from the Southern Ute Reservation, right?"

Joe nodded. "Yes. They share a border, but the Southern Ute Rez is much more affluent." He turned back to Hawk and continued. "His mother left the Rez when she was seventeen and went to Albuquerque. Met some guy there and got pregnant. Stayed in Albuquerque a while after she had Jay. After a few years, she decided she wanted to come back to the Rez. Her clan took her in, but she felt there was resentment towards her son because of his father."

I wanted him to fast-forward his story. I didn't want to hear

Gary's life history. I wanted to know how Joe knew who he was. However, there was no menu button, no remote arrow to push.

"So, why did his mother give him a name like 'Carrot Eater'?" I asked instead.

"She didn't. The kids nicknamed him *Yampa*, because the clinic nurse told him to eat carrots to try to improve his eyesight. He was always eating carrots." Joe paused and sipped his coffee. I regretted the interruption, because he took forever before he decided to continue.

"You know how mean kids can be. Rumors started. He was too stupid to attend class, crap like that. He became a recluse, got into the habit of wandering between the two Reservations and in the mountains around Wolf Creek Pass. Sometimes he'd be gone for weeks at a time. He disappeared altogether when he was fifteen." Joe paused again. I took a sip of what tasted suspiciously like black petroleum and could not suppress a reactive scowl.

"So, how did you know about this guy if he lived on a different Reservation than you did?" I asked him, setting the cup down and hoping I wouldn't offend the man if I didn't drink any more of his undrinkable coffee.

"Because of the pranks he started pulling on the school children on both Reservations," he answered, looking at my cup then grinning at me. He understood my actions, and I felt my face turn red.

"And how did you ascertain that Gary and this Jay Wild Horse Houser were one in the same?" Hawk inserted.

Joe drank some more coffee, proving at least to me that he had no taste buds and a stomach with an iron lining. "The scars on his face. Jeremiah suspected they were one in the same when he met him at your folks' funeral."

I gaped at him. "What? Are you telling me Jeremiah knew Gary?" I broke off my next question when Hawk's fingers curled around the nape of my neck.

"Any more questions, and you will be gagged and trussed and left in a corner."

I clenched my teeth and swallowed hard, wished Hawk was on the other side of the globe, and leaned my elbows on the table. *Get on with your story*, I silently fumed. Hawk's fingers relaxed, but did not release me.

Joe continued. "Carrot Eater became quite a marksman by the

time he turned fourteen. He practiced on prairie dogs to begin with, then on children in the school playground."

I clamped a hand over my mouth. Joe shook his head.

"He used a twenty-two rifle with a silencer. He could shoot a hole in a winter hat without hitting the child's head. Created absolute chaos whenever he got it into his head to have some fun. No one knew where he was. Often his prank wasn't even noticed until he got someone's attention by shooting out a window or two."

"But you just said his eyes were bad," I blurted.

Hawk grunted. "A good scope would compensate."

"How did they know it was him? Didn't he get into trouble for doing that?" I asked, despite the squeeze of Hawk's fingers on my neck.

Joe's face remained sober. "He called the school afterwards. And yes, he would have ended up in jail, but they had to catch him first. There were similar incidents of children getting sniped at after he disappeared off the Rez. Walsenberg, the Southern Ute Rez, even Alamosa and Pagosa Springs. The sniper hid behind the dome of the courthouse in Walsenberg. Police found a few generic cartridges. No one could give a description."

"And no one saw him?" I asked, incredulous. Hawk's fingers tightened. I clenched my teeth again in an effort to control my mouth. I did not want to end up in a corner, and I wasn't sure Joe would stop Hawk if he decided to carry out his threat.

Joe shook his head. "Nope. I suspected Carrot Eater was responsible, but didn't have any proof."

"Does Jeremiah know Gary's background?" Hawk asked, while I sat there in sudden disbelief.

Jeremiah had known who Gary was at the funeral and had not told me.

"He vaguely remembered Gary. He called a while back and asked about him. When he described the man he met at the funeral, I told him I thought it was Carrot Eater." Joe sounded like he was hedging around the truth. "All the children were afraid of Jay Wild Horse. That's why the rumors ran rampant."

Hawk dropped his hand from my neck. I missed the next bit of conversation. I was too busy concentrating on unpleasant insight.

My brother-in-law was tied to both Ute Reservations and an international assassin network. My husband knew who he was from the Reservation stories, yet had chosen not to warn any of us.

Joe was answering Hawk's question. "...If you choose to

spring something in that area, you'll be on his turf. Jeremiah knows the area well, but not as well as Carrot Eater. I'd give Carrot Eater the upper hand at this point." Joe nodded towards the rifle leaning against the table. "You'll need every advantage you can get."

"Unless we can contact Jeremiah," I interrupted. "Let him know we know what's going on."

Hawk turned his head towards me. "Assuming Jeremiah is still capable of answering his mobile."

I stared at the man. He stared back. It was now Tuesday evening, over two days since Jeremiah had last been seen or heard from. Dread oozed through me, but before I had a chance to respond, Hawk turned back to Joe.

"How much ammo have you?"

"I have a stash in the barn." The two men rose and disappeared through the front door. I trailed behind, engrossed in rapidly forming thoughts.

Had Gary recognized Jeremiah at the funeral?

Mud Rain had been at the reception. Jeremiah had been at his side. It would have taken very little for Gary to put two and two together. Given Gary's behavior so far, the only reason I could think that he would have wanted to take the boy with him to Colorado would be to use him to bait my husband. Besides me, Mud Rain was the only person outside the reservation whom Jeremiah cared for. A call about Mud Rain would get him on the road without a second thought.

What if Angela had realized the same thing?

Her first thought would be to get to Mud Rain, then try to get the boy to Jeremiah.

Why not go to the authorities, or to friends?

Because they might not have believed her, and they might not have immediately put Mud Rain into some kind of protective custody. An investigation would have been started, sure, but as long as Mud Rain was in the vicinity, Gary would have had an opportunity to snatch him.

And Angela had not been willing to risk that chance. She had experienced first-hand Gary's ability to lie and manipulate.

I thought over what Jeremiah had told Joe. Angela, weakened by starvation and God knows what else, had realized Gary was planning on kidnapping Mud Rain. He may even have called the Parsons with some excuse about taking the boy to meet Jeremiah for a trip to the Reservation. She had managed to get away, had no doubt disguised her condition well enough not to arouse Becky's suspicions, and had gotten Mud Rain first. She had taken off with Jeremiah's little brother, hoping to reach Colorado before Gary intercepted her. Angela made it to Limon before her last bit of strength gave out.

I turned on my heel and headed over to the station. There was a phone in the front. I was alone for the first time since I had met Hawk. It was time to get the police involved with chasing down Gary, and to find out whether Mud Rain had been with Angela when they took her to Denver.

Chapter Twelve

Lingering clouds created floating black shadows across the sky lit with pale, luminescent moonlight. Distant, faint pink spidery threads flashed in the southwest. A slight breeze stirred, touching my face with high desert coolness. Wet grass and mud rendered my footsteps silent as I made my way toward the station.

When I reached the corner of the building I glanced over my shoulder, expecting to see a dark form coming after me.

If Hawk caught me making a phone call....

Thoughts slid to my husband. Jeremiah was somewhere in the middle of the mountains tracking down Gary and Mud Rain, and my sister lay critically ill in a Denver hospital. Here was a chance to get badly needed information without Hawk's interference. The opportunity might not present itself again.

I slipped over to the red phone booth. The interior remained dark after I stepped in and closed the door, so I squinted up at the light fixture. No light bulb. I thought about trying for the operator and making a collect call, then reconsidered. No one at the hospital would accept a collect call anyway.

I exited the booth and darted into the store, spotted an aisle with automotive gadgets, and found a small packaged penlight that came with a set of batteries. I tore open the hard plastic and took out the contents, discarded the refuse in a trashcan behind the counter, then loaded the batteries into the small cylinder. When I switched it on, a bright LCD beam lit up the room. Swearing to remember to pay for the thing, I darted back to the phone booth.

I stood in the dark interior, vacillating. A pesky inner voice was ranting, warning me strongly against breaking the silence Hawk had gone to such measures to establish. If this Charlie Network really had the kind of resources Hawk hinted about, then no doubt someone would be monitoring incoming calls to my office and home, as well as my cell phone. While Hawk had blocked the last source of a trace, calls to either of the other two risked setting up a connection to locate us.

But I needed information. Hawk had flatly refused to help me, so whatever damage I might incur was really his fault, I argued back at the voice in my ear.

Should I call the police? Would the county sheriff listen to a phone call from a pay phone way out in the boonies?

Probably not. Or at least not until an officer met me out here, or I came in for an interview. The only numbers I had memorized were ones that were totally useless at the moment. Well, except for one, and the person behind that number would blow Hawk's covert efforts clear to Montana.

I stood there and wasted several precious minutes racking my brain, but I could not think of a safer, less conspicuous person to call. I picked up the receiver and dialed zero, then waited for an operator. Using the brilliant glow of the penlight, I peered at the number of the payphone. The operator came on line, and I told her the number I wanted. I flashed the light on my watch dial. Eight-thirty. *Please still be there*, I prayed.

"Colorado Springs *Daily News*, Jason Matthews."

"Collect call from Mattie Taylor. Will you accept the charges?" the nasal voice of the operator asked.

There was a beat of dead silence, then Jason's voice replied, "Yes. Yes, of course I will."

The operator connected us. Jason's voice jumped through the landline. "Mattie!! Where in the hell are you? Are you all right?"

The intensity of his reaction startled me. Before I could reply, he went into a tirade.

"Your car got blown to hell and back Sunday evening! The cops just released information today saying no one was in the car. Where in the hell are you, and why was your car parked in that empty lot? I've been trying your cell phone ever since we got word it was your car. The Denver dicks have been down here trying to locate you. What in the hell is going on?" When he paused to catch a breath, I jumped in.

"It's a long story. I'm…I'm sorry, but I don't have time to explain right now." I hesitated a fraction over whether to report Hawk to him, then decided to leave that until last. "Look, I need a favor."

I explained the situation surrounding my sister's condition, the reasons I suspected her husband, and the fact he might also have been connected with the car bomb.

"That's a lot of coincidence," Jason observed. I heard the rustle of paper in the background and figured he was jotting notes like mad.

"Not when you consider the amount of inheritance involved. And I need the cops to start looking for Jeremiah. He's in the southwestern side of the state, around the Wolf Creek area. He's tracking Gary. Gary may be using Mud Rain as a hostage to corner Jeremiah."

More rustling in the background. "They're not going to do much until you come in and talk to them. Have you filed a Missing Persons report?" he asked.

"No, and I'm sort of…restricted at the moment. I'll get into that in a minute. Right now I need you to contact the county sheriff and the State Police. Say you got an anonymous tip that Angela's condition isn't accidental. Tell them to do a background check on her husband, and while they're at it, tell them to contact Becky Parsons down in Norman, Oklahoma."

"Slow down," Jason complained. "I'm writing as fast as I can. Who was the last person?"

I repeated the information, adding, "Becky is taking care of Mud Rain, Jeremiah's younger brother. I'm guessing that Angela somehow managed to pick him up from Becky's house and had him with her when the ambulance came and got her in Limon. Gary must've found him at the hospital, probably in the ER waiting room. I'm hoping someone in the department will remember Gary, or maybe surveillance tape picked him up. Tell them there's a connection between Angela and my car getting blown up, and give them this number." I read the numbers off the pay phone.

"Lord, Mattie. According to the area code, you're in the middle of nowhere. Do you have a contact number for this Becky?"

"I don't have my cell with me, so the only number I have off the top of my head is the one for the Prediction Center." I gave him the number.

"Why the hell don't you have your cell? Wait. Did you leave it in your car again?"

I ignored his question. "If the police miss me, tell them to talk to Joe."

Jason sounded more than a little confused. "Joe? Joe who?"

"Joe Healing Water," I explained.

"Hang on a sec. I need another note pad." More paper rustling.

"Hurry up. I don't know how much time I've got left to talk."

I needed to get back to Joe's adobe before either he or Hawk realized I was missing.

Jason started to say something else when a movement caught my eye. An arm snaked in from behind me and disconnected the call.

"Just what the bloody hell do you think you're doing?" Hawk's voice raised the hairs on the back of my neck. He caught my arm and pulled me out of the booth, then spun me around. "Answer me, damn you!"

I tried to think of an explanation that he would accept, but all I could think about was the fact I was alone, and that he had blocked my every effort to get back to my sister and to get help to my husband. Six months ago I lost my parents. For all I knew, Jeremiah was lying dead somewhere in the mountains around Wolf Creek.

Hawk shook me. "What calls have you made?"

To my dismay, the pay phone started clanging. Must be Jason calling back to see why I had cut the call. I waited for Hawk to release me and answer the phone. When he didn't, I grappled with how much to admit.

Hawk shook me again. "Damn it all, Mattie, whom did you call?"

Recklessness replaced caution. "I called the hospital!" I lied. "I found out what's going on with my sister. She's still alive, but not for much longer. I need to get back to Denver."

Hawk's fingers tightened so fast, tears sprang to my eyes. The phone continued to jangle away.

"You're lying, Mattie. Whom did you call?" He sounded desperate. I had been a fool to make the call. When investigators finally made it out here, I was suddenly sure they would find my mangled body in one of the dark corners of the barn.

Too late now to wish I had listened to the inner voice of wisdom.

"J-just the hospital." My voice shook despite my efforts to stay strong. "They need me back there to talk to the police." Surely, I could fake it enough to convince him without admitting the truth.

Abruptly, Hawk released me. "You're a bloody fucking bad liar, Mattie." He spun on his heel and strode towards the barn.

Stunned with his sudden change in behavior, I hesitated, then followed. The phone continued to ring behind us. I wished Jason would give up and cut the connection. "Since you're not helping me get back to Angela, I'm doing it myself!" I shouted at the retreating man ahead of me.

Hawk spun around. "Whom did you call? The police?"

The phone quit ringing. Anger, frustration, and grief jumbled into a reckless, and foolish, mix.

"My friend at the paper!" I yelled across the field at him. "And I told him where we are, and where Gary is! I gave him everything but the description of your car, damn it, and if I'd been thinking straight, I would have given him that, too! That was him trying to call back! He'll be on the phone right now to the state police and the county sheriff! With any luck, someone will be out here before morning, and I can get some help tracking down Jeremiah and get back to Denver where I should be, instead of clear out here in the middle of nowhere!"

Hawk's voice floated across the distance separating us. "Well, the best of British luck to you. And American luck. You'll bloody well need both."

I jogged over to stand in front of him. "Why?" I demanded. "We're out here in the middle of nowhere. No one has followed you, no one knows where you are. How could my phone call possibly put you or me in danger?"

Hawk ran a hand through his windblown hair. When he spoke, desperation laced his words. "Mattie, the Charlie Network will have tapped into every source connected with you, including that bloody daily. They will trace any calls you make to get a spot on where we are. And now, you have handed them our location on a bloody platter. At this very moment, they've notified one of their team. Your Yankee bobbies won't be able to stop a sniper bullet."

He turned and strode for the black outline of the barn. "All their snipers need is one clear shot, Mattie. *One chance.* Their shooters can hit a *tomato* dead center from a *thousand meters*," he threw over his shoulder.

I had to run to keep up with him. "It'll probably be morning before even the police show up! You've got time, it's dark, it's been raining ..."

Hawk shook his head. "They've got all the equipment they need to handle whatever conditions exist," he spat. "Once they have our location, they've got resources to chopper in one of their own."

"We can stay here with Joe until the cops show up," I pressed. "He's said that he's good with a rifle. If anyone shows up, we'll see them from miles away out here."

"You stay with Joe if you want," Hawk answered. "But Joe's going to be finding a place to hide, too." He broke into a trot. I followed as best I could, thinking that he was way over-reacting, but realizing that arguing the point further was not only useless but probably dangerous. Joe might not think I had anything to fear from this man, but his anger scared me.

Weak yellow light shone through cracks and holes in the barn. Joe stood beside the Mercedes and looked up when we entered.

"We've a change in plans. Mattie has blown our cover," Hawk strode over to the Indian. "You'd better go underground for a few days. Charlie will want things tidy. They won't risk leaving behind anyone who could be a witness." He spun to face me. "Your choice. Go with me, or stay with Joe."

Joe shook his head. "No choice in that. She's going with you."

When I started to argue, Joe cut me off. "Hawk here has infinitely more resources at hand to protect you. Get in the Mercedes and don't argue."

I started to balk at being treated like a truant child, but considered the fact Hawk did at least have reason to be angry with me this time. I nodded and moved towards the front passenger door. I unclipped my belt pack and tossed it into the back, then pulled off the hoody and climbed into the car. From the corner of my eye I watched Hawk stride to the makeshift target and haul bales of hay back into the corners of the barn. Joe ambled over to the open passenger door, his eyes drifting to the dirt floor. I watched him lean over and pick up an empty cartridge, then straighten and lean against the car.

"I'm late this year making a trip to the Rez. Guess now's as good a time as any to go." he murmured, rolling the cartridge between his fingers. I stared at the object in his hand. When I looked up, his black eyes were on me.

"Joe, why didn't you pack up and follow Jeremiah after he told you what was going on? Why didn't you give him that phone?"

"Too old to be useful. I would have been a liability anyway. He knew that Gary would know my grandson's name and make the connection back to me."

"Why didn't you call the cops?" I pressed.

Joe snorted. "You know from Jeremiah's stories the problems with jurisdiction, especially on that part of the Rez. They would have come in and fouled up Jeremiah's chances of getting to Gary before he kills the boy." His last statement hung in the air like a terrifying, giant monster.

"It's been over two days since...since..." I couldn't finish.

Joe's gnarled hand reached in and gripped mine. "Your advantage is that Gary loves games. He likes to drag things out, show how smart he is. He likes to torture and maim before he kills."

I didn't think that gave us much advantage, and Joe's description gave my imagination ample fodder concerning what Gary might be doing to Mud Rain and to my husband.

But Jeremiah was good. Really, really good. He was a crack shot, his hunting kills were always clean. And in the seven years we'd been married, he had never come home from a hunting expedition empty-handed.

"Joe, I'm...I'm sorry about breaking the silence, but I had to contact someone to get some help with all of this, and for Angela." As trite as my words sounded, it was the truth. I started to say more, but he released my hand and waved me quiet.

"Danger is relative. So is family."

He was being as obtuse as Jeremiah. I opened my mouth to ask him what he meant, but he continued before I could get any words out.

"That minivan family will find themselves facing a lot bigger problem than hail damage, if they get towed back here." His eyes drilled through mine. "They know the make and model of your car."

I slumped against the seat and stared at him. "Is that why you don't want me with you?"

Hawk reached the driver's side and slid behind the wheel. The powerful engine purred to life, and I swung my car door closed as we rolled into the middle of the barn. Without a word, he cut the engine and got out. I twisted in my seat and watched him stride to the back and open the rear hatch. Heavy clunking told me he had removed the flooring to access the compartment underneath. Moments later he reappeared holding a wad of clothing, which he deposited on the driver's seat. I averted my eyes when he began stripping off clothes. Cloth rustled, zippers zipped. When I looked around again, he was dressed in full camouflage, complete with a vest full of pockets and compartments. He went back to the rear of the car and pulled out another vest.

"Here, put this on." He tossed the vest through the open driver's door. Probably twenty pounds of heavy cloth and full pockets dropped into my lap. I slipped my arms though the oversized vest and looked for ways to help it fit better. The heavy thing dragged on my shoulders. I wouldn't be able to run very well with it on. Carrying the rifle I had seen in the trunk earlier, Hawk walked over to where Joe stood. He nodded towards the rifle Joe held.

"You'd best keep that. I appreciate your offer, but I don't want to leave you without a means of defense."

Joe shook his head and held the weapon towards Hawk. "For Jeremiah. I have other resources." After a moment's hesitation, Hawk took both weapons and strode over to the car, carefully laying the rifles down on the floor behind the front seats. Joe followed.

"You'll want to follow one-sixty west," Joe advised. "That's the straightest route from here over to Walsenberg and the Pass. Gary knows Wolf Creek Pass well. It was his favorite retreat. I'll scout around on my way to the Rez. I'm friends with some of the rangers. They might have seen something."

I held my breath, realizing Hawk represented my only option for going after Jeremiah. As mad as he was, he might nix following my husband and look for a way to get rid of me instead.

Hawk nodded. "I'll leave the mobile on. If you come upon any leads, contact me."

I watched Joe give Hawk another of his white-toothed grins and thought about his earlier words. Joe Healing Water had to be pushing seventy or more. He'd already said he wasn't up to tramping around the mountains, that he'd be a danger rather than a help, if he went looking for my husband and a psycho.

Joe disappeared into the darkness. Hawk returned to the Mercedes, climbed in, started the engine, and rolled out of the barn.

"I've blown your cover." As bad as things were, I did not regret calling Jason. Knowing that someone now knew my predicament was minutely consoling.

"Too right you have." Yeah, Hawk was pissed. We bumped roughly over the damp field behind the gas station.

"So we're going after Jeremiah?" I crossed mental and physical fingers. He threw me a cold look as we bumped onto county pavement.

"Might as bloody well," he muttered.

Anxiety spurred me to ask another question despite the look on his face. "Will Joe be okay?" I thought about the family in the minivan. What if they ended up back at the station because of damage from the storms that passed through earlier?

They would at the least find themselves stranded before a locked up building. They might also find themselves facing a killer, if Hawk's suspicions were accurate. I muttered prayers that if Lee or someone else from the Charlie Network showed up at Joe's place, the police would already be there.

Hawk's head turned briefly in my direction, then back to the windshield as we gained speed along the thin ribbon of roadway. "He knows how to hide. Probably better at it than I am."

Jolted out of my thoughts, I couldn't remember what I had asked, but decided not to request clarification. I searched for something to defuse the tension.

"I think when Gary showed up at our apartment on Saturday, he thought Angela and Mud Rain were with Jeremiah and me."

Hawk was silent for so long that I decided not to attempt any more conversation. "Go on."

"Mud Rain wouldn't have enough knowledge not to go with Gary. He doesn't know him well, but he knows Angela ..."

Hawk finished my thought. "... and when Gary found him in the Emergency department waiting area, he no doubt told him that Angela sent him to pick him up."

"Yes." If only I had known then what I knew now, I thought bitterly. I would have checked the emergency department before going to Angela's room.

Hawk continued. "Angela was trying to protect Mud Rain from Gary."

I nodded, remembering Joe's conversation. "That's why she was driving out to Colorado. I wish she had called me, told me what was going on."

"Would you have believed her?"

"Of course I would have!" I snapped. "Why would you ask me something like that?"

Hawk flicked his eyes in my direction. "I find it intriguing Angela called your husband. Your husband, rather than passing on the information, chose instead to pass along a red herring."

I looked out the passenger window at the darkness. "He hesitated before he told me that Becky called him. He's not a natural liar, like some people." I shot a look across at Hawk.

He must've seen my expression despite of the darkness. "I have not lied to you. I have, admittedly, withheld information."

I looked out the window again. "Angela called Jeremiah, and Jeremiah must have called an ambulance, but didn't make it to the hospital before Gary. And Gary would have known immediately where Angela and Mud Rain both were, when the ER tried to contact him."

"And after Gary picked up Mud Rain at the hospital, he realized how he could control Jeremiah's movements." Hawk's eyes constantly checked the rearview mirror.

I stared through the windshield at the surrounding darkness. Surely being out here in the middle of the Comanche National Grasslands would make it harder to track us down. "And when Gary called Jeremiah and told him he had Mud Rain, Jeremiah took off after Gary."

"Yes." Hawk's voice lowered, and I got the strong impression he was thinking along lines I didn't want to consider. "Heading toward the Reservation puts Gary in familiar territory."

In familiar territory, Gary could easily ambush Jeremiah.

Fear gripped me. Had Gary planned to go after my husband all along, and had hired someone through the Charlie Network to get rid of me? Was he not only after both Angela's and my trust funds, but also bent on some personal revenge against Jeremiah? His aptitude for violence frightened me beyond thinking.

Angela tried to get Mud Rain away from Gary, and Jeremiah was trying to protect me by keeping me in the dark. But Gary so far had out-flanked all of us. And now he was in territory familiar from his days on the Reservation.

And Gary would be counting on the jurisdictional problems that plagued the area, knowing if Jeremiah tried contacting authorities, both sides of the border would be slow to get involved.

Chapter Thirteen

I tried not to stare at the vast empty darkness as we drove along the narrow two-lane highway. We were the only vehicle in sight, our headlights the only illumination for as far as the eye could see. Low clouds had rolled in and now hid the moon, the stars, leaving the night blacker than black. It would be all too easy for Hawk to pull over, put a bullet through my brain, and leave me for the buzzards and coyotes to chew on.

Yet, Joe had said to trust this man.

"Were there any unusual circumstances surrounding the death of your parents?" Hawk's question startled me, and I turned to face him. He sat behind the wheel, shadowed and indistinct. Power hummed under the hood as the car sped along one-sixty across the empty Comanche National Grasslands.

I swallowed. "No. According to the truck driver, Dad swerved into his lane and the guy didn't have time to react."

"Where did the accident occur?" He asked.

"Along US fifty, close to Dodge City, Kansas. They were on their way up to Colorado to visit Jeremiah and me."

"And Gary had been dating your sister for how long before the accident?" His question pricked a nagging suspicion I'd been trying to deny.

"What are you getting at?" I stalled.

"I don't believe in coincidences," he muttered.

"Yeah, so you've told me now a million times." Okay, I believe in coincidence, but not when they begin stacking up one on top of another. Uncle Bernard's death, Mom and Dad's death, then Gary elopes with my sister two weeks later, and within six months my sister ends up in ICU?

Uh-uh. Not that many coincidences, which begged the next question. Had Gary been involved with my parents' death? Would it be too late to find out? What could he have possibly done that would have caused a fatal collision?

As if reading my thoughts, Hawk answered several of my questions. "Gary may have been planning on an inheritance for a while.

You mentioned he's a representative for a drug company. He would have innumerable options at hand, most of which would be difficult to trace unless a coroner knew what to look for. That they were both killed in an accident was a stroke of luck. As long as the bodies were not cremated, reviewing their autopsies might be informative."

I thought back to the police report. The trucker had sworn that my father had swerved into the oncoming traffic too late to avoid a head-on. He had also seen a glimpse of my father through the windshield just before the impact. According to the trucker, my father's head had been slumped forward. The state patrol assumed he had fallen asleep at the wheel.

What if he had suddenly lost consciousness instead?

Doubt crowded in. "Angela told me that Gary hadn't met our parents. How would he manage to slip them something?"

"Through Angela, no doubt. Not having met them would hide his involvement." Hawk made the whole idea sound academic.

I balked. "He would have to assume an awful lot. Like the fact Mom and Dad would accept something from him without ever having met the guy. And it would have to be something they would eat or drink. He would have to know they were going on a trip. And that Angela would give them whatever he gave her, and that they would eat it, that Angela wouldn't eat or drink some of it herself. That's a lot of things that could go wrong."

Hawk tapped a finger on the steering wheel. "Does your sister like everything your parents do?"

I scowled at him. "Well, of course not. But Gary hadn't met Mom or Dad. He wouldn't know what their likes and dislikes were."

He glanced in my direction. "He would if he asked the right questions of your sister."

The silence that followed seemed awfully loud.

"You really think it's possible Gary was responsible for Mom and Dad's death," I muttered, mostly to myself because I didn't want to hear his answer.

The dash lights emphasized the grim lines around Hawk's mouth. "More than probable, given Gary's history."

I didn't want to believe all of this was about money. "How would he know about our family? About our money?"

Hawk turned his head in my direction for so long that the car drifted off the pavement and he had to whip his head to get us back on the road before we ended up in a cow field. "Are you being quite serious?" He sounded incredulous.

"Internet, I suppose," I grumbled, feeling my face heat. Thank God it was too dark for him to see my embarrassment.

He wasn't ready to drop the subject. "You've not researched your family name?"

I shook my head. "I suppose you have?"

Hawk filled me in. "Your family has quite a background, all nicely presented under your father's surname. Your family's history, worth, the Alabama plantation, the properties, including the current one in Shawnee, the structures your parents have listed on the National Historical Building registry. Anything you would like to know about the Lamonts. Even your full name."

I winced at the thought. To my dismay, Hawk was not about to pass up the opportunity.

"So, you didn't want to answer to 'Marigold', 'Annabelle', or 'Tessence'?"

"Oh, shut-up." No, I had not wanted to go by any of the names given me at birth. For all of my parents' wonderful traits, picking names had not been among them. Being the first-born, I had been saddled with maternal family names passed down through four generations. The names had not improved with age. By the time I was six I refused to answer to anything except the name my initials spelled. Thus, M.A.T. became "Mattie."

I scowled at him again. "When and where did you have access to a computer?"

"Who in bloody hell designed this nonsense?" Hawk complained, abruptly slowing to negotiate a (literal) ninety-degree bend, one of several that one-sixty makes on its way across the empty national park. He managed to keep us on the road. "While you were asleep in the motel. A bit of cash and a smile worked wonders with the receptionist."

I rolled my eyes and wondered how men like Hawk could stand to be around themselves.

It was closing in on the early hours before sunrise when Hawk pulled over east of Trinidad. "Bathroom break and nap time." He opened the driver's door and got out, then poked his head through the opening when I didn't move. "We'll be no use to Jeremiah if we're physically and mentally exhausted."

With reluctance, I exited the passenger's side and stretched. I squinted in the darkness for a clump of bushes. Clouds had cleared and billions of stars twinkled, but didn't do a thing to lighten the pitch darkness that engulfed me. I spotted some dark shadows about twenty yards to my right off the road and made my way towards the clump.

The shadows rose and ambled off. They were cows, not bushes. I muttered an oath and stumbled along until I found a rocky outcropping. I remembered the penlight I had taken from the station. With that thought came the realization I had not paid Joe for the thing. Great. I could now add shoplifting to my list of less-than-pleasurable experiences. Reaching under the vest, I felt for the light in the hand-warmer.

Nothing.

I searched my jeans pockets, but it wasn't there, either. Maybe it had fallen on the floorboard. I made a mental note to look for it when I got back to the car.

After I made my way to the side of the road, Hawk waved me into the back of the car. My muscles quivered with fatigue, and my head throbbed. Memory of the barn incident slid through my thoughts when he slipped in beside me.

I needn't have worried. Gun in hand, he closed his eyes. Within thirty seconds, his breathing slowed and his muscles twitched.

The sky had lightened with the gray of pre-dawn when Hawk roused me from sleep. As I climbed out of the back of the Mercedes, Hawk's vest emitted a soft two-tone ring. He took out the satellite phone and turned away. I picked up muted words and faint squawking. He returned the phone to a vest pocket and turned to me, his expression covert.

"That was Joe, wasn't it?" We were standing at the back of the car. No traffic was visible in either direction.

Hawk's brows twitched, and he studied the surroundings. I took his non-answer as an affirmative. "Well? What did he say?"

His gray eyes met mine. "The police notified his grandson a while ago of an incident at the station. They asked whether he knew Joe's whereabouts."

Uh-oh.

"What…what sort of…incident?" And did I really want to know?

"A minivan crashed into the building and caught fire. Blew the petrol lines, too."

I turned away and covered my mouth with my hand. My eyes

closed against the scene my brain envisioned. "Were there...did they find...?" I trailed off, unable to finish the thought.

Hawk spoke from behind me. "Bodies were found in the remains of the van. Joe's grandson said they're suspecting arson over accident."

I turned towards him and felt my face go white. Hawk gripped my shoulders to steady me. My ears were working fine, but I couldn't seem to see anything.

"There's more."

I squeezed my eyes and rubbed my face with the sleeve of the hoody. I took a long, shaky breath, then opened them and studied a zipper on his vest. I couldn't bring myself to make eye contact.

"Joe got information from a ranger friend who spotted Jeremiah's Jeep along a four-wheel track on the east side of Wolf Creek Pass."

I jerked my eyes to Hawk's. "He did? Did he give you directions?"

Hawk dropped his hands and turned towards the steadily brightening scene around us. "He gave landmarks just now to locate the access road." He slid his hands into his pants pockets, his eyes on the horizon.

I wasn't about to let him drop the subject. "Did he see Jeremiah? Does he know where he is?"

Hawk swiveled his head and met my eyes. He was withholding something, I could see it in his expression. Urgency swelled, threatened to choke off my ability to breathe. "Tell, me Hawk. What did he say?"

Hawk looked away.

In my agitation, I started jumping up and down. "Hawk! Tell me what he said, damn it!"

Instead of answering me, he turned on his heel and reached into the back pocket behind the driver's seat. When he pulled out the packet of pictures he had shown me the other morning, I almost lost it.

"Tell me what you're not telling me!" I yelled at him.

He shook his head. "We need to find a photo shop and get copies of Lee and his twin to some top brass." With utter calm, he began flipping through the pictures, handing the pictures to me as he went. If I hadn't been a professional photographer, I would have thrown the things on the ground and stomped on them.

"You're being obnoxious and stubborn, and you know it!" I seethed, trying to pull my voice back down from the upper stratosphere. "Tell me what Joe said! Did the ranger see Jeremiah? Was he with the Jeep?"

When Hawk's body tensed, I thought that maybe, finally, I had hit a nerve. He stood rigid, his eyes staring at the picture he held in his hand. A fine tremor shook his fingers.

"Bloody hell." Hawk's voice was hardly a whisper.

I went up on my tiptoes to get a look at the picture in his hands. "No, no. That's the wrong one." I shuffled through to find the correct one and held it out. "Here's the one of Lee and his twin."

Hawk stared at me, his face so white I couldn't see the outline of his lips. "Is this the same day? At the game?" He was holding the picture of the boy asleep on the man's chest.

Nonplussed, I looked at him. "Of course it was. You mean you didn't see it?" Memory slipped in. "Well, these two," I pointed to the two pictures he held, "they were stuck together behind another picture. That's why you must've missed them. I don't see what you're so worked up..." I trailed off as the pictures slipped through Hawk's fingers and fluttered to the ground. He looked like he might fall over.

"Hey, easy there." I grasped his arm to steady him. "What's the matter?"

Hawk bent and gathered the scattered pictures, slipped them and the negatives into the photo packet, then tucked the packet into an inside pocket of his vest. Without a word, he walked to the driver's side of the car. I ran around and climbed into the passenger's side. Hawk started the engine, then sat motionless. I watched him, not understanding what he could possibly have seen in the picture of the father and son.

"Talk to me, Hawk. What's wrong?"

His eyes flickered to me, then returned to stare out the windshield. Several minutes passed before he answered. "I've just realized that the man who saved my life is the mole."

"Well, yeah. I think we figured that one out back at Joe's station." I was having trouble keeping my voice calm.

"Not Lee." His gray eyes resembled chipped ice. "Max." Hawk reached into a vest pocket and retrieved the satellite phone. He punched in numbers, his fingers steady. He paused, watching the screen.

The phone squawked.

Hawk's voice was cold, authoritative. "Joe, get lost. Very, very lost. Not even your grandson should know where you are. There's a CIA mole behind all of this. He'll have access to any information the police pick up on our whereabouts."

The phone squawked back.

"And Max will have the information about the petrol station soon, if not already." Hawk ran a hand over the black stubble on his face.

Squawk, squawk.

"Bloody-fucking breadcrumb path." Hawk cut his eyes in my direction. "I'll send copies of Max and Lee and his twin to senior brass on both sides, but there's no guarantee the post won't be intercepted. Get rid of your mobile, Joe, and go deep." He punched the little phone, then tucked it into an inside pocket, shifted the car into drive and pulled onto the pavement.

In the meantime, I was totally lost. "Hawk, please tell me what's going on."

Hawk began to explain, but to my frustration, not about the picture he had been holding, or about what Joe had said concerning Jeremiah. "Lee was my senior intelligence officer when this whole Charlie Network started. We could not figure how their shooters were consistently getting past security detail, getting beads on targets. No matter what we tried, we could not break into their network. We could not protect whomever they targeted. It was bloody infuriating. Then Max came in. Told us we had a leak. I'd known Lee a long time, his background, his habits. He gave absolutely no indication that he was working both sides."

"Okay, what has that got to do with the picture of the father and the son?" I asked, confused. "It sounds like Lee is the mole, the guy with the twin no one knows about, not this Max guy."

Hawk nodded. "That's what I thought, when I saw the shot of him with his twin. I also assumed his twin was a trained killer. It makes sense. He could swap spots with Lee and get in close. Lee was lead in more than one security detail that failed to protect a figurehead the Charlie Network took out."

I could not understand why Hawk was reacting to the wrong picture. Maybe he was cracking under the strain. "So, Lee is connected to this Charlie Network."

Hawk shook his head. "Max used him as an informer. He

would have used the threat of exposing Lee's secret twin to keep Lee quiet and cooperative. Max set both of us up that day at the ballpark. Question is, *why?*"

I threw up my hands in frustration. "Who the hell is Max?"

Hawk answered, his voice dead calm. "The CIA chap who got me to Denver."

I narrowed my eyes at him. "Are you talking about the man with the little boy asleep on his chest?"

Hawk didn't answer. I didn't like the implication. The car hummed as we approached Trinidad.

"Please, Hawk, please tell me what Joe said about Jeremiah." I needed some modicum of reassurance in the middle of everything that seemed to be falling apart.

Hawk was following his own train of thought. He began muttering, talking to himself. "When Lee saw you taking a picture of him and his twin, he would have suspected Max set him up. He followed you to the hospital, no doubt saw where you left your car. He would not have had time to wire your car, but he could get rid of you, at least. I imagine he was too panicked to think things through."

Maybe all of this would lead back to information about Jeremiah, so I went along with the subject. "So, Lee's the one who blew up my car."

Hawk shook his head. Tension whitened the knuckles of his hands. "No. Max was behind that one. Just like he was behind the car bomb that almost killed me."

I released an exasperated sigh. "So does this mean this Max guy is after Jeremiah, too? Or is he after just us?"

Hawk's expression closed down. "We need to find a photo shop."

His abrupt change in subject threw me. "Why a photo shop?"

Hawk was sounding almost rattled. "I need to get copies of Lee and his twin, and Max, back across the waves to some top brass."

"Yeah, well you burned the negatives of Lee when you torched your pictures. You could have just sent them," I pointed out.

Hawk grunted. "I switched the strips."

I stared at him for several minutes. "Are there any other secrets you'd like to share?"

"There's water in the pockets behind the front seats, if you need a drink."

"You're not answering my question." I accused, frowning. "What about a bathroom break pretty soon?"

Hawk shook his head. "In the car and moving, we're relatively safe. This car is custom, and among other things, the glass is bullet-proof. If their snipers follow normal routine and use a bolt-action single shot, we stand a chance. If any one of them uses an automatic, we're history."

"Okay, okay." I tried again to understand why he'd reacted to the wrong pictures. "Do you think Lee and Gary are working together to get Jeremiah?"

"You mean Max. He's after you because of the pictures you took of the three of us."

That didn't clear up a thing. I threw him a puzzled frown. "Is *any* of this connected with Gary?"

"Based on the fact that all of the above persons are killers, I cannot rule out the possibility that all of them may be involved with the Charlie Network."

That made about as much sense to me as washing my car during a rain storm. Frustration started morphing into something more like horror. "I think it's past time we get help from the police."

Hawk grunted. "No bobbies. Particularly now that I know Max's involvement. My gut says follow Jeremiah's trail."

I rolled my eyes. "Your gut?"

His eyes flickered over and held mine for an instant before returning to the road. "It has kept me alive to date." The conviction in his voice was unmistakable.

Damn. I didn't want to head into the mountains without the help of some sort of law enforcement. The idea seemed suicidal at this point. I whipped my head around and stared out the window as desperation boiled around my insides.

We drove through Trinidad and picked up Interstate Twenty-five north. Traffic was minimal, and we exited at Walsenburg and headed west again.

Hawk looked worried.

"What?" I asked after a while.

"We're limited in our choice of routes. That'll narrow Max's search." He leaned forward to scan the sky around us.

The bright mid-day sun beat down when we located a photo stand outside of Walsenberg. Hawk pulled into the gravel lot that serviced a small gas station and grocery. A tourist shop sat nearby and displayed an indoor sign that read "Develop your film here. One hour service." Hawk pulled out the photo pack, and I followed him into the dimly lit store. A middle-aged, bald man sat behind the cash register. He peered at us through large square-framed spectacles perched on the end of his nose.

"Afternoon folks. What can I do for you?"

"How fast can you reprint some pictures for us?" Hawk asked before I could open my mouth. "We're in somewhat of a hurry."

"Well, my assistant has gone to lunch. If you want to leave it here, she'll be back after a bit. Say, two o'clock?"

Hawk shook his head. "No good. Thanks anyway." Taking me by the elbow, he steered me back outside.

"Bloody hell," Hawk muttered when we climbed into the Mercedes. He started the engine and guided the car back onto the highway, heading west.

"What?" I asked.

He nodded back towards the little shop. "Good spot, that."

I sighed. He'd reverted to Cryptic Brit again. "How so?"

"Excellent visibility in all directions," he muttered.

I waited for him to explain. Mused for a bit over how much easier things would be if he and my husband learned how to adequately express what they were thinking.

"And...?" I prompted after a long, irritatingly silent mile.

Hawk threw me a look, then acquiesced. "Nice flat, open terrain. No elevated building to climb and pick us off."

"We've been driving almost non-stop since last night. There's no way anyone could be after us," I argued.

Hawk said nothing and kept going.

"You know," I ventured after a while, "If we had a cell phone, we could take a picture of the pictures and text it or email it to whoever you want to show it to."

Hawk nodded. "And give Max and his jolly crew a pinpoint on our location."

The flat valley floor slipped by as we approached Alamosa. The inside of the vehicle chilled with the drop in temperature over La Veta Pass. Scattered patches of snow gradually converged into large white sheets. Since we didn't reach timberline, aspens and evergreens lined the slopes. The majestic Spanish Twin Peaks jutted to our left, while to our right Blanca Peak soared above fourteen thousand feet. Despite the fact it was the third week into June, snow squalls still presented a threat in this area, especially around the passes.

I rested my head against the back of the seat and tried to imagine what Jeremiah was doing. He always came to this area in the fall to hunt, had grown up on the Reservation located just south of Wolf Creek. Did my husband have as intimate knowledge of these mountains as Gary did?

I fervently hoped so.

I didn't realize I had drifted off until I felt the car slow. I opened my eyes and peered around. We were on the western edge of Alamosa.

"There's a Wal-Mart over there. Do you want to try their photo center?" I asked.

Hawk shook his head. "Closed-circuit cameras." We passed through Alamosa and headed for the pass.

As we neared the base of Wolf Creek Pass, I spotted a tourist photo-shack standing in the middle of a graveled parking area that hosted a gas station and a small grocery store.

"How about that one?" I pointed. Hawk pulled over and parked between the wooden building that was the store and the small cubicle that housed the photo stand. He cut the engine, then sat immobile for several minutes, his eyes scanning the slopes and houses that rose around us. The faint sound of a helicopter echoed through the small valley we were in.

"I've a bad feeling." He reached into his vest, brought out a slender monocular, and panned the area.

I watched him, trying to understand what he was thinking. "What are you looking for?"

"That chopper, among other things," he said, his voice curt.

I relaxed a bit. "I bet it's a search crew looking for lost hikers. That's pretty common this time of year."

Hawk continued to scour the area. "Impossible to pick him up, if he's holed away in those hills." He lowered the glass. "But sitting here gives him time to set up and pick us off. Let's go."

His uneasiness made me nervous. I exited the passenger's side, and he escorted me into the little store. The familiar odor of chemicals permeated the air. A young Hispanic woman smiled at us from behind the counter, her thick, jet-black plait trailing down to her waist.

"Good afternoon. How can I help you?"

This time I beat Hawk with the answer. "How fast can you scan and reprint two prints?"

She smiled at me, her wide black eyes friendly. "Probably about ten minutes."

Hawk removed the pictures and handed them to her. "We'll wait." He draped his arm around my shoulders and steered me away from the windows, towards the back next to a display case containing various sizes and makes of cheap one-touch digital and disposable cameras, shelves of frames, and photo albums.

Personally, I figured the grueling pace he had driven since last night gave us several hours lead-time. Lee and the Charlie network could not find us. How could they have followed us all the way over to the western corner of the state?

"We need to get over that pass," Hawk said after a bit. We were standing behind the last shelf at the very back of the little store.

I looked at him. "How in the world are we going to find Jeremiah?"

Hawk's eyes flickered from the scene beyond the windows to my face, then back again. "Joe briefed me on the area last night."

The girl reappeared behind the counter with the pictures. Hawk pulled out cash to pay her. "Have you a scanner and a Fax?"

The girl behind the counter shook her head. "You might try the Wal-Mart in Alamosa."

Hawk shook his head. "Then I'll need two photo flats, please."

The girl reached under the counter and produced two rigid photo envelopes. Hawk addressed both, then slipped in the prints and handed them to her.

"Post these ASAP," he instructed after he had settled the bill.

"I'm going to lunch soon. I can mail it then," the girl replied.

Hawk paused in the act of slipping his wallet into a back pocket. "Do it now." His tone and expression raised the hair on the back of my neck. "And close down for the rest of the day."

A worried frown creased the girl's forehead as she backed from the counter, and I sensed her alarm would lead her sooner to calling the police than mailing the envelopes. Personally, I wouldn't mind getting the police involved, but I also felt it important to get the packets in the mail.

"We don't have time to explain right now, but we wouldn't ask you to close down unless it was really important," I explained, trying to assuage her unease.

She glanced at me, then Hawk. "It's been really slow. I guess I could go home," she said but I sensed her uncertainty.

"Please. It really is important," I told her, trying to sound calm while still giving her the urgency of the situation.

When we exited the small store Hawk sprinted to the car. I ran to catch up as he unlocked the doors, and we slid onto the leather seats. I heard his audible sigh of relief as he swung the driver's door closed.

S-M-A-C-K.

"Bloody fucking *hell*," he swore, jamming the key into the ignition. The engine turned over. Tires spun on the loose gravel as the Mercedes tore a one-eighty in reverse, slinging me out of my seat and practically into his lap. He threw the car into drive, and we shot out of the small lot. I stared at the glass in the driver's side window.

A crater the size of a half-dollar marred the polymer surface, directly in line with Hawk's left temple.

Chapter Fourteen

I expected Hawk to make a beeline for the two-lane highway. Instead, he swung the Mercedes onto a steep, narrow town road. We wound around several large homes and through groves of pines and aspens until we topped out at a wooded ridge overlooking the tiny shopping area we had just left. He parked the car near the sheer drop-off, then reached into his vest and retrieved the monocular. Silence hung between us as he scanned the area below. Wind currents wafted through the hole in Hawk's window and I heard the soft whisper of surrounding trees.

"Where are you, you bastard," he breathed. I waited for him to spot the man and grab a rifle, but he remained motionless.

"Aren't you worried he'll try another shot at you? Surely, he sees us," I ventured after a moment.

Hawk grunted. "We're out of range."

"Then why are we sitting here?" Out of range or not, I still felt like a sitting duck.

"Knowing someone is watching lessens the chance that he'll take out the girl. Max won't risk witnesses." Hawk trained the monocular towards the small shopping center we had just left.

The coldness of his voice sent chills rippling through me. I leaned over his shoulder and peered through the window, wondering whether the girl in the photo shack was about to walk into a head shot.

Minutes crawled. Fear jolted through me when the ant-sized figure of the girl appeared and started walking to a dark blue SUV. Just as she opened the driver's side door, a black-and-white local police car pulled into the parking lot behind the photo shack. A cop unfolded from the driver's side, then disappeared into the grocery store.

Go find the cop.

Despite my frantic mental signals, the Hispanic girl ignored the cruiser and climbed into the SUV. The door shut and a few minutes later the vehicle drove off. A sudden bout of faintness hit me, and I realized as I released a lungful of air that I had been holding my breath.

"What about the cop down there?" I pointed towards the black-and-white cruiser still sitting in front of the grocery. "We can tell him what's going on. He'll get help, especially when he sees the window."

Hawk didn't answer. His attention remained on the view through the monocular.

I jabbed his shoulder with a finger. "Did you hear me? He needs to see that bullet hole. The local authorities need to know there's a sniper in the area!"

"No." Hawk slipped the monocular into his vest, then straightened and shifted the car into reverse. We backed onto the pavement, turned around, and started down the hill. The faint sound of a helicopter drifted from the far side of the opposite ridge.

Hawk threw me an I-told-you-so look. "It would appear as though your rescue crew hired out."

"Yeah, right. Lee would have to climb a tree for them to reach him." I didn't want to think the sniper guy had use of a helicopter. If he did, then that meant we were at a significant disadvantage.

"You mean Max." He swung onto the two-lane highway. "And it's picking him up. We need to make it over the summit before he gets it in his head to use the bloody chopper to come after us."

"I thought Lee was the one after us. The twin," I argued.

"Before I saw Max's picture, I thought the same," he muttered as he pushed the speedometer needle way beyond the local speed limit.

We shot past the grocery store and the police cruiser. I stared at the black-and-white, willing the cop to appear from the store, see the speeding Mercedes, and take off after us with lights flashing and siren screaming.

No cop. No lights. I grabbed for the overhead handle when he swung round the first bend. "Hey! Slow down!" I shouted as the tires took the first curve with a faint squeal.

Hawk ignored me. "Lee pushed you into the front of that lorry when he realized you snapped a picture of him with his twin. If Max had been claiming to be hiding his brother all this time for reasons unknown, at least to me, then Lee would assume you were working for Max."

The man was nuts. He had to be. Just to humor him, I asked, "So why were he and his twin at the game on Sunday? And Max?

And you?"

The next several twists forced Hawk to slow down, albeit not by much. He kept weaving between our lanes and oncoming traffic.

I gripped the overhead handle until the cut on my palm burned. "You know, we generally drive on the right side around here. We're going to end up plastered against an eighteen-wheeler if you keep this up." My fingers were cramping due to the death grip I had on the overhead handle. The healing cuts on my hands were going to re-open if I didn't let go of the damned thing.

Hawk leaned into another curve. "It's your own bloody damned fault for driving on the wrong side of the road."

"How are you coming up with Max being behind all of this?" There had to be a reason that would prove Max an innocent by-stander. Max had been spending the day with his son.

Hawk didn't answer because we nearly went flying off the edge of the road through the next set of switchbacks. "Because Max saved my life two years ago," he finally said.

I decided that somewhere between the photo shop and the sniper attempt Hawk had totally lost it, and his driving proved my point. We wheeled around the tight curves and passed slower cars as though we were the only ones on the road. I glanced down at the river that the pass followed and refused to make a bet with myself on how soon we would end up in it.

"Max must have done the same with Lee's twin brother several years ago," Hawk mused, breaking the silence. "That's how he was able to smokescreen Lee. I'll lay odds Lee's been under extortion. Max threatened to report his brother to authorities. What I still can't figure is why he arranged for us to be at the game. We were practi-cally in the same section."

I shook my head and tried to talk some sense into the man. "But Max has a son. He was there enjoying the game, having some father/son time together. He wasn't part of whatever you and Lee and his twin are involved in. He just can't be." The whole thing seemed ludicrous.

We passed through an avalanche shed, then a tunnel. When we came out on the other side, Hawk slowed and guided the car off the road onto a wide dirt parking area that stretched around the outer rim. As he circled around the outside of the tunnel, a narrow forest access road appeared to our left. The river rushed along in a deep arroyo on the same side. Hawk followed the thin strip of red dirt as it wandered along the side of the ravine, then disappeared around a blind corner. As we came around the bend a small one-lane bridge, built from whole tree trunks and spanning the chasm, came into view. Neither railings nor steel reinforcement protected us from the raging rapids far below.

There was no cover, either, to protect us from flying helicopters with snipers shooting at us from above.

It was a long way down to the roaring water. My imagination painted too clearly a picture of the Mercedes careening off the side to fall, fall, fall....

As the vehicle's tires bumped onto the wooden structure, I squeezed my eyes shut and held my breath. Suspended over a drop of several hundred feet in plain view with nothing but Colorado pine between us and raging Colorado rapids was *not* my idea of intelligence.

"We're in plain sight on this bridge," I complained, though Hawk probably couldn't hear me. The roar of the river drowned out all noise, especially approaching helicopters. I gave up any pretense of courage and bent double, cowering behind the dash as the car lurched and swayed across the uneven bridge.

"I'm counting on it."

I jerked my head up to gape at him. "But they'll see us. Which means they'll follow us."

Hawk nodded. "Precisely."

My heart did several double-flips. "You *want* him to follow us? Oh my God, Hawk, why?"

His eyes flickered to mine, then back to the bridge. We were almost across. "It's best to know where one's enemy is."

I scowled at him. "Yeah, well, this enemy took a shot at you. You'd be dead, if it wasn't for the bullet-proof glass."

Hawk shook his head. "He's re-conning to determine our direction. Now that he knows we're off the main road, he'll get ahead of us and look for another opportunity. He won't bother with a single shot next time."

My heart banged against my ribs with such force that my chest hurt. "And you want him to follow us?"

His cold gray eyes cut to me. "Two can play this game."

To say I wanted out of this mess was the understatement of the century. I'd rather be facing the lava flow of an erupting volcano. We were in way over our heads, yet Hawk actually sounded pleased with the situation.

The tires bumped onto the dirt on the other side, and I heaved a shaky sigh of relief. Hawk concentrated on the lane in front of us, his expression void of emotion.

The dirt road had been well maintained despite being deep within the pass. The reddish-brown ribbon hugged the side of the mountain, winding on a ledge that traversed deep chasms and impossibly steep slopes. Pines and aspens encroached, providing better coverage than the winding pavement of the pass we had just left. Maybe that was the reason Hawk had turned off the main road, I thought in retrospect. Maybe he knew what he was doing after all.

I watched the road disappear around another blind curve ahead of us and wondered whether the route had originally been a railroad bed. During the gold rush years, narrow gauge had been popular in these mountains because of the terrain. In confirmation, a short tunnel appeared around the next bend, a ten-yard hole that had been blasted through solid rock over one hundred years ago. As we crept through I saw the black soot that stained the ceiling, silent testimony of the thick smoke that had chugged from engine smokestacks.

About a mile beyond the tunnel, Hawk slowed and pulled over to the side of the road. We were at a bend hidden in both directions by aspens. A steep drop-off fell away on my side.

"Crawl over the back seat and get out on this side." Hawk indicated the door behind the driver's seat. Remembering my conversation with Jason about getting photographic evidence, I grabbed my digital camera and the belt pack.

Hawk shifted the car into park, retrieved the two rifles from behind the front seat, and exited the driver's side. I expected him to dig out equipment from the back of the car, but instead he stood beside me. The car idled on the narrow shoulder, the right side tires sitting at the edge of the steep drop-off.

"This way." He turned away from the vehicle and crossed the dirt road. I followed him, thankful to be away from the sheer slope and wondering what on earth he was up to. I opened my mouth to ask when he turned, pointed the key fob towards the vehicle, and pushed a button.

The car rolled forward. Before I could shout a warning, the front tires tipped over the steep embankment and the Mercedes slipped over the side. I ran to the edge of the road and watched in shock as the vehicle bumped and careened downwards, then tumbled into a roll. Sounds of snapping branches and screeching metal echoed against the mountainside. The gas tank blew with a dull *boom* that shook the ground beneath my feet. The car came to a stop on its crumpled hood, flames licking around the undercarriage. From where I stood I could see the passenger compartment, though damaged, remained intact. Airbags deflated like miniature balloons.

"What do you think you're doing?" I demanded, throwing the words over my shoulder because I refused to turn around. Instead, I stood there staring at the wrecked vehicle and the blatant truth that we were now reduced to hiking through these mountains. I spun around as implication hit. "You're setting us up! How do you expect us to get out?"

Without a word, Hawk turned and began climbing the steep slope. I stood at the side of the road and contemplated a long list of very uncomplimentary, colorful adjectives.

"Hawk, answer me!" I yelled after him. "We're in the middle of nowhere, there's a guy with a gun after us, and you just destroyed our only means of transportation!"

"Follow me and keep as quiet as possible," he called over his shoulder, his voice drifting down the steep distance between us. Anger pushed me into following, though I paused long enough to snap on my belt pack and sling the camera across my chest. The camera and belt pack added weight to the already heavy vest. I wondered how my muscles would hold up under the strain if he planned to hike out of here.

Cool mountain air hung beneath the evergreens and aspens while recently melted snow dampened the ground. My butt and calves tightened as I trekked up the impossibly steep terrain. Because of the incline I fell behind. By the time I reached the spot where he had paused to wait for me to catch up, my breath was coming in short, painful gasps. Ten thousand feet is hard on the lungs. I rested my dirty bandaged palms against my knees and turned to gaze down the mountainside we were on. From where we were I could see the ruined Mercedes, now just a smoking black speck, through a break in the trees. Smoke drifted upward in a thin, gray line. The fire didn't look like it was consuming the entire vehicle and I figured that it would smother itself out before long.

Hawk turned and began to climb again. I straggled behind, wishing he would at least give some clue to the reason why he had stranded us in the middle of these mountains.

I stopped again and gulped air that was way too thin for the amount of exertion. "Did you do that to attract someone's attention in the forest service? Are you signaling to bring in help for Jeremiah?" I asked between breaths.

He didn't answer. I wanted to think it was because he didn't have enough air to make conversation, except that he didn't seem to be winded and he had yet to break a sweat.

Damn the man.

We continued up, up, up, until we reached a ridge that perched about five hundred yards above the road. I sat down on the rocky outcropping and tried to get air to my screaming lungs. Hawk had finally started to pant.

"Jeremiah's Jeep should be on the other side of that mountain." He pointed north. I squinted against the afternoon glare and spotted a tiny red ribbon of roadway that disappeared around a bend.

Hawk removed his vest and set it on the ground. "That's our goal, after I've addressed a bit of unfinished business."

"What…what unfinished business?" I didn't like the implications.

Hawk surveyed a large boulder that formed part of the ledge I sat on, then disappeared around the underside. Curiosity won out over exhaustion, and I heaved myself onto my complaining legs and followed to see what he was up to.

Hawk was on his knees, bent over, using the butt of one of the rifles as a makeshift shovel to dig the loose, damp earth from beneath the large boulder. The other rifle, muzzle pointing skyward, rested against the rock.

"What are you trying to do?" I asked as I watched him. If the nut wanted to send the boulder down the mountain and onto the road, he would be digging for a couple of years.

"Making a place for you to hide." His voice sounded flat against the rocky surface.

He had to be kidding. "Hide? Are you planning on hiding in there, too?"

Hawk didn't answer. He just barked out more instructions. "Hunt around for loose debris. Don't drag or disturb anything around the area where you collect things." He looked up and swung his arm in a large arc. "And avoid picking up anything in the immediate vicinity. Go down closer to those trees."

Instead of following orders, I planted my feet. If he thought I was going to crawl into a hole while he ran around the mountains, he was going to get an earful.

"Hawk, I'm staying with you. If you want me to hide in there," I pointed to the underside of the rock, "then you need to be telling me why. And it had better be damned good."

The space underneath the rock muffled his answer. "I'll explain later. Right now, do as instructed...please."

Sighing, I turned and worked my way down the slope into a grove of spruce mixed with aspens. There wasn't much of what I thought he would be looking for. This was summertime, after all. The rocky mountainside would have more debris come fall. I had to hunt around a good bit, but eventually I came back with some dead pine brush and a tangle of old leaves and twigs.

"How's this?" I asked, setting the items down beside where he sat on his heels.

He didn't answer, but began arranging the stuff around the shallow hole he had made. He leaned back and frowned at the results. "It'll do," he muttered, then waved a hand at me. "Your camera and belt pack. Hand them over."

I shook my head and started to refuse.

"*Quickly!*" He barked.

I unsnapped the belt pack from around my waist, then removed the camera from my shoulder.

Instead of tossing the items into the hole, he set the camera and belt pack beside the rifles. He waved his hand at me again. "Now, crawl in."

I stood there. "No. I'm not crawling into any frickin' hole under a rock."

His hand whipped out, caught my wrist, and jerked me onto my knees. The scowl on his face reminded me only too clearly who was in charge. He used his free hand to unzip my flak jacket.

"Take it off, or you won't fit properly under there."

I shrugged my arms from the flak jacket. Hawk had to release my wrist momentarily and I thought about bolting, saw the warning in his eyes, and stayed put instead.

"Get in." He clapped a hand on my shoulder to guide me under the rock. "Max is likely in the area," he said under his breath.

"Okay, okay." Squirming under his grip, I eased into the space, barely fitting lengthwise into the hole he had made. He began covering my legs and back with dirt.

"Aren't you getting in, too?" I demanded, my heart jolting into my throat as he continued to shift dirt and brush around me.

"No."

I shook my head and swore. "Damn it, Hawk, I'm not staying in this hole all by myself." I started brushing off the dirt he had been throwing over me. "No way," I repeated emphatically. "If there's some nut running around these mountains after us, then I'm sticking with you."

He paused in the act of throwing more dirt over my legs, his eyes meeting mine. "You'll stay here and do as you're told. Any movement or sound, anything at all, and you will compromise my position. Is that clear?"

His bullish behavior set off my mutinous streak. "No, Hawk. I am not going to lie under this rock, half-buried, when you haven't bothered to explain why you want me here in the first place. Besides, I have to pee. Come in here with me and cover yourself up with dirt, and I'll be glad to stay." Okay, I was lying about my bladder, but I couldn't think of another immediate reason to justify wriggling out from under the rock.

Hawk started arranging some of the debris cover my hiding place. "Do not move until I come back for you. If you have to pee, do. You're jeans will dry. I'll be doing a spot of hunting."

I stared at him. *"What?"* Are you nuts? I'm not staying here while you go traipsing around these woods looking for whoever took a shot at you! I'm coming...."

Hawk dropped to his stomach, scooted in until our eyes were inches apart, and gripped my mouth with hard, grimy fingers. The rest of my argument turned into so much mumbling. His voice was a bare whisper when he spoke.

"Do not make yourself expendable." The look in his eyes made the threat in his words crystal-clear. I trembled and nodded against his palm. He released my mouth, picked up a handful of dirt, and smeared it all over my face. I spat out granules, muttered a few curses. He started to wriggle backward.

I reached out a hand and caught his arm. "Hawk."

He stopped. Our eyes met. I squeezed his arm. "How long do I have to stay here?"

Hawk didn't move. "Until I come back for you."

I fumbled around for a way to ask the next question without sounding panicked. "And…and what if he should…get you first?"

His voice was devoid of emotion when he answered. "He'll eventually find you. You won't feel a thing."

I tried to swallow and didn't succeed. I relaxed my death grip on his arm and withdrew my hand. As I rested my head against the cool damp earth I caught sight of the hiking boots Hawk wore and thought about the Nike cross-trainers he'd had on earlier. Obviously, he had changed his footwear. Must've done that when he changed into the camouflage clothes back in the barn.

Long shadows created illusive images. From my position, I could see about thirty yards down the slope, but no one from the outside could see me. Further down, the red dirt road wound its way around the mountain.

Whoever had shot at Hawk was somewhere on that road.

And somewhere to the north of us, Jeremiah's Jeep had been seen on a dirt track. So close, yet here I was, stuck under a boulder for God only knew how long, unable to do anything to protect myself, much less try to find my husband.

Minutes ticked by, and small twigs and pine needles made their locations known. I had folded my hands beneath my head, and my shoulders began tingling from being in one position. I thought about the possibility of snakes, then realized that all the digging Hawk had done would have agitated any in the vicinity. Spiders and other creepy crawlies came to mind and I broke into a mild sweat hoping nothing of the multi-legged variety would decide to join me under my rock. The weight of the dirt Hawk had thrown over me dampened my clothes, and I grew chilled. It was already afternoon. Sunset would bring a significant drop in temperature. At this altitude, dressed as I was, hypothermia posed a threat.

How long was I supposed to wait here? The question kept popping into my mind no matter how hard I tried to push it away. Bird songs and the normal rustle of small wildlife reached my ears, and I tried concentrating on them to calm myself down. Everything sounded normal beyond my hiding place. My restlessness grew and the small pricks and pokes became unbearable irritations. I don't handle inactivity well to begin with, and lying here not knowing what was going on was driving me crazy. I tried shifting to check my watch and hit the boulder hard enough with the back of my head to bring tears to my eyes.

Damn it all, if Hawk didn't show up soon, I was crawling out of this stupid hole.

My imagination invented mirages in the shadows, jolting my heart into my throat before I realized that the figure I thought I saw was only darkened air. The urge to escape increased exponentially.

A squirrel came into my field of vision, inching along the ground, stopping every few steps to lift a tiny nose into the air for a sniff. I wondered whether he was looking for food or for suitable material to build a nest. The thought of food made my stomach growl, and I realized I was starving. Fast upon that thought came the realization of how thirsty I was. Shadows floated over the ground and I shivered. Afternoon thunderstorms, even snow, might be on the way. A cool breeze picked up, swaying the evergreens and whispering secrets through the aspens. The squirrel continued on his little hunt, wandering around the small clearing between my hiding place and the trees, his tail jerking with light grace, his little whiskers quivering. The scent of rain touched my nostrils and I ached for some water. In an effort to distract myself, I turned my thoughts to Angela.

Bad, bad idea. The image of Angela lying in that hospital bed brought tears to my eyes, and my chin started to tremble. I sniffed, tried to move an arm enough to wipe my nose on the sleeve of my sweatshirt, but didn't have enough room to do that, either. My parents were gone, and my sister soon might be, too, all because of Gary. Was Jeremiah lying dead in these mountains because of that bastard?

I squeezed my eyes shut, felt tears trickling down my cheeks. The man could have my trust fund and the entire Lamont fortune if he would just leave Jeremiah and Angela alone.

When my eyes opened the squirrel was paused on hind legs. I figured it had detected my presence either from my scent or the noise I'd made trying to sniff so my nose wouldn't drip. I watched the animal scamper up the trunk of a large pine and decided that I'd had enough of this hiding under a rock and started to brush the dirt and debris out of my way when something shifted to the right, at the very edge of my peripheral vision. No doubt it was Hawk, circling around to see whether I was still in the hole. Maybe this was his way of getting rid of me.

The casual thought made my blood suddenly run cold, and I reconsidered what my inner voice had just suggested. If Hawk had indeed left me here, his plan to get rid of me was brilliant. I had no identification, no camera with its digital pictures, no food, no water...

Shit. Had I just been left to die in the middle of Wolf Creek Pass?

I forced my thoughts to slow down, remembered the sound of the helicopter, the bullet hole on Hawk's side of the car.

You need to trust him. Joe's words filtered into my head.

Well, it's hard to trust someone who's just buried you under a flipping rock, I argued back.

I looked to my right, straining to see whether the movement I thought I'd seen was Hawk returning to get me. I reached again to haul the dirt and debris out of my way so I could crawl out of this damned hole. I realized I was panting and closed my eyes in an attempt to calm down. Hyperventilating while buried under a rock would not improve things.

Something disturbed the lose terrain to my right. Something large, like maybe a deer.

Or maybe a coyote, or a mountain lion, or a bear, I thought as my heart jerked into my throat again. The rustling leaves almost hid the sound. Whatever it was, it wasn't moving normally. The sounds were intermittent, stalking.

Why would Hawk be stalking so close to me without alerting me first?

Fear turned to anger, and I opened my mouth to yell his name when I caught a brief glimpse of black combat boots among the trees. My mouth snapped shut and I stared.

Hawk had been wearing *hiking boots.*

Fear does amazing things. Seconds ago I was ready to leave this stupid hole under a rock. Now I felt helpless, exposed. I dared not shift further back against the overhang. My eyes widened as a man's leg appeared, close enough that I could make out every detail of the boot and bit of his pants leg. The man was dressed in camouflage similar to Hawk's.

The boot disappeared. Leaves trembled in the breeze. A man's hips, torso, and shoulders came into view on my left, then vanished. I pressed my face against the ground as raw terror welled up and consumed every fiber of my being.

The man had a rifle tucked against his shoulder.

Jeremiah's voice whispered in my memory. *Animals sense when they are being watched. Humans have retained the same instinct.*

I squeezed my eyes shut, every muscle tensed against the cool, damp earth, and tried to imagine myself a part of the boulder.

The soft rustle of cloth reached my ears. I opened tentative eyes, directing my gaze to the left, where the squirrel had disappeared up the tree. I looked for the boots but could not see anything.

Was I visible? Would he be able to see me in the shadows? Would he walk up and crouch for a closer look? Or would he just assume that Hawk was hiding under the rock and start shooting?

"Come out from under the rock," a strange male voice commanded.

I jerked so badly I almost let out a scream. My eyes scanned the trees below, but I could not see the man who belonged to the voice.

Do not move until I come back for you.

Hawk's command rang in my ears so loudly, I thought he had shouted it. I lay utterly still, not even daring to breathe. Surely, the stranger was guessing. Animals could have made the disturbances on the ground. He had no proof there were any humans here. He would not shoot without knowing first what he was shooting at. Besides, I still had to get back to the hospital. I had to find that asshole brother-in-law of mine and kick his murderous butt all the way to Cañon City Maximum Security Prison.

Clothing rustled and boots thudded against the earth. My eyes snapped open...

...and stared straight down the black muzzle of a rifle. I saw combat boots and most of the body of a crouched man, watched as his finger curled in slow motion around the trigger, stared with crystal clarity at the weird looking cylinder that elongated the barrel. A scream welled up, ready to rip from my throat.

Thwuump.

My eyes went blank, my throat filled up, tears sprang onto lashes, and I felt...

...nothing.

I realized my eyes were shut and cracked one open. I watched the rifle drop and the man slump onto his back, his feet bent awkwardly beneath him. I stared at the motionless heap, expecting the man to jump to his feet, pluck up his rifle, and shoot me. The longer I stared at the lump, the more still it seemed to become.

My other eye opened. A pocket flap fluttered as the breeze

brushed the man's motionless chest. Scattered raindrops smacked down into the brown earth, dampened the material of his camouflage clothing. I trembled under the rock and decided that I would not move until someone woke me up from this nightmare.

I don't know how long I stared at the body when I heard a disturbance somewhere nearby. A pair of familiar hiking boots dropped down from the top of the boulder and landed lightly onto the ground. The figure crouched down. Familiar fingers searched the dead man's vest. Then the boots pivoted in my direction and a set of gray eyes peered under the boulder.

"Mattie," Hawk said gently. "You can come out now."

Chapter Fifteen

I didn't want to move. Well, if you want the honest truth, I *couldn't* move.

Hawk shifted away from the body, knelt down on his knees, and reached into where I lay. Catching hold of my wrist, he gently pulled me out from underneath the rock. The light breeze brushed against my cheeks as I stood up. A surge of dizziness hit, and I swayed. Hawk gripped my arm until my vision steadied. When the trees quit spinning before my eyes, I found myself staring at the dead man lying on the ground.

There was a large, bloody mess where his head should have been. Bits of rich, dark red hair stuck out around the man's annihilated features, splattered blood stained his camouflage jacket. His long, muscular arms lay at unnatural angles, his legs bent equally unnaturally beneath his body.

The sight curdled my insides as childhood memories slammed before my eyes. I shook off Hawk's hand and stepped carefully around the dead man. On shaky legs I stumbled over to the pine tree that the squirrel had scampered to, then collapsed down to my knees, gripping the sticky, sappy trunk with shaking hands. My gut wrenched with spasms so violent I could hardly breathe. I eased over to the slope-side of the tree and sat on the damp ground, my back pressed against the rough, sticky bark. Emotions whirled with such force, I thought my head would rip open. I pressed my hands against my eyelids and tried to blank out the black hole of that rifle, that bloody, headless corpse, the blood and guts of the neighbor all those years ago.

I heard footsteps, then the rustle of clothing. Glancing up, I watched Hawk kneel down in front of me, peering at my dirt and tear-streaked face. I could not bring myself to make eye contact.

"You were brilliant," he murmured.

I leaned my head against the sticky bark of the tree and squeezed my eyes shut again.

"I...I never expected...h-him to show up where I was." I felt my hair sticking to the tree sap, smelled the resin mix with other high altitude forest scents. "I...I thought you were staying between h-him a-and m-me. I th-thought you would b-be...p-protecting m-me."

I heard Hawk release a slow, measured sigh and opened my eyes. He looked away. His vest was gone. I wondered why he had taken it off.

His eyes scanned the surroundings. "I used the wreckage to lead him up the mountain."

I noticed how well his clothing blurred into the surrounding foliage. Maybe that was why he had taken the black vest off. With just his camouflage he would have been invisible, melting into the terrain like a rattler among the rocks.

I wiped my face with the dirt-encrusted sleeve of my sweat-shirt. "W-why didn't you shoot him d-down there? Around the c-car?" I shut my eyes again in a futile effort to block the image of the black hole of the dead man's rifle. If I could just shut things off, quit thinking about it.

Hawk released a slow sigh through his nose, which sounded inordinately loud to my ears. "Because he knew better than to leave the cover of the trees. He could survey the inside of the wreck from a distance and see that it was empty."

I stared at the side of his head as he scanned the trees around us and got the sudden impression that he was the one avoiding eye contact. "S-so how did he know s-someone was under the boulder?"

Hawk didn't reply. A gentle wind breathed softly through the aspens, and the pine shuddered faintly against my back.

The silence continued. I was staring at the back of his head when he snapped his eyes to mine. He finally answered, his voice very even. "Because I left subtle leads."

Everything went still around us. The breeze stalled; leaves quieted, animal noises ceased.

Or maybe I couldn't hear any of it because of the roaring in my ears as I stared at him, incredulous. His eyes bore into mine without apology, without the least sign of contrition.

"You...you mean...." I trailed off, unable to bring myself to verbalize what I thought he was saying.

He said it for me. "I set up an ambush."

I finished it for him. "And used me as bait."

Sitting with my back against the trunk of the pine tree, I stared at the man who set me up to be shot. He handled my life with the same callousness as the other day when he pulled his gun on me in the middle of northeastern New Mexico.

If I opened my mouth, I would start screaming and would not be able to stop. Instead, stiff and grimy, I rose from my protective, knobby tree. Hawk stood with me. Because he was on the down slope, our heights were even. And because I didn't know what was coming myself, I inadvertently added the element of surprise.

I felt my right hand curl into a fist as I went straight at him, throwing all my weight into my shoulder and hip. My eyes focused on his mid-section as my fist made contact, hitting him dead center in his solar plexus. The impact against his hard muscles shocked my arm all the way through my shoulder. He gasped, his eyes widening, and staggered back on the steep slope. I stepped in, cocked my left arm, and with every ounce of strength I had, jabbed the heel of my hand straight towards the bridge of his nose.

Surprise caught him off guard with my first blow, his professional training reacted before I could land the second. His left hand whipped up and caught my wrist just before I made contact, his vice-like fingers wrapping around my fragile bones. We froze, arms in mid-air, the pressure of his hold forcing my fingers open. I recalled his cruel strength the times he had twisted my arm behind my back and waited for his flash of anger and dangerous retaliation, and wondered whether my attack might result this time in a broken arm rather than simply strained muscles and joints. Silent tears ran down my cheeks as I glared at the man with outright hatred. I didn't give a *damn* how badly he hurt me.

With a slow, deliberate movement, he lowered his arm, taking mine along. When he got to the point where he might jerk me forward, his fingers loosened. He released me and took a careful step away.

I heard myself gulping air, realized I was hyperventilating, and shut my mouth in an effort to slow my breathing. Hawk stood poised, feet braced, arms ready at his sides, but he did not move a muscle.

I backed away, then turned and began making my way down the slope in the direction Hawk had indicated earlier where the forest ranger had spotted Jeremiah's Jeep. I did not look back.

Hawk did not make a sound or movement to stop me.

I stumbled down the steep gravelly surface, almost toppled over onto my face because I was concentrating on blocking out the memory of the dead man and the live one instead of the dangerous terrain. Muttering curses, I focused on the terrain and forced my thoughts forward, though I doubt I would see a grizzly jump from behind one of the stubby trees.

Find my husband. Get back to Angela. Rescue Mud Rain. Screw the order.

Stumpy evergreens swayed with stunted aspens at this altitude. Despite being hot and sweaty, I shivered in the cool mountain air as perspiration dampened my skin and clothes. Shock created part of the problem and the clothes I wore sorely lacked enough protection from the wild fluctuations in weather and temperatures. I had to find someplace warm before night came. Light retreated rapidly in the mountains. I didn't have much time.

I reached the bottom of the first slope and began working my way up the steep incline of the next one. My thoughts turned inward, as the need for flight drove my legs on, despite intensifying pain throughout my body. I was fast running out of strength and my lungs and muscles felt seared from too much exertion in the thin air.

I had to reach Jeremiah's Jeep before sunset. What time was it now? I glanced at my watch. Five-thirty. I had no more than three hours of daylight remaining to try to find him. Three hours max before I found myself facing serious trouble trying to stay warm through the night.

Max…max, max, max. Thoughts shifted to the man lying dead on the mountainside. I struggled to block out Hawk and his games.

How would Jeremiah be moving in this remote backcountry? I forced myself to think about what Jeremiah had told me of his hunting experiences. How he kept his pace slow, steady, kept his eye on the sun, his ears alert for surrounding wildlife.

Bottled up panic swelled, threatened to seize control of my legs and send me crashing around like a frightened elk. But if Jeremiah's Jeep were in the area, Jeremiah and Gary might be as well. I had to use common sense and what I remembered from Jeremiah's stories. I tried to imagine myself as Jeremiah, tried to picture him slipping through the trees, tracking a mule deer. Struggling to slow my pace, I looked for ways up the mountain that would provide concealment and minimal disturbance. I sorely missed my hiking boots, which were sitting in my closet back at the apartment. The sneakers I wore had no tread, and I tripped and slid my way upwards along the steep, loose terrain.

Was my husband lying dead in the Jeep?

Of course not, I argued against another wave of hysteria. Jeremiah was way smarter than Gary.

Unfortunately, my imagination suggested all sorts of reasons why Hawk had not mentioned my husband's whereabouts after his conversation with Joe. I lost concentration, my feet slipped on the crumbling granite, and I landed hard on all fours. I knelt there, gasping, cursing, before struggling back to my feet and over to a pine tree. I needed to stay closer to the trees. The ground was firmer around the trunks, and the small branches provided something to hang on to. But that meant more weaving back and forth, rather than the direct route I had been trying to maintain. Switchbacks would take more time out of the sun, time I didn't have to spare.

Why hadn't Hawk told me more about Joe's phone call? Had the ranger seen Jeremiah driving, or had he seen the Jeep abandoned?

Oh, God, *please* don't let me find a body.

I didn't know whether Hawk was following me and I refused to waste energy looking back. As far as I was concerned, his part in this mess was officially over. He had no reason to involve himself in the situation between Gary, my husband, and me. I didn't care what Joe Healing Water thought. I wanted absolutely nothing to do with that man, his guns, or his ambushes.

The top of the hill seemed to retreat further with each change in direction. My legs burned, my head felt light as air. I could only manage to breathe in short, painful gasps, while my hands and knees burned after repeated falls onto the loose, crumbling earth. I ground my teeth, lowered my head, and kept taking one more step. Maybe I would glimpse the red Jeep through the trees when I got to the top. I didn't look up, but gauged my progress by the incline. Jeremiah and I had done a lot of hiking around the Springs, including the climb to the summit of Pikes Peak. If I could manage the Sixteen Golden Stairs at fourteen-plus thousand feet, I could make it over a couple of hills to get to my husband.

The angle leveled, and I felt relief all the way down to my toes. I glanced up from the ground to see how far the crest stretched and released a frustrated groan. The terrain ran flat for about a hundred yards, then dropped into a steep ravine. I crossed the distance and glanced down. A several hundred-foot drop and a large snowdrift stretched along the bottom. There was no way to attempt a descent. That meant going around. I looked left, then right, but could not see where the chasm narrowed. I moved to a fallen rotted tree trunk, pushed it with my foot a few times to make sure no wildlife was present, then eased down, testing for stability before I rested my full weight on it. I practically doubled over because of the pain in my lungs. I needed water, but didn't have any with me. I thought about eating snow but decided not to risk it. I studied the filthy bandages on both palms and wondered whether it would be a mistake just to take them off.

I was sitting there wishing my lungs would quit hurting when a small water bottle appeared on my right. Startled, I jerked, tumbled off the trunk onto the ground, then scrambled to my feet.

Hawk, his breathing labored, stood just behind the fallen tree trunk. The altitude had gotten to him, too, which gave me immense satisfaction. Both rifles jutted behind his shoulders. He had his black vest on, and my belt pack was clipped to one of the pockets. My camera hung around his neck and the vest I'd been wearing hung from one of his shoulders.

I really wanted to scream at him.

"What…." That's as far as I got before the pain in my lungs bent me over again. I braced my hands on my knees, closed my mouth, forced myself to breathe through my nose.

Hawk did not utter a word. After several minutes, I glanced over at the water bottle he still held out. I straightened and reached out, took it, then turned around and sat back down on the tree trunk. Yes, I was being rude. No, I didn't care. I unscrewed the cap and tipped some of the clear, cool water into my mouth, holding it there until it was warm enough to swallow. My throat ached and I groaned. I hadn't been maintaining a steady pace to keep my breathing even, and I was paying for it now. Hawk took the half-full bottle from my shaking fingers, tipped the rest into his mouth, then tucked the small bottle into one of his vest pockets.

Sitting here was wasting precious daylight, but my legs felt like two tons of solid lead. I looked out over the ravine and wondered whether I should go left or right to try to get around it. The deep rift might go on for miles, and there might not be a way to cross it.

At that thought, anger rose and leaked some energy into my aching limbs. I stood. There had to be a way around that damned ravine.

There was movement beside me, and Hawk appeared. I opened my mouth to cuss him out, but he spoke first.

"Mattie, you need to trust me."

If my legs weren't so exhausted, I would have started stomping the ground. "Trust you? *Trust you?* You set me up! I was lying under that rock and wondering whether you'd just gone and left me there! You should've told me what you were planning!"

Hawk's gray eyes met my green ones. "Would you have followed directions, had I told you why I wanted you under that rock?"

I opened my mouth to yell at him that, yes, I would have stayed under that rock, then slowly closed my mouth again when the truth made itself clear. Reluctantly, I admitted to myself that had I known I was being used to bait the killer hunting us, I would not have had the courage to stay under that rock and stay quiet. Not even Hawk's threats would have been enough to make me cooperate.

Images of rifle muzzles, blown off heads, and ballgame pictures mixed and swirled until I lost the ability to think straight, so my next comment sounded like I'd dove straight off the deep end of a shallow cliff. "That man had a son."

"And quite likely a wife." His calm observation floated between us. "He has also led an assassination network for the better part of a decade."

I fisted my hands in my hair, felt pain streak across my palms, and refused to cry. "How can you know that? You're basing your assumptions on three pictures I happened to take at a damned ball game. How do you know you're assumptions aren't all dead wrong!" I winced. Wrong choice of words.

Hawk's eyes flickered over the rugged terrain. Several moments passed before he replied. "If Max was innocent, then why was he ready to shoot you with a silenced rifle on the side of that mountain?"

"Maybe he thought you were hiding under a rock ready to shoot him? How the hell am I supposed to know? I don't even know whether my husband's still alive!" I clamped my mouth shut. I sounded hysterical. I needed to get a grip.

He held out the vest I had been wearing. "You'll want this."

I wanted to hit him again. Instead I spun around, clenched my fists and winced at the pain that streaked through my palms, turned to glare at the yawning breadth of the ravine to hide my grimace from Hawk. Crossing it seemed impossible, and I slumped onto the fallen tree trunk.

"How much pain are you in?"

I ran shaking fingers through my tangled hair, hating his as-tuteness, not wanting to admit the toll terrain and altitude were tak-ing on body parts. My head definitely did not like the exertion. "Things hurt," I admitted.

"Your palms. Let me see them." He came around, dropped the vest at my feet, then crouched in front of me. My emotional whirlwind had spun itself out, and I sighed and held out my hands. Pulling a utility knife from a pocket, he sliced through the worthless bandages and exposed the cuts on my palms. The edges had turned an angry red, but no icky drainage was visible.

"Allow me to re-dress these before we move on." His was a statement rather than a request, so I sat there and watched him pull a small first aid kit from a vest pocket. He cleaned the cuts with an alcohol wipe, then applied salve and wrapped clean white gauze around them. I grit my teeth and refused to admit how much the alcohol and salve stung.

Still crouched, Hawk glanced up, our eyes close. "There's ibu-profen in a small first aid kit in the top right pocket of your flak jack-et. Take some now."

I didn't want to follow his advice. If I wanted to keep going, however, I would need some help in the pain department. I rum-maged around the pockets of the vest at my feet and found the small first aid pack. I removed a package of painkillers, tore open a corner, and popped both pills into my mouth, swallowing them with my spit.

Hawk straightened and looked down at me. "Mattie, put the flak jacket on. It'll keep you warm."

Of course his logic was impeccable. I hesitated, then shrugged into the thing and tightened the Velcro straps, wondering how I was going to manage climbing downhill with the extra weight.

Hawk surveyed the terrain. "If we follow the ravine down to the road, we may find an area narrow enough to cross without risk-ing Gary's crosshairs." He shrugged the rifle with the silencer from his shoulder, then turned and began picking his way down the slope on a parallel course with the ravine.

I fumed over the fact he possessed infinitely better outdoor skills than I did. But the cold truth was I needed his help if I hoped to find Jeremiah. I swallowed my pride and started after him, trying to ignore the screeching protests of muscles and lungs. I prayed my knees would hold out. The slope was insanely steep, rough, a nightmarish fall waiting to happen. I stopped, thrust out my hand. "I want my camera and belt pack."

Hawk paused a few yards down from where I stood, turned to face me, and shook his head. "The jacket is already hampering your balance. Keep moving." Without waiting for a reply (he probably figured I'd try to argue anyway), he turned and resumed his trek down the mountain.

True to prediction, my knees began to give out before we had made it down fifty yards. Even using switchbacks, the pressure exerted on my kneecaps and lower joints made me gasp with pain. I paused and leaned against a pine, shifting my weight from one leg to another in an effort to give each joint a modicum of relief. I glanced back up to the crest of the hill. My mistake, because I realized how little distance we had traveled. The sun dropped towards the western horizon. We were never going to make it before dark. I wasn't even sure I could make it to the bottom of this hill.

Hawk paused, waiting while I rested. I massaged my knees, trying to ease the pain, and started again.

To the left five steps, then switch, moving to the right for five more. Make it six next time, I told myself. I made up an imaginary obstacle course with each switchback, adding a step each time I changed direction. When I reached ten, I could take a thirty-second rest. Sitting down didn't help my knees, nor did bending over. All I could do was stop and straighten them as much as possible. If I paused for any longer, I wasn't sure I would start up again.

The next time I looked up, we were about halfway down the mountain. The sun threw ominously long shadows in the rapidly cooling air.

I kept talking to myself. To the right, now switch back to the left. Over and over, step by painful step, I kept working my way down the impossibly steep mountainside until at last the slope lessened, then flattened out. We were deep in the trees, and a ribbon of rusty red dirt road peeked through the branches. The drop into the ravine had closed to about a hundred feet, but continued all the way down the mountain. An old railroad bridge spanned the yawning chasm, the red ribbon of dirt road meeting the bridge and continuing on the opposite side.

Holding the rifle in loose readiness, Hawk halted under some pines about twenty yards from the near side of the bridge. He leaned against a trunk for a long time, studying the bridge and listening.

"Crossing the bridge will expose us to anyone watching." His eyes cut over to the ravine, then to me. "But I'm not sure how much more descent you can handle, and trying to cross the ravine will expose us anyway." He spoke so low as to be almost inaudible.

Along the bottom of the chasm, the snow had tapered to a narrow belt and conceivably we could have climbed down, then up the other side. But large, jagged boulders lay in heaps all along the rift, creating an obstacle course that would hamper our progress and eat up precious time.

Hawk's eyes conducted yet another gradual sweep of the surrounding terrain. "Gary chose well. The bridge and the ravine limit access to the other side." He paused, and I got the strong feeling that he was choosing his next words carefully. "Jeremiah's Jeep should be just past the bridge, on a side track."

I started to ask if he thought Jeremiah might be in the vehicle, but changed my mind before the words formed on my lips. I would be finding out soon enough anyway, provided we made it across the bridge.

Shadows lengthened and before long we would lose sight of the bridge altogether. I started to mention that crossing it in the dark might be to our advantage, then remembered the existence of night scopes. I wondered whether Gary had one.

Hawk's hand pressed down on my shoulder, forcing me into a crouch. He leaned his head close to mine and whispered, "I'll go first. There should be just enough light for you to see me reach the other side. When I get there, dart across as fast as you can, crouching as low as possible."

I nodded, even though my current position started the hot screaming sensation in my knees again. I gritted my teeth and stayed put. Hawk tucked the rifle into his shoulder, then slipped out from the cover of the trees.

I thought it would be easy to detect his movement across the bridge, but the man blended into the wood and steel framework and I lost track of where he was. I gave up trying to follow his movement and kept my eyes on the other side. I still couldn't see anything, even though the opposite side was visible in the rapidly fading light. In the end, I had to guess he had made it across and started to follow. My knees would not move in a full crouch, so I ended up sort of bent over. Fine butt shot, if anyone was aiming. At least it wasn't my head. I couldn't run in that position, so I scooted my feet along the bridge, praying no cars would come.

Praying no bullets would either.

I didn't realize I had reached the other side until a hand caught me by the arm and pulled me into the dark safety of the trees.

"Good girl." Hawk released me, turned, and slipped among the pines and aspens. I followed, or tried to. Even with me close behind him, he melted so well into the increasing darkness that I had a hard time keeping up. We topped a small rise, and he stopped. I came up beside him and looked down.

Jeremiah's red Jeep lay on the driver's side, almost on the hood, in a small ditch beside the narrow tract of a dirt road.

I inhaled to yell his name and started to leap down the hill. Hawk's hand clamped hard over my mouth, smothering me. He jerked me back, pinning my head against his chest. Thrown off balance, I landed with a soft thud on my backside.

"Not a good idea," he hissed in my ear. I froze. He dropped his hand, and I clamped my own hand against my lips, silently swearing not to make a sound or a move before he did.

Again, he crouched motionless, rifle ready, for what seemed like hours. Full dark surrounded us now, and the red color of the Jeep faded to a dark gray shadow. No movement or sound disturbed the intense stillness around us. A cold breeze whispered through the tops of the trees, bringing the smell of rain…or snow, if any storms came through. My hands and face chilled and I shivered.

At long last, Hawk stirred and began making a slow trek down the incline. I followed, as noiselessly as possible, trying to match where he stepped. When we made it to the rear of the vehicle Hawk paused again, listening, rifle ready.

Pock marks from the hailstorm Saturday night marred the top of the vehicle. The back window had been broken out and safety glass scattered over the ground. I glanced through the interior of the Jeep towards the front and saw a spiral-shaped fracture in the windshield, fanning out from a bullet hole on the driver's side.

No bodies, or awful smells, filled the shadows.

Tears sprang and I choked on a soft sob. Hawk's hand gripped my mouth again, and his head leaned against mine as he whispered, "He was alive after he crashed. The pattern of the glass on the ground proves it."

Thunder rumbled across the tops of the trees.

"Get inside." His hand moved to the back of my neck. With

firm but gentle pressure, he guided me through the broken back window. Pens, notepads, old coffee cups and floor mats lay strewn around, dislodged when the Jeep toppled over into the ditch. I crawled over the back seat, then reached under the driver's seat where Jeremiah always kept his handgun.

Nothing. I prayed Jeremiah had it with him, but feared Gary had found it when he searched the wrecked vehicle.

I spotted Jeremiah's black leather jacket on the floor under the dash and leaned over to retrieve it, remembering vividly the way he had shrugged into it before leaving for work Saturday night. I slipped my arms through the sleeves and pulled the jacket close around me, feeling Jeremiah's essence, smelling his scent. It fitted loosely over the heavy vest and gave reassuring weight and warmth. He always kept a gym bag in the Jeep in case he got delayed in Boulder or on the way back to the Springs. Now the bag lay open, it contents strewn about the floor behind the front seats. I stared at his deodorant, gym towel, spare pair of shorts and thought about his habit of neatness and keeping everything in its place. To have everything strewn about like this meant that something had been very wrong. I glanced closer and inhaled sharply as I recognized dried blood. A lot of it.

The space became cramped when Hawk crawled inside. He fumbled with the back seat, found the handle, and collapsed the back forward. Then he picked up the thick blanket Jeremiah always kept in the car. "Curl up in this and get some sleep."

I took the blanket, wondered how he thought I could sleep right now, and sat down on the passenger window behind the driver's seat. I leaned my head against the folded down back seat and tucked my legs beneath me. Raindrops splattered against the undercarriage. I turned my head and looked at Hawk. He had propped himself against the tilted floor behind the rear seats. One rifle rested against knees bent almost to his chin. The other lay by his feet. Visions of my sister, Mud Rain, and headless bodies swam around in thoughts too fatigued to make sense.

"Hawk?"

It was too dark to see his expression, but I caught the motion of his head and sensed his eyes on me. "Mm?"

"Do you think Jeremiah's still alive?"

I heard him release a slow sigh. "Get some sleep."

I stared at the angled top of the Jeep and wished my husband were here instead of the man who was. The cloth of the backseat brushed roughly against my cheek. The warmth of Jeremiah's jacket gently wrapped around me as I huddled beneath the blanket

Please, Jeremiah, I prayed into the darkness, *please don't be dead.*

Chapter Sixteen

I slept the sleep of the dead. I didn't dream. I didn't wake up. I didn't even shift my position. My subconscious and my bladder finally nudged me back into the world of the living.

When I opened my eyes to the gray of pre-dawn I hadn't a clue where I was at first. Realization settled in, and I looked around for Hawk, who had disappeared. Stiff and cold, I struggled to unbend my legs, and then crawled through the back window. Pins stabbed my calves and thighs as impaired circulation got going again. I stood up on the cold ground, my breath fogging in the early morning chill, and tried to locate the man, but he was nowhere in sight. Patchy snow collected in spots where trees thinned, utter silence surrounded me. My parched throat ached from too little moisture, too thin air, and way too much exercise yesterday. Miraculously, my knees seemed to be in good shape. I pulled out the first aid kit and downed two of the remaining ibuprofen, then searched for suitable cover to do my business.

When I got back to the Jeep, Hawk was still nowhere in sight. I picked my way along the left side of the ditch to the front of the vehicle and took a closer look at the bullet hole.

The windshield had buckled with the impact, had almost shattered. I skidded down into the ditch until I faced the grill and stared at the driver's seat.

Large, dark blotches stained the cloth on the left side, and I stamped down hard on the panic that surged into my throat.

Jeremiah had been shot.

"He got out," I said aloud. "He got out, which means he can move. He's hurt, but he's alive."

My racing imagination wasn't listening. How much blood had he lost? What if he was lying in the forest somewhere bleeding to death? What if some wild animal had followed the scent of blood and taken him down?

What if Gary had shot him a second time, after he escaped from the Jeep?

"He was hit. Probably a flesh wound by the location of the

stains." Hawk's voice said from behind me.

I jumped so badly I almost fell into the front of the Jeep. I spun around with the unpleasant memory of his sneaking up on me in the barn. I scowled at him, but kept my thoughts to myself. "Do you have any idea which direction he went?" I asked instead.

Hawk glanced to our left, in the direction of a nearby summit. The dark shadow of a beard roughened his appearance. After a few moments he turned to me.

"I brought breakfast."

He set the rifle he carried against a tree, then pulled out the small water bottle, which he must have filled somewhere in the vicinity. He pulled two oblong foil packets from a vest pocket and offered one to me.

I refused to have my attention diverted. "Hawk, what have you found?"

His lips formed a thin line. "Nothing to indicate that your husband's mortally wounded."

I realized I would have to be satisfied with his answer for the moment. I glanced down at the foil packet he proffered.

"What's this?" Though hungry, I was still a day or so away from eating tree bark.

"You Yanks call them M.R.E." He tore open the top of the one he held. When I hesitated, he explained. "'Meals Ready to Eat'. Add water, break the small casing to mix the chemicals so that it gets hot, and there you are. Enough calories to get you through a brisk morning march." He pulled out a small camping spoon from the depths of his vest and held it out.

"Got any toilet paper stashed in there?" I asked as I took the utensil.

The corners of his mouth twitched. I tore open the package with my teeth, then held it out for him to pour in some water. He broke the capsule for me, and the foil package began to warm. Before long, faint steam rose from the open top. I dipped the spoon in and came out with something that looked like a cross between casserole and soup. Smelled like heaven. My mouth watered and I gingerly sampled a bite.

"Umm, I never thought portable food could taste so good." I ate some more. I was careful not to eat too fast, first because I wanted to enjoy the sensation, and second because I didn't want my empty stomach to cramp. I watched him eat a few mouthfuls, then forced out the question that gnawed at my brain.

"How badly hurt do you think Jeremiah is?"

Hawk's jaw worked as he chewed, his eyes scanning the surroundings. "Not seriously enough to impair his mobility. He's wounded, which makes him more dangerous."

I stared at the bullet hole in the windshield of the Jeep. "All he has with him is his father's old army forty-five."

Hawk directed his attention back to me. "And a hunter's instinct. Gary may be an excellent marksman, but he'll need to be sharp on tactics to maintain the advantage, even if he's got more fire power." His eyes were on mine, but I got the feeling his thoughts were elsewhere.

"What makes you say that?" I asked through another bite.

He regarded me in silence for a moment. "Because even wounded, your husband has left very little sign. Tracking him will be a challenge."

"If Gary was close enough to shoot him through the windshield, he could have followed him and…and tried shooting him again." I shuddered.

Hawk shook his head. "We haven't found Jeremiah's body in or around the Jeep. The bullet hole in the windscreen indicates Gary tripped the ambush. He had a clear kill shot. He would still have had the advantage while your husband was trying to escape from the Jeep." Hawk frowned as his gaze slipped back towards the summit he had scanned earlier. "The bullet hit the windscreen straight on. He had a clear kill shot," he repeated, muttering through another bite.

I swallowed hard as insight hit. "You were expecting to find a body here yesterday."

Hawk's eyes cut to mine. "It was a reasonable assumption."

I fought back the image of Jeremiah lying dead somewhere and tipped the foil package to my lips to drain the last bit of liquid. Energy seeped into my muscles and limbs. Hawk took the empty packets and stored them in a vest pocket.

"So, what now?" I asked when he offered the water bottle. I took a couple of swallows, then handed it back. He drained the rest and put the bottle back into the (seemingly) infinite pockets of his vest.

"We track your husband."

I held out my hand. "I can carry my belt pack and camera

now. You have enough on your hands."

He unclipped the belt pack, then handed it and the Canon to me. I strapped the belt pack around my waist and slung the camera across my shoulder and chest until it tucked snuggly against the back of my arm. Hawk checked the weapons he carried, then shouldered one. Holding Joe's rifle in the crook of his right elbow, he motioned for me to follow. We began climbing towards the summit that had held his attention earlier, eventually reaching a small ridge that paralleled the dirt track, being careful to remain crouched within the cover of the trees. Not much moisture had fallen during the night, and the early morning air sat around freezing. Jeremiah's jacket hugged me with warmth and a strange sense of reassurance. The vest still hampered my movements. I wondered whether it had any bullet repelling capabilities. I had no idea how far we had gone when Hawk stopped for a break.

"So, are these things bullet proof?" I asked, indicating my vest.

"The Kevlar will slow a bullet but not stop one," he explained. Slipping over to a small stream of snow run-off, he pulled the bottle from his vest, dipped the bottle into the water, added an iodine tablet and shook it up. The clear water tasted cold, refreshing. I drank half; he finished it off. I thought about the day before. Curiosity stirred me into asking details I didn't really want to know.

"So, did you just leave that guy where he fell?" I asked as Hawk tucked the empty bottle back into a pocket. He checked the weapon he carried, adjusted the one across his back. The breeze lifted his disheveled hair when he looked at me, his eyes cool. "I buried him under the rock and notified one of your agencies to send a clean-up crew."

I gaped at him. "You mean I was lying in…in a…." I tried to verbalize the word. It refused to come out of my mouth.

His eyes narrowed on mine. "In a holding area."

"I'm glad I didn't know that when I hid under there," I muttered. "What about his rifle? Why didn't you take it with you?"

"Not enough ammo to divide between three weapons. I disabled it, then buried it with the body."

I shuddered and looked away to study the surrounding terrain. Time to quit thinking about corpses.

A narrow canyon dipped below us, rising in a barren, rocky incline about a half a mile away. I adjusted the camera around my chest. On an impulse, I took it off, fished around my belt pack for the zoom lens, recoiled when my fingers touched the handgun, then pulled out the lens and screwed it on. I brought the camera up, turned it on, and zoomed in on the surroundings. Rugged terrain leapt through the lens in sharp detail. I panned over the mountainside opposite us, my view blocked whenever I passed a tree trunk. Weak sunshine shone through stratus clouds, though I predicted the sky would clear as the atmosphere warmed. The sheer surface of the southern-most ridge presented a rock climber's dream. I hoped we weren't heading in that direction. The vertical drop defied a way down without equipment. I followed the cliff to a rocky base that met the tree line. Even though we were still below eleven thousand feet, barren terrain far out-stretched wooded sections.

I directed my attention to the opposite side of the canyon and focused on a dark gap between two boulders.

"I think I see a cave." I lowered the camera and offered it to Hawk for a look. He took a turn studying the overlay, focusing last on the dark slit between the rocks. He handed the camera back to me and brought out the monocular. Several minutes passed while he examined the area.

"I would have to agree." He lowered the glass and worked his way carefully to the left. He put the glass back into his vest, then raised the rifle he carried and peered through the scope.

"I wonder if that's one of the hideaways Gary knows about from his days on the reservation." I recapped the lens. I started to unscrew it from the camera base, then thought better of it. I slung the camera back over my shoulder and chest.

"It would narrow our search." Hawk concentrated on the canyon below us. My thoughts wandered to Mud Rain, and then another face slipped across my thoughts.

"Why was it Max, Hawk? Why wasn't it one of the twins?" I heard the plea in my voice, tried to block the sleeping child's peaceful face from my memory.

Hawk lowered the rifle. I looked away, embarrassed for asking such a moronic question, knowing he probably wouldn't bother to answer.

"Why is it Jeremiah and Gary we're hunting now? Why not someone different?" His voice was neutral.

I stared at the ground, feeling incredibly stupid for the emotions interfering with logic. "But it was Lee who tried to kill me. We don't know for sure Max planted that car bomb. Lee could still be up to his neck in all of this. What are you going to do about it?"

"Nothing, until the time comes." He turned and continued along the ridge, staying well-hidden behind available foliage. I followed, still plagued by questions. When he paused again, I came up close beside him.

"Wouldn't be better now to call in the cops? Can't you call whatever agency you contacted and tell them what's going on?"

Hawk turned his head to study me. An eagle's cry echoed off the canyon walls below us, the stark, lonely sound reverberating as it traveled down the valley.

"No."

"Why not?" I asked, frustrated with his reluctance to ask for outside help.

Hawk released a sigh and turned his head away. "Because as of yesterday, I was supposed to be headed to Denver for a debriefing."

When he shifted his feet to start off again, I put a hand on his arm. "Are you saying that you're AWOL at the moment?"

Hawk's eyes flickered in my direction then back to the seclusion that surrounded us. I took his non-answer as an affirmative.

"Why, Hawk?" I persisted, refusing to accept silence as an answer. "I mean, none of this concerns you."

He swung his eyes back to mine with hot intensity. "Because I've a problem with a man who poisons his wife, then kidnaps a defenseless boy." He pulled his arm away and I dropped my hand. "We need to keep going if we're going to locate your husband."

We moved onward, our bodies crouched, our footsteps careful. I glanced down at my filthy sneakers, uncomfortable with the irony that without Hawk's help, I would probably be dead by now with or without the threat of killers on the loose.

We stayed just below the rise except when Hawk paused to reconnoiter. I crouched beside him, sensing the hunter instinct that made him so dangerous, feeling compelled to tell him what was on my mind.

"I…I could not have made it this far without…without your help." I stared at his profile. "When you said earlier you were supposed to be headed back to Denver, does that mean your cover, or whatever you call it, is blown?"

I heard him grunt. "Probably." He directed his attention through the scope again, despite the fact he had just lowered the rifle. I wondered whether my question had made him uncomfortable.

"Does that mean Lee knows you're alive now, too?"

He regarded me for several very silent moments. I stared at his cool gray eyes, feeling an alien tinge of concern.

"Undoubtedly," he answered, his expression bland.

I wasn't sure I wanted to know any more about what he was thinking. I did know that I wouldn't trust a man who had hidden a twin brother from government officials. That had to mean bad news. And I didn't want to consider what Hawk's future might hold since he now knew about Lee and his twin's cover up.

Hawk glanced towards the canyon, then shifted the rifle against his shoulder and turned. I stared at his back before starting after him.

"You know, you sort of destroyed our transportation when you trashed the car," I said as I followed. "How are we going to get out of here?"

"We worry about that when the time comes," he replied over his shoulder.

I sighed. I should have known he wouldn't tell me what he was planning. At least he was consistent.

We continued along the ridge, Hawk pausing often for long periods to study the ground. The sun rose higher, warming the thin atmosphere as morning grew to mid-day. I reached into my vest and retrieved a package of hard tack, and the resulting energy boost got me over the next ridge. I noticed that Hawk did not drop down into any of the shallow valleys. At regular intervals, he brought out the monocular and surveyed the area around us. We had drifted away from the ridge that held the cave, and a strong nagging sensation kept telling me to go back.

"Can we backtrack to the ridge where the cave was?" I asked during another one of our rests. I expected him to brush me off.

"Why?" He tipped the water bottle I had just drunk from and finished off the rest.

This time I was the one who didn't answer. As I gazed over the slopes, a small herd of elk appeared from underneath an aspen grove. When they paused to graze, everything looked peaceful, undisturbed.

The nagging feeling persisted, and I turned in the direction of the ridge, which now lay behind us, trying to identify the reason why I felt we needed to return to where we had spotted the cave.

"I don't know. I just have a strong feeling we should go back."

Hawk sighed. "Well, I've lost your husband's trail anyway. I'd hoped he continued along the higher ground, but I haven't picked up anything for the last hour."

We turned and made our way back with the same caution as earlier. Since the slopes we traversed were relatively gentle, my stamina remained strong, my breathing controlled. My mind began to wander as I followed Hawk. Was Mud Rain still alive? Had Angela's condition stabilized?

I couldn't handle the thought of either of them being dead, so I focused on memories of both of them alive and well.

The sun slipped into the western sky, and I began to dread spending yet another night in the wilderness. If all of us got out of this, we would spend a week at a spa.

"Do you go with your husband to the Reservation?" Hawk's question penetrated my thoughts. He had paused again and had the monocular out, directing his attention towards a thick grove of aspens below us.

"No…" I trailed off, thrown a little bit by his question. "I've gone with him a few times," I corrected.

"Why not?"

Good question, I thought. I didn't have a solid answer. "He always takes Mud Rain with him. They go at least once a year, to the annual Bear Dance that's held every spring."

"You're avoiding the question." Hawk lowered the monocular and studied my face, waiting for an answer.

"Jeremiah usually asks to go alone with Mud Rain. I'm probably considered an intruder, even though everyone's always really nice." I sounded defensive.

"What do you know of his background?"

I wondered why he seemed curious all of a sudden. "You mean before I met him?"

He nodded.

I shrugged. "He graduated from OU a few years before I did. Got his degree in meteorology. He grew up on the Southern Ute Reservation." I stopped. I knew there was a gap in his twenties that he had never explained. I had quit asking.

Hawk let the subject drop. We continued our way along the ridge and eventually reached the spot opposite the cave. I removed the cap from the zoom lens of my camera, focused in for a look. The afternoon sun shone almost straight at us, throwing shadow over every detail. I panned over the expansive rocky surface, then returned to the cave. I was about to lower the camera when I caught a shimmer of movement.

"Hawk, there's something in the cave," I whispered, unaware I had shifted to the cover of a pine tree. He crouched low, the scope already lined up with the cave, which would offer a natural home to any number of wild animals, so I told myself I had seen a coyote, a bear, or maybe a mountain lion.

We spotted it at the same time. A small face framed by a dark thatch of disheveled black hair. Just a quick glimpse against a rocky surface before it disappeared again into the dark recess.

Both of us also saw a small puff of dirt spit up not a foot away from the young boy's face before he darted back into the safety of the cave.

"Mud Rain," I whispered.

"Gary," Hawk murmured at the same time.

I examined the area around the cave. Gary had chosen well. Any possible cover lay at least two hundred yards away. There was no way to get to the cave without being seen.

And Gary could keep Jeremiah's brother trapped by sniping at him every time he tried to come out. It was a terrible game, and I suspected Gary had only one finish in mind. I looked around the base of the canyon but could not locate him. Beside me, Hawk muttered an oath.

"He's well camouflaged in the trees. I can't get a spot on him from here."

"Where is he?" I asked, still searching with the zoom.

Instead of answering, he lowered the rifle and backed deeper into the trees. I followed. Hawk leaned against the bark of a pine and regarded me with grim eyes.

"Well, we know where Mud Rain is. We also know your husband is likely in the area. He's had ample time to assess the situation."

"But if Jeremiah tries to get to the cave, he'll be in plain view. Gary can pick him off without a second thought," I whispered back.

Hawk nodded. "I suspect Gary has equipment should your husband try a nighttime approach." He lapsed into silence for several minutes. "That explains why he didn't take out your husband at the Jeep. Bloody bastard."

I glanced around as a faint awareness prickled the nape of my neck. "What do you mean?"

Hawk jerked his head in the direction of the cave. "He's playing cat-and-mouse. He could have easily killed that boy just now. He ought to have killed Jeremiah when he shot him through the windscreen. Evidently, he enjoys making sport with his victims." He paused, then added, "Did you snap a shot of Mud Rain?"

I nodded. "I got one just as Gary shot at him. I caught the puff of dirt, too."

"Brilliant." He nodded grimly. He didn't say why it was brilliant. He didn't have to. If Mud Rain didn't make it, I had evidence he had been alive on this mountain.

We were so preoccupied that neither of us heard the quiet footsteps behind us. Before either of us could react, rough hands shoved me away from Hawk and sent me sprawling to the ground. A blurred image leapt past me and onto Hawk's back, propelling him forward into a tumble down the steep slope. I stifled a scream as both figures rolled down the hill. At first I thought they were out of control, but then I realized Hawk's attacker was directing their fall. The two figures slid to a stop amidst a small cloud of dust. I gasped when I caught a clear view of the attacker's face.

Jeremiah.

Realization slammed in and I scrambled down the steep slope.

"Jeremiah! No!" I hissed, aware sound carried for miles in these mountains, and Gary was located just beyond the nearest crest.

My husband did not hear me. His left hand jammed Hawk's shoulder against the ground. In his right was his father's old semi-automatic. He whipped back the slide, then pressed the muzzle against the base of Hawk's skull. Frantic, I tried to think of something that would startle my husband into looking up.

"Black Bear!"

At the sound of his native name, Jeremiah's head jerked up, his black eyes staring coldly straight through me.

"Jeremiah! No! He's on our side!" I pleaded in a strained whisper. I jerked to a halt, frozen by the ferocity in his eyes. It was then I noticed his blood-soaked shirt, the bloody rag wound around his shoulder, the bloody bandage that circled his head. I wondered wildly whether his head injury had caused some sort of amnesia.

"Jeremiah," I coaxed softly. "It's me, Mattie."

His eyes narrowed with unmistakable recognition. I trembled under their hard, accusing stare.

"Who...is...he?" He spaced the words, his voice as deadly cold as his expression.

"He saved my life," I replied, keeping my voice soft.

Hawk had not stirred, and I wondered whether the fall had knocked him unconscious.

Jeremiah's attention returned to the man beneath him and the lethal muzzle pressing against the base of Hawk's skull. Terrifying seconds ticked by. I remained frozen in place, afraid to move, afraid to say anything because I didn't know what might spur my husband to shoot the man.

With deliberate movement, Jeremiah shifted the gun to the right, then gripped Hawk's right shoulder and rolled him onto his back. Hawk's eyes flickered and he appeared dazed as he lay motionless beneath my husband's weight. Jeremiah lowered the gun muzzle until it nestled against Hawk's Adam's apple, his eyes narrowing with unconcealed, murderous intent.

"You have thirty seconds," my husband whispered, "to explain what you are doing out here with my wife."

Chapter Seventeen

My initial shock of seeing Jeremiah alive vaporized days of anxiety into anger.

"You shoot him," I hissed, "And Gary's going to know we're here. It'll take thirty *minutes* to tell you what's been going on, since you never bothered to answer your damned cell phone!"

Jeremiah's eyes swung to me then back to Hawk. He stood slowly, keeping the muzzle of the gun steady. Hawk struggled to a sitting position, his movements slow, labored.

In the meantime, I was just warming up. "He probably heard the commotion you made anyway, crashing down the side of the mountain like that. After all the effort Hawk here has forced me to suffer through, you've made enough noise to scatter every living creature within ten miles!"

Hawk stumbled to his feet. The rifle on his shoulder jutted skyward, and I wondered whether the weapon had left bruises during his tumble down the mountain. When Jeremiah motioned with his gun, Hawk carefully removed the rifle and laid it carefully onto the ground. Jeremiah's expression was void of emotion. I slid down to the earth beneath one of the trees and watched the two men eye each other. Jeremiah's cold eyes swung to mine with such intensity, I was thankful I was sitting down.

"You should not be here. Gary will kill you, if he knows you are in the area."

I jerked my head in Hawk's direction and opened my mouth before thinking. "Well, after the near-death experiences with him I'm used to it." I managed to close it before blurting that he almost shot me in the middle of nowhere, came on to me in Joe's barn, and used me to bait an ambush.

Fresh blood oozed around the darkly stained socks that bound Jeremiah's head and the bloodstained T-shirt wrapped around his left shoulder. I realized he had used spare clothes from his gym bag for make-shift bandages. I remembered Hawk's comment about Jeremiah being more dangerous because he was wounded and silently admitted that he looked half crazed at the moment. I didn't give Hawk very good odds, so I decided I had better do something to try to defuse the tension.

"We ran into Joe Healing Water near one-sixty. Hawk met him. Joe gave him his rifle."

Jeremiah turned to Hawk. "You have met Joe?"

Hawk nodded, his expression looking more alert, though he swayed slightly on his feet. He had been holding Joe's rifle when Jeremiah attacked him, but now it was gone. I glanced up the slope and spotted a dull reflection against the red-brown earth about midway up the rocky surface. I rose to my feet.

"Leave it," Hawk muttered when he saw my movement.

At the sound of Hawk's voice, Jeremiah's eyebrows jerked upwards. "You are British." He sounded puzzled as he studied the man.

"Bloody astute of you," Hawk retorted, shifting his feet to a wider stance in an effort to steady himself.

Jeremiah glanced up to where the other rifle lay, then at Hawk. "You have been protecting her?"

Hawk nodded and slowly brought up a hand to massage the back of his neck.

Jeremiah watched him. "From Gary?"

Hawk released a slow sigh. "Among others." He threw me a look when he dropped his hand, and I remembered with a sharp thud of my heart the weapon tucked at the small of his back. Hawk's arms hung loose by his sides, and I realized that had Jeremiah been thinking clearly, he would have searched Hawk for weapons. Because of me, Jeremiah had made a lethal mistake and Hawk could kill him before I would be able to shout a warning.

Jeremiah's eyes narrowed. "Who?"

Hawk explained, but I was too preoccupied about what he might do to immediately realize something was going on between the two men. Gradually, I recognized that Hawk was using military jargon I'd heard on television but did not fully understand, summarizing events in a few curt sentences. I stared at Jeremiah, wondering whether he comprehended what Hawk said. Apparently he did because he studied me, then with a small nod lowered his handgun and tucked it into the waistband of his black jeans. Fearful, I glanced at Hawk and admitted to myself that I really didn't trust that man. Not at all.

With cat-like agility Jeremiah darted up the slope, plucked the second rifle off the ground, then cut to the right and back into the trees, all without a sound, not even a whisper of feet against the loose terrain. I watched in amazement until I lost his shadow among the trees. I whipped around and confronted Hawk.

"Just what did you say a minute ago?" I demanded, annoyed that the two men had omitted me from the conversation.

Hawk regarded me with shrewd eyes. "You neglected to mention that your husband has military background."

I was ready to retort I had no idea he was military when Jeremiah emerged, rifle in hand, from the tree trunks nearest us. He held Joe Healing Water's rifle out to Hawk. "He entrusted you with this."

Hawk gave him a surprised look but took the weapon, and reaching into his vest, pulled out several magazines, which he handed to Jeremiah. My husband tucked the magazines into what pockets he had, including the front of his denim shirt, which hung loosely over the black Polo shirt he wore, then picked up the other rifle and conducted a quick check. He glanced up, shot me a cold look the likes of which I had never experienced from him.

"Mattie, come with me." He spun on his heel and strode several paces into the trees.

I didn't understand his attitude towards me, his apparent anger over the fact that I was with him now. All the worry and fear of the last few days compacted into what would have rivaled a nuclear explosion.

But I had to stay calm. I reeled in the tantrum and sealed down the lid, then followed my husband through the trees. He stopped beneath a very skinny blue spruce. I came to a halt a few paces away. The muscles along his jaw clenched, the only outward sign of his anger. In all the time I had known him, Jeremiah had never shown even the slightest irritation towards me. All at once I felt a threat from him as potentially dangerous as Hawk.

"You're angry with me," I acknowledged, hoping that getting it out in the open would dispel some of his emotion.

"You should be home, not here," he accused.

"Yeah, well stewing about it won't make me magically disappear," I retorted. "I've traipsed over this damned mountain to find you, to make sure you were alive, and to help you get Mud Rain." Tears started down my cheeks, and I swiped at them with the sleeve of his leather jacket.

"You will not go near the face of that mountain," Jeremiah hissed, turning his cold, black eyes angrily towards Hawk.

"Shooting it out with him isn't going to make me magically disappear, either," I snapped, stepping between the two men. I didn't know how to convince Jeremiah to take me along and I didn't want to waste time thinking about it. My eyes wandered to his bloody shoulder, then to his bloody head, and pent-up emotion began cracking despite my efforts to control it. I swiped my face with the sleeve of his jacket again as tears started pouring down like a crack in the Hoosier Dam. "I...I thought you were dead...when I saw the Jeep ...I thought..."

Jeremiah stepped close and wrapped his good arm around me.

"How do we get to Mud Rain? How can we help Angela get well?" I choked out, leaning my head against his uninjured shoulder.

"We cannot help Angela," he murmured. "Your...friend and I will get to Mud Rain."

I lifted my head and met his eyes. "Yeah, well you better count me in. After everything I've been through, I'm not going to lay half-buried under another damned flipping rock."

God, his strength felt good. With shaking fingers that felt like icicles I touched the stiff bloody rag that wrapped his head, then the bloodied makeshift bandage around his shoulder. As I started to withdraw my hand, he caught my wrist and stared at the bandage wrapped around my palm. I held up my other hand.

"Twins," I shrugged for lack of anything better to say. "The cuts aren't deep, and Hawk's the one who's been tending to them." I stepped away when he released me and shrugged out of his leather jacket.

"Here. You need this a whole lot more than I do." I held it towards him. When he shook his head I gave him a rough shove. "Quit being so damned stubborn and put this on. I'm not the one wearing half my blood on my damned shirt." My voice shook. "Besides, I'm having a hard time looking at what Gary did to you."

Jeremiah relented, grimacing when he eased his left arm through the sleeve. He zipped up the front, then looked at me, a hint of a smile on his face. "Better?"

"Infinitely." I felt my expression relax. "All I need now is a beanie to hide your head."

Jeremiah's eyes met Hawk's. "This is not your battle."

Hawk shrugged. "You need back-up."

I chimed in. "Damned right you do. From both of us. Gary thinks you're alone out here, so that should give us at least some advantage. Right?"

My husband threw me another cold look. I could see the answer already in his face, but I plowed on anyway.

"Jeremiah, I can't handle not being able to help, and worse, not knowing what's happening. I'm an advantage. Use me. Tell me how to get over to the cave. While you and Hawk create a diversion with Gary, I'll get up to Mud Rain."

My statement earned a full two-second stare of disbelief.

"Absolutely not," he retorted.

I barged on anyway. "I've lost my parents because of Gary. And now my sister is critically ill because of him." I glanced at Hawk, then back to my husband. "Gary will focus on you. If I can get up to that cave, I can keep Mud Rain safe until one of you takes out Gary."

I'm not sending you out there without backup.

Joe Healing Water's words whispered inside my head. "Hawk can provide the kind of support you need to nail Gary, but it'll take all three of us to help Mud Rain."

I sensed the struggle in Jeremiah. My point about helping Mud Rain had gotten his attention.

"He needs only one shot, and you would not have means to protect yourself." He was talking himself out of the idea.

I jumped in. "Yes, I will. You and Hawk. You just need to find a way to distract him so he doesn't spot me when I make a break for the cave."

Jeremiah stared at me for what seemed like a long time. I got a strange sensation his spirit had penetrated my chest to beat next to my heart.

"*Please,*" I whispered. "I can't handle the thought of that man killing someone else I care about."

Hawk had remained silent during our exchange. I nodded in his direction. "Hawk is good. But it'll take both of you to flush out Gary."

Jeremiah's eyes narrowed intensely at mine, then swung to Hawk. I saw the expression the two men exchanged, sensed a hunter-like telepathy pass between them. He turned to me. "You will do exactly what I tell you, without argument."

I nodded. Jeremiah waved his hand. "I have until sunset to get to my brother. Follow me."

We made our way back towards the saddle-back Hawk and I

had traversed earlier, staying well below the crest. Jeremiah led the way, I followed, and Hawk brought up the rear. Both men kept rifles against their shoulders when we reached a cleft in the ridge that created a passageway through to the canyon. Crouching low, the three of us slowly made our way along the narrow ledge of a tremendously deep ravine until we reached the canyon wall that faced the side of the mountain with the cave. When Jeremiah raised a hand I stopped and peered over his shoulder. The eastern face of the mountain with the cave lay in growing shadows as the sun dipped towards the western horizon. Towering thunderclouds rose from behind the summit. Already the air had started to chill and a cool mountain breeze brushed my face. A horrid thought clenched my stomach.

Were we too late?

Jeremiah raised the rifle and peered through the scope for several silent minutes. Hawk crouched to his right and copied his actions.

"He is still there," my husband breathed, and from the obvious relief in his voice I realized he had feared Mud Rain was already dead.

Without any visual help, all I could see was a black hole on the face opposite us. I estimated that about a half mile separated us straight across. The trek down into the small valley and up the other side made the distance at least twice as long. A thick grove of aspens provided cover until the last two hundred yards.

Jeremiah faced me, his black eyes staring into mine, all emotion carefully concealed. "We will work our way to the north end of the canyon. Do not move for thirty minutes. After that, make your way down the valley and up the east side until you are level with the cave entrance, then wait at the tree line for my signal. I will watch you."

"How will I know when to head for the cave?" I whispered, acknowledging the need for silence now that we were in the canyon.

"I will fire my rifle to distract Gary. Gary and Hawk have silencers on their rifles. Once he knows I have better firepower, Gary will keep his attention on me."

Hawk nodded and murmured, "I'll move around and try for a shot while he's distracted."

Jeremiah was staring at me, and I knew he was fighting the image of me in clear sight on the side of the mountain. "When you hear my signal, sprint as quickly and with as little noise as possible. If

Gary spots you, I will warn you with two rapid shots and try to redirect his fire." He paused.

I gave him a grim nod. "Don't second-guess this, Jeremiah. Think of your brother."

His black eyes stared hard into mine. My attention turned to Hawk, who had slipped a hand into his vest and was pulling out a magazine. "Here. You'll want to load your handgun before you go anywhere."

Startled, I looked at him as he handed the magazine to me.

He shrugged. "Didn't want to risk you accidentally shooting yourself."

"Or turning the damned thing on you?" I asked, feeling more than a little stupid. I had forgotten about the handgun in my belt pack.

Without another word, both men turned and disappeared into the dark shadows of the scraggly pines. I stared across the chasm that separated me from Mud Rain and prayed to God to keep all of them safe. I glanced at my watch. Six-thirty. Jeremiah had said to wait for thirty minutes. I peered down the steep incline to my left at swaying pines that thrust into the thin air, their dwarfed branches sticking out from skinny trunks. Evergreens were ugly at this altitude, there was no getting around it. They were nothing like the majestic hardwoods that grew down in Oklahoma. The aspen groves were little better, but at least they looked prettier.

Oklahoma. Home. Those thoughts forced to mind facts I had been trying to ignore.

Jeremiah had known who Gary was at the funeral and had told neither Angela nor me about him.

And why would my husband hide a military background from me?

No mail, no calls, no contact from any military establishment had ever crossed our doorstep. He had purposefully hidden a former identity from me. Just like Gary Tacque had hidden who he was from Angela and the rest of us.

Just like Max would have hidden his involvement with an international assassin network from his family, including the redheaded young boy asleep on his chest.

I flinched at the comparison and glanced at my watch again. Six thirty-five. Only five minutes? I stared at the second hand to make sure the damned thing was working, then gave myself a violent shake. Now was not the time to be casting stones at Jeremiah's behavior. I needed to be figuring out a way down the mountain.

I surveyed possible routes into the valley and then across to the tree line on the opposite slope. My efforts were mostly worthless, as I could not see the terrain further than about fifty yards down. No way to know what kind of obstacles I faced.

The heaviness of my belt pack pulled my attention to what I had forgotten lay under the zoom lens.

Should I take the handgun out and keep it ready? I stared at the magazine I still held in my hand. Memories of how easily the thing went off and the raucous noise convinced me otherwise. Best leave it alone. I tucked the magazine into my belt pack, then glanced again at my watch.

Six thirty-nine.

Thirst, hunger, fatigue, fear. I had lost count of how many days now all four had been my constant company. Mud Rain would be feeling them, too.

The thought of that poor boy's situation galvanized my determination. I fumbled around the various vest pockets and took inventory of their contents. Then I tucked everything back into the pockets of my vest, removed the lens cap from my camera, and took a closer look at the approach to the cave.

If I was going to make it to Mud Rain, I needed to start thinking like Jeremiah and Hawk.

Chapter Eighteen

Impatience won out. I packed the lens into the belt pack, snugged the camera across the vest, and climbed off the ledge into the trees. I descended on hands and feet, my palms stinging with the pressure despite the bandages. But the four-point stance kept me low and in firm contact with the ground, and I sought cover from the trees as much as possible. I could not afford to slip and slide halfway down the mountain. Noise would echo plainly in the thin air.

Twenty minutes later I traversed an easier slope, midway between the cleft from where I had started and the floor of the valley. I was making good time, my legs felt strong, though my head throbbed, probably residual effects of the concussion combined with the high altitude.

I ran into problems trying to reach the tree line below the cave. A deep wash spiked with boulders and jagged rocks cut a widening tear down the slope. Out of breath, I gulped in air as I surveyed the ravine. It narrowed further up the hill, but I seriously doubted I was fast enough to make the detour and still make the tree line in time. I looked at my sneakers and grimaced, longed for the millionth time for my sturdy hiking boots, then maneuvered my way down into the rift, picking my way around jagged, jutting rocks, hoping the thunderclouds wouldn't crest the summit with a rainstorm and send a flash flood my way. The sun dipped inexorably towards the western horizon. Impatience ground away with increasing pressure.

By some miracle, I made it to the opposite side of the ravine without injury or a rainstorm and clawed my way to the top. Significantly cooler air washed over me, and I glanced up and saw dark clouds thickening over the bald crest of the mountain. Pausing deep within the trees, I listened to the soft whisper of evergreens and aspens. The wind currents carrying the clouds over the summit had not reached the valley, and I hoped that the incongruity meant the storm system was not yet developed enough to bring rain. Please, not an afternoon storm. Not now. Rain in these mountains at this altitude meant flash flooding down steep inclines, dangerous lightning and rapid hypothermia. I shivered as the colder air eddied around me. Maybe the clouds would hunker over the summit and hide the cave and my approach. After all, I silently prayed, was it too much to ask to hold off on the wet stuff until I made it to the cave?

I peered at the rocky cave entrance. Gary could not have chosen a better place to stash his hostage. Crumbling granite made the terrain between the tree line and the cave impossible to cross without making all kinds of noise. There was not a single bit of cover. The slope climbed steeply from the tree line for the first hundred yards, then leveled out. The last twenty yards or so ran almost flat, creating a slender ledge to the entrance. Once I reached the safety of the cave and found Mud Rain, finding another way out would be our first priority. While Gary guarded this opening, he could not watch other accesses. And he obviously had banked on the fact Jeremiah's little brother would not understand the necessity of finding another way out. I scanned the northern side of the canyon as encroaching shadows darkened the valley and the increasing clouds hid the late afternoon sun. A hawk screeched somewhere overhead, echoing against the canyon walls. Where I stood, the tree line marched in lines so straight they seemed artificially created.

Could either Jeremiah or Hawk see me? Should I step from the trees? What would they do in my place?

They would stay hidden, I reasoned. Jeremiah knew where to look for me. If I stayed at the edge of the trees, he would spot me. I would not risk stepping out into the open, not with Gary in the vicinity.

Between the cave entrance and where I stood, the steep barren incline rose like a great rock giant, daring me to cross its treacherous stretch. The dangerous terrain was a slide waiting to happen. A slide would create noise.

Noise meant death.

Stay here, in the trees. You'll be safe.

But staying in the trees meant death for Mud Rain and Jeremiah, I reminded myself coldly. I hated the panic that threatened. My fingers tingled, my knees felt stiff, awkward. The vest dragged at my shoulders, focusing my attention sharply on the extra weight I carried.

Should I remove the vest and leave it here in the trees? I would be able to run much better without it.

I remembered Hawk's comment about the Kevlar's limited

protection against bullets. Well, I reasoned, limited protection was better than no protection at all, even if it meant dragging extra weight when I made my break for the cave. I glanced down at my belt pack and camera. I could at least take those off. I unzipped the belt pack and removed the handgun and the magazine, then found a vest pocket to store them in. Then I unsnapped the belt pack from my waist and laid it and the camera at the base of a pine. If things went well, I would come back and retrieve them later. I closed my eyes and focused on the image of Mud Rain's face, then pictured myself climbing up the rocky surface, watching where I placed each foot, moving quickly, silently, just like Jeremiah had when he re-trieved the rifle earlier.

I jumped when the hard crack of a rifle shot echoed around the canyon, jarring my heart into the base of my throat.

Don't think. Just run.

I hit the open face of the mountain as Jeremiah's signal faded with eerie echoes down the valley. My worthless sneakers slipped on the granite. The moment I felt my footing shift, I sprang forward another step. In theory, that should have meant I could maintain momentum.

In reality, I ended up on my hands and knees more than on my feet. The brittle rock slipped beneath me and rattled down the slope, picking up pebbly companions and creating all kinds of noise. The vest hampered my agility. I scrambled, hit a section of solid rock, scrambled another twenty yards.

Jeremiah's rifle cracked again. Was Hawk firing at Gary, too? I wouldn't hear his rifle because of the silencer. I wouldn't hear Gary's rifle, either. Would Jeremiah or Hawk be able to neutralize Gary's weapon? Would they have to kill him? Gary had no idea two men were after him. Surely, that increased the odds in our favor.

My lungs ached, I couldn't get any air. A glance up towards the cave told me I hadn't even made a third of the distance yet.

Faster, go faster.

My imagination started working against me. I pictured Jeremi-ah dead among the trees, Hawk dead, too. When I pictured myself lifeless just outside the mouth of the cave, I almost sobbed.

Another shot rang out.

Not two shots, I prayed. *Please, don't let me hear two shots.*

I kept throwing out another foot, taking another leap. A stiff headwind suddenly swirled around me, slowing me down, impeding rather than helping. Another ten yards and I hit crumbling granite again. I didn't fall as much this time because the terrain had leveled out.

I glanced up. The cave was closer. I had covered over half the distance.

Another shot cracked, the ominous echo bouncing off rocky walls, dying as it traveled down the canyon. I wondered why Jeremiah was still shooting, and thought with a jolt that Gary might be trying to reach a position to fire at the cave. Jeremiah was still firing single shots, letting me know he was protecting me, helping me to reach the cave entrance and his younger brother.

His continued shots also meant that Gary still posed a threat.

My feet slipped again, and I landed hard on my hands and knees, brutally jarring my attention back to the mountainside as the impact stung my palms and other recent injuries still trying to heal. I scrambled up and pushed my tiring legs another stride.

Thunder rumbled with ominous proximity. I glanced towards the cave, stumbled, felt my lungs cramping in the thin altitude, tried to go faster. Adrenaline hurtled through me. I was going to make it.

The violent report of Jeremiah's rifle rang through the canyon.

A second shot split into the first echo.

Even before I heard the second report, I knew. Instinct screamed primal alarms. I could almost physically feel Gary's rifle pointing at me.

With a splintering *snap*, my right leg buckled underneath me in an explosion of pain so intense I saw brilliant stars. I fell full force onto the side of the mountain, my face and chest crashing hard onto the granite. I choked and writhed, my throat convulsing. Every fiber of my body shrieked. I started to slide off the small ledge onto the steep slope that would send me plummeting down the side of the mountain. At the last moment, I gripped a jagged, stable rock with my fingers. My right leg dangled, useless.

Lightning sizzled, then cracked in a hard concussion, the brilliant flash momentarily blinding me. Ozone assaulted my nostrils, and I knew the bolt had struck nearby.

Get up! I begged through painful gasps. My muscles quivered, too shocked to respond. I tried again, but could not get anything to move. Two more shots rang out. Another explosive crack of thunder shook the ground as lightning flashed. Cold, fat drops of water splattered down around me, and my weather experience warned of the possibility that hail was on the way. I lay there, utterly helpless, knowing Gary had me in his crosshairs, and in a few minutes, I would probably be dead either from his bullet or from a hailstorm. I heard the pounding approaching, then gasped with surprised relief when cold, hard rain fell in a dense gray curtain, soaking me within seconds, hiding me from Gary's crosshairs.

With agonizing gasps I pulled my left leg underneath me and worked my way into a wobbly three-point stance on my palms and left knee. I squinted through the pouring rain and saw the yawning cave mouth barely ten yards away.

Fighting the faintness in my head, I started to move. Sight faded to black again when my shattered knee banged against the hard rock. Nausea rose hard and fast. Retching, choking, coughing, my insides tried to heave themselves right out of my mouth. I clawed forward a few inches, choking on acidic bile that burned my throat. Rain pounded my face and body with ruthless intensity.

No closer. I wasn't getting any closer. Could Gary see well enough to shoot me again? Any minute, and the rain might taper just enough to allow him another chance. All he needed was one more chance. If the storm cleared I would be completely exposed. Had he intended to maim? Would he kill me, or put a bullet through my other knee?

Why in the hell hadn't Jeremiah or Hawk shot him?

Visions of corpses wove through slipping awareness as I inched forward on my hands and my left knee, trying to maintain a line towards the black hole. Another streak of pain ripped through my body and a soul-wrenching sob escaped my lips, the sound lost amid the downpour. Another lurch…another sob…God, another slam of pain so hideous, every muscle fiber threatened to seize. My eyesight went black. The cold, gray torrent made the rock slick as glass. I glanced up again, trying to see through the downpour.

The black hole beckoned.

I wriggled closer. I thought I heard Jeremiah whisper.

Just a few more feet.

He couldn't have made it to the cave before me, could he? Was I hallucinating? Or had Gary shot him and now his spirit was hovering over me? My hands reached the opening, then my arms. With agonizing slowness, I twisted and pulled the rest of me into blessed cover, out of the rain.

Away from Gary's rifle.

I had not heard any more shots. Or maybe I couldn't hear them because of the storm. The rain had hidden me from Gary, but it also now blinded everyone with a rifle. Would the rain cause a misfire? Would Jeremiah or Hawk use the rain to sneak closer to get a better shot? Or had Gary done the same thing and permanently silenced my husband?

I lay there, gasping, sobbing, cursing every word I could think of and making up a fair share in order to chase away the pain, panic and blackness. Lightning sizzled and thunder crashed again as rain pounded the outside of the cave. I shivered uncontrollably in my wet clothes. God, it felt as though my whole right leg was on fire.

I reached out with shaking hands and pulled myself along my left side until I butted against the cave wall. I lay there, my back against the cold rock, my head swimming with dizziness so intense that I thought the world would explode.

"Mud ...." My voice broke. I cleared my throat and tried again. "Mud Rain!"

The thunderstorm outside drowned both the sound of my voice and any answer Mud Rain might have attempted from deeper in the cave.

Despite the whirling in my head, I pushed my arms beneath me and tried to lever myself into a sitting position. Horrid pain shot through every fiber and I collapsed hard onto the rocky cave floor.

I wasn't going anywhere with a shattered leg. Gary would make it to the cave soon, and then he would shoot me and Mud Rain. He had already killed Hawk and Jeremiah....

"*STOP IT!!!*" My voice echoed weakly against the rock. My head felt like it would spin right off my shoulders.

I yelled with pain, frustration. The sound came out guttural, animalistic. The dizziness lessened and the pain seemed to shrink just the tiniest bit. Resolve seeped into my weak arms and I pushed myself into a sitting position with my back against the wall, my oaths and guttural shouts growing stronger with repetition. I strained to see into the darkness, hoping to pick up some small movement that would indicate that Mud Rain was close by, possibly too scared by the sight and sounds of me to respond.

Empty blackness stared back. Even if Mud Rain were near, he wouldn't be able to help me. I was supposed to have come to help *him*. Thanks to my murderous brother-in-law, I was useless.

You're going to die out here. Shock and blood loss. No hope. Hawk and

Jeremiah are dead, you'll soon be dead, Gary has won….

I swore, vilely, violently, and steeled myself to look at my leg.

Blood soaked the cloth from the knee down. Okay, I'm bleeding, I thought. I need to stop it. Think.

First aid pack.

My numb fingers fumbled around with vest pockets, my teeth chattering so hard I thought I would bite my tongue. Great. The shock from blood loss was getting worse, and my soaking wet clothes were not helping the situation. Between the two, my odds of survival probably rated less than zero. I located the red nylon First Aid case and pulled out a small pair of scissors and a slender package that felt like it had sand in it. I bent forward, found the hole where the bullet had pierced the fabric, worked my finger into it, and began cutting the cloth away with the scissors. I squinted at the instructions on the packet, then tore it open with my teeth and poured the contents over the bloody mess that had been my knee. I gasped as sudden, blinding pain seared right through my leg, ripped an agonizing sound from my throat, then slammed blackness down.

~ * ~

The sound of trickling water woke me up. Something cold pressed hard against the left side of my face. I tried to open my eyes, saw nothing but black, closed them again. Distant thunder rumbled, and I vaguely remembered running, feeling pain ripping through my leg, falling…falling….

When I became aware again, absolute silence surrounded me. Memory seeped back. I was in a cave, crumpled over on my left side. It felt pleasantly numb, lying this way.

Cold, still cold.

Something snagged the fingers of my right hand. Curious, I bent my elbow, bringing my hand close to my face. A pair of scissors bumped my nose.

Oh, yeah. I had been cutting my way through the jeans leg and then had poured some kind of stuff into the bullet wound. Holy shit, the instructions hadn't warned about how awful it would feel. I lay there on the cold, dry earth, wondering what I was doing here. I had to find something…someone….

"Mud Rain!" Fear and urgency choked my words. My voice seemed to bounce back at me with a bluntness that did not echo.

Where was Mud Rain? Had he been shot, too? Was Gary near?

What would I do if he suddenly appeared in the cave?

Angela and I had been brought up around compassion and honesty, helping those who needed help. I'd never experienced the side of Life that rips out humanity, leaving only the merciless, vicious wolves hiding within sheepskin personalities, stalking the weak and the unaware.

Gritting my teeth, I pushed myself upright until I could lean my head against the cold rock wall, then forced my attention back to wreckage that had once been a leg.

"For the amount of hurt that stuff caused, it had better have worked," I muttered. I peered down. No evidence of continued bleeding. I leaned forward and used the scissors to cut through what was left of the material, exposed the extent of the damage. I started trembling all over again, and the dizziness returned. The bullet had missed my knee, impacting instead on the bone just below the joint. It was a clean break, although the white of the bone was showing through a gash in the skin. I slid back down on my side, closed my eyes, and tried not to think about what I had just seen.

Okay, so my leg's broken. At least the bleeding stopped. Dark red, jelly-like clots crowded around the gash in my leg. The sight brought back memories of the faceless, bloody corpse on the mountainside, then the headless corpse of our neighbor, splattered clumps of brain matter and bone fragments all over their back porch all those years ago.

Ick. Ick, ick, ick. Why had I tried to become a photojournalist when I couldn't stand the sight of anything gory and destructive? If I ever got out of this alive, I would take pictures of flowers, happy people, lots of sunshine. To hell with real life and news.

At the moment, what I needed most was some help.

"MUD RAIN!" I yelled through gritted teeth. Where was that kid? I had to find him, but in order to do that I needed mobility. The only way to achieve that was to make some sort of splint long enough to reach from my thigh to my foot. With a splint and a makeshift crutch, I might be able to limp around. I remembered the ibuprofen in the First Aid kit and retrieved four of them, swallowing them down with my spit. I listened for movement in the shadows.

The silence was absolute. Wherever Mud Rain was, he wasn't close. Nor were there any sounds of wildlife, not even bats. My thoughts returned to Mud Rain, and I refused to consider any possibilities other than the one assuming he was alive.

Think. Solve the problem. My thought processes unlocked and an idea began to form. I could use strips of the jeans material to pad the break and hold the clots in place. But I would need something hard to act as a splint. I sat up, rummaged through the pockets of the vest and came up with a small roll of duct tape and a small flashlight. The bright LCD beam gave me a jolt of mental strength, and I began searching the dirt floor nearby for something that would make a suitable splint. As I swung the beam around, the bright light revealed several dried wood fragments. I inched my way over to the cluster of branches and chose two pieces roughly the diameter and length I needed. I fashioned and applied a splint, using the cloth to wrap the site of the break. The exertion warmed my limbs. Duct tape wound tightly around the two sticks and my leg. I reached for another sturdy-looking stick. Using it for support, I struggled to my feet. With an exhausted sigh, I leaned against the cold rock and closed my eyes, listening to the silence outside.

A coyote howled, then several more. The yipping abruptly ceased when the lower, longer cry of a wolf echoed around the canyon. How ironic, I mused, shivering as the sound died, that it was the human predator I feared the most right now.

With that thought came the worry Gary might be making his way to the cave now that the rain had stopped. Stiff and shivering, I braced one hand against the rock wall and clung to the walking stick with my other. I found I could shuffle along fairly well with the makeshift crutch. Pain still shot up my leg, but with less intensity than earlier, and I figured the ibuprofen had kicked in. I bent over and picked up the flashlight. I needed to find Mud Rain.

I had neither seen nor heard a sign of the boy. Reluctantly, I faced the options. Had he run back into the cave and injured himself? Had he found another way out?

With the flashlight jammed into my left armpit, I limped along the passageway, the damp air chilling my already wet clothes.

"Mud Rain?" I called out, not too loudly because I didn't want an echo to frighten him. As I limped along, the light revealed cylindrical holes high up in the wall at regular intervals, proof that miners had used dynamite to blast through the rock, and I realized the cave was really an abandoned mine. I limped a good hundred yards along the tunnel, then stopped and shut off the flashlight.

Utter blackness wrapped around me. Not a breath stirred. No shuffling feet, no shortened breathing. Not even a solitary animal sound disturbed the silence. Strange as it might seem, I heard better with the light off, so every few yards, I sank myself into darkness to listen. I continued further down the rounded passageway, feeling totally isolated from the rest of the world.

The floor sloped suddenly downward, and I misjudged my next step and toppled over onto my face. Pain scorched up my leg, through every fiber. My curses bounced off the tunnel walls. I struggled to sit up, then leaned against the rock, my forehead breaking out in a cold sweat. I turned off the flashlight, felt darkness wrap around me like a thick cape. I wondered how far this tunnel went and began to worry why I hadn't yet found Mud Rain.

A sound trickled across my ears. I held my breath, unable to identify the soft, continuous noise. The sound echoed gently...not behind...in front...?

Water.

I turned the flashlight back on and directed the beam toward the sound. The floor of the cave dipped several feet, then disappeared. Scooting along, I followed the noise down the slight decline, holding the light steady as I went. When the floor leveled out, a small stream trickled along the left side, curled around another gentle slope in the dirt, and wandered off down a tunnel to my left. My spirits leapt.

The water was not pooling. That had to mean there was another way out.

I shone the light around. Additional passages veered off into the darkness. It would be too easy to get lost down here. God only knew how long these other passages went, or how many passages branched off of each of these. If this area had been mined for a while, prospectors could have dug numerous holes to follow whatever veins they came across. I had to find a way to mark my way, give myself a trail to follow back to the main entrance.

I went through more pockets of the vest and found a tube of phosphorescent paint. Thanking Hawk for his insistence I wear the vest, I unscrewed the cap from the tube, squeezed a generous amount of paint onto my finger, then wiped it around the tunnel I had just come through. I repeated the action until a thin white line of paint glowed eerily in the darkness. I grinned, absurdly pleased with myself. When I came back to this juncture, the paint would show me the way. I wiped my fingers clean on my jeans. Then, using the wall as support, I clicked off the flashlight, leaned on the stick, and listened.

The gurgle of the stream echoed all around me and I realized if Mud Rain had followed the sound of the water, he would not hear my calls. Unfortunately, that also meant I could not locate him by voice. With so many branches to choose from, how in the world would I ever find the one Mud Rain used?

Follow the water.

I started to flick the light back on, then paused. In the otherwise absolute blackness, a ghostly, wispy white mist floated against the ceiling, as moisture from the small stream condensed in the cool air of the tunnel. The mist lay absolutely still, silent proof there were no drafts. I flicked the flashlight on, and the mist faded. I turned the light off, wondering why the mist was more visible in the darkness. I watched the phenomenon for a while, checking for any signs of circulation, but the mist remained absolutely still.

No drafts meant no air circulation.

No air circulation meant no other exits.

Chapter Nineteen

I found Mud Rain about fifty yards from the tunnel junctures. He must have followed the sound of the water, using the wall that led him into a small recess originally used as a shelter when miners dynamited the rock. The beam of the flashlight first revealed a couple of large rusted metal blast shields, then his small, huddled figure. When the flashlight beam illuminated him, I thought I had started hallucinating. I swung the light back to the small form tucked tightly against the wall. A pair of frightened black eyes in a hollow, white face stared back.

"Mud Rain? Mud Rain, its Mattie." I kept my voice low and shone the beam on myself so that he could see me.

"Maddie." His hoarse, shaking voice echoed eerily with the gurgling water. His small frame unfolded, and I backed against the wall for support when he threw thin arms around my waist. Damp, dirty, tangled black hair hung around his face and neck as he clung to me with desperate strength.

"I'm here." I dropped both the flashlight and my walking stick, and circled his shaking body with my arms.

"Big noise, big noise," he cried, and I realized why he had fled into the depths of the tunnel. Mud Rain became hysterical whenever he heard thunder. When the storm came over the mountain he had run to get away from the sound. The water would have soothed him, so he had followed it.

"It's all right now." I continued holding him, waiting for the shock of seeing me to wear off.

"Ang-ie," he mumbled against my sweatshirt.

"You were really brave to go with Angela."

The warmth of Mud Rain's body helped lessen the chill of mine, and he seemed content hugging me, so we just stood there, absorbing each other's presence in the dimly lit tunnel. I left the light on because I was afraid the darkness would upset him.

When he pulled away, he looked down and pointed a grimy finger at my splinted leg. "Owwie. You have owwie."

"Yes, I hurt my leg. But I'm okay." I smiled down at him. "Are you hungry?"

He nodded. He was fourteen, stood just under five feet tall, had the mental development of a first-grader. He had on blue jeans, an OU T-shirt, and OU high-top leather basketball shoes that had probably been very new and very white before Gary had snatched him.

I fished around the vest until I located the packets of GU. I tore one open and handed it to him. "Suck on it. It's good. Like Jell-O."

Mud Rain took a tentative taste, and his face screwed up into a wide grin. He sucked down the rest, held out his palm for a second one. He handed me the empty packages, which I stored in my vest. Then I pulled out a plastic bag from among the seemingly endless vest pockets.

"Go fill this with some water." I handed it to him, then shone the light towards the stream so he could see where he was going. He walked over and squatted, his movements deliberate, as though he was holding a fragile piece of crystal. When the bag was full, he rose and walked carefully back. I dropped a tablet into the water, waited until it had dissolved, then stirred the contents with my pinky finger, since it seemed the only one on either hand that was relatively clean.

"Drink some. Not too much, or you'll get a tummy-ache."

He did as instructed, then handed the rest to me. I finished it off and folded the bag into a pocket, thinking of Hawk and the way he had made sure I stayed hydrated during our trek through the mountains. He had been a good teacher. I prayed desperately he and Jeremiah were still alive.

Ignoring the message of the mist still hovering above us, I pointed in the direction the stream ran. "Let's go this way. Maybe there's a way out."

There *had* to be another opening.

Without a word, Mud Rain took the flashlight and directed the beam in the direction I pointed, slipped his free, small, hand into my left one, and stayed at my side as I limped my way along the passageway. His blind trust in me steadied my nerves. The stream gurgled along, providing a strange sense of comfort. The rocky passage did not narrow or widen, and I marveled at the determination of whoever had blasted their way through this mountain to create so many tunnels. Then again, greed was a powerful motivator.

So was my survival instinct.

Because we couldn't see anything to gauge either time or distance, I lost track of both. At regular intervals I asked Mud Rain to shut off the light. Each time, darkness enveloped us like a living creature, but all my ears picked up was the gurgling of the small stream. Try as I might, I could not detect any change in the pitch of the running water.

Doubt began nudging in. Surely there had to be an alteration in the pitch and flow of the water soon. I started rationalizing why we weren't seeing a lightening of the absolute darkness around us. I didn't think I would see an opening while it was dark outside, and clouds might very well be hiding the moon. I clung to those thoughts and ignored the irritating voice that asked why I hadn't noticed a change in air quality, or the presence of a breeze, or a drop in the pitch of the trickling water. We continued along the tunnel, blackness always just ahead.

At last, the pitch of the water dropped, the trickling slowed. I stopped, my relief so intense I forgot about the pain in my leg. "Mud Rain, shine the light on the water."

He shined the beam downward, and I felt like dancing when I saw the small stream had widened.

"Turn it off for a moment." Once again utter darkness surrounded us. The gurgling was now a whisper, and seemed to fade altogether a little further on. I stared hard at the blackness in front of us, expecting to see a change in density.

The encroaching blackness remained thick as ever.

I put a hand on Mud Rain's arm. "Let me have the light for a minute. Hold onto my shirt and don't move." I flicked the light back on and shined the beam ahead of us, wishing it reached fifty yards instead of five.

"Stay right behind me, Mud Rain." I limped forward, sweeping the light along the wall and then across the floor. Mud Rain's small fist clung to the back of my sweatshirt.

Black oil appeared suddenly, oozing across the entire width of the floor from wall to wall. We seemed to have left the manmade tunnel and entered some sort of natural chamber, which didn't make any sense to me at all. Confused, I shone the light along the stream, allowing the beam to follow its progress until it disappeared into the oil.

Not oil, but water…a pool.

A very black, very large, very still pool. Alarms clanged in my head, and I searched the ground for something to throw. Laying down my makeshift staff, I reached for a rock about the size of my hand. After a slight hesitation, I tossed it underhanded towards the middle of the pool.

An ominously deep *ker-pluunk* echoed around us. Frustrated disbelief surged to uncontrollable levels. Even if there was an exit further down, we had no way of getting there. There was no way I could swim across, not with my injured leg, and I wasn't about to let Mud Rain try, even though he was a strong swimmer for his age. Not to mention the temperature of the water this deep inside the mountain probably hovered around freezing.

All of which meant we had to go back.

At that moment, the flashlight flickered and perceptibly dimmed. I slid down to the ground and fought back the urge to cry.

"Mud Rain, stay with me," I said, though he had not moved from my side. Images of him running towards the black water and falling in whirled through my head.

"Sit down here beside me." My voice shook despite my efforts. Obediently, he sat down.

As the beam of light flickered and weakened, I remembered the penlight I had used to light the inside of the phone booth. I rummaged through the vest pockets. No penlight.

I emptied pockets, searching, trying to maintain outward composure even though inside I was falling apart. I pulled everything out and laid it carefully onto the ground in front of me, squinting in the rapidly fading light, feeling panic churn my stomach as I sought to find the pen light. My fingers groped through pockets and the warmer of my hoody with increasing alarm.

Where was the penlight?

I patted all the pockets of my jeans. The last time I had wanted it was in the middle of that cow field, and it hadn't been in the warmer of my hoody. Closing my eyes and feeling the pit of my stomach drop a couple of floors, I remembered thinking about looking for it when I got back to the car....

"Bad! *Bad-bad-bad-bad!*" Mud Rain jumped up, his small hands flailing in the weakening light. In horror I watched him scoop up the handgun, fling his arm back, then throw the weapon away from him with every ounce of strength in his small thin body.

"NO!" My cry came too late. I watched our only means of defense go sailing through the encroaching shadows. The gun arched

over the black water, then raced downwards. With a sickening splash
it hit the surface and disappeared. Mud Rain turned white-rimmed
eyes to me.

"Mud Rain…" I clamped down on the scolding I wanted to
give, tried to maintain outward calm as my insides imploded.

Why, why, *why* hadn't I had enough presence of mind to realize the sight of the gun would set him off? He understood enough to
know what the weapon represented. I struggled to hide the tears.
Seeing me cry would only upset him further.

Mud Rain sank back down at my feet and gave me a look of
pride for getting rid of something he thought endangered us both.
With trembling fingers, I stowed away the now useless magazine
along with the other items, then struggled to my feet. Mud Rain
picked up the weakening flashlight and whacked it against the palm
of his hand a couple of times, which did no good whatsoever. He
looked at me, then held out the flashlight.

"You fix."

"We'd better head back." I didn't try to explain why the light
was fading. I barely kept my voice steady as it was. I didn't want him
to pick up on the fear in my voice if I tried to say anything else.

The flashlight gave out before we reached the main juncture.
Mud Rain was walking in front of me, guiding the way. I hadn't
thought to time my progress to gauge the distance I traveled, so I
had no idea how much further we had to go. If Hawk or Jeremiah
had been with me, they certainly would have been on top of something that important.

Mud Rain whimpered when the light flickered and died, and I
heard him hitting the thing against the palm of his hand again.

"Wand lighd back." His voice was low, scared. His trembling
hand found mine.

"I do, too." I gave his hand a reassuring squeeze. "Stay behind
me and hang onto my shirt." I guided him until he was behind me,
then pressed his left hand to the wall and felt him take a fist full of
my damp sweatshirt.

I tried to crouch as I felt along the wall, but maintaining that
kind of position was difficult with a splinted leg, and I kept banging
my head against the low tunnel ceiling. Panic hovered like a black
specter, growing more powerful each time I smacked my head. I felt
like we were enclosed in a tomb. What if we never made it out? I
shoved away thoughts of doom and death, slamming mental doors

on the raw terror that threatened to cripple my sanity.

I thought my eyes were seeing things at first when a pale circle broke the absolute blackness. As I stopped to stare at it, brain cells reluctantly chugged out the reason.

Thank God for phosphorescent paint.

Limping against the wall in a sideways crabwalk, I felt along the cold rock with my left hand, tracing the luminous circle with a finger. I couldn't tell whether the utter blackness in front of me was solid rock wall or the opening to another tunnel. Tentatively, with Mud Rain in tow, I took a step forward, then another step, following the rocky, uneven floor that was still under my feet.

I stumbled when the floor slanted upwards, and Mud Rain's grip on the back of my sweatshirt save me from a painful face plant. I sat down on the ground, turned around, and instructed Mud Rain to pull my shirt as we worked our way up the small incline. I had to drop my walking stick and use both hands to lever myself up, pushing with my left leg, making sure the walking stick stayed between the wall and me. The cuts on my palms definitely did not appreciate the exertion. When I planted both hands on the wall to my left and turned my head over my shoulder, I couldn't believe what my eyes saw.

A tiny, miniscule pinpoint of light shone against the blackness. It was the mouth of the cave. But why could I see it if it were still dark? I glanced at my watch. Four a.m. The moon must be out.

"See the light? We'll be out of here before long." As an afterthought, I added, "The noise is gone, Mud Rain. No noise now."

Please, God, no more gunshots, either.

We stood again when I felt the floor level out, but uncontrollable shivering made it difficult to hold onto the walking stick. I kept knocking the top of my head against the rocky ceiling. Very slowly, the pinprick grew to a dot, then to the size of a pupil.

Why couldn't it start getting bigger faster? Where was Jeremiah? He should have followed me into the cave, I thought as fear stabbed again. Had Gary killed him? Had Hawk killed Gary?

Had Gary killed them both and was now waiting for us at the cave entrance?

Maybe we would have been better off staying with the stream. We could have followed it and found the source. Getting lost in the bowels of the mountain seemed infinitely more appealing than facing a bullet, especially from someone who enjoyed inflicting pain before death.

My shivering stopped and I started feeling warm again, finally. Sleep beckoned, and I thought that perhaps we should lie down and get our strength back before we went any further.

"Maddie. Maddie, wake up."

Mud Rain's voice seemed close to my ear. A small hand tugged at my shoulder. Pain ground through my bones as I pulled my hands towards my face, tried to lift my head from the dirt floor.

"It's okay." My words came out in a croak. I coughed and tried again. "I'm okay."

"You faw down. Wake up now." He shook me.

"I'm awake. Thanks." I struggled to a sitting position. I couldn't stop shivering. I felt around for the walking stick, found it, then glanced towards the small dot of gray light and wondered whether I should try scooting along the ground instead of limping.

"Up, Maddie, up." Mud Rain's hands gripped my shirt as he tried to pull me to my feet.

So much for scooting.

I gritted my teeth, pressed my left hand on the rock wall, gripped the stick with my right hand, pushed myself to my left knee. Each movement took enormous effort. My head started to spin, and I waited an eternity before things settled. I couldn't get off my left knee without using my right leg. My arms just didn't have the strength.

Small hands pushed my right hip, so that it was Mud Rain who helped me make it shakily to my feet.

"Wawk, Maddie. Wawk." His voice did not echo in the tunnel, and his single-mindedness gave me strength.

Leaning on the stick and bracing against the wall, I shuffled towards the light again. Mud Rain's hands stayed in constant contact, steadying me when I wavered, always pulling me another step towards the growing light. I couldn't remember where we were, or why we were here. I really needed to lie down and sleep, but for some reason, I kept putting one foot in front of the other, taking another step.

I fell again, conscious this time I was going down. The hard earth knocked the wind out of me. I lay there gasping, thinking how much warmer it seemed lying down. Mud Rain's small hands started pulling on my vest, and some deep instinct warned me not to stay here.

Leave me alone, I thought wearily. *Let me sleep for just a little while.*

It was while I lay there, shivering, trying to open my eyelids, that a strange, freeing sensation floated through me, breathing strength into my arms and legs. Immediately, I knew what it was, what it meant.

Angela had died.

The sensation faded, leaving behind a gaping emotional hole and an overwhelming urge to get back on my feet. I opened my eyes. Standing took all I had, and I leaned against the rock wall and tried to remember what I'd been doing.

Mud Rain pulled on my sweatshirt. "Wawk, Maddie."

Why wasn't he home, in bed? I wanted to ask him, but couldn't organize my thoughts enough to form the words. It was dark. I should be in bed, too. I was cold, exhausted, in pain. All over, pain stabbed and sucked on every muscle.

I took another step, dragged my useless leg, clung to the walking stick. I kept going in the direction the small hands pulled. The next time I looked up, the dim light in front of me was huge. I sagged down to the ground and leaned my back against the cold rock wall.

Angela was dead. I had not made it back to the hospital. She was gone, and I hadn't been there. As I crumpled over onto the dirt, a shadowy movement appeared in the middle of the round circle of light. My heart froze when my eyes focused on the rifle the figure carried.

Rifle shots…pain…Mud Rain's frightened face … Jeremiah's bloody shoulder and head … Angela. The images swam around my head as the figure stepped closer. My teeth were chattering so badly that I couldn't utter a sound.

When the shadow crouched down next to my head, Mud Rain leapt to his feet.

"Miah! Miah!"

Jeremiah. I couldn't work my mouth to form his name.

My husband's warm, strong fingers pressed against the underside of my jaw, then he began loosening the vest around me, removing it and then my sweatshirt and short-sleeved shirt I'd had on underneath. Something warm and heavy draped over my exposed chest. With gentle hands, he guided my arms through soft, toasty sleeves.

"Lie still." Jeremiah's long, strong body stretched beside mine, his arms wrapping around my chest and pulling me into a cocoon of blessed heat. Mud Rain snuggled against me. Jeremiah's strong arms fiercely rubbed my back and arms until I felt the resulting friction heating my skin. My teeth quit chattering, my muscles relaxed, and I inhaled sharply.

Jeremiah stopped massaging and squeezed me hard. "You are going to make it. Just relax," he whispered. I thought I heard his voice crack.

Gradually my orientation returned, and I remembered the chain of recent events.

"Is…is Gary dead?" I stammered.

The long pause that followed did not bode well. "No." His arms resumed their rubbing.

Silence.

"Then how did you get up here?" I asked, confused. The moonlight would have made Jeremiah's approach to the cave clearly visible, and Gary would never have allowed him to reach the opening.

When Jeremiah inhaled slowly, I felt his chest expand against mine. "When Gary left his position I ran for the cave."

My teeth started chattering again. "I t-t-tried…." I broke off.

Jeremiah's arms paused. "The storm prevented Gary from shooting you again."

I tried to distance myself from the memory of being shot, decided to change subjects. "I looked for another way out."

His arms resumed massaging my back. I curled my arms against his chest and wished we were in bed in our Colorado Springs apartment.

"I know this cave. Miners used it for a long time. There are no other exits." Jeremiah's warm, strong body pressed against mine. I felt him tense, knew that he had bad news.

"Gary shot Hawk, then left his position in the canyon to confirm his kill."

"You mean…you mean Hawk is *dead*?" I choked.

He bent his head close to mine. "I tried to spot where he had fallen, but I could not see his body."

I felt a flicker of hope. "So does that mean he might not be dead?"

Jeremiah shook his head against mine. "If he was wounded and Gary found him, he is now."

I refused to believe him. "But if he's wounded and conscious, maybe he can still take out Gary."

My husband didn't answer. I remembered the rifle he had carried with him into the cave. "At least you have your rifle, if Gary tries to come after us."

"No ammunition left." Jeremiah's flat statement killed any sense of relief I may have felt.

My slender thread of control snapped. "*Shit.*"

Uncomfortable silence fell, and I remembered the sensation that had passed through me. "You should have told me you recognized Gary. It might have been enough to protect...." I trailed off as tears rolled down my cheeks. "Angela's dead," I whispered. I fisted my hands against his chest.

Jeremiah didn't say anything. Needles prickled all over my thighs and calves, and my right leg began to throb.

My fists moved to his shoulders, and I lifted my head enough to meet his eyes. "You should have told me what was going on. Damn it, I've been your *wife* for the last seven years."

Mud Rain's small body snuggled closer against my back, reminding me abruptly that he needed attention. "Is he all right?"

"Seems to be," Jeremiah murmured. "He about hugged the life out of me earlier."

"Well, we need to get him out of here. We need to get all of us out of here." I tried extricating myself from Jeremiah's arms.

"Not yet." His arms loosened. I felt the heaviness of his leather jacket as he eased away from me and lifted the vest that lay on the floor of the cave. A grimace of pain crossed his black brows when he eased the vest over his left shoulder.

I realized with a jolt I could see his features. Pre-dawn lightened the sky, threw dim luminescence into the cave. I sat up and looked down at the heavy, black leather jacket, which Jeremiah had put on me backwards. I shrugged out of it, turned it around, stuck my arms back through the sleeves, and zipped it up. Gingerly, I shifted my splinted leg until it rested in front of me, and then leaned my head against the rock. Mud Rain continued to sleep in a tightly curled ball beside me. I was careful not to disturb him.

Jeremiah looked at me from across the floor of the cave, pain and sympathy in his expression. "I...I am sorry about Angela."

Staring at the rocky ground beneath me, I couldn't control the tears that flooded my eyes, began tumbling down my cheeks. "I couldn't get back in time. I needed to be there, and I couldn't get back in time."

"There was nothing you could have done." Jeremiah's voice was soft. I looked up when he continued. "When she called me, she told me she was dying. By the time Gary planned to steal Mud Rain she had weakened to the point she could hardly stand. She knew he intended to kill Mud Rain, too. She knew going to friends or authorities might protect her, but she was afraid Mud Rain was at risk as long as he stayed in Oklahoma, so she tried to get Mud Rain to me. She made it to Limon before her strength gave out. She called me, but she was so weak…" he trailed off. He crept over, cupped my chin in his hands and lifted my face until our eyes met.

"When I told her Gary stopped by our apartment, she begged me to keep you out of it, to keep you safe. I told her to hang on and called nine-one-one and got an ambulance dispatched."

Our faces were close. Jeremiah continued in a whisper so low, I could hardly hear him. "I headed to Denver, hoping to intercept Angela and Mud Rain in the Emergency Department. Gary got there first and found Mud Rain in the waiting room. He called me, told me he had my brother. I am sure Angela thought Mud Rain would be safe. She would not have thought Gary could get to him in the hospital."

I looked into his black eyes. "So you went after Gary."

Jeremiah released me, sat back on his heels and rested his hands on his thighs. "Yes. He kept calling me, putting Mud Rain on the phone and teasing him until he became hysterical." He paused. I waited for him to finish. "He threatened to kill him if I tried notifying the police."

I stared at him, at the dried blood on his shirt, then the crusted, bloody socks tied around his head. "There was only one bullethole in the Jeep," I said slowly. I returned my gaze to his face. "You tried to get to the cave, didn't you?"

He nodded.

"And you only had a handgun." I shook my head. "You had no way to get close enough to get a shot at Gary."

Jeremiah looked away. "As a youth, he could shoot out the eye of a prairie dog without maiming the skull." He swung his eyes back to me. "After he called, I could not risk you getting in his way."

"And that's why you didn't return any of my messages?"

He nodded. "Once I knew you were aware of Angela's illness,

I hoped you would stay at the hospital until I contacted you." His attention suddenly jerked to the cave opening.

"What is it?" I asked.

Jeremiah raised a hand, signaling silence. I listened, and after a bit thought I heard what had caught his attention. "Sounds like a chopper."

Jeremiah nodded. He stood and moved to the edge of the cave mouth. The sound of beating rotor blades grew louder, and I caught sight of a tiny orange blimp in the gray sky.

"Who would have called them?" I asked as I watched the orange speck grow larger. It seemed to be heading straight towards us.

Jeremiah's attention focused sharply downward, to somewhere below the level of the cave, and he stepped back into the shadows.

I tensed. "What do you see?"

Jeremiah ignored my question. He drew his old Army semi-automatic handgun from his belt. I heard him pull the slide before stepping over and holding the gun out to me. When I shook my head at him, he took my hand and wrapped it around the butt of the gun.

"The safety is off. When you shoot, shoot to kill." Before I could ask what he meant, he gave me a soft kiss. I inhaled sharply with alarm when I saw a strange, desperate look in his eyes. Before I could ask him what he intended to do, he stood abruptly and strode from the cave into the early morning light. Lifting his uninjured arm, he began waving with large, exaggerated motions. I watched the chopper drop altitude as it neared.

We were going to be rescued. Finally, the three of us were safe. I squinted at the gun in my hand, carefully avoided the trigger guard, and fumbled with the safety so the damned thing wouldn't accidentally go off.

No noise alerted me, no report of a rifle. One second Jeremiah was standing, waving his arm. The next instant, with a choked gasp, he collapsed backwards onto the ground, crumpled and motionless.

Chapter Twenty

I clamped my hand over a scream. The bright orange helicopter dipped into the canyon, dropping almost to the level of the cave, then abruptly swerved out of sight. The thumping rotor blades faded into silence.

"Jeremiah?" I didn't understand what had just happened, didn't understand why he was lying so awkwardly on the ground. A memory of Hawk's words oozed through my shocked haze, something about the Charlie Network having resources to chopper in one of their own.

Had Jeremiah just been shot by someone in the helicopter?

Mud Rain whimpered and wriggled behind my back. "Miah?" His thin voice sounded scared, and I feared that he would cry out.

"Be still," I whispered, squeezing his hand. I dragged myself towards Jeremiah's motionless form.

"Jeremiah, answer me." My voice sounded so thin, so weak, I didn't think he heard me. As I reached the opening, I looked out over the canyon and wondered where that helicopter had disappeared to. Then I looked down.

Gary, rifle in hand, was making his way up the incline towards the cave, his head lowered, his attention on the steep, loose terrain.

I withdrew into the shadows until I felt the cold rock of the cave wall against my back, shock and anger surging from deep within my gut. Jeremiah's handgun and empty rifle lay on the floor.

Why hadn't my husband waited until Gary was in range and shot him?

The answer dawned slowly. Gary would have been concealed well out of range of Jeremiah's handgun. He would have fired shots into the cave, probably would have fired at the helicopter. Even if he didn't hit any of us he would have kept us pinned until we died of thirst.

By stepping out, Jeremiah had forced the situation. Gary would know I was seriously wounded, possibly dead, and therefore would believe that neither Mud Rain nor I posed a threat.

I dragged myself over to Mud Rain.

"Get behind me," I whispered. I heard the fear in my voice, saw the reaction on his face. "Be very quiet." I tried to sound calmer than I felt. After a slight hesitation, he nodded. I scooted until I felt him tight against my back, then reached over with both hands and picked up Jeremiah's handgun, used my thumb to switch the safety off, then pointed it towards the opening. The gun barrel shook abominably, so I bent my good leg and rested my hands on my knee.

Recalling how easily Hawk's gun had gone off, I kept my finger out of the trigger guard. I prayed with all my soul Gary was out of ammo, that he'd had a miraculous change of heart, that he was climbing to the cave to help Jeremiah, to help us, that he was climbing to the cave for any reason other than with the intent to hurt us. I wanted to believe someone from the chopper had shot Jeremiah and the threat was now gone.

I jolted when pebbles rattled down somewhere just outside of the entrance. There was no way I could tell which side the sound had come from. I pressed my back against the wall and felt Mud Rain squirm. If he made any noise at all, Gary would know where we were.

A shaft of brilliance pierced the darkness of the cave, illuminating the ceiling. The ray of dawning sun broadened as it scattered the heavy blackness, exposing us with brilliant light. Visions of a slowly receding shadow down the eastern face of Pikes Peak slid through my thoughts, and I marveled in a detached sort of way how my brain could think of something so peaceful in a moment of such utter terror.

Without warning Gary stepped into view, sunlight creating a halo around his straggly hair. I watched in morbid fascination when he moved to Jeremiah's still body. He shifted the bolt on his rifle, sliding the mechanism home with a lethal snap, then slowly raised the weapon to his shoulder, the barrel mere inches from my husband's head.

"NOOOOOOOO!" My eyes squeezed shut, my finger jerked the trigger. The gun kicked hard as it fired, my ears rang with the brutal report. The acrid smell of gunpowder assaulted my nostrils as I fired again. I kept curling my finger around the trigger, the gun recoiling against my knee, the sharp, ear-splitting report ringing in my ears over and over.

Finally, the gun clicked. I jerked against the now immobile trigger a few more times before I realized the weapon was empty. I realized that my eyes were still closed and slowly opened them. The haze of gunpowder filled the mouth of the cave, stung my eyes. Feeling heat radiating from the barrel, I dropped the weapon, heard it clatter against the rocky ground. Mud Rain, curled in a tight ball behind me, whimpered and trembled, tears streaming down his pale cheeks, his hands clasped tightly against the sides of his head as he rocked back and forth on the ground.

I dragged myself over to Jeremiah. Gary lay next to him, a little further out on the ledge. The metallic, sickening stench of blood flooded my nostrils, and my throat constricted as my stomach lurched. Blood soaked the ground. I willed myself not to throw up and focused on my husband. My vision blurred, and I swiped away the tears that flowed down my face.

Jeremiah lay on his back, his legs bent awkwardly beneath him, in much the same way as the body of the man Hawk had shot on that mountainside.

A strangled gurgling sound penetrated my shocked eardrums and I glanced around.

Gary had turned his head towards me, and our eyes met. His were glassy, unfocused, as he sucked weakly against the blood that filled his mouth and ran from a large gash in his throat. He gurgled again, more faintly than before. Then, gradually, his eyes went blank and the horrible noise ceased. The blood that flowed from him began to pool.

I closed my eyes and turned back to Jeremiah, sobs racking so hard I couldn't breathe, couldn't sit up. I bent my head down to Jeremiah's chest. Blood oozed around the hole in the vest he wore.

The Kevlar will slow a bullet but not stop one.

It took several moments before realization hit. I jerked my head up and stared at my husband.

His wound was *bleeding.*

He was alive, though for how long I had no idea. Blood covered him, and I thought with a jolt of hope that some of it was probably Gary's. I folded my hands against the hole in the vest and pressed as hard as I could. Jeremiah stirred and moaned, then became still again. I prayed the vest would save his life, the same damned vest Hawk had so stubbornly insisted I wear.

~ * ~

I lifted my head when my ears caught the sound of the helicopter returning, and I watched the bright orange machine circle the canyon, then hover close to the side that held the cave. Figures dropped from the dark inside of the chopper and scrambled across the bald summit to the cave, where I sat pressing Jeremiah's chest. Gentle hands pulled me away, and I watched the rescue crew strap him into the wire basket they had carried across. Four of them carried him to the hovering chopper, snapped the basket into a harness, which lifted him up and inside. The helicopter lifted, swung a one-eighty, and flew away.

After a while more rescuers came on foot, bringing more metal baskets, which they strapped Mud Rain and myself into. They produced a large body bag for Gary.

One of the rescuers knelt beside me. "This yours?" She held out a small black object.

It was the satellite phone Joe had given to Hawk.

"Where did you find it?" I croaked, bound and wrapped in straps and blankets.

"A call came in from this phone, then the user quit responding, but left the phone on. We used GPS to get a fix on its location. We figured the man lost consciousness, but we haven't found anyone else in the canyon. Is it yours?"

"I borrowed it…from a friend. I must have dropped it when I was climbing up to the cave." Fleeting thoughts of Hawk wandered through the haze in my brain.

"It was a man who made the call." The lady's expression told me clearly that she knew I wasn't telling the truth. When I shrugged and refused to clarify she added, "We'll need to keep it while there's an investigation going on."

I nodded. Another rescuer found my camera and belt pack. They kept those, too.

The county hospital admitted, sewed and casted, fed and washed us, then let us sleep in borrowed beds. Officials came and went. I answered questions, was told Mud Rain was being taken care of and Jeremiah had undergone a long surgery.

Bill and Becky Parsons came into my room the following afternoon. Between them, Mud Rain stood holding their hands. Bill, standing beside my bed, looked worried.

"How you feeling, sweetie?" he asked as he carefully extracted his hand from Mud Rain's grip and leaned down to give me a kiss on the forehead. He looked worn and his clothes were wrinkled, a far cry from his normally impeccable appearance. I smiled, but asked what was uppermost in my mind.

"How's Jeremiah? Have you seen him? Is he going to be okay?"

I knew from the way Bill looked at his wife that something was wrong.

"What is it? What's happened?" I started to sit up. With a gentle hand, Bill pressed me back against the mattress. His eyes watered, and he swiped a hand against his face.

"He's gone."

"You mean…you mean…" I could not bring myself to utter the rest.

Becky moved to the side of the bed, pushing Bill aside. Bill stood back with Mud Rain, who took his hand again.

"No, honey, he doesn't mean that. What he means is that Jeremiah has disappeared. The doctors and the nurses who were taking care of him…" She paused. When she continued, her voice shook. "The nurse couldn't find him this morning when she came in to check on him. They moved him out of ICU late last night to a private room."

"But…but…where is he? He's alive, right?" I couldn't understand what she was trying to say, what she was trying to tell me.

"They've notified the police." She was crying now. "No one has any answers."

No one had any answers the day the hospital discharged me, either. The police asked me a few questions about Jeremiah's background, whether he had family on the reservation. No one offered any explanations concerning his disappearance. All they said was that they were investigating the incident and would let me know as soon as they got any leads.

After I was discharged, Becky drove me back to the apartment. I felt as though I'd been gone a year rather than little over a week. Becky answered email, phone, and the doorbell non-stop for the next couple of days. I hobbled around the apartment on crutches because there wasn't enough clearance for a wheelchair. Bill returned to Norman, Oklahoma, with Mud Rain.

The nightmares started the second night I was home. I was sleeping on the couch because it was easier to keep my leg elevated than trying to stack pillows on the bed. I awoke in the early hours of the morning to find Becky kneeling beside the couch.

"You were crying in your sleep," she whispered, caressing my forehead.

"Where is he?" I felt like I had been sobbing forever. "Where is Jeremiah?"

"They're looking, honey. The detective said as soon as they know anything, he'll call."

He called, but he couldn't (or wouldn't) tell me anything.

Thursday I submitted my resignation to the paper, refused to attend an exit interview, stowed the Canon (returned minus the memory card), lenses, and the boxes of photographs in the spare bedroom closet, then answered questions about details concerning funeral arrangements for Angela. The hospital released her body and sent it to Shawnee, where the funeral would be held.

Early Friday evening Becky and I flew to Oklahoma. Irma Greenbeck, one of Mom's life-long friends, met us at Will Rogers International Airport in Oklahoma City.

"Dear, dear Mattie," she sniffed, taking the handles of the wheelchair from the flight attendant before Becky could step forward. The short, energetic woman began to bulldoze through the crowd of pedestrians. Irma and wheels was a bad combination, I realized with a nervous swallow as we careened through the airport, disrupting the pedestrian flow and generating startled shouts and hand gestures. At this rate I would end up in the hospital with matching casts. Miraculously, we made it without casualties to curbside pick-up.

"Honey, we've handled all the funeral arrangements," Irma pressed. "All of your parents' friends are lining up to help you. You're just too upset to worry about any of this."

Bernie, the family chauffeur for as long as I could remember, stood beside Mom and Dad's crimson and cream Mercedes sedan. He took Becky's and my suitcases and slipped them into the trunk. I flashed back to the image of Hawk's black Mercedes bouncing down the mountain and squeezed my eyes shut. I stood on my left leg, hopped with Bernie's assistance off the curb to the open car door, and carefully slid onto the soft supple leather of the backseat.

Irma turned to Becky. "The girls and I'll get notices in the paper."

"Thank you, Irma." Becky squeezed her hand, then slipped into the front passenger seat. I stared at the back of her impeccable, thick, snow-white short hair as we traveled along the interstate to

Shawnee. I couldn't bear to watch the fresh green of summer sliding by through the tinted windows. The estate gardens would be in full bloom now. Jeremiah and I had discussed whether to keep the staff intact at our parents' house after their funeral, or to close the house up and wait for advice from the estate lawyers. Now, I sighed with relief that we had opted to keep it occupied.

Air-conditioned coolness washed over me when Bernie wheeled me through the wide front entrance. William smiled at me through his moist eyes and took the wheelchair from Bernie. Flowers and potted plants overran the large entryway. I stared at the plants and wondered whether insanity might bring oblivion.

Monday morning I found myself in church, sitting in my wheelchair beside the hard wooden pew I had occupied during Mom and Dad's funeral. Despite the chair being a good deal softer than the pew, my backside was as numb as the rest of me, while my heart tore into little bits. My cast, white plaster of Paris, peeked out from the bottom of the long black cotton dress I wore. I stared at the elaborate urn that held my sister's ashes, then lifted my eyes and stared at the intricately detailed stained glass in the window behind the altar.

Preacher Pat rose from the chair he occupied behind the altar and approached the pulpit. I refused to look at him, because nothing he could say would console me.

After the service, tearful eyes and wet faces greeted and hugged me. I sat in my wheelchair, feeling numb and alone, and ignored all of them. I wanted to fly back to that small community hospital and grill the staff on the disappearance of my husband.

Irma and her (seemingly) endless friends had planned a reception at the estate. Becky insisted the collective energy would help lift the morbid atmosphere that seemed to have permanently settled over the place. But I saw only the cold wealth that had generated enough greed in a man to drive him to kill every member of my family. As William wheeled me through the crowd of bodies, people turned my way and gave me sympathetic pats on my shoulder, hugs that felt awkward because they had to lean down, hand squeezes and kisses on the cheek that made me want to hit them. I didn't bother to paint a polite reaction or grateful disposition. My face hurt too much from crying.

"Mattie, dear."

I glanced up. Irma stood beside me, holding two wineglasses.

She pressed a glass into my hand.

"Drink this, honey. You need something to help your nerves."

As I raised the glass to my lips, my focus drifted towards the far side of the room. Bodies parted for an instant and my eyes widened. I jerked, and wine sloshed all over my hand and down my black dress.

Hawk stood against the far wall, in his hand a whiskey glass filled with golden-yellow liquor and ice. He was dressed in a black turtleneck and black trousers. His gray eyes caught mine and held them. Then bodies eddied, blocking my line of sight.

"Hold this." I shoved my glass towards Irma and wheeled through the crowd, not caring whom I clipped on my way.

There was no sign of Hawk when I reached the far end of the room. I looked around, but the crowd blocked my sight in every direction. I wanted to scream at everyone to leave.

"Mattie, dear, are you all right?" Irma asked from behind me. She leaned down and peered at me. "You're white as a sheet."

I gave her Hawk's description and she immediately strode off, calling his name from room to room, her foghorn voice sounding clearly over the noise. I figured she would run him down quicker than anyone else in the place, but she returned alone after a long interval.

"I'm sorry, Mattie. I didn't find him." She opened her mouth to add something else, then abruptly closed it, but I knew what was on her mind. I wondered the same thing myself.

Maybe I had just imagined the whole thing.

Gradually the rooms emptied and the line of parked cars outside shrank. I shook hands, endured more hugs, pats on the shoulder, squeezed hands, and kisses on my cheek. After the last guest departed I wheeled myself into the music room. I really wanted to crawl under the pianos and never come out again.

Angela's urn sat atop the nearest piano. I heard William running the vacuum over the carpets, the soft clinking of china, crystal, and silver dinnerware from the direction of the kitchen as his wife, Anna, cleaned up the dishes. I rose from the wheelchair, hobbled over to the nearest bench, and sat down. Staring at the lid that covered the keyboard, I remembered Angela's and my conversation the day of our parents' funeral. I lifted the lid, pressed a few keys. Lonely, discordant tones whispered from hidden strings. I rested my head against the music stand and closed my eyes. My fingers stilled. The dissonance stopped.

I don't know how long I sat there when I got the eerie feeling that I was not alone. The staff had left, and Becky had driven down to Norman to check on Mud Rain, so I should have been the only one in the house. I glanced up.

Hawk stood near the door.

A shiver ran through me as I straightened. I had not heard him enter the room, had not heard the door clicking shut. I wondered seriously whether I was hallucinating.

His steady gray eyes blinked. Okay, maybe he wasn't a hallucination. I spotted a long, stapled incision that ran the length of the right side of his jaw.

"What are you doing here?" I asked into the stillness, more curiosity than accusation in my voice.

When he continued to regard me in silence, I began to doubt my sanity. Maybe hallucinations *did* blink. I didn't know. I'd never had one before.

"Are you really here?" I asked.

"Yes." His whisper barely broke the silence. I stood, pain jolting up the cast when I tried putting a little weight on it, so I leaned against the piano.

Hawk folded his arms across his chest. "You look like you've seen a ghost."

I frowned. "Well, you're acting a lot like one. Disappearing off mountainsides, out of one room and re-appearing without a sound in another. Excuse me if I'm not quite sure you're real."

A wry smile flickered across his lips. "I'm already dead, remember?"

My leg throbbed. I sat back down on the bench, the cast sticking out in front of me. The throbbing did not improve.

"Where's Jeremiah?" I asked.

Hawk's expression closed. He uncrossed his arms, slid his hands into the pockets of his dark trousers.

"Where is he, Hawk?" I repeated angrily.

"I was not at the hospital." He watched me with steady eyes.

"You're not answering the question," I accused. "I want you to tell me where he is and whether he's okay."

Instead of answering, he changed subjects. "You present rather a problem."

I glared at him. "What?"

"Since you are alive still and in relatively good health, that is." He was being as obtuse as Jeremiah, and I was sick of it.

"What are you talking about? Is this another British thing?"

"Lee and his twin. You're an eye witness." He remained by the door. I wondered why he seemed reluctant to move.

"Don't change subjects on me." I rose and limped to the wheelchair. My leg definitely did not appreciate the weight I put on it and upped its complaints to teeth-grinding level. Time for some more pain medication, which meant a trip to the kitchen for some water. I sat down, then scowled at the man leaning against the door.

"Jeremiah's room would have had an officer posted. How did someone manage to get in and get him out without anyone knowing about it?"

Hawk did not move. "That's need-to-know."

I wanted to choke him. Healing bone and tissue ached and throbbed. To make matters worse my head started to hurt as badly as when I'd banged my head against the pavement in the middle of that damned boulevard. One memory led to another until Jeremiah's words in the cave drifted through my head. I broke from my thoughts and turned to Hawk. "What happened out there, on the mountain?"

Hawk withdrew his hands from his pockets and straightened. "Gary shot and disabled my rifle. The bullet deflected and hit me in the jaw. Knocked me senseless for a bit."

I pondered that for a bit. "You called the rescue chopper?"

He nodded.

I circled my hand at him. "And then?"

Hawk released a slow sigh, walked with slow, measured steps towards me. "And then I left."

"Why didn't you stay and help?" *Why didn't you stay and shoot Gary?* That was what I really wanted to ask.

Restless, anxious, and uncomfortable, I stood again and hobbled to the piano, my back to the man across the room. I leaned my forearms on the ebony lid and wished with all of my heart that Angela was sitting at the piano instead of on it.

"I...I shot Gary." The words slipped out, barely audible. I tried to suppress the memory, the horrific odors, the ungodly scene.

"Be glad you did." His words came from right behind me. "Gary had everything all nice and tidied up. With the three of you dead, he would have gained access to the entire Lamont estate despite whatever investigation might have followed."

He had a point. The hospital staff had not found anything indicating criminal behavior, despite Angela's condition.

His hand reached for mine. "He would have fabricated some story about the three of you not returning from holiday, knowing full well your bodies would never be located." He turned my wrist to expose the healing cut on my palm. I stared at the thin, pink scar until he gently twisted me around to face him. I stared at the fabric of his turtleneck and thought it too hot a garment to wear in Oklahoma in June. Thinking back on it, I realized he'd worn long sleeves to the Sunday afternoon ballgame, too. I wondered whether his burns had messed with his body's ability to maintain a normal temperature.

"And then there's Joe Healing Water," he continued, touching beneath my chin with a finger until my eyes met his.

I didn't want to listen to what he seemed to want to say.

"He no doubt would have come forward to provide witness that Gary should be a suspect. What do you think Gary would have done to him?"

Gary would have found a way to make his death look like an accident, too.

"There was...so much blood." The memory twisted my stomach into hard, uncomfortable knots. Raw with the impact of lingering images, I leaned my forehead against his thickly muscled chest and wished he were Jeremiah.

"I didn't shout a warning. I didn't give him a chance to put his gun down." I wasn't sure he understood what I'd said because my words came out more like garbled mumbles against his shirt. My voice was shaking. Tremors started racking through me, violent and cold.

"Be thankful you didn't." His voice was soft, his arms at his sides. "The three of you would be in urns just like your sister."

I turned my head towards his shoulder. I was slobbering all over the man. "I...I wish you had shot him. Why didn't you try? Why did you leave?"

I heard him sigh. "I'd never have made it to the cave in time. I wasn't terribly steady on my feet. All I had was my Glock, and Gary was out of range."

Several minutes passed before Hawk whispered, his words barely audible even though his lips brushed my ear. "I was still in the area when you took him out. I knew you had it in you to do the job."

I lifted my head from his chest. "He would have tracked you down, too, wouldn't he?"

Hawk stepped away. "Quite likely. Lee and his twin would have appreciated that."

I didn't want to think any more about killers and guns. I'd experienced enough in the previous week to last me the rest of my life. "I...I keep seeing Gary's eyes, all that blood, that awful gurgling sound."

Hawk's expression seemed oddly neutral. "You'll come out on the other side."

Maybe a change in subject would help dispel the mental pictures. "So, why are you here?" I asked him.

His cool, gray eyes regarded me. "Because it's not over yet."

Those weren't the words I had wanted to hear. "You mean, about Lee and his twin?" I thought I began to understand why Jeremiah had disappeared.

Hawk's jaw clenched. He seemed tense. "Among others." He retrieved the wheelchair, motioned for me to sit down.

I didn't move. "Are you kidnapping me again?"

My comment should have generated a smile or at least a hint of humor. Hawk's expression remained closed. His mood had changed. He seemed distant, closed off. "In a manner of speaking."

I looked at the wheelchair, then back to the man standing behind it. I inhaled deeply, thought about all the crap he had put me through, the injury he had sustained fighting a battle he had no reason to engage.

"You need to trust me." His comment broke the silence that had fallen between us.

"Whatever happens, remember that." He raised a hand and pressed his ear.

I waited for him to explain his cryptic comment, released a sigh after he remained stubbornly silent, and frowned.

"You know, you and Jeremiah both would make my life a lot easier if you would learn how to carry on a normal conversation."

About the Author

F.L. Godfriaux (Lynn Godfriaux Maloy) has spent most of her adult life raising her two children and teaching piano. She received both a Bachelors and a Masters in piano from the University of Oklahoma and is an active performer, adjudicator, and presenter. Her writing career began through poetry and culminated in her first book, *The Well-Tempered Poet: 24 Pictures and Poems*, which was published in 2010. She has written articles about dyslexia in the music field in the CSMTA newsletter and *Clavier Companion*. Now that her family has grown, Lynn is focusing on writing, performing, and spending time with her husband and with her horse.

More mysteries await in these books from WolfSinger Publications

da sticks – Rich Kisielewski

Not long ago, Harry had moved back to the town where his ex-wife and kids reside and was trying to rebuild his life. The "work hard and play hard" attitude that carries Harry through life is balanced by the softness evidenced in his dealings with his children. Once again, he was going to have to be away from them and the new life he had been trying so hard to establish.

Going undercover at MechInsCo, Harry gets exposure to executives within the company including his lifer accounting boss, the psycho senior finance executive and a frantic company president. They all paint the same picture-a company losing money with no idea how, or why. His stint at MechInsCo supplies Harry with some raucous times: large amounts of information, booze and ladies provide him with much more than he signed on for.

da bug – Rich Kisielewski

Harry Mickey Shorts gets a call from M. Randle Trundle, a New York business tycoon, who is in need of Harry's help. Without a thought, Harry drops what he is doing and races off to help his benefactor, and his friend.

Trundle is a part owner in Board Room Farms—a horse racing stable—which is run by his brother, Danny Trundle. He informs Harry the stable's stud breeding stallion was found dead in his stall and Trundle feels something is wrong. Harry agrees to help Trundle with the case and does what he does best by going undercover and begins digging into the world of thoroughbred horse racing. Having bet on more than a few nags before in his lifetime, Harry is comfortable around the track and blends in very smoothly.

During his investigation, Harry forms an alliance with the ranch's female vet—in more ways than one. She agrees to provide needed intelligence on the current and prior goings-on at Board

Room farms. Along the way, she becomes a serious love interest in Harry's life. Unfortunately, that conflicts with Harry's renewed part-time interest in his ex-wife that may prove to be a "pick one" dilemma, sooner, rather than later. His love for, and continued attempt to become part of his two children's lives, remains paramount in Harry's thinking.

da nuts – Rich Kisielewski

Harry Mickey Shorts, street wise private detective, gets a call from Max who just happens to be his favorite as well as his only son. Max doesn't ask his dad for much but he and his buddies are in need of Harry's help. Without a thought, Harry drops what he is doing and races off to help his son and his friends.

Max informs Harry he would like him to investigate the untimely events that prohibited Clint, their current cult hero, from participating in a first ever poker tournament. Clint had played over a quarter of a million hands of poker by the time he had reached his eighteenth birthday and, as evidenced by the size of his bank account, he had won a lot more of those hands than he had lost. All of that meant nothing when he turned up unconscious in his hotel room on the morning of the first day of the inaugural "Under 18 World Championship of Poker" tournament.

During his investigation, Harry uses his expertise that sets him apart from other private investigators and goes undercover to explore the world of internet poker. The twist with this version is only kids between the ages of sixteen and eighteen can participate and all winnings may only be paid to higher institutions of learning for the kid's college education. Once he uncovers the wrong-doings of the unscrupulous masterminds behind this scheme he partners with his benefactor M. Randle Trundle, a New York business tycoon, to set things right and preserve the previously dashed hopes of the winning poker teenagers. Harry's renewed part-time interest in his ex-wife and his love for and continued attempt to become part of his two children's lives complicates his own life but remains paramount in Harry's thinking.

The Dolmen – Matt Bille

When attorney Julie Sperling's fiancée is murdered while researching a controversial museum exhibit, she calls on her ex-lover, science writer Greg nightmarish pursuit as very real predators from ancient folktales try to hunt down anyone with knowledge of their existence.

For Greg and Julie, the City of Angels has become the gateway to hell…

In Adam's Fall – Phoebe Wray

Old New England towns are infamous for their odd murder stories, but that had never happened before in Halton, Massachusetts.

When history teacher Nikki Sheridan trips over the dead body of a young Muslim girl in her backyard she finds herself at the center of a murder mystery. A mystery that will take her on a perilous journey with the police, the FBI, a nervous town ready to point fingers at neighbors who seem different, and a man calling himself 'the Patriot': a dangerous zealot whose hateful agenda could destroy the small town or bring them even closer together as they face a homegrown terrorist in their midst.

Murder Most Howl – Margaret H. Bonham

Dog Mushing Can Be Murder

For Stephanie Keyes, noted sled dog racer in Colorado, sled dog racing can be dangerous enough. But when a fellow musher and rival is found murdered and she's a prime suspect, Stephanie races to find the killer before he can strike again.

Missing sled dogs and deadly goals abound in this super sleuth tale—or is it tail?

www.ingramcontent.com/pod-product-compliance
Lightning Source LLC
Chambersburg PA
CBHW051506260626
47162CB00008B/2842